FINALLY BAR-LEV RAISED HIS EYES.

"Time is the problem, Daud. If we had the time, we could work out the settlement issue. Your people and mine can exist together as God intended. But the time must be bought."

Qidal nodded.

"I wish to buy that time. I know you do also. But your people are in an even worse position to buy time than when Arafat led them. With him, I could not deal. *We* could not deal. With you in charge, I can come to make a bargain."

"A bargain?"

"You must have a homeland," Bar-Lev continued. "We know this. But we will never allow a hectare of Israel to become Palestine again. *You* know this." He paused.

"With the right hammer, a good carpenter can build anything. I wish to give you that hammer, Daud. So you can build your homeland."

"A hammer," Qidal repeated. "What do you mean, exactly?"

"I mean a nuclear weapon."

AIRBURST

Steven L. Thompson
AIRBURST

WORLDWIDE®

TORONTO · NEW YORK · LONDON · PARIS
AMSTERDAM · STOCKHOLM · HAMBURG
ATHENS · MILAN · TOKYO · SYDNEY

AIRBURST

A Worldwide Library Book/February 1988

ISBN 0-373-97056-0

AIRBURST

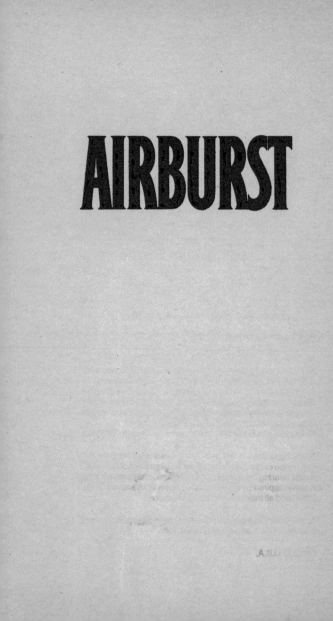

PROLOGUE

HE TIRED OF READING, and looked up from the Recital of the Prophet. A fly caught his eye. It droned heavily in the little room, a sound at once lethargic and ominous. He laid down the Koran and gave himself up to the observation of the fly. It lit on Ali's AKM automatic rifle barrel and began to wander the brutal blue-black metal in search of whatever flies seek. Ali, sitting just inside the narrow little door with the AKM across his fatigue-clad knees, ignored the fly. He gazed across the valley, keeping watch with the intensity of youth. Qidal studied Ali with the same detachment with which he had observed the fly. The young man's passionate nature was written in his features.

Was I once that young too? Was anyone? Even as he thought it, Daud Qidal smiled inwardly. The musings of an old man. Would *he* feel the same? He was older even than Daud—and Daud could still recall how he felt when he was Ali's age; men as old as he was now were almost beyond comprehension for him—as he must be for Ali. Yet he commanded Ali, as al-Raquim had commanded him. He thought for a moment more on the circles of life, until the fly suddenly began droning again. He blinked and sat straighter. He could not afford such empty philosophy. He was no longer a scholar. Just as *he* was no longer a fellow professor, but a powerful member of the Knesset and the secret intelligence committee.

Irritably now he looked out the door of the shepherd's hut at the valley. Where was he? Would he not, after all, come, despite his solemn word? Heat boiled up from the narrow little valley in visible waves, distorting the very light reflecting from the copper-colored stone. The faint, dull clanging of the sheeps' bells on the steep hill below seemed to be absorbed by the superheated air.

Ali suddenly stirred. He blinked away the sweat that collected below his checkered burnoose and peered into the glare.

"He comes," Ali said.

Qidal's heart beat faster. His mouth went dry. Perhaps there was hope after all.

"You are sure?"

"Positive. Do you not hear? It is an Israeli scout car."

Now Qidal could hear the rumble and rasp of the vehicle. He had heard many like it, but did not have the youngster's discriminating ear. To him it was just another military vehicle. He cared nothing about what kind it was. He only hoped it contained the man who had convinced him to come here to the Valley of Stone with only Ali by his side. It was a gamble that they would not take him prisoner. But it was a gamble he had to take. The starving children made that inevitable—so silent, so gaunt, their huge eyes so terribly accusing to every adult, and especially to their leaders. Especially to him. He straightened his clothes and listened to the scout car approach.

Ali got to his feet and went outside. He hoist.
AKM across his chest and stood, legs apart, a sen
outside the little hut. Qidal waited.

He heard the car slow, then halt. The engine rasped
and barked as the driver shifted gear. Finally it shut
down. A voice called out in bad Arabic, *"Essalamu
'alekum!"*

"Allah has indeed given us a good morning," Ali
replied dryly. Qidal smiled. No less a nomad than his
Palestinian forebears, though deprived of their centuries of dignity, Ali retained a touch of Bedouin wit
and all the desert nomad's caution. "What do you
want?" Ali challenged the visitors.

"Is Dr. Qidal inside?" The words were Arabic, the
voice Israeli. Qidal's smile widened. He *was* here. The
thought of seeing David Bar-Lev again was sweet to
him, and he got to his feet and went to the doorway.

The sun struck him like a fist. He squinted out at the
shadowy scout car.

"Yes! By Allah, David, it is I!"

A hatch clanged open. A young Israeli Defense
Force soldier climbed out, matching Ali's AKM with
his own Uzi. The IDF man swung his legs over the side
of the hot armor plate and rested his hands on the
weapon while the other hatch swung wide.

Bar-Lev struggled free of the small hatch. Qidal was
struck by how he had changed since last they had met,
twelve years before. No longer the swift ferret of a
man he had known in Jerusalem, Bar-Lev was
stooped, fat and gray. How must I appear to him?
Qidal wondered. Finally Bar-Lev stepped off the car,
puffing, and strode forward, hands outstretched in
greeting.

The Arab and the Israeli clasped each other like the old friends they had been, and for a moment neither said a word; each man kept his own thoughts to himself.

"It has been too long, my friend," said Bar-Lev at last. He looked hard up into the tall Qidal's black eyes. "Far too long."

Qidal nodded his head. "Yes. Yet you are the same. And so am I."

Bar-Lev took his arm and began walking to the hut. "Perhaps. And perhaps not. Too much has happened. Most of it bad." He blinked as he entered the relative cool of the spare little room. "Or maybe these are just the bitter thoughts of an old man."

Qidal motioned him to the other crude chair. "No, David. We are old, but things are bad. And they can get much worse. That is why I am here."

"And it is why I am here, old friend." Bar-Lev looked at Qidal for a long moment. "It was not easy to come."

Bar-Lev glanced at the door, where Ali's shadow announced his station outside the hut. Qidal followed his look. "Ali," he said quietly, "we must be alone."

The young man nodded and moved away. He sat on the ground five meters from the door, between the Israeli soldier and the hut. His AKM lay across his knees.

Qidal poured some tea from the battered silver teapot into a pair of glasses and offered one to Bar-Lev. The Israeli took the glass, sipped some tepid sweet tea and set it down on the uneven dirt floor.

Bar-Lev put his hand on his knees, staring down at them. Qidal waited. He knew the pose, having seen it a hundred times in the faculty club at the university. His friend was not to be rushed. Finally Bar-Lev raised his eyes.

"Time is the problem, Daud. If we had the time, we could work out the settlement issue. Your people and mine can exist together as God intended. But the time must be bought."

Qidal nodded.

"I wish to buy that time. I know you do also. But your people are in an even worse position to buy time than when Arafat led them. With him, I could not deal. *We* could not deal. With you in charge, I can come to make a bargain."

"A bargain?"

"You must have a homeland," Bar-Lev continued. "We know this. But we will never allow a hectare of Israel to become Palestine again. *You* know this." He paused.

Qidal didn't reply. Sandwiched between the warring factions of Islam and the might of Israel, his Palestinians were lost, less than humans in their misery, made into a battle cry of convenience for the madmen on both sides.

Bar-Lev wiped a gnarled hand over his bald head. He stroked his gray beard and peered through thick lenses at Qidal. His voice was like gravel on metal. Qidal suddenly realized, as if by revelation, that Bar-Lev was dying. He did not know how he knew this. But he knew it.

"With the right hammer, a good carpenter can build anything. I wish to give you that hammer, Daud. So you can build your homeland."

"A hammer," Qidal repeated. "What do you mean, exactly?"

"I mean a nuclear weapon."

Hard training and long years of rigid self-control froze Qidal's response. "Proceed," he said at length.

"From this moment, Daud, we are co-conspirators. If I continue, the speaking of the words alone will bond us together, possibly against our own peoples, who would almost certainly not understand why I would entrust you with the knowledge I have, nor why you would take it from me and make the pledge I will require of you in return. Shall I go on?"

"Proceed," Qidal said again quietly. He felt no emotion. Reality was a string of dirty camps, beset by disease and hostility. Reality was never-ending wanderings, ceaseless combat. This was fantasy. He shifted in the hard little chair and waited.

Bar-Lev pointed out the door, almost due south. "In the Midbar Paran, 350 kilometers from here, is Har Mughara. You have heard of it?"

"The Mountain of the Cave? No."

"Good. Our security is working. Har Mughara is one of our greatest secrets. There we have our nuclear weapon storage facility. It is, for most purposes, an impregnable fortress.

"Yet there is a way a determined group of men who knew some secrets could infiltrate Har Mughara and take one of our bombs."

"But the world believes that Israel does not possess any nuclear weapons," Qidal said without emotion.

Bar-Lev raised his shoulders lightly and let them drop. Then he continued talking. "Once these men had taken such a terror weapon, who knows? Perhaps they might use it to force certain changes in the situation."

"David. When you asked me to come here, I hoped we might discuss seriously how we two old friends might help the terrible fate of my people. I had hoped we could discuss issues of substance. When your messenger stipulated a meeting here with only a single companion, I hoped the secrecy meant you would be bringing a message from the Knesset. Instead—" he spread his hands eloquently "—instead you are discussing some kind of crazy military adventure. Forgive me, my old friend, but you do not seem entirely well. And these seem the delusions of a sick man."

Bar-Lev peeled off his thick glasses and wiped them elaborately with a white handkerchief. "You were always too good a lawyer. Too observant. I *am* a sick man, Daud. But these are not delusions. The delusion is yours if you think the Knesset will ever agree to serious changes inside Israel. Do not hope for sanity."

"Very well. For what am I to hope?"

Bar-Lev replaced his glasses, leaned forward and stared intently into Qidal's eyes. "Hope for fear. Hope for blackmail. Hope for whatever it will take to turn your hammer into a mallet large enough to shape a nation for your people."

"So a determined band manages to steal one of your nuclear weapons. What then? How would they use it? Would Israel shiver in its boots and beg us not to use it?" He snorted. "Now it is you who do not know your own countrymen, David. They would defy us to use it, and if we did, they would weep, bury their dead, cordon off the radioactive zone, make it a me-

morial and charge American tourists to observe it. But
long before that, your Mirages and Kfirs would have
killed many thousands of my people in revenge. This
is not much of a hammer.''

Bar-Lev stood up and went to the door. Ali glanced
at him, as did the young IDF soldier. He clasped his
hands behind his back and looked out at the shimmering valley of rocks. ''This part of Lebanon is poor,
Daud. But you well know that much of southern Lebanon is well watered. Were it not for the war—''

''Brought on by your invasion.''

''Perhaps. But in any case, a population like yours
could easily live here, as long as it had the right security. God has given this land a great deal. Only man
makes it hostile.''

''I'm sorry, David. I do not see your point.''

''My point is this,'' Bar-Lev said as he turned back
to Qidal. ''You are correct in thinking that you would
achieve little with a single small atomic bomb. After
all, what we store at Har Mughara are not launchers,
only warheads, so you would then have somehow to
convince the generals that even if you had it, you
could deliver it against a city like Tel Aviv or Jerusalem. But what if you used it elsewhere? What if you
used it not to threaten Israel, but some other place? A
place inhabited by people who would not defy you to
use it—but would probably give in to your demands?''

Qidal poured some more tea into the two glasses. He
stood and carried Bar-Lev's glass to him. Together
they sipped, looking out across the valley. ''And the
demands one would make of these unfortunate people?''

"More bombs, alas. And launchers. With them, you would have forged a mighty mallet. With enough nuclear weapons, you might force not just Israel, but Syria, Jordan, even Egypt to accept what you would propose."

"And that would be?"

"A new Palestine. Carved from the chaos of the old Lebanon."

The sheep downslope, suddenly startled by some sheep phantom invisible and inaudible to humans, jangled their bells as they ran with their awkward gait toward a young shepherd. His soothing calls echoed across the valley. Soon the bells quieted and the sheep again grazed on the scrub. Qidal turned from the doorway and gently set down his glass on the ancient silver tray. He sat heavily. The crude old chair creaked.

"It is a desperate thing," Qidal said.

Bar-Lev also sat down. He studied Qidal. "You are not desperate? *I* am. As long as your people provide the madmen with an excuse to rally the Arab world against us, my people will not know peace. Desperation is called for."

Qidal thought for a moment and then said, "You spoke of a pledge."

"It is this. That you will promise me never to use the bomb, or others it may spawn, against us."

"I can promise, David. But the militarists—"

"Don't come the lawyer, Daud. I am asking you as a man. A friend. A leader."

Qidal considered Bar-Lev. "Tell me truly, David. Why do you come to me with this? Why do you make yourself a traitor to your nation?"

Bar-Lev grimaced again. "My nation! You know how I have fought for her. How I have bled in three wars. I love Israel. But I have seen a change. My countrymen now talk calmly of an empire, of Greater Israel. This is not why we struggled in the camps. We must find a way. Otherwise we will all perish together." He paused. When he spoke again, his gravel voice was softer. "And there is this, to be truthful. They say I am dying. This time I believe them. Too many cigarettes, too much rich food. A man has only so much time, Daud. I wish to use mine well, if I can. Do you understand? Do I have your word?"

"You have my word."

Bar-Lev slowly smiled. "So, we have a bargain?"

Feeling foolish and a little giddy, Qidal smiled back. "We have a bargain."

Bar-Lev stood and, seized by the moment, so did Qidal. Bar-Lev embraced him, then stepped back.

Laughter rolled from the hut, spontaneous and pure. Outside, both Ali and the young Israeli soldier glanced at the doorway. When their gazes met again, both wore tiny smiles they could not suppress.

WHEN THE MOMENT CAME to meet him, Qidal was calm. Hassan el Jazzar, the man styled himself, Hassan the Butcher, Hassan the terrorist hero-commander of the Islamic Jihad, Hassan the slayer of unbelievers, Hassan the invisible, Hassan the omnipresent. Qidal had hated him for years. The Jihad publicly and piously proclaimed its solidarity with the Palestinians while actually seeking to liquidate the Liberation Organization's leadership and to turn the young Palestinians into brainwashed Jihaddin, loyal only to the

Iranian ayatollahs. But now Qidal had to deal with el
Jazzar, as he had had to deal with Bar-Lev.

The door burst open and the Butcher entered, preceded by six of his black-hooded bodyguards. Qidal
pointedly remained sitting. His own men shifted into
positions of tension, their AKMs at the ready, their
eyes picking targets even as Hassan's men covered
them warily, guns all but raised.

Hassan halted before the table. Qidal sat at one end
on one of the two chairs that were, with the scarred old
aluminum table, the only furnishings in the crowded
room.

El Jazzar did not look like his reputation. He was
only of medium height, with a slightly oily olive skin.
A fine gold chain hung around his neck and was visible below the open collar of his red cotton sport shirt.
Sweat stained the short sleeves. His face was unreadable, his eyes opaque in their blackness. He wore his
hair short, and cut like a European. He seemed to be
unarmed, his large hands—uncallused, Qidal swiftly
noted—hung easily at his sides as he stared at Qidal.
More like one of the Shah's Iranian bankers, Daud
thought, than the ayatollah's most feared Jihaddin.

"Welcome, brother," Qidal said evenly.

Hassan eyed him a second longer. *"Allah il allah,"*
the Iranian said. He paused, as if waiting for something. Qidal let the silence stretch. A Shia, in any
dress, is still a Shia, he sighed to himself.

"Yes. God is great. Please sit down."

Hassan made some tiny movement, and one of the
guards leaped to pull out the chair.

"You are ready to commit your people to the Jihad?" There were no inflections at all in Hassan's

tone. Somehow, this chilled Qidal more than the rantings of a hysteric.

"No. You know that is not why I asked you to join me here. Surely my messenger—"

"Your messenger is dead. May Allah forgive him his unwillingness to join the true believers."

One of Qidal's men jerked as if jolted by electric shock. Qidal's messenger had been Ali. His brother, Ahmed, stood only an arm's length from Hassan. Qidal raised a warning hand as Ahmed, gasping, slid back the bolt of his AKM. Instantly, the Jihaddin cocked their weapons and tightened their group.

"Hold!" barked Qidal. He looked sternly at Ahmed. "Compose yourself, brother. Remember the words of the Prophet." He shifted his gaze to Hassan. "May Allah forgive you, el Jazzar. It is not young Ali ibn-Assoud who needs his forgiveness. This was treachery."

"It was necessary. We could not be sure he spoke the truth until Allah took him. That is why we are here. Otherwise, you may be certain we would not be."

Qidal's stomach churned. This madman represented everything he hated about radical Islam. Yet he needed him. Desperately. Without his organization— its trained troops, its spies, its money, its worldwide contacts—he was powerless to use Bar-Lev's precious information.

"So. You are here. At the moment, that is all that is important. But what I have to say is not for any ears but your own, Hassan el Jazzar. These men must leave."

El Jazzar looked impassively at Qidal for ten long seconds. Then he leaned forward and spread his hands on the table. "Yes. Mahoud, take the men outside. Wait."

Mahoud went immediately to the door, motioning the others to follow him. Qidal waved Ahmed and his four comrades out. The two groups went into the huge, empty hangar outside the little office. The Libyans had deserted this training site weeks before, taking with them everything not nailed down. Had Qidal known he would not have Libyan troops on site to protect his little band of twenty men, he would not have come. Yet it was too late when he found the desert base all but deserted, only the maintenance crew and the liaison officer present. Only Libya's great desert afforded the secrecy and neutrality they needed for this meeting.

After the door closed, Hassan raised his hand. It was a gesture at once insolent and sardonic.

"You are not joining the Jihad. Yet you ask us to join you."

"Yes."

"Is there an operation?"

"Yes."

"And you need our men."

"Yes."

"What else do you need?"

"Everything."

"And in return?"

"A solution to the Palestinian problem. A new Palestine."

Hassan blinked slowly. He looked, Qidal realized, like a huge lizard. Finally a corner of his mouth lifted. It might have been a smile.

"This is desirable, of course. But the aims of the Jihad—"

"Include an end to my people's agony."

"Of course. This is why we have been, ah, trying—"

"El Jazzar. Your butchers have been attempting to beat us into submission to your ayatollah for years. When subterfuge has failed, you have tried combat. Do not fence with me."

The faint smile faded from el Jazzar's lips. "And do not consider me a fool, Qidal. Until you are prepared to accept the true way—"

Qidal held up his hand. "Enough. I am prepared to bargain for your aid. But you must understand that what I offer you is not plunder for your Jihaddin, but survival. If you do not join me, you risk annihilation."

Hassan cocked his head slightly. "These are big words."

"Yet they are true. We have no more time for your assaults or your connivance with the Syrians to destroy us." Qidal reached into his flapped shirt pocket and withdrew a small scrap of paper. He slid it across the table to Hassan. "Do these coordinates mean anything to you?"

Hassan glanced at the paper and started. He tried immediately to compose himself, but it was too late.

Qidal smiled. "I see you understand their meaning. We have spies too, Hassan, and sources of information you do not dream of. Here is my bargain. Help us, and what lies at this location—and the eleven others you thought were safe and secret—will not be disturbed. Refuse my offer, and I pledge that even if you kill me instantly, my men in Lebanon will see to it that the Iraqis, Israelis and Americans get these before the sun is up tomorrow. You know what that means. These are assets you cannot move. Refuse me, now or for the duration of our agreement, and the Jihad will be all but wiped from the face of the earth."

Hassan stared into Qidal's face a long time. Daud did not flinch. He admired the man's composure. Faced with such a threat, he would not have been as stolid.

"You offer a bargain, but hold a dagger at my throat."

"Yes. Because I know your true goal."

"Where unbelievers are concerned, our goals are identical. To harm us is to harm yourself."

"Do not evade me, el Jazzar."

"My superiors—"

"Have ceded the Jihad to you in all but name, Hassan. Agree for them or see your lifework eradicated. This is your choice."

As a successful lawyer, Qidal knew how prudent men of power react to ultimatums. Agree to anything, was the rule, and then argue, fight or apologize later, all in the name of the higher morality of self-interest.

"Allah is merciful," Hassan said.

Qidal allowed himself a smile. "Yes. That is why we call our plan the Love of Allah. Will you join us?"

"I have no choice." Hassan's voice was barely audible.

"No. You have not. Unless you wish to suffer as my people have suffered for half a century."

El Jazzar stiffened. A wildness came into his countenance, a sudden flash of widened eyes and stretched lips. It was the look of the true madman, Qidal knew. But then it was gone. Whatever forces warred in Hassan el Jazzar had fought themselves to a standstill. When he spoke again, his voice was even, his gaze level. "The Love of Allah. It is a good name. I hope it is also a good plan."

"It is," Qidal said. "A *very* good plan."

SLEEP WOULD NOT COME. He lay awake on the tiny cot and stared at the ceiling. The Americans had built this barracks, as they had built everything else here, during World War II. Qaddafi had added nothing not essential to training his "liberators." The desert wind whispered on the hard gray sands outside the window. Cold seeped through every crack of the collapsing walls. But Daud Qidal did not feel it any more than he felt the onset of sleep.

El Jazzar had left committed to the plan. It was in motion. Would it work? Perhaps. But not even Qidal expected it to succeed fully. But a man had to do something. A man cast by fate into his position had to act. He *had* to.

For the thousandth time that night he closed his eyes to seek the succor of sleep. But sleep would not come. The wind whispered on the sand, the sound of restless souls roaming.

CHAPTER ONE

"A *CORVETTE*? Is this *yours*, Max?"

In spite of himself, he grinned. "Yeah. Like it?"

She pulled open the door and got in, somewhat awkwardly. The tall doorsills of the car made it hard for women in dresses to get in any other way. Max suspected the car had been designed that way on purpose, to penalize women and reward men. A subtle, coded reminder from Corvette designers to Corvette buyers that this was, by God, a *man's* car. Or maybe not. Maybe it was just another manufacturer's ergonomics screwup.

She grinned back at him as she wriggled into the leather-clad racing-style bucket seat. "Yeah, sure. My brother had one. I used to drive it all the time."

He snorted inwardly. So much for the men-only car.

"Ready for some conch chowder?" he asked.

"Always. That's one of the main reasons why I come down here."

Max started the car. The faraway rumble of the big fuel-injected and turbocharged V-8 spoke of unlimited power. Considering what it cost, it damned well ought to, he thought.

"What about you?"

"What?"

"Why do *you* come down here?"

He flicked the light switch. The panel display dimmed and the big one hundred-watt Hella halogens swiveled up. They painted the pink stucco walls of her hotel in dazzling white light that completely overwhelmed the glorious Florida sunset.

"Why?" He paused while the idle steadied. "Easy. It seemed like the right thing to do at the time."

She laughed, a tinkling kind of coquette laugh, the slightly nervous laugh of a good-looking young woman on her first date with a stranger. Which made sense, because she was a good-looking young woman and he was a stranger to her and this was their first date. If people in their early thirties can even have "dates," he mused. Come to think of it, he was even a little nervous himself. How, exactly, did you go about this business of dating, when most people your age were all married with kids or divorced with kids or something else with kids, and you were still a bachelor? Like this, he thought. Just like this. You found a girl like Kelly here, on a snorkel diving expedition out of Key Largo, you got to know her a little during the forty-minute ride out to the Pennekamp Reef, dived as her buddy for half an hour over the coral and barracuda, then agreed during the forty-minute ride back that a date was in order. Next thing you knew, you were wearing your long-ignored wool slacks, Harris tweed jacket and loafers on your way to dinner at the Plantation Key Yacht Club. Easy.

"Good line. Got more?"

"Lots more, sweetheart. Just stick with Rocco, baby, and you'll see."

"Whoo! Edward G. Robinson, right?"

"Bogie."

"Not bad. Not great, but not bad. Got any more?"

He chuckled as he swung out onto the Keys Highway, the narrow umbilical linking the long chain of little islands where people from the north landed every winter, to be grudgingly welcomed by the locals with the epithet, Snowbirds, and where the locals in return were referred to as conch-heads or crackers by the Northerners. Traffic was light, this being an early spring evening. Things wouldn't get crowded until the night wore on and both crackers and snowbirds got looped and loose on the ribbon of asphalt.

"Yeah. Got a million of 'em. Too many."

"Ever do any work onstage?"

Max grinned ruefully. He thought about Camp Peters, where they'd tried to make him learn the skills of a spy. And about a road long ago and far away in East Germany, where he'd fooled some Russian sentries with an electronically amplified White Russian accent, picked up lesson by lesson over four years from Yaakov Pechaver in the same musty classroom in Berkeley. Some stages were more dangerous than others.

"Nah," he said, easing the 'Vette onto the road. "Just an amateur smart mouth, I guess."

Kelly glanced at him, a movement he caught out of the corner of his eye. Just as Ike had taught him all those years ago. Never miss anything, kid. What you miss'll ruin your whole goddamn day. Her look was appraising, slightly leery. He found to his surprise that his palms had gone suddenly a little damp, as they always had just before the flag dropped in a race. And sure enough, his damned mouth was desert-dry. He felt like a kid out with the prom queen. It irritated him.

"Well, it was a good Robinson, if not a Bogie." She paused, sensing his nervousness, maybe feeling some herself. "Mind if I try the radio?"

"'Course not. Have at it. Volume's on the left, the stations are preset. Tapes are under the armrest."

Kelly busied herself with the radio, trying each station in sequence. The small passenger compartment filled successively with the crisp sounds of Top-40 rock hits, classical music, country and western, Motown, white jazz and news as the traffic built up in the gathering darkness. Bugs splattered on the windshield, dying in huge, sometimes eerily fluorescent globs. Max listened to her search for acceptable music with interest. Another compatibility test.

Kelly was maybe five years his junior, an obviously vivacious and ambitious midlevel manager in some financial operation he'd never heard of in Boston. She was neither stunningly beautiful nor plain as Jane. She wore what seemed to be her naturally blond hair in a modish, flip manner that had attracted his eye at once on the benches of the dive boat. Her confidence as she stripped off her pastel outer gear to reveal a pert, fit figure in her wet suit had made him admire her even before they spoke. Most of the other women had been nervous about stripping for the dive, even though they all wore suits under their street clothes. Max hadn't exactly been looking for companionship in joining the dive boat at the last minute, but he realized by the intensity with which he'd watched Kelly that it was too long since he'd been with a woman—in every sense. So when she boldly and smilingly returned his interest, he'd realized they were feeling each other out for a possible relationship. Hence their long conversation on the way back from the reef, playing do you know? and have you been to? to establish personal values, life-styles and landmarks. He had played it close to the vest—she'd never believe the truth anyway—but enough compatibility had been established to allow them this date. And now the music test. She didn't seem to be having much luck, scanning furiously.

"Here," he said, flipping up the armrest and withdrawing a tape. "Try this one."

She looked at it curiously. Like all his personally recorded tapes, it was unlabeled. She shrugged and slipped it into the tape slot.

After a faint hissing, Luciano Pavarotti filled the cabin. She glanced at him, obviously surprised.

He saw her look and nodded. "Yup. *I Puritani*. Story's a real downer, but the tunes are great. And old Luke Highsquawker really gets into this one, don't you think?"

She laughed. "Pavarotti. In a Corvette!"

"Sure. Why not? Don't like opera?"

"No, no—love it. It's just that—well, you know..."

"Yeah. I know. Guy with a 'Vette ought to be a Beach Boys man. Well, I've got 'Little Deuce Coupe' if you'd prefer—"

"No, no! I love it! Sorry!" She laughed and waved her hands in mock surrender. The tension in the car slid away with each mile and measure of the opera. Max relaxed and concentrated on driving at the speed limit, which was not an easy thing for him to do. Nor was it any easier for the other cars on Highway 1 that evening; those ahead pulled slowly away, going maybe ten miles per hour more than the limit. And those behind slowly closed on him. One by one, they passed him, some darting curious glances at the fire-red Corvette poking along at fifty-five. Head against the headrest, absorbed by the music, Kelly didn't notice.

Max did. Just as he noticed that one set of headlights did not close on him, slow, follow and then jerk past as the others had. For some men such an event might have meant nothing. And Max knew that it might mean nothing to him now that he was out of the game. But years spent behind the wheels of Mission vehicles, thousands of miles spent in pursuit or escape with a stomach knotted tight had taught him a different set of responses.

Headlights that wouldn't pass might be nothing. Or they might be everything. They might be anything. He felt the calm descend, the flood of adrenaline so familiar and so vital. He tuned out Kelly and Pavarotti, scanning his instruments, flicking glances at the road, the environment, even the weather, trying to recall the map. Ike's voice haunted him: *Where are you, boy? Where the hell you going? Where you been? What's around you? What's up front? In back? Open your eyes, kid! Clean out your ears! This ain't a fuckin' playground!* He licked his lips, eyes once again on the headlights. Long-dormant mental processes clicked on automatically as he sought to type them.

A Mercedes. Probably a 560 SEC. Flanked by aftermarket driving lights. But too low by about four inches. In the light of an oncoming truck, he caught vital clues. Highlights on fancy bodywork—chin air dam, widely flared fenders, the hint of a tall wing mounted on the trunk. Not just a Mercedes, then. A boy-racer Mercedes, something like an AMG special. The favorite tools of the very rich. And the very nasty. As in Mafia. As in coke kings. Whoever it was could have blitzed by without a second's delay, miles ago. But chose instead to tail him.

Okay, Max thought. Okay. The map in his head told him he was a few miles from any decent side roads. Which meant the escape routes were restricted to the highway and the tiny clumps of scrub and crushed coral on either side. Until they got to Plantation Key, he was hemmed in badly.

Kelly continued to gaze out the translucent moon roof, absorbed in the music. Max shelved the idea of telling her to hold on, to be ready for anything. Nothing might happen, and she'd think he was a fool, or a loony. The guy back there in the trick Benz might be just some drunk, target-fixated on Max's taillights. Gently, Max picked up the speed.

As if magnetized, the Mercedes's headlights swept up ten feet, now only five feet behind his rear bumper. Max's heart rate accelerated. He checked the road ahead and picked up another five miles per hour.

The headlights followed. Now they were uncomfortably close even for Kelly. She frowned and craned her neck to look around.

"Don't!" Max barked. She blinked and looked at him. He seemed a different man. His close-cropped but unruly black hair now framed the face of a man in combat. His pale green eyes were narrowed, constantly in motion, checking the road, the mirrors, the instruments. His normally pale skin was taut, tiny wrinkles at the corners of his eyes, small scimitars of concentration framing his narrow lips, which were drawn into a grim horizontal line. The tiny slanted scar on his chin stood out in white relief. A muscle twitched in his cheek. She opened her mouth to ask a question, then closed it. He radiated tension of a wholly different sort than they had experienced a few minutes before. She caught something of his mood and gripped the door handle instinctively. It occurred to her suddenly how little she really knew of Maxwell Taylor Moss.

"Okay," Max muttered, "okay. Let's see what you've got." And before Kelly could ask what he meant, Max slammed a lightning-quick downshift and floored the accelerator.

The Corvette lunged ahead, pinning them both to their seats with 500 horsepower. The muted rumble of its engine became a roaring bellow. Speed gathered so quickly the huge green digital speedometer simply flashed a confusing tumble of meaningless numbers. The engine screamed up to its redline, and Max moved the gearshift to fourth so quickly it seemed to Kelly the car had shifted by itself.

Max checked the rearview mirror. The Benz had initially been taken by surprise, then had kicked in its own considerable power. He glanced at the tachometer. The speedo was useless, but he knew he had to be closing on 135 mph, at which point he'd shift to fifth gear. Then it would be a flat-out drag race between the Benz and the 'Vette, before the next key, where he could get off the road and try to get behind the guy. That was still some miles ahead. He loosened his grip on the thick leather of the steering wheel, deliberately forcing his hands to relax, steering with pressure not on the wheel but behind it, with fingers and not palms. He felt the car come alive as the speed built, shaking

off the effects of days spent idling around the town of
Key Largo. Unnoticed by either of them, the automatic sound-level compensator of the sound system
kept pace with the increasing wind, engine and tire
noise, ratcheting up the volume of Pavarotti as he
belted out the lament of the Puritans. Max ignored
him as he now ignored Kelly. He glanced at the speedo,
which had now settled down. It showed 155, and was
still moving up. He recalled in a flash the words of the
guy who'd taught him how to drive the huge banked
tri-oval at Daytona: "Just keep one thing in mind,
boy. Above a buck and a half, things get real serious." It had taken him a second to understand that the
Virginian's buck-and-a-half was 150 mph. But it had
taken him less than that to know what he meant once
he got his racer up to that speed on the steep banks.
He'd never forgotten the advice. And it had saved him
more than once.

He kept the throttle down and hoped the road
would stay clear. The headlights behind dropped
slowly back as the speedometer nudged 167. Had he
had the concentration to spare, he would have grunted
in satisfaction. The tricked-up Mercedes behind was
plenty fast, with slippery bodywork, to be sure. But it
was still a sedan. And he was in one of the fastest
production cars on earth. That was why it had seemed
the right thing to do to buy it back there in Mobile.

The satisfaction faded as he crested a gentle rise and
saw taillights far ahead. The noise changed abruptly
as he dropped onto one of the long causeway sections
of the Keys Highway, the singing of the crushed coral
of the roadbed through the huge tires now accompanied by the howl of the air shoved up against the

Armco guardrail, which was all that was standing between them and the dark water a few feet below. The
taillights drew closer rapidly. Max darted a glance in
the mirror and confirmed what he guessed by the
brightening glare of the lights in his cockpit; the guy
in the Benz had somehow found some more speed. He
was closing. The speedo now rested on 173.

Max swiftly considered his options. He was sure
that the guy in the Benz had stuck with him too long
to be considered simply a harmless, boozed-up street
racer out to prove he was top gun on Highway 1. He
had to follow through with his evasion plan. But to do
it, he had to get to Plantation Key. And between him
and the Key was the car with the taillights. His only
hope was to get past that car before the other guy
could block his pass. He grimly kept the throttle
down, and the 'Vette crept toward its ultimate redline
while the headlights behind him burned ever nearer.
He started to call an explanatory phrase to Kelly over
the perfectly reproduced tenor of Pavarotti, but as he
opened his mouth he saw the twinkling of oncoming
headlights. He clamped his mouth shut and, just as he
was setting up to blow past the car in his lane—now
looming frighteningly quickly in the blaze of his Hel-
las—instead jumped on his brakes.

The antilock braking computer calculated the required data in microseconds and translated his three
hundred pounds of muscle power into maximum
stopping. It regulated the flow of the silicone brake
fluid to the four huge disk brakes with precision un-
available to any human, and the big Corvette slowed
as if it had run onto a road made of quicksand. Kelly
gasped as she lurched forward into her seat harness,

which locked solid under the g-loading. Acrid smoke filled the cockpit as Max slammed downshifts, desperately hoping the oncoming car would pass before the Benz rammed them or—worse!—slipped into the overtaking slot.

A Honda Civic full of wide-eyed passengers whipped past just as Max's bumper almost kissed the rear end of the Chevy pickup truck ahead, and the instant the Honda was parallel to his door, Max jerked the wheel left and floored the accelerator, trying to get around the slow truck.

He almost made it, but the Benz was there first. Max caught the nose of the sleek black Mercedes in his peripheral vision and jerked the wheel right again. The Mercedes accelerated past, filled the left lane and stayed there, pacing the truck—which had sped up to about seventy—and keeping Max locked behind.

The tape clicked over to the other side, and Pavarotti was replaced by the Beach Boys. Max swept the road ahead, looking for a way out. If he tried a handbrake reverse, the guy could be on him in a second. He would either have to wait until the key ahead or—

"Hey!" Kelly said weakly, "Max—this is crazy. I—"

"Quiet!" Max growled. He kept his eyes on the situation ahead. The truck driver was slowing down, obviously trying to get the black Mercedes to pass him. An arm waved out the window. There was no response from the low Mercedes.

"Yeah!" Max breathed as he spotted what he'd been hoping for. Ahead, the Armco had been taken out on his side, probably by an accident, and it had not been replaced. There wasn't much room. But it might be enough.

"Hold on," he grunted, and kicked the Corvette's throttle to the floor. At this low speed, the car slewed from side to side under full throttle like a freight car about to go off the rails. He held it under control and aimed for the right side of the pickup. It looked as if no more than five feet lay between the truck's flank and the steep bank of the levee road. Beyond that was nothing but crocodiles.

Kelly gulped as the 'Vette roared past the truck. Max felt the car slipping on the soft shoulder. For a moment it wallowed and lurched, the wide right side tire spinning, the left one still on the asphalt. The truck driver panicked with cars on both sides and swerved right. Max hit the air horns and the shriek made the driver swing left. As soon as Max saw the truck's front wheel deflect he hammered the throttle again and suddenly they were past the truck and the Mercedes. He kept the throttle down and didn't let up. After a few seconds, he checked the mirror.

The Benz and the truck were tangled in a mess of headlights and dust. Max looked until he was sure it was just that and not a major accident, then shifted again, eased off the throttle and coasted back down to 100 mph. Whoever that guy was, he thought, and whatever he was trying to do, it would be a while before he got his fancy Mercedes extricated from the Chevy pickup. He smiled thinly and looked at Kelly.

She stared straight ahead, eyes wide, lips trembling. She clutched the door grip with her right hand and the edge of the seat with her left. Oh, shit, Max thought. He thought about what to say, how to explain, and just came up blank. So he just drove for a moment, slowing again. Suddenly he realized the Beach Boys were wailing about their four-speed dual-quad Positraction 409. It seemed singularly inappropriate. He reached out slowly and turned off the tape deck.

Ahead, Plantation Key appeared as a constellation of lights.

Kelly slowly released her grip on the seat. Not looking at Max, she said, "I *hate* the Beach Boys."

They drove the remaining mile to the yacht club in silence.

As Max pulled the big car into the parking lot, Kelly began shaking visibly. He switched off the engine and looked at her.

"Hey, you need to understand—"

"No. I don't need to understand. I need to go home. I think I'm going to be sick."

In the multicolored light thrown by the Chinese lanterns over the porch of the club, she did look pale. Max cursed himself silently. What a way to begin. If only he'd—

"So thanks for the ride, Mr. Moss. But I think I'm calling it quits here. I'll get a taxi." She pulled at the door handle and just as awkwardly as she had got in, struggled to swing her legs up and out.

"Listen. Taxis are pretty scarce out here. I'll take you..."

But as if God had decided to make his night perfect, a yellow Ford sedan with the indisputable word, Taxi emblazoned on its rooftop light bar crunched up on the porte cochere driveway and disgorged two old ladies. Kelly whistled, got the cabbie's attention and started walking a little unsteadily to the Ford.

Max jumped out and ran to her. They walked slowly in silence—she stonily, he miserably.

"Look. I don't drive like that for *fun*," he said as she halted by the cab. She fixed him with an icy glare.

"And I don't ride like that for fun, either. You want to show off, get another girl. When I die, it's not going to be because some yo-yo in a machomobile couldn't resist a race. Even my damned brother grew out of *that* stage."

He was finished. They were finished. Yet still she stood, hand on door handle, facing him, as if not quite convinced that he was a dangerous lunatic. Maybe there was a chance.

"It's like this. See, it's the business I'm in. Or was in. You couldn't take chances. We—that is, they . . ." His voice trailed off and he looked at her.

She might have softened her look. Or then again, she might not have. In the crazy red-green-yellow light of the club's lanterns swinging gently in the Keys breeze, it was hard to tell. She opened her mouth to say something. But before she could, a commotion on the road nearby interrupted her.

The black Mercedes slid to a halt. Its engine sounded like a slightly muffled turbojet. Max turned to face the shiny black car, now ruffled somewhat with dust, a torn-off section of air dam and a little crease in the right front fender. The blacked-out windows didn't allow them to see inside. Max felt for the 9 mm he had been carrying until recently and suddenly remembered where he was. Who he was. And now, who he was *not*. He was no longer a guy who carried a

9 mm. He stepped slightly in front of Kelly, large
hands slowly knotting into fists.

The Benz sat still a moment more, then the passenger window hissed down. The light from the club was
strong enough to show that the passenger was a beautiful Hispanic woman, heavily made up with blue-
green eyeliner and flame-red lipstick. What probably
were very large diamonds sloped around her neck and
dangled from her earlobes. Her expression was inscrutable.

But that of her driver was not. He leaned across her
to look at Max. He wore pink-shaded sunglasses, a
blue silk shirt open to the breastbone and a white,
rough-cut silk jacket, collar standing up, sleeves
jammed up his brown arms. Under his thick black
eyelashes and swept-back, oiled hair, his black eyes
were flaming, his nostrils flared wide. Max watched
his hands. The right one seemed to be on the passenger's seat back, the left one—

The left one was pointing at him.

"Hey, asshole! Next time you want to race with
José, make sure you got the balls to go all the way!
¿Comprende?" Then, before Max could reply, José
threw him the finger and the window hummed back
up. In a second the engine snarled and whined, and the
Benz's tires spun on crushed coral before laying thick
black streaks on the road. After a moment, the Mercedes was gone toward Key West.

When Max turned again to Kelly, she smiled coldly
at him. A smile of certainty.

"What was this about your... *business*?"

Max suddenly felt tired, alone and frustrated, as he
had felt for a long, long time. He saw in his mind the

effort it would take to convince her that he wasn't just
a middle-aged street-racing egomaniac—the humble
half-revelations, the drinks, the dancing, the slow
melting of her hostility and deserved fear—and wondered whether it was all worth it.

She decided for him. He had somehow missed his
cue. She jerked open the door of the cab and slipped
in while he stared blankly at her.

"Don't call me," she said frostily. "I'll call you."
Then she rolled up the window and tapped on the
cabbie's shoulder. The Ford clunked into gear and left
Max standing in the porte cochere. In a moment, the
taxi, like the Mercedes, was gone.

As his mind was accustomed to do, it grabbed the
least obvious thing to focus on. The Mercedes. It *was*
a street racer, and the guy—a Cuban, probably, and
given his outfit, probably also deep into the drug
business—*was* just racing him. It *was* as innocently
stupid as it seemed. He had *not* been engaged in combat with the real bad guys. Only a sort-of bad guy, a
common criminal rather than gents trained in Lenin-
grad and Omsk and Karl-Marx Stadt. He considered
the implications. They were all bad.

He had been out almost two months and was still
acting and reacting like he was still in. His hair was
longer, he didn't carry an ID card with "Moss, Maxwell T., Capt., USAF" on it, and Blackie Lundberg's
special phone number in Arlington was no longer issued to him monthly. As far as he could tell, when
he'd called Landreth a pissant martinet and handed in
his papers back at Camp Peters, that was it as far as
they were concerned. He was out of their game, out of
his former life.

But it was obviously going to take more than a few months of hanging out in Key Largo, blowing separation pay on condo rental and gas for a Corvette to get him really out of it. He was in most ways a normal thirty-four-year-old American male. But there were ways he was not normal, and he knew it, as Kelly now also knew.

Kelly. He winced and shook his head as he ambled back to the car. She seemed like a nice lady. He slid behind the wheel and stared into the darkness down the long, straight Keys Highway. Where to? his eternally wired driver-mind asked his confused socialmind. Anywhere, was the answer. Anywhere at all.

Anywhere, fifteen minutes and about as many miles south, turned out to be Mike's Place. Driving in a bemused daze, he'd noticed Mike's because of the car parked in front of its typically seedy Keys-bar stucco facade. The car was a 1963 split-window Corvette Stingray in atrocious condition. It attracted his attention because it was worth so much and because its fiberglass body was so badly in need of paint and TLC. He slowed his own 'Vette to a walking pace as he drew near the bar and the car. One perfectly complemented the other. The flickering red neon sign—which read M k s Pla e—threw a sickly glow over the peeling paint of the low, windowless building, and coated the car nosed up to the cheerless door with a tint of red that only made it seem more distressed than it might actually have been. The effect was heightened by the proximity to the '63 Stingray of a brand-new Ford pickup.

He was parked and getting out of the 'Vette before he even thought about whether stopping here was the

right thing to do. He was determined to switch off his
mind. He was tired, hungry, thirsty and lonely. But
not necessarily in that order.

Behind the door lay a scene common in the Keys.
This was no upscale dating bar where bright-eyed
young professionals came to discuss wine and BMWs
and AIDS. This was the kind of bar where men like
him—hurt men, angry men, exhausted men, confused men who didn't know what was wrong and
couldn't explain it even if they did know—came to lick
their wounds. It was a locals' bar, local in these parts
being defined as anybody on the Keys who wasn't a
snowbird.

Nobody looked up as Max walked in. Not even the
bartender, an older, balding guy wearing half glasses,
tiredly hunched over a glowing calculator and a stack
of receipts, gave him a glance. In the darkest corner of
the dark, beer-smelling room, a television flashed
meaningless pictures of a world nobody in here wanted
to see. The sound was turned off, but an old-
fashioned, much-pounded-on jukebox in the other
corner played "Stand by Your Man."

The only light inside came from the long, tired fluorescent tube that hung above the mirror behind the
bar and two conch lamps hung on adjacent walls. A
few battered wooden tables were scattered around the
small floor, and seven stools at the bar. Two guys sat
at one of the tables, desultorily sucking beers and
playing cards. Another sat at the fifth stool at the bar.
Max plonked himself down on the third stool.

After a moment, the bartender peeled off his glasses
and came over.

"What's your pleasure?"

"Dos Equis. Got any chips?"

"Sure." He reached below the countertop and slapped a napkin and a bag of chips on the bar, then pulled a bottle out of the beer cooler. He popped off the top and thunked the bottle and a mug he pulled deftly from a freezer in front of Max. Max pulled a five out of his money clip, and laid it on the bar. The barman glanced at it, slipped his glasses back on and sat heavily at his calculator again.

Max poured his beer and munched a chip. It was stale. The beer was not prime. What the hell, he thought. He munched and drank for a while, the music a perfect accompaniment to his mood. Nobody spoke for a long time. Then the barkeep tugged off his glasses, sighed and came over.

"More?"

"Not yet. Thanks."

The barman turned to the other guy at the bar. Max had ignored him and the other two, lost in his musings. Now, pulled by the barman's attention, he glanced at him. Something about the man made Max sure he owned the Stingray. He was in his late fifties, maybe early sixties, to judge by his thinning silver-blond hair. His skin was the color and texture of weathered leather, his face a road map of deep creases and wrinkles. Even with a glance Max could tell the effects of a broken nose set badly long ago. He was a big man. But he did not have the look of a boxer or onetime tough.

He wore a simple blue sweatshirt, sleeves raggedly cut off at the biceps. There was some kind of insignia or logo on the shirtfront, something that might have once been gold. Below the sweatshirt were faded canvas shorts, hairy, muscular and very tanned legs, and docksiders worn almost to disintegration. "Charlie?" said the bartender.

"Sure, Mike." He slid his glass over and the barman filled it again with draft beer.

"Thanks. *Kempei.*"

"Hai. So des," said Mike absently and sat down once again, to do battle with the calculator.

Because Max was tired of contemplating his own shortcomings and lack of prospects to change them, the brief interchange caught his attention. A lot of crazy talk goes down in bars. But they'd taught him enough in all those months of intel classes to spot a few things. These guys were obviously old friends. Both of them spoke enough Japanese to be unconsciously comfortable with it. He looked more closely around the bar, and at the men called Charlie and Mike.

The bar gave nothing away, save for a small photo in the corner by the TV and the sign for the toilet. The photo seemed to be of an airplane. Curious, Max set down his beer and threaded the tables to the bathroom, pausing to look at the poorly framed photograph. It was a faded color photo of a Navy Corsair, the gull-winged single-seat fighter used in World War II and Korea. Two smiling young guys in Navy tan flight suits and Mae Wests knelt before the huge old four-bladed prop. A scrawled inscription read, "Mike: Good luck and keep it close—Charlie." There was no date on the photo. Max went to the john.

When he sat down again, Max took a pull on his beer and looked two stools down at Charlie.

"That your Stingray outside?" He kept his voice neutral. Bars like this one were not places to be misunderstood. Charlie nodded, not looking over at Max. "Yep."

"Nice car."

"Was."

This was obviously intended to halt further conversation, not encourage it. Somehow, it irritated Max.

"Probably all it needs is restoration."

For the first time, Charlie looked at Max. His eyes, deeply set in a sea of wrinkles, were ice-blue and penetrating, not at all the eyes of a rummy.

"Lot of things need restoration, mister, but that old split-window isn't one of them."

Something about the edge in his voice rang a bell with Max. And something about the intonation of "mister."

"Oh? Body looked kind of shot."

Charlie smiled thinly. "You know, a lot of ol' boys around here used to think that car ran the way it looked. Now they know better."

"Can't judge a book by its cover, eh? Well, maybe. But maybe you can."

Charlie held his eyes a moment longer, then took a pull on his beer. "You a good judge of cars?" He asked it coolly.

"Sometimes."

"Lots of experience, have you?"

"Some."

"Ah. Some." Silence fell. Charlie drank some more beer. So did Max. This was the classic bar confrontation, he realized. Like the race with José, like just about everything in his life, it was a showdown of sorts. Maybe Kelly was right about him.

Charlie swiveled on his stool and scrutinized him. "Son," he said at last, "about here is where I usually get kind of mad about what some young guy says concerning my car. But tonight I'm too damn tired. Tonight I just don't feel up to it. So if you don't mind we'll leave out the gunfighter shit and just drink in quiet comradeship. That okay with you?"

Max slowly smiled. "That's fine with me, Captain." He knew as he said it that he'd scored a bull's-eye; he'd finally recognized the grimy logo on the sweatshirt. It was the U.S. Naval Academy crest. Odds were this guy was a retired naval aviator.

Both Mike and Charlie looked sharply at him, then exchanged glances.

"You Navy?" Mike asked, looking at him over his glasses.

"Air Force. Was, anyway." He paused, then smiled again. "Career got cut short by a run-in with my CO."

Charlie grinned. "Bad run-in?"

"Bad enough. If I hadn't turned in my papers, I'd have popped him."

Mike chuckled. "Just like you, Charlie. Just like you."

Max raised an eyebrow.

"Not quite. If you'll recall, Michael, I actually did pop Nichols."

"Yeah—but not until *after* you'd done his wife!"

Both men burst into laughter. Max smiled and drank his beer. For the first time that night, he began to relax. And then he realized that it wasn't just the first time that night. It was the first time since he'd gotten out.

Mike and Charlie were still chuckling. Max held his glass out to Mike, who took it, grinning. Max looked at Charlie. "Sounds like a good story," he said.

Charlie smiled wide. "Hell, son, it'll *kill* you. But it's a long one, right, Mike?"

Mike nodded and handed Max his beer. "Hell of a long one. About twenty years' worth."

Max held up his glass in salute. "Fire away."

Charlie shrugged and returned the salute. They both drank, and when he put down his mug, Charlie looked up at Max, blue eyes twinkling. "Now *this*," he began, echoing every story told by every pilot in every officers' club in the world, "is *no shit....*"

CHAPTER TWO

DURING A LONG NIGHT FLIGHT, a man has a lot of time to think thoughts that the sun dispels as it does the morning fog. Hadj al-Shiran knew that well. He had almost as much flying time at night as during daylight. He had learned to distrust the heightened emotions of the night. Yet even so, he could not fully suppress the elation he felt as the shoreline—and the state of Pennsylvania—drew near. He knew that to feel it too keenly was in some way a kind of multiple betrayal. A betrayal of his vows as a Jihaddin. A betrayal, too, of his oath to avenge his brother, himself, his race. And last, a betrayal of the unwritten code of the other brotherhood of which he was still a proud member, the brotherhood of professional aviators.

But the dim line of creamy waves ahead that marked the end of Lake Erie and the beginning of the Commonwealth of Pennsylvania evoked something too strong for him to control. He checked his course again, knowing it was perfect. He checked the fuel flow, knowing it was perfect. He checked the time, knowing he was, as always, right on schedule.

In the faint light cast by the quarter moon, he guided the little Cessna Turbo 210 toward the grass airstrip near a dilapidated old farm fifty miles inland.

There the next stage of his long journey would begin. It was, like his whole life, a pilgrimage. As the shoreline approached—rapidly, because of his low altitude and 170-knot airspeed—he prayed for guidance on this pilgrimage, just as his mullah had so thoroughly instructed him to pray for Allah's aid in all his work. He muttered the lilting Arabic swiftly, eyes darting around the cockpit and scanning the coast ahead. He was here. At last. His heart beat more quickly and he muttered his prayer a little louder a second time.

"In the name of Allah, the compassionate—" he began again. A flash of pain, almost too quick to be felt, slid through his head. He blinked in surprise and shook his head as if to toss off a clinging demon.

"In the name of Allah—"

The pain stabbed again, a jolt that he knew all too well. The sweat came almost in torrents now and he gritted his teeth, focusing on the demands of the low-flying airplane.

"In the name—" he shouted it this time, and the pain did not come "—of Allah, the compassionate, the merciful—"

In the name of Allah, the compassionate, the merciful: Why should we believe you, unbeliever? Why should Allah take you under his care? Will you renounce your unbelief and accept the way and the truth and take up the righteous sword? Will you do all this for love of Allah?

Jefferson Paul Jones knew that sometimes things got a little weird for him. He knew, vaguely, that he wasn't like other men, not even like other bloods, in the Army or back on the street. Paul had known that, too. He was *special*, his brother had told him, when

not even Mama had understood why he had to fight
the four white kids from Northeast. It wasn't just
black pride. It was . . . what? Even now, now that he
had renounced Jefferson Paul Jones as a slave name,
a relic of the unbelieving white man's onetime power
over him and his people, even now that he had truly
become Hadj al-Shiran, he wasn't sure. But he was
sure he was still special. The voices told him so. Paul's
voice. And the Other, a strong voice, a calming voice
that might have been the father he never knew but was
more probably Allah Himself. Al-Shiran was careful
never to tell even the mullahs about the Other, just as
he'd been careful never to tell the medicos in the green
machine. The voices were too special, like him.

He was destined, the voices whispered to him, to do
great things. And now, at last, as the coast slipped
under the Cessna's wings, he was about to do them.
He was about to avenge Paul and, with Allah's grace,
to begin the final liberation of his people. For a moment, the dark, rolling coastal countryside shim-
mered in his sight, and a Garden of Eden seemed to
replace it. He shook his head and cleared the vision,
while mentally uttering a prayer of thanks to Allah for
showing him again why he had been put on earth. The
prayer was interrupted by human voices crackling
through his headset.

"Beechcraft One-Niner-Foxtrot, say position and
altitude."

"Nineteen Fox is at ten point five, seven southwest
of Alky intersection, Center."

"Roger, One-Niner-Foxtrot. Contact Erie Approach on one-two-five-point-five."

"Twenty-two-five. So long, Center."

The Center controller clicked his mike button twice, and al-Shiran's headset went quiet again, the VHF net hissing faintly, barely audible over the drone of the big six-cylinder Lycoming pulling the 210 through the night. There had been little chatter on the net, but he'd monitored each appropriate frequency as he penetrated each new sector. They didn't know where he was—his transponder was dead, turned off, and he flew too low for their radars to spot him. At least, he thought so.

Allah was on his side; he knew that as he knew he was the best pilot in the world. Yet Allah helped him who helped himself. That was why he had the AN/ALQ-696 strapped awkwardly into the right seat. When they had told him in Qom of this plan, he had made certain demands, despite his humble position. One was that they obtain this special electronic countermeasures black box. He knew that the F-14Ds shot down over Lebanon had carried them, so unless the swabbies had been more efficient than they usually were at ensuring post-ejection destruct, there had to be some around. He'd been fairly certain that if the mullahs could pull the political strings, he could get the protection from the U.S. and Canadian customs and their secret military airborne backup that he'd need to penetrate undetected. The mullahs of course had the pull, and when he took off from Tehran on his long flight to the tiny strip that awaited him, Allah flew with him, but he was also aided by the best that Litton and Westinghouse could devise to thwart detection by radar. As long as the AN/ALQ-696 stayed quiet, he was safe from the prying eyes of the Citations and CH-53s and cutters that prowled the increasingly well-protected borders of the country he'd once called home. And so far, it had emitted not a single peep of alarm, not even when he'd veered close to the secret Naval air station in Maine, driven off course by an ominous wall of clouds. Like him, the trip was special. Blessed by Allah.

Read, acolyte, and bless Him who made you. Read from the Repentance, chapter 9, verse 4: "When the sacred months are over slay the idolators wherever you find them. Arrest them, besiege them and lie in ambush everywhere for them." And: "Those that have embraced the faith and fled their homes and fought for Allah's cause with their wealth and their persons are held in higher regard by Allah. It is they who shall triumph. Their Lord has promised them joy and mercy, and gardens of eternal bliss where they shall dwell forever. Allah's reward is great indeed." And heed His word to Mohammed: "Prophet, make war on the unbelievers and the hypocrites and deal rigorously with them. Hell shall be their home: an evil fate." Do you understand this, who seeks enlightenment and favor with Allah? Do you see how your path lies down the way, through the faith and the sword of truth? Do you embrace Allah?

When they had told him he would share his airplane with more than just the big fuel cell, he was not happy. When they told him what his cargo would be, he was even less happy. One hundred pounds of pure heroin would bring in a great deal of money for the cause, they had said. And the drug would go to those who had rejected Allah's word: the already damned, the sons and daughters of the Great Shaitan. He had obeyed. But he was still uneasy. Much, he knew, would find its way not to the comfortable white suburbs, there to hasten the demise of the damned, but also to places like his old street in Washington, D.C.'s poverty-stricken Southeast. Many black brothers and sisters would suffer. In his cubicle at Qom, he had spent many a night after prayer, tormented by the thought that he was hurting the very ones he was sworn to aid. The pains had come often on those nights, and the voice of the Other had not guided him.

But his mullah, Ayatollah Hassoghi, had eased his conscience, explaining how it all fitted into Allah's plan. Hassan el Jazzar had made it even plainer: if it pleased Allah to allow him to fall into the enemy's hands, the explanation of his flying the airplane to avoid detection would be readily ascribed to the heroin. He would be treated simply as a drug smuggler, and not what he truly was: a Jihaddin. This deception would please not just the ayatollahs of the Jihad, but also Allah.

Al-Shiran reluctantly agreed to sacrifice his concerns and sixteen gallons of fuel to their heroin. But he could not wait to land, consign it to those who awaited him, collect the money and be on his way, free of the dreadful drag of its presence behind him in the small cabin.

Maybe it was because as Chief Aviation Warrant Officer J. P. Jones, holder of a DFC with silver oak leaves, Silver Star and Bronze Star, two-time Nam veteran, he knew too well what such drugs meant. Old J. P. Jones had *done* shit like that. Or maybe it was because the pigs had claimed what happened to Paul and Anita and Leslie was "drug-related." But maybe it was because some part of him, deep down, down even past Hadj al-Shiran, wondered if the end did justify the means. He believed it now, or so he thought. But he recalled uneasily that he had once also believed, or at least not disbelieved, something much like it twenty years earlier when they had first let him fly.

The instrument scan that was so much a part of his life, like breathing, like swallowing and smiling, happened by itself. All normal, his eyes told his brain, which then told his hands and feet how to work the rudder pedals and control yoke to keep it that way. Hadj al-Shiran or even J. P. Jones wasn't even home. That was part of what had happened to him; part of Nam and Charlie and the unit. Part of 1968.

The haze came as the memory chain activated. It always did. He just couldn't remember some things. Even some times. Weeks, maybe. Months. Occasionally flashes of scenes, startlingly real, in brilliant color and sound, would rip through his mind. Sometimes when one of the pains came, or when he was sleeping, sometimes even when he was awake, usually on a long flight like this one. They shook him. Bad. Like the pains, they remained his secret. He never told anyone about them. Not the mullahs, not the flight surgeons, not even Paul. They scared the shit out of him, he had grimly admitted to himself. The worst part was that once they'd come and run through his brain while he watched like some dude strapped into a chair in a movie theater, after he'd fought like a crazy man to be free, after he'd sweated and screamed for release, they'd just go away, and he'd remember nothing but the fear. He'd never worked out a way to stop the flashes. They just came when they wanted to. He thought, Allah is punishing me, and said a prayer, willing the flash to go, but it never worked. He gripped the yoke and tried to will the flash to stop.

"In the Name of Allah, the compassionate, the merciful—"

It was the little kids again. Hak Do. Sweltering weather. The gunship—his gunship, his pride, his first air love—was at fifty feet, swiveling slowly, the Gatling chewing up parts of Charlie and his village. Sweeney was screaming in his ear. About the little kids. But he felt the pure sweet rush of sheer power as the big turbine did what *he* wanted, the big rotors listened to *his* commands, and the perfectly oiled, perfectly lethal chopper lifted and danced and killed at *his* behest. The sight, vibrating slightly, swung across the old woman with the AK-47 and she disintegrated in a shower of red and black. He was with the rhythm, the real rhythm, the killing rhythm. Drums beat and only he heard them. And the sight kept moving as *he* made everything happen. No more the poor black boy from Southeast. Now the head motherfucker in charge. Now the man upstairs, the decider of everything for everybody. The gun sight sliced across the burning huts, and there was the little girl, clutching her little brother and looking up in stupefaction at him and his huge black gunship, oblivious to what was really happening.

He blew them away, not even thinking about it. One minute, little kids clutching each other. The next, shards of skull and flesh and spouts of blood. No big deal. The rhythm had him and the drums pounded and *he* was *in charge*, man, in charge. And Sweeney screaming in his ear, some dumbass white-boy shit,

some redneck cracker crazy shit, some *stop-stop-stop*
kinda shit. Sweeney shit. He ignored Sweeney—as always until he'd had to chop him too to shut him up—
and kept the trigger down until there was no more. No
more huts, no more Charlie, no more indigenous per-
sonnel, no more anything. Just smoke and fire and red
and black and drums, drums, drums. He felt good. He
felt righteous. He felt better than he'd ever felt. He felt
high and mighty and he didn't give a slippery shit
about any of *them*, no more than he had about the
white kid at 13th and T, who'd looked at him like he
couldn't believe it when J.P. had slid that nice butterfly knife from Manila right between his ribs. No more
than when he'd used napalm to grease a whole rag-
head clan ten years later, like some kind of avenging
angel as they were cooking their dinner by the river,
ten years after Hak Do in the north of Iran, when the
Unit was sent in secret to help the Shah.

He *never* gave a shit. Not until they got Paul. Then
it all changed. Everything. Forever.

The little girl left him alone and he was back in
command of the Cessna again, the scene faded already. He wiped sweat from his hands and face and
willed his heart to slow. Still on a night flight. Still no
piece of cake. Still the low-level nav to do. He blinked
away sweat and focused on the ground rushing by only
fifty feet under his Cessna's belly.

All at once, the landmarks were there, exactly as
he'd been briefed. The moon showed them clearly to
his night-adjusted eyes. The silo to the northeast. The
power lines south. The long, flat field. He lined up on
the field and zoomed over it, looking west, as planned.

Automobile headlights flashed on. Once, twice, three times. He pulled up and circled while switching on his red and green nav beacon lights to answer the signal. He kept the 210 in a tight climbing spiral over the field, looking down. The headlights came on again, and a man stood illuminated, holding out a long white nylon streamer. It fluttered eastward, showing him the wind. He clicked off his lights as he reached one thousand feet, and so did the car.

He ran through the landing check, another task made automatic by twenty years of flying, while he rehearsed the night landing. The field was long, with a gentle upward slope, clothed in short alfalfa planted in firm black soil. He would have to adjust his eyes to the moonlight, then line up and drop in without lights. At the end of the field was a huge old barn where the Cessna would be parked, the heroin pulled off and the AN/ALQ-696 removed. They hadn't told him what would happen to the heroin or to the Cessna, and he hadn't asked.

The landing was routine for him. He pulled back the power, dropped the flaps and gear and eased the 210 onto the earth. The drone of the Lycoming was replaced on the landing roll by the rumble and clank of the mostly empty airplane coming to a halt. He spotted the black shape of the old barn and taxied slowly to it. Once there, he idled the engine for a moment to cool the turbocharger, then pulled back the mixture, let the engine die and toggled off the master switch. The night closed in as the gyros slowly whined to a halt. He popped the door and got down on slightly unsteady legs.

The sedan that had illuminated the field for him pulled up, lights out. He braced himself on his wobbly legs and stared at the car. He knew what was supposed to happen. But years of combat had taught him that what was supposed to happen rarely did. These guys with the cash and the car were not Jihaddin, just common thugs. They worked for nebulous "interests" in New York with connections in Iran, which had been exploited to put together this deal. There were guarantees, they'd told him, that these people—mafiosi, al-Shiran suspected—would do what was expected. But he stood on the balls of his feet anyway as a figure emerged from the moonlit car.

The figure approached, a short man in dark clothing, wearing a dark watch cap. Moonlight hooded his eyes and revealed less than it obscured. His hands were thrust into his jacket pockets. He halted four feet from al-Shiran and cocked his head a bit.

"You're fuckin' late," he grated in a Bronx accent.

Al-Shiran became J. P. Jones. It was easier than he'd thought. He eased his torso forward and thrust out his chin at the small man. This was a ritual with which he was all too familiar. On the street it happened every day, a dozen times.

"The fuck you say, white boy. My ass is on time, to the motherfuckin' *second*. You got a problem with time, you want to check your Mickey Mouse watch, sonny."

Tension crackled around the dark little man almost visibly. He jerked upright, shifted his weight as if to do something—al-Shiran could guess with what, the "what" being in the right pocket of his jacket—and then relaxed.

"Okay. No sweat. We was gonna give you another five minutes then blow. You're lucky we held on." Al-Shiran stepped forward. He hadn't intended this to get out of hand, but the little shithead was taking it too far, insulting him not just as a man, but as a pilot. The small man stepped back as he came forward, but al-Shiran's long reach and swift moves caught him before he could get out of reach.

Al-Shiran grabbed a handful of his nylon jacket and jerked upward. The guy fought to get his hands out of his pockets, but the gun and al-Shiran's grip trapped him. He made a muted "awk" noise as the jacket squeezed up around his neck. Behind him, a door slammed as al-Shiran lifted him clear off the ground.

"Drop him!" another Bronx voice called. It was underlined by the unmistakable sound of a weapon being cocked.

Al-Shiran thrust his face close to the small man's, ignoring the threat. He saw fear in the tiny eyes, now widened. The pale, pockmarked face twitched. Al-Shiran knew that he was a terrifying presence when he was angry; he knew because as J. P. Jones he'd beaten every man who'd ever crossed him, and had seen that same look of terror on each face. Maybe it was because he stood six foot three, was not a pretty black, but a dark, blue-black, with a wide, flaring nose and huge eyes that seemed to swell as if they would explode when he was angry, as he was now. He smiled a vicious smile.

"Get this straight. I was on time. I did my part. You twinkies going to do the same?"

"Hey! I said—"

The little guy got his left arm free and waved a cool-it wave to his pal, now crouched behind the sedan's open door, the gun aimed at what he could see of al-Shiran. Since al-Shiran was holding the man he had tagged Little Shit directly in front of him, blocking his pal's aim, there was very little of him exposed—and Little Shit knew it.

"Gawk," choked out Little Shit. Al-Shiran grinned and loosened his grip, allowing him to breathe easier and his feet to touch the ground.

"Yeah, okay, okay, you was on fuckin' time. What's the big deal?"

"No big deal. Shall we get on with business?"

Little Shit finally untangled his right hand, pulling out a chrome-plated .357 Magnum, with which he was planning to impress al-Shiran. Instead, it caught on a torn pocket lining in his jacket and twisted out of his grip. It fell to the ground, and Little Shit stood looking at it as if he'd never seen it before. Al-Shiran knew that the other guy had him covered now, so he deliberately turned away and unbuttoned the Cessna's cargo door. No sense in pressing the little men too far, he thought.

Hurriedly scooping up his big revolver, Little Shit collected himself and stood warily a few feet from al-Shiran as he pulled out the plastic-wrapped cartons packed with pure heroin. He worked quickly and methodically and soon had the cartons stacked in front of Little Shit.

"This is it," he said.

"Yeah. I can see that. How do we know—"

"Look, boy. I just finished a long flight. I'm tired. I don't have time for you and your gangster shit. You know this stuff is the real thing and I know it. So stick it wherever you're gonna stick it, give me my money and the car, let's get the airplane parked and get on with it. Okay?"

"Got it all figured out, don't you?"

"Yeah. All figured out. Now, are we going to do business or am I going to kill you and your pal over there? It's all the same to me. And like I said, I'm tired."

The cool night wind, smelling of earth and life, plucked at al-Shiran's clothing as if to remind him of Allah's grace. This was just another test to be passed, another test of his worthiness to be a Jihaddin. It would be gratifying to J. P. Jones to kill both these men. But Hadj al-Shiran had other duties. He waited for the little man to feel strong enough to allow the business to proceed; he had obviously lost so much face that it was a supreme struggle. But he too had duties; he too had overlords, who would not take kindly to his screwing up this particular deal. El Jazzar had smiled secretively when al-Shiran had asked how they might be certain of the drug sellers' cooperation. "We can be sure of few things in this life, al-Shiran, but we can be *certain* of that," he'd said. So the mullahs had some hold on the shadowy figures far above these scum—and they definitely had the power of life and death over Little Shit and his pal.

The impossibility of smoothing his ruffled feathers as he so dearly wished finally sank into Little Shit's brain and he lowered his .357. "Okay," he ground out. "Yeah. Sure. Let's move it."

The work was done in minutes. They loaded the heroin into the Chevy sedan, then rolled the 210 into the huge old barn. Little Shit's pal, whom al-Shiran tagged Big Shit because he seemed to weigh almost 250 pounds and moved like a clumsy bear, tugged at a rusted iron bar on the sliding barn door, and it moved noiselessly down a well-oiled track. The tumbledown appearance of the old barn was not reflected in its interior. Even in the moonlight, it was obvious that this barn was well used, and well maintained, and not as a storage area for animal fodder.

Al-Shiran pulled the Cessna into the barn with the nosewheel tow bar, an easy task once the wheels bumped over the door track, since the floor inside was smooth, spotless concrete. He chocked the wheels, grabbed his bag and flight gear, made a swift inspection of the cabin to insure that he had left nothing incriminating behind, then closed the Cessna's door. As he did so, he felt a little pang of remorse over the fate of the airplane. Like sailors, airmen grow fond of good ships, and this one had been good to him. He had flown it from Iran to Pennsylvania, and it had performed flawlessly, day after day, hour after hour. He straightened up as he walked from under the wing and surveyed the dimly lit barn.

"Where's the car?"

"In the corner," said Little Shit. "Where's the keys to the plane?"

"In the ignition. Money in the car?"

"Yeah. You wanna count it?" he sneered.

"No. Either it's right, in which case you live for a while, or it's wrong, in which case you die before tomorrow night. Makes no difference to me."

Little Shit tensed visibly again, and al-Shiran knew he was walking the line very closely. But he *was* tired, and he did not like dealing with these men. He had a pure vision of his goal here in America, a shining vision of revenge and liberation, and these vermin sullied it. He not only hated them for being what they were, he resented them for making it difficult for him to be what he wished to be.

Little Shit finally relaxed again. "You are one tough dude, aren't you, Mr. Badass? Well, maybe. But maybe not. You just watch it if you ever cross into my territory. Got that? Just watch it." He waited for al-Shiran's reaction. Seeing none, he reached in his pocket and tossed some keys on the ground. They clanged on the concrete.

"Your chariot awaits you."

Al-Shiran ignored him and plucked the keys off the ground. He hefted his bags and turned away, heading for the dark corner where he saw the old Toyota gleaming dully. Behind him, Little Shit fingered the trigger of his .357, just as al-Shiran knew he would. But just as he expected, fear moved the finger off the trigger. Fear and Allah's will.

He had his gear in the trunk in a moment, and saw the nondescript Reebok jock duffel standing there, too. He unzipped it swiftly, riffled the stacks of greenbacks sufficiently to satisfy himself that however much money had been placed in the bag, it was more than he'd ever seen before, then slammed the trunk lid down and slid into the driver's seat.

The Toyota was not quite a beater, but it had been through the mill. It had the stale disinfected smell of a well-used rental car. He couldn't have cared less when it started on the first turn of the key. It ran. And it would take him to the next stop on his pilgrimage. He put it in gear and rolled slowly toward the door.

Little Shit stood in his way, gun aimed at him. Al-Shiran kept rolling forward, until at the last second, Little Shit danced out of his way, raising his revolver. As al-Shiran passed him, he called, "*This* time! Just this time! Next time—"

But as he hit the open field, al-Shiran pushed down the accelerator and Little Shit's words were swallowed by the noise of the old Toyota's exhaust. Hadj al-Shiran had already left him and his world behind. His eyes guided him down the rutted old farm road, lights still off, to the little-used county lane a mile away, where he would turn on his lights and make for the motel where he was expected. But his mind's eye was not seeing the moonlit Pennsylvania farmland. It was fixed on the blazing glory of Paradise.

CHAPTER THREE

TO AN INTERESTED potential opponent, the Israeli military activity near the 555-meter tall mountain called Har Mughara would be explainable as the maintenance and manning of the nearby observation post. And in Syrian, Egyptian, Iranian and PLO intelligence reports spanning a decade and a half, the few lines accorded the site simply noted the presence of a few Israeli Defense Force soldiers and their equipment, living dusty and uncomfortable lives in the handful of prefab buildings of the Observation Post. Although Har Mughara's position in the chain of rugged, barren mountains near the Israeli-Egyptian border in the Sinai gave it some possible importance, any military man could see at a glance that it was too far from the border and too deep in almost impassable terrain to be either a prime asset of the IDF or a prime target for those who might again fight the IDF. It was the Israeli equivalent of an outpost in a quiet backwater of the American frontier. Or so it had seemed until David Bar-Lev told Daud Qidal the truth of it.

The truth was that inside the large motor pool building was an entrance to the subterranean cache of tactical nuclear weapons Israel was not supposed to have. The cache was built into some of the caves that had given the mountain its name, and was protected not by massed soldiery but by sophisticated electronics. This was a gamble whose implications the Israelis well understood; but it was a gamble they had to take, according to Bar-Lev, since of the two elementary choices for protection of such an asset as a nuke—concealment or fortification—concealment best suited Israel's needs.

It also suited Qidal's needs, because it simplified his assault problem. Had the weapon he sought been stored at a fully fortified IDF base, he would have stood no chance—even with Bar-Lev's connivance—of getting it. But Har Mughara was different. To one who knew its secrets, it was vulnerable.

Hassan el Jazzar knew its secrets. He knew the code needed to deactivate the explosive devices that would detonate in the event of an unauthorized entry into the caves. He knew the routine of the guard detachment, and knew when they would be most open to assault. He knew enough to make the Love of Allah a reality, if his men did as they were expected.

As the sun sank behind the stark hills, el Jazzar swept his field glasses across the hilltop post one more time. In the blood-red light of the fading sun, the radio tower glinted crimson. In eight hours, they would strike, before the watch changed, when the guards were dull and the world half-dead. They would have only thirty minutes at the outside before the radio check disclosed something wrong at Har Mughara. Thirty minutes to silence the guards, enter the vaults, find, detach and retrieve the bomb, then meet the Iranian helo at the rendezvous. Not much time,

even for men who are ready, who have practiced until
they can do it blindfolded.

He glanced at his men, almost invisible in the swiftly
darkening rock and sand of the wastelands. They had
practiced, and they were ready. He handed the field
glasses to his lieutenant and slipped down the rocky
scarp to where the forty-two men merged with the
desert wilderness.

Like any commander, he was preoccupied with the
worrying details of the mission. Just getting the men
trained and in place had been grueling. Penetrating
Israel had been comparatively easy, thanks to the
Iranian navy's efficiency in getting them ashore undetected on the Egyptian side of the border at Taba,
on the Gulf of Aqaba. But the last day and a half of
old-fashioned desert soldiering had been tough. It had
been thirty-six hours of ceaseless movement—by
truck, first, along the old military road, northward to
El Kuntilla, and then on foot at night through the
small break in the almost sanitized border. But the Jihaddin were up to it. These men were not the barely
bearded boys who were fed into the slaughter at the
front by the Revolutionary Guards. These were experienced, battled-toughened commandos. He felt a
flush of pride as they went about their bivouac chores,
each movement efficient, virtually noiseless. The Israelis on the hilltop were garrison troops, expecting
nothing more than boredom. Hassan el Jazzar smiled
at the thought. Before dawn broke again, they would
be anything but bored.

A NIGHT ASSAULT had been foreseen as a real possibility when Har Mughara was secretly built in 1979.

The gamble to defend the place with a few troops augmented by a great deal of electronics had been taken only because the designers had faith that the electronics were triple-redundant and essentially fool-proof. As a result, the first layer of defense for Har Mughara was actually the communications network itself. It was expected that intelligence would alert border and near-border stations like Har Mughara well in advance of any actual contact with an enemy. In addition, Har Mughara was encircled by four rings of invisible trip wires. Lasers, infrared and micro-waves were beamed from point to point around the perimeter of the station at varying heights above the ground. With a secure power supply—which the fa-cility had—there was no reason to expect a genuine surprise attack, because surprise was declared techni-cally impossible.

The same was true for air attack. Although the site had no radar of its own—such emissions would belie the putative purposes of the base—it was data-linked with the superb nationwide network of active and passive radar that kept Israel's border the most closely watched on earth. So as he retired to the spare little dining hall for the evening meal, the commander of Har Mughara felt nothing but a vague kind of contin-uing confidence in the impregnability of his mini-fortress. That night, his biggest concern was whether Goldberg, his electronics wizard, would be able to pluck the direct-broadcast "Dallas" episode from the air with the new descrambler the young draftee had built especially for the purpose.

THERE IS A TIME before dawn when the human bio-
system is barely functional. Research has proved what
military commanders have known for millenia: between three and four in the morning, an unalerted enemy, even if awake, is really only half-effective. A
man's eyes may be open, but his brain is mostly asleep,
and his body sluggish, its core temperature down, its
hormonally regulated chemical factories off duty.

Hassan el Jazzar had never read the research, but he
had been fighting his whole adult life. He knew the
"dead zone" well, and knew how to prepare his own
men to withstand the onset of its creeping fatigue.
When his watch glowed with the numerals 0330, he
motioned to Mahoud and stood up.

Behind him, forty black-clad Jihaddin did likewise.
Ahead, a hundred meters away, el Jazzar knew that his
team of electronic sappers was ready to defeat the four
rings of the electromagnetic fence. He waited until the
combat teams were assembled. When he saw, in the
predawn blackness, the quick red flash of the signal
from Mahoud, he turned and aimed his own flash-
light at the spot his sappers occupied.

Another red glow answered. He held up his watch,
finger on the chronograph button. When he got two
red flashes, they would signal the defeat of the system, and the half hour would begin.

Time stretched, as it always did in an operation. But
nobody moved. The desert wind sighed among the
rocks, gusting occasionally with a stinging handful of
sand. Now, he thought, now we will see whether we
have been betrayed by Qidal. The PLO chief had delivered, as his part of the assault bargain, incredible
detail about the defense system—including precisely

how the "fences" could be fooled by a sophisticated feedback-loop circuit introduced at one of the hidden relay points. These relays were very cleverly dug into the rock, hidden well from a would-be infiltrator and protected by automatic defenses such as mines and machine guns. Furthermore, each was monitored from the OP by a remote camera and other sensors, all in turn tirelessly overseen by a computer programmed to alert the watch in the event of any anomaly, from wandering sheep to lost hermit.

The prime contractor for the defensive system had been an American company, which designed and built the hardware and software not knowing the location of the site it was to protect. Only a few members of the IDF's electronic warfare cadre knew everything there was to know about the Har Mughara defenses. One of them was the colonel who had briefed the secret Knesset committee overseeing the huge expenditure for the system. And the chairman of the committee was David Bar-Lev.

The two flashes blinked from the darkness, almost catching Hassan by surprise. He had no real idea what had been involved in defeating the system. All he knew was that of all the men with him tonight, the two he could not afford to lose were those who now worked their modern magic with their portable computer, wire harnesses, reflectors and antennas. He also knew that in the endless practice runs with another system rigged to duplicate the American "fences," the two-man team had never failed to make their system work. So it was tonight. The red light blinked and Hassan's finger pushed down the button of his chronograph. He turned and flashed the go signal to the forty silent troopers in black.

THE TELEPHONE THAT RANG near Stein's bed was not of the chirping-bird variety. Moshe Stein detested only a few things about the modern world. Chirping phones were on that short list. A telephone was supposed to ring. Loudly, annoyingly, demandingly. So his phone, although fully as sophisticated as any in the Mossad's extensive array of gadgetry, *rang*.

He jerked it off the cradle and glanced at the clock as he answered, a habit learned in the Six-Day War.

"Stein."

"Colonel. We have a situation."

"Go ahead."

"It's Lorelei, we think."

Stein closed his eyes and thought furiously for a moment. He'd been at it too long. There were too many files, too many operations. His memory wasn't what it had once been. Finally the code word opened his mental file drawer. He jerked upright and leaned against the rosewood headboard. He checked the bug monitor. Nobody was tapping him today.

"Lorelei? Are you certain?"

"It looks like it, Colonel. General Avrams says—"

"I know what he says. Get me transportation. Now."

"On its way, sir. The helo will be at your pad in four minutes. Then to the site, if it's okay with you."

"Perfect. Shalom."

"Shalom, Colonel."

Savyon was the Beverly Hills of Tel Aviv, the suburb of choice for those who had made it in Israel.

Lavish estates vied with one another as banker sought
social supremacy over film producer. It was not a
place of neighborliness, so nobody in Savyon was
surprised when Moshe Stein, a tall, sandy-haired,
cheerful-countenanced middle-aged government
mandarin of some kind moved into their midst. At the
club bar, the word was that Stein played at the government the way some men played chess—as a serious hobby. He was single—divorced, the word was—
and he had money—*lots* of money—from the States,
where the Steins had made it big in the last century in
some kind of manufacturing. It was not much re-
marked upon, because the story was a common one
among those who lived in opulence in Savyon.

Thus the sometimes strange events at Stein's geo-
desic home and its well-guarded grounds disturbed
nobody. He drove—or was driven, mostly—in a black
Mercedes with blacked-out security windows, like
many of those in Savyon. And even the appearance of
a helicopter over his tennis courts at an outlandish
hour of the morning was nothing to comment upon.
Many of the richest in Savyon preferred the convenience of a private helo to the danger and discomforts
of an automobile trip—even the short trip into down-
town Tel Aviv.

Perhaps his neighbors, even had they been able to
penetrate the acre of strategically planted orange trees
and usefully tall and artfully arranged walls, would
not have been surprised to see Moshe Stein standing at
the edge of those tennis courts wearing not the leisure
gear of his class or the business attire of the government, but the rumpled khaki of an Israeli Defense
Force colonel. Many, if not most of those who lived

in Savyon, had reserve commissions activated during emergency.

Had they known of Stein's real job, even the world-weary cynics of Savyon would have paused. Stein was not just the scion of a wealthy American family. He was not just a government type. He was the head of Section Four of the Mossad, the department of the Israeli secret service charged with protection of the most valuable of Israel's assets. Among those were the nuclear weapons the nation was publicly sworn not to possess.

The helo—a big American RH-53—touched down noisily, and Stein ducked his head instinctively, waited for the door on the fuselage to slide open and ran forward when it did. A crewman gave him a hand up. He jumped in and buckled himself into the webbed seat. Across the boxy fuselage from him sat his aide, Captain Chaim Chafaz.

The captain waited until Stein had buckled in and slipped on his headset, then handed across a small file as the helo lurched back into the air. Stein took it, flipped it open and scanned the pages.

"This is all?" he said into the mike of his headset.

Chafaz's voice was made tinny by the interphone, but there was no mistaking the emphasis.

"No more, Colonel. We only got this after a team from Mizpe Ramon went down when the radio check came up blank."

"No survivors?"

Chafaz's scarred visage did not change. The captain had been severely wounded in the invasion of Lebanon in '82, while trying to halt the excesses of the Christian militia. He had been taciturn before, but after the plastic surgery he had become the most reluctant of speakers. It was perhaps a personal tragedy, but it made Chafaz a perfect Mossad man.

"None. They were taken almost all by complete surprise."

Stein dismissed the tiny twinge of emotion that stubbornly welled up in him. Har Mughara had been commanded by an old friend. A friend who never knew that Stein was using him as bait. He said nothing and again scanned the brief, hastily written report. There was nothing useful in it. The men from the base at Mizpe Ramon were not trained to know what was important in this case. All they saw were their slaughtered comrades—and the door to the vaults standing open. At least their commander had had the sense to keep them out of the vaults.

Stein checked the time. It had been an hour since the Mizpe Ramon team checked in. His people had moved fast. But was the trail still warm? What could he discover?

"You have the terminal?"

Chafaz nodded and pointed to the battered black aluminum case stowed on the webbed seat next to him.

"Good. We'll need it. Contact Ygal at Mizpe Ramon. Tell him to have a company of his boys meet us there. Tell him we want only the best guys. Tell him we need people who'll keep their mouths shut and their eyes open. We'll need them for at least two days on-site. And keep the others out of our hair. No replacements for the OP yet. Has General Avrams issued the order to the zone commander?"

"Yes, sir. You have full authority. I have a copy of the twix. And I've already contacted the zone people.

Also, I asked air defense to have a sitrep for us, and then let us tap into their net when we get there.''

"Good. Did you bring the Lorelei file?''

Chafaz reached into his scarred old leather brief-case and withdrew a plain buff file envelope. He handed it to Stein. As Stein took it, Chafaz held his eyes.

"I hope we get the bastards,'' the captain said. Even in the headset, the intensity of his voice was clear.

Stein looked at Chafaz for a moment. "Family?''

"My brother, sir. Had another week to go before his time was up.''

Stein tore his gaze away from Chafaz's burning eyes and opened the Lorelei file. His own eyes automatically raced ahead, reading the first lines of the op-plan overview while he thought of something to say to Chafaz, who had now lost every member of his family to Israel's enemies. His wife and baby had been murdered in a kibbutz raid three years before, his mother and father killed in '73 and now his only brother had been butchered in his sleep.

Stein reread the report's opening words:

Operation name: Lorelei
Operation purpose: Detection and elimination
of internal security threats in nuclear program
Operation priority: Unrestricted
Operation access: Mossad/4 only

Stein looked back at Chafaz's stony, ravaged vis-age.

"We'll get them,'' he said.

CHAPTER FOUR

AFTER THIRTY-FOUR YEARS of living, Max knew only a few things for certain. One was that most American men are more comfortable with machines than they are with one another. To this scrap of hard-won wisdom he could add only one corollary: it was even more true of him than of most of his contemporaries.

He had always been a loner, and deliberately so. It was not so much that he disliked his fellow man, but that he felt little in common with him. Partly this derived from a childhood spent being flung from one Army base to another, following his father and his father's mania. Maxwell Taylor Moss, therefore, grew up as an only child who learned early that if you made friends, they would be taken from you, or you from them, by unseen, unstoppable forces.

And partly Max was a loner because what he thought about, and what he did as a result of his thinking inevitably set him apart. He learned quickly the need for camouflage for his differentness, and thus became that unusual combination: a socially adept man, capable of managing himself well in any society, yet a man with few real friends and even fewer lovers. Knowing this about himself did not make living as himself any easier.

Maybe Charlie Barton somehow sensed all that as he warmed to his topic and to Max as his audience. And maybe Charlie himself was like Max. Moss didn't know, and didn't ask. He simply listened to Charlie's wild tales of life in the Navy, of flying and fighting and drinking and screwing, laughed in the right places, bought the right number of rounds and went home to his condo from Mike's Place unaccountably cheerful, considering the events that had driven him to seek it out. He had managed entirely to forget Kelly and the Plantation Key fiasco for five whole hours. Only the solitary drive back to Key Largo caused the smile to slip from his face.

Opening the door to his little rented place was the grimmer because of the unlooked-for surcease at Mike's. There is an odor to a cheerless home, a peculiar scent that is two parts chemical and eight parts emotional, and Max's condo had that unmistakable smell, the smell of a widow's cottage, of a divorcée's apartment, an orphan's bedroom. It was the smell of despair, and nothing in the condo—not its bright colors or new rattan furniture or wide-screen TV or compact disk player—could dispel it. Only Max could change it. And in the weeks he had been seeking the purgative power of idleness, he had been unable to.

He tossed his tweed jacket onto a chair, pulled open the new refrigerator and jerked a can of beer from the shelf in one continuous motion. As if he cared what he was doing, he flopped into the rattan TV chair, punched the remote control and sucked on the beer as the screen sprang to life. Images flickered across the screen in perfect, cable-fed fidelity, and he looked right through them. The sound system faultlessly rep-

licated the sound track, and he did not hear any of it.
He pulled on his beer, not tasting it, and wondered.

Mostly he wondered at himself. What the hell am I
doing here? The thought ran through his head for the
thousandth time. And for the thousand-and-first time,
there was no decent answer. He swigged the beer
again.

There were reasons, of course. One event led in-
eluctably to another, a relentless chain of circum-
stances that defined not what he wanted to happen,
but what had happened. Maybe it was the same for
everybody.

But not everybody wound up sucking bad beer in
Key Largo, staring into a future that consisted entirely of fog. Not everybody managed so completely
to burn his bridges to possible alternatives. He thought
about who he had been, and when, and what he had
thought his alternatives were. There had not been
many, it seemed.

When he left Berkeley with his engineering degree,
the last thing he had wanted to do was work for his
father at Moss Electronics. The first thing was to race
cars, an alternative he'd been introduced to by chance,
and whose crazy dimensions his skill had opened up
after his first improbable race and his equally improbable success. Then there was the Air Force, an
alternative again—this time to being coerced back into
working with Eric Moss. It had seemed a sweet sort of
thumbed nose at the time, peculiarly effective against
a father who had retired a major general in the Army
and who detested the Air Force. Yet four years of sti-
fling boredom resulted. And the alternative to that had
been the Mission. And Recovery work. Ultimately, the

Defense Intelligence Agency and Camp Peters and the final showdown. Leading, inevitably, right here. Sans prospects, sans decent alternatives. And sans friends and lovers.

Max morosely recognized the building inertia of the tiresome cycle of self-recrimination and punishing hopelessness. He snorted aloud.

"Bullshit. Get that? *Bullshit.* You made your bed, bozo. Now lie in it, and shut up." He grimaced at the absurdity of talking to himself. He was exhausted. He slugged down the rest of the beer, tossed the can into a wastebasket and staggered off to his decorator-coordinated bedroom. His intention had been to undress and crawl between the cool sheets. But intentions are a lot like wishes, and when he sat down on the bed to take off his shoes, he simply lay back and fell instantly and dreamlessly asleep.

He awoke with cotton in his mouth and ringing in his ears. It took him a few seconds of confused semi-awareness before he understood that the ringing was real, even if the cotton was not. He lurched upright, winced at the crick in his neck and grabbed for the phone. On the second swipe, he got it.

"Yeah," he grunted into the receiver.

"Hey. This Max Moss?"

Max blinked and rubbed his eyes furiously. He squinted at the clock. It was barely seven. Remorselessly, the brilliant Florida sun poured in his window. He swallowed and tried to concentrate.

"Uh, yeah. Who's this?"

"Charlie, man. You know."

"Charlie. Yeah. I guess." A pain something like an embedded ax head lodged precisely midway between his eyes and about two millimeters above his eyebrows. He rubbed it furiously.

"You *guess*? Shit, boy, don't you remember?" The voice chuckled, a not entirely pleasant sound.

He did not remember. He recalled Charlie, of the Corvette and the crazy stories. But—

"Hell, Moss, we're goin' *flyin'* today! Unless you wimp out on me, that is."

Flying. Vaguely, Max remembered something about flying. Something about him flying. Something to do with—

"My SNJ, boy. Best damn airplane ever come out of a tin bender. Hey! You there? Click the mike twice if you can't talk."

"Yeah, yeah, I'm here. Was that *today*? You sure?"

"'Course I'm sure. Hell, I've been waiting for almost half an hour. So you coming or not, Air Force?"

Max thought creakingly about telling Charlie to go buzz the lagoons himself so he could sink back into his interrupted sleep. Before he could answer, Charlie spoke again. This time, the mirth was gone from his voice, as was the shit-kickin' bumpkin delivery.

"Sounds to me like you're not up to this, Mr. Moss. Well, sorry I intruded. Last night, I took you for a man serious about his hardware. Guess I was wrong."

A flash of anger shot through Max. It woke him up finally. "Not at all, Captain. Forgot to set my alarm is all. See you there."

The line hissed for a moment. Then Barton said, "Okay. You know where to go?"

Max furrowed his throbbing brow, but couldn't withdraw the information from his sluggish memory bank. "Uh..."

"Thought so. Take 1 south to Duck Cay. Turn right at the green motel. Can't miss my place. Look for the wind sock by the cattails. Got it?"

"Got it."

"See you in twenty. Okay?"

"Okay. I—"

The line went dead. Max dropped the receiver in its cradle and closed his eyes. He tried to remember why he had volunteered to go flying. But that information, too, refused to surface. He sighed and heaved himself to his feet.

What the hell. He had nothing better to do anyway.

The drive to the Barton's private airstrip gave him back his memory of the previous night. As the Corvette idled along at fifty miles per hour behind the snowbird traffic, he recalled how he had expressed interest in a ride in Charlie's other pride and joy, his 1951 North American SNJ trainer. How he had agreed that maybe he ought even to try the stick. And finally, about beer number eight, how yes, by God, it sure would be a fine thing to learn to *fly* Ol' Blue, as Barton tagged his ancient trainer. Now his bluff was being called.

Barton's directions, though succinct, were excellent. Twenty-two minutes after he hung up the phone, Max rolled up next to Charlie's battered old Stingray and saw, parked not fifty feet from the weed-strewn parking lot, the faded old SNJ. It was pointed into the sporadic wind, whose direction was shown by a dispirited wind sock hanging from a pole where the alleged airstrip met the parking area. Charlie slumped in a lawn chair under the wing, a baseball cap with NAVY emblazoned on it, gold on blue, pulled low over his eyes, and what seemed to be the same clothes he'd worn at Mike's.

Max sighed, shut off the engine and climbed stiffly out. As he walked across the weeds, he saw a giant television antenna rising from the side of a single-axle Airstream trailer that had seen better days. A dog barked somewhere, but without enthusiasm. The heat was already building, the sun already no longer friendly. Charlie ignored Max as he crunched slowly over to the airplane.

"Nice plane," Max said. He stuck his hands in the pockets of his faded jeans and eyed the crazed Plexiglas of the canopy, the oil-slicked underside of the fuselage, the homegrown repairs to the places where the skin had been damaged. It was indeed blue, but definitely *old* blue. Under the paint job, a U.S. star could be clearly seen on the aft fuselage, along with the registration number on the tail.

"Glad you could make it," Barton grunted. He looked pointedly at his watch, an old stainless steel Rolex, also with a crazed crystal. He didn't wait for Max's reply, getting to his feet surprisingly easily for such a large man slumped so apparently permanently in the beat-up lawn chair.

"Yeah," Max said. His mouth still tasted like cotton, and the coffee and doughnut he'd bolted on the drive down began to form a cannonball in his gut.

Barton picked up the chair by the top rail and paused near Max. He stared hard into Moss's face, as if looking for something. Just about at the point at which Max would have to react, he smiled thinly and kept moving, plopping the chair down a few feet from the rough surface of the runway.

"Yeah," Charlie said. He turned back to Max and crossed his arms. "You were some kind of racer, you said."

"Right. Stock cars."

"Any good?"

"Fair."

"How fair?"

"Won the Sportsman at Daytona."

Charlie cocked his head. "No shit?"

"No shit. Look, am I here to fly an airplane or make out a loan application?"

"Hey. Sorry, Moss. It's just that I don't offer just anybody the chance to go up in Ol' Blue, see? Especially not the chance to handle her."

"Fine, Captain. Understood. Let's get on with it, shall we? But let's assume I know something about high performance machinery. Because I fucking well do. And if I didn't, believe me, I wouldn't be here now."

Now Barton stiffened, the smile frozen on his face. Max cursed himself for his quick temper. Must be the damn coffee, he thought. Or maybe the lack of sleep. This was a hell of a way to get off with your flight instructor-to-be.

"Maybe you'd like to explain that, Mr. Moss, before we get on with our little flight." Barton's voice was cool, almost icy.

Max sighed. "Okay. You deserve some civility. Frankly, I'd forgotten about the flight and I didn't have too great a night. But the reason I came down is your 'Vette, not your BS war stories."

"My 'Vette."

"Sure. I figured, how many guys would drive a Corvette as valuable as yours, and keep it as deliberately ugly as yours? And how many guys would keep it in as good mechanical shape? You got what we call a Q-ship there, Cap'n Barton. Sucker bait. I could tell you got the right stuff under that messed-up paint and dinged fiberglass. I didn't know why, but when every twerp with a good credit rating can drive something he doesn't even faintly deserve, well, I figured your car—and you—were kind of interesting. So here we are."

Barton stared at Max a moment, then broke into a grin.

"Goddamn. You ain't as dumb as you look, Air Force. For your information, I keep the split-window ugly for very definite reasons. Same goes for my humble abode there—" he waved at the Airstream "—and Ol' Blue. Not many people can see beyond the paint. Not many at all." He paused. "Mr. Moss, you and I just might get along." His smile widened into a grin. "But Ol' Blue—she's something else entirely. Not many get along with her. You ready to try?"

Max answered his grin with a small smile of his own that probably looked more like a grimace, since his face hurt when he tried it. "Yeah. Ready as I'll be today."

"Good. We'll start with the preflight. Follow me."

Max followed. Then, and during the next thirty minutes of careful inspection of the airplane, the twenty minutes of serious detailing of the plan for the flight, the ten minutes of strapping in and plugging in helmet interphones and the two minutes of actual engine start-up. Once involved with the airplane, Barton lost his ersatz country-boy persona and became all business. It was a transformation Max had seen many times with racing automobiles and the men who cared for and drove them. As his long-ago mentor had said, above a buck and a half, things get serious fast.

Although he had spent years in the Air Force, Max cared little for aviation or its icons. He knew this airplane was one such icon to the true believers; the SNJ was also the T-6, the Texan, the Harvard, the Flying Classroom, the terror of World War II and Korean War Air Force and Navy flight students. Its big old radial engine was supposed to have a dozen killer quirks, its tailwheel-configured landing gear was reputed to be the screen that separated the flying men from the boys; he knew this much about it, but until he started the big round engine and used the huge aluminum rudder pedals to steer the little tailwheel, he had not cared. But now, suddenly, he cared very much. His heart thumped in his ears, adrenaline once again racing through his system as it had so many times before when he sat behind the wheel of a race car or a Recovery vehicle. Max began at last to understand some of what bewitched men who loved flying more than anything on earth.

He discovered the rest when, coached by the careful, severe words of Barton, he caressed the round throttle knob forward with his left hand, held the stick slightly aft of neutral with his right and danced on the rudders to keep the nose aimed down the short, weedy runway as the old SNJ gathered speed. Magically, at about forty knots on the airspeed indicator, the tail came up by itself. Magically, as he put a tiny bit of back pressure on the stick, the nose lifted a bit farther, and they were flying.

Awestruck with the winelike air flowing past the canopy and the powerful throb of the engine only a few feet ahead of him, Max did exactly as Barton asked of him. He lost track of time as they climbed through the morning haze over the Keys and Barton coached him through a basic set of maneuvers, each time improving his coordination of throttle, stick and rudders. Barton said nothing about his performance, and Max cared nothing of it. He had flown many times before, but always as a passenger. Having the airplane in his hands, feeling it talk to him as his cars did brought him a kind of elation he'd felt only rarely in his life. And the sense of soaring above it all, of leaving the earth and his troubles far below, intoxicated him more than any amount of booze.

Barton rarely touched the controls, not even when he talked Max through his first landing simulation at three thousand feet. And when Charlie brought them back to the airstrip, navigating Max knew not how, he allowed Max to try the landing itself. Still drunk with the experience, Max eagerly agreed, and did precisely what Barton demanded, so that when Ol' Blue touched down her main gear on the crushed coral and weeds of Barton's strip, she did so gently, right on the edge of a stall, her tailwheel kissing the earth only a fraction of a second after the mains. Barton even allowed Max to brake the big airplane, only taking over when Max pushed too hard on the port brake just as the airplane was slowing to a halt.

"I've got the airplane," Barton said tersely, and Max, as briefed, raised his hands above his head to show they were off the controls, and took his feet from the rudder pedals. He sat transfixed as Barton expertly turned the SNJ around on the narrow strip and taxied back to the parking place by the Airstream.

Max simply watched the big two-bladed prop spin as Barton went through the shutdown procedure. Finally, it whuffed to a halt. The gyros whined loud in the sudden silence, and the dry click in his headphones told Max that Barton had disconnected. Max fumbled with his own plugs, but found less trouble with the seat straps, since they were much like those in racing cars. He peeled off his helmet and levered himself up in the cockpit, looking around for Barton.

The SNJ rocked and Max realized Barton had already gotten out. As he continued to clamber from the front cockpit, Max saw Charlie striding purposefully across the sun-drenched lot to his Airstream. Max shrugged and continued deplaning. He followed Charlie, wiping sweat from his brow. He no longer felt ill. As he walked through the warm Keys air, he realized he felt absolutely wonderful.

The screen door of the Airstream banged open and Charlie came out, clutching a can of beer, even though it was still before noon. Max smiled at him, ready to thank him. But the smile died on his lips.

Barton swigged hard on the beer and glared balefully at Max. Shit, thought Max. What the hell did I do wrong this time? He smiled again and held out his hand. "Hey. That was great. I just want to—"

"Can it," Barton said gruffly. "Just tell me this. I don't mind being made a fool of. But I would like to know how much time you got in T-6s."

Max blinked. "What?" His hand dropped. "What do you mean?"

Barton took another pull on his beer. "Come off it, Moss. The game's over. How much time you got?"

Max shook his head. "If you mean, how much flying time, the answer's just what I told you: zip. Nada. Zilch. This was the first time I ever laid hands on an airplane's controls. Why?"

Barton stared at Moss over his beer can, then slowly lowered it. He cocked his head again and narrowed his eyes.

"Once more, or I swear, I'll get nasty. *How much time?*"

Max reddened. "And for the last time, none. What the hell's the problem, Barton?"

Barton tossed away the can after a moment and looked out at his airplane. He glanced again at Max, adjusted his cap and scratched his chin. He folded his arms and unfolded them. Finally he faced Max again, hands on hips.

"Because, mister, you flew that goddamn bird like somebody with more than a few hours in her. And that means—" he shook his head and spit at the ground, as if he couldn't believe what was happening to him "—that *means* that you are either the lyingest son of a bitch to ever get in my cockpit, or you are one *hell* of a natural pilot." He glared at Max defiantly. "So which is it?"

Max flushed. "Neither. I didn't lie to you, and I'm not a natural pilot, whatever that is. You just told me what to do, and I did it."

The color slowly drained from Barton's flushed features. He cocked his head again at Max for a moment. The anger slowly left his face. "Jesus. Jee-*zus*. Is that true? I mean, the game's over, okay? You can share the joke. Really."

Max handed him his helmet. "True. No joke. What's the problem? I didn't fly the thing—you did. You talked me through everything. No big deal."

A laugh welled up in Barton and boomed out, then another. "No big deal? Sierra Hotel, Mother! *No big deal!* Christ, Moss, you just climbed cold into the toughest airplane in the whole fucking world and flew it like you were born in it—and that's no big deal?" He laughed again, almost helplessly, as if it were the funniest thing to have happened in the Keys in twenty years. After a moment, Max grinned, too.

"Good, huh?" he said.

Barton wiped tears from his eyes and laughed again. "Good? Jesus, if I'd flown like that, I—well, yeah, you could say good." He stopped laughing and slapped Max on the back. "I owe you an apology. And you owe me some story. Step into my office and we'll deal with this like the officers and gentlemen we are, over a cold one." He pulled open the screen door to the trailer again and elaborately bowed Max inside.

Max nodded and halted at the doorway. "One small correction."

"Shoot."

"Like the officers and gentlemen we *were*."

Barton's big laugh boomed out again across the weeds and crushed coral, and Max suddenly realized as he stepped into the tiny, tidy trailer that although the night before had cost him a lover, it had gained him a friend. It was a realization he cherished even more than the memory of the flight.

CHAPTER FIVE

HE AWOKE SCREAMING, of course. He almost always did after these two months back in America. Luckily, there was nobody to hear him. He lived in a run-down farmhouse in the tiny community of New Hope, a few miles southwest of Frederick, Maryland. New Hope was a black town of maybe 150 souls, dwindling fast. Like his reserves of energy.

Al-Shiran wiped his face and drew a long, shuddering breath. It must have been the Nam again. It usually was. He uttered his quick prayer to Allah and closed his eyes. Maybe he could sleep.

But Allah was not a sandman. The events of the day, of the week, of his whole sojourn in Maryland flicked through his mind like phantoms, unstoppable. He turned on his side, grunting, and tried to stop thinking. It didn't work. Finally he opened his eyes wide, threw off the covers and got to his feet.

The little farmhouse was cold, despite the warm autumn temperatures. It had belonged to some poor old black sharecropper whose death had been followed by more tragedy when the bank foreclosed and forced out his family. Like most of New Hope, it was now owned by a white real-estate management com-

pany down-county. The rates, of course, were usu-
rious.

He pulled on a worn robe and went into the kitchen.
A scuttling noise told him the rat he'd seen the day he
moved in was still in residence. And why not? Al-
Shiran had made no effort to rid the place of the vermin. He had bigger vermin to exterminate.

The single sixty-watt light bulb cast wan light on the
bleak kitchen. He turned on the gas, lit the flame under the teakettle and settled heavily in the ripped plastic chair by the rickety table. He watched the blue
flame dance under the teakettle, a little advance
warning of the fires of hell. A teaser. A reminder.

He did not need reminding. He felt more lost every
day. Two months, and no word from the Jihad. He
had followed instructions to the letter. As arranged.
County Aviation at Frederick Airport had hired him
quickly as a flight instructor. Slade, the white boss of
the fixed-base operation had been blunt: Jefferson was
expected to work as a qualified charter pilot, ferrying
people and canceled checks and ball bearings on the
increasingly profitable short-haul runs with the twin-
engine airplanes owned by County. He was also
expected to draw into flight training, if he could, some
of the newly affluent black people spilling out into the
Washington suburbs of Montgomery and lower Frederick counties. He was the token black; there wasn't
even the hint of camouflaging that. Slade had made it
perfectly clear; Jefferson had been hired because Slade
had this vision of himself capitalizing on the upward
impetus of the suburban blacks. They were breaking
into all the once-forbidden institutions of the D.C.
suburbs in increasing numbers, and Slade saw no rea-

son why he shouldn't score some money off them. Al-Shiran inwardly seethed as Slade matter-of-factly detailed his business plan and showed Jefferson on his personal computer the five-year profit projection he'd worked out should his guess prove correct.

The first month had not been promising. But there had been flickers from the wealthy down-county area. One doctor who worked for the huge Kaiser health organization had driven up from Rockville in his BMW and talked loudly of "getting his ticket." A shy young bank manager from Gaithersburg had timidly come during a "free ride" day and left clutching a packet of propaganda. And there had been a lawyer.

Al-Shiran had almost not survived the lawyer. She was a stunningly beautiful young black woman, maybe ten years younger than he, who worked for a major D.C. firm handling contract law. She was a perfect prospect; bright, aggressive, well-heeled, she vibrated with the need to show her white competitors that she was not only as good as they, she was better. She had already learned to sky-dive, and drove an expensive Porsche in local autocross events. The learn-to-fly ad in the *Washington Post* Weekend section showing a smiling Jefferson standing next to a Cessna 152 had worked for her, and she zeroed in on Jefferson without delay.

The teakettle blew its little whistle and al-Shiran reached over to the old stove and turned off the gas. His hand dropped and in the early-morning silence the hissing of the kettle filled the room.

She had of course been sent by Satan. He knew that now. She was just another test of his will, his loyalty, his love of Allah. But at first he had been so stricken with her that he was almost blinded to his true duty. The memory of Paul saved him, even if it lost her as a lucrative student, much to Slade's fury.

It had not taken her long to turn the student-teacher relationship on its head and begin probing him. And he had to admit his sheer lust for her perfect body made it easier for her. His mind and heart were cautious, but his body was heated by her presence. So when she began to evince real interest in him, he had been powerless to halt his response.

Had she not begun to speak of her own life and work—all, he saw now, as part of her role as succubus—he might have done something foolish, even dangerous. But that brought up, again against his will, the subject of Paul. And his work. And death.

He poured hot water into the chipped old china cup, dipped his tired tea bag in it and stared as the gray-brown stain slowly spread through the water. It had been over a postflight glass of iced tea at the decrepit little Frederick Airport restaurant that she had relentlessly pulled out Paul's story.

"Your brother was a lawyer?" she'd asked.

"Yes," he'd said, hoping she'd stick to talking about her Porsche. "But he died," he'd added.

"How?" she'd asked.

"Murdered," he'd said. The word had escaped him in spite of himself. He had struggled to keep his mind clear, but all those old images came back.

Blood on the carpet. Blood on the walls. Blood on the sofa. Blood everywhere. Little Leslie battered beyond all recognition, a tiny pulped doll smeared across the pink-flowered wallpaper of her room, the room Anne had been so proud of fixing up. And Anne naked, tied to the bed, mutilated so badly they had to use her dental records to establish her identity. And Paul.

They'd gone beyond anything he had ever seen in Nam or Iran with Paul. They'd killed him slowly, expertly, probably making him watch as they raped and tortured Anne.

He'd only seen the photos when he came back on emergency leave the second day after the murders were discovered. The photos and the bodies, made antiseptic in the morgue's fluorescent pallor.

He'd stayed cool until they showed him the photos, as he demanded. The D.C. homicide chief hadn't wanted to let him see them, but he grew so violent they finally showed him. And then he'd gone crazy, grabbing the lieutenant and lifting him to the top of his filing cabinet and yelling at him until he was hoarse that they had to do something.

And they'd done nothing. Nothing. They fussed and made statements and reassured him that the killers would not get away, and of course they had. By the time he had run out his leave, the cops had nothing and the TV people and the newspapers had forgotten the "incident." "Drug-related," they told him at the station in his last interview. Happened all the time, even in the best neighborhoods of Southeast. And after all...Southeast was still Southeast now, wasn't it? the lieutenant had smirked at him. As in: Paul Jefferson Jones got what he deserved, trying to be something he shouldn't have been...couldn't have been.

He wasn't just a lawyer, just like he wasn't just the smartest kid—black, white, green, yellow, whatever—they ever saw in school. He was special. He was energy and guts and hope and a leader. He was getting set to be the next Martin Luther King, the next black leader, maybe even the first black President of the United States. They knew it when they let him into Georgetown University, they knew it when they gave him all those scholarships to go through law school, they knew it at the minority-owned law firm he joined fresh out of the bar exam. Paul J. Jones was somebody. He was going places.

And he went. He specialized in promoting black business, and it led him to contract law, concentrating on government contracts. He was a one-man lobby for black businesses, on the Hill, everywhere. He was asked to the best parties, he was offered partnerships in white firms, he was given a shot at the golden apples. And he turned them all down.

He stayed in the ghetto. He bought the worst house on the block and renovated it, inviting the winos and pimps and street people to join him in regaining dignity and pride. It seemed to be working. The pimps went elsewhere, the winos followed. Shamed, other upscale blacks timidly moved not to the suburbs but to his neighborhood. And his business boomed. He landed one fat post office contract for one of his clients, and the word was out: P. J. Jones could do anything. Anything.

Drug-related? Al-Shiran had sat in his cheap Arlington motel room that last night, nursing his Jack Daniels and staring at the TV, still angry, still heart-dead, still unbelieving. He had nobody now. Mama dead for years, Daddy gone who knew where twenty years before that, and now, no Paul and Annie and

Leslie. But he had nothing to do but swallow liquor and try to forget those awful photos.

Until Stick knocked softly on his door. Stick had tracked him down somehow, God knew how. Stick was street. Stick was everybody's intelligence officer, Stick was knowledge. The cops knew it, the dopers knew it, everybody knew it. J.P. hadn't seen him for ten years when he showed up at the Motel 6, a pair of sunglasses, a crooked grin and a body so thin the name Stick only started to define it. He'd slid into that little room and cased it and sat down before Jones even really knew he was there.

"Crazyman, they got your brother," he'd said, instead of Hello, or Good to see you, or whatever.

"Yeah, they did," he'd said, "and nobody knows who or why," he'd said.

"*Shit*," Stick had snorted, "I tell you who and I tell you why, and I do it for him. But once you know, it won't do you no good."

"Try me," he'd said.

"Crazyman, your brother was no kind of scared of anything or anybody. But he ought to been. Because he was messin' with the big time. And it got him."

He'd just looked at Stick, not understanding through the booze and dope. So Stick had continued.

"Man who knows says Paul scored one from a major league defense company. Got a federal contract for the bloods. Big time company didn't like it. They thought it was theirs. Now, we're talkin' *major* league, and we're talkin' *billions*, and this big company, they rented up some muscle, and they did it to him. And everybody gets the message. Pretty soon the contract goes back to the big company and everybody knows the score."

"Everybody but me," Jones had grated.

Stick had shrugged. "What you expect, Crazyman? You're in the *Army*," he'd said. And before he'd had a chance to make Stick explain some more, Stick was out the door and gone, just as if he'd never been there at all. And sometimes al-Shiran wondered about it—maybe he'd dreamed the whole thing.

But the next day, before he got on the bus to go to Dover Air Force Base for his MAC ride back to Tehran, he'd phoned Paul's law firm and asked the edgy partner about the contracts and found out that everything Stick had said was true. And after that, there was no going back to America for J. P. Jones. Only for Hadj al-Shiran.

"MURDERED?" SHE'D SAID, the veneer of sophistication cracking just the slightest bit.

"Yeah," he'd said and tried to put some sugar in his iced tea. But his hand wouldn't stay steady so he just flipped the sugar package back and forth until she said again, "Say, your brother wouldn't have been Paul Jefferson Jones, would he?" And the way she said it, he knew she knew something big went with the name, something ugly and so powerful you just didn't fuck with it. When he nodded, it was like something snapped in her and all that upscale black-woman-of-the-new-age stuff just evaporated, and suddenly she looked scared, and he knew she was not going to hang around to learn to fly from him. Maybe it was better for everybody concerned, because she made him think of Paul and that made him lose control, bit by bit, and losing control was something that neither J. P. Jones nor Hadj al-Shiran could afford. So when she hurriedly paid her bill and climbed into her white Porsche he knew she was gone for good, because Stick was right: the word had gone out, years ago, and it was still in force.

The tea had grown cold. He shook his head and sat heavily back in the chair. The strain was almost too much. They had warned him it would be hard, his mullahs severely testing his will with simulated attacks on his belief. They'd told him the citizens of the Great Shaitan would tempt him, bit by bit, back into life as Jefferson Jones, but he had held out. Now, though, it was different. Sometimes, during the day, when he was working with his beloved airplanes and being an aviator and not a Jihaddin, he would grow terribly confused, the pain would come into his head and he would have to chant inwardly his true name over and over again until he was back in control. He was an actor on this stage, and he had to force himself every waking minute to remember his role and his lines, and it grew increasingly difficult. He was a strong man, but he was weakening, and he admitted this to himself only reluctantly. He needed guidance. He needed the Jihad. He needed a sign from Allah to keep his faith alive and his mission working.

He realized with a start that dawn had come while he sat in a daze at the kitchen table. He blinked and looked out at the ragged little garden, now painted in gray light. The aviator in him estimated the conditions while the Jihaddin reminded him that he had to monitor the radio frequency they had decided on in case there was a message for him. He had risen every morning at this hour just to listen, and it was part of his disappointment that there had never been anything. Just the hissing of the shortwave.

The battered old Zenith World Band Radio would have attracted no one's interest, but it served his purposes well. Radio Tehran could broadcast its SW programs to America at that time of day relatively free of solar static or other interference. He went into the tiny living room, flopped on the threadbare sofa and toggled on the radio. He slipped on the headset and carefully retuned the frequency. He checked the time. If there was to be a message, it would come in one minute, and then be repeated at the same hour for the next two days.

The empty hissing of the shortwave band filled his ears. He closed his eyes. *In the name of Allah, the compassionate, the merciful—*

A strong, clear tone broke his intonation. He hurriedly checked his watch. An "action" message was preceded by a tone, then the Morse code letter *A*, then the voice message.

The tone held for thirty seconds. His heart began beating like a jackhammer.

The tone stopped. In its place came the Morse code. Sweat poured suddenly from his palms. The letter repeated three times.

A voice—clear, calm, surely that of his own mullah!—spoke in English.

"Allah is love. And for the Love of Allah, man must do what he must do."

Al-Shiran gasped. It was precisely as they had briefed. If the operation was to proceed, this was exactly the phrasing he would hear. The mullah's recorded voice repeated the words twice more, then the signal disappeared into the ether.

He pulled off the headset and let the thought wash over him: Allah had heard his prayer! Now, *now* he knew the operation was blessed, as the mullahs had promised him. Whatever shards of unfaith he had left were seared out of him by the blinding fire of truth that the message sent through him.

He faced Mecca and fell to his knees. As he bent forward to touch his forehead to the worn carpet, Hadj al-Shiran no longer doubted that Paradise awaited him after his holy mission was done. And he no longer feared that Jefferson Paul Jones would regain control of his mind and heart.

The Jihad had come, at long last, to America.

CHAPTER SIX

THERE HAD NOT BEEN MUCH to go on at Har Mughara, even for Moshe Stein's experts from Section Four. They had the usual detritus of a Jihaddin raid; spent cartridge cases, corpses and stolen hardware. In this case he had been forced to report to his superiors that something very special had been stolen: the Judah IV, a ten-kiloton tactical nuclear weapon. It was a warhead package only, not yet inserted into a bomb or a missile, and without any means of delivery. But, as his report to the Knesset committee sourly disclosed, in the hands of anyone with the slightest nuclear-weapons experience, it could be easily armed to explode through a variety of means. And since it was so small—only forty kilos, in a large aluminum container not unlike a small casket—detection and recovery was going to be extremely difficult.

The committee had been duly alarmed, but procedures long in the planning had come smoothly into play, and Stein was able to tell them about his plans for coordinating a discreet search using all available assets. At this, the committee had been somewhat mollified, and Stein had emerged with a guarantee of a free hand and a liberal budget without oversight—and that was precisely what Lorelei demanded.

Stein had few contacts close to the Jihad that were of any real use. But those few had all agreed that something big was in the air; more than just another airport terror assault or hostage attempt. In the weeks after the Har Mughara theft, he patiently collected data, trying to track not just where the Judah IV had gone, but how the Jihad had known its location and all the codes necessary to defeat the electronic cordons at the site. It had to be someone privy to the Judah file and the site file. That narrowed the field considerably, to a few men in Israel and a handful in America, people whose help had been unavoidably necessary in building the secret nuclear weapons. People who were supposedly loyal to Israel above and beyond their loyalty to America; scientists and a few engineers who had heretofore been utterly silent about their role in Judah.

Stein sat at the console of the powerful computer in his home in Savyon and sipped wine, staring at the screen as he scrolled through the file. He could assign his people to checking the Israelis. Clearing the Americans would require him, in person, and someone else. Someone American. Someone whom he could not allow to report to the American intelligence agencies. Ever since the deplorable Pollard affair, intelligence relations between Israel and America had been erratic. He needed trained American help, and quickly. But he could not reveal why.

He reclined and pondered the glowing letters and numbers. He had access, through this terminal, to incredible computing power and worldwide data bases. But computers couldn't do everything. And with the American security system in disarray, remote data sharing, even via secure satellite link, was virtually impossible. There was no alternative: he had to leave for the States immediately.

His decision made, he leaned forward, scowled momentarily as he tried to recall the secret code and the file name and rapidly tapped the keyboard. He would not be able to do it alone. He would need the help of a man whom he trusted more than any other American. After a few seconds, the screen cleared and a name appeared. He grinned at the name, glanced at his watch, did a quick calculation to check time zones, called up the communications program, typed in the initials of the entry and picked up his telephone as the computer dialed the U.S.A.

The phone rang twice. Then it was answered in the same way it had always been, with a voice he recognized instantly, though it was more than a year since they'd last spoken.

"Colonel Chester," the gravelly voice said.

"Shalom, Mat," Stein said, smiling into the mouthpiece, "this is Mo. Listen. Something's come up. What are you doing for lunch next Tuesday?"

THE PHONE BUZZED. She ignored it and continued staring into the computer terminal, trying to make the connection she knew was there between the figures in the left column and those in the right. The left listed dates of movement of the latest batch of conscripts in the Soviet strategic rocket forces, and the right detailed truck and transporter production quotas and actual rates at the four Soviet plants that built for the rocket forces. It wasn't just that she knew how much effort had gone into getting the numbers that made her frown and blank out the phone—how much sheer sweat on the part of intel types like her, maybe even how much unknown bravery on the part of moles or their own agents. It was that making useful connections between such apparently unconnected data was her specialty. She was the best, and she knew it as well as her bosses in the Defense Intelligence Agency knew it. She had not only the training, but the unquantifiable knack of the ace analyst. It was why she was here in Arlington, working with Mat Chester's secret interagency focus group. And it was why she allowed herself to ignore the phone's buzzing.

Finally she sighed and touched the answer bar on the speakerphone. "Captain Koppel," she said, still eyeing the glowing columns of numbers.

"Sandy. Glad you answered. I was just about ready to send an MP over there." She smiled slightly at Chester's only half-jesting tone. As a colonel's daughter, she well understood what her mother had despairingly called "the chicken colonel syndrome." Refusing to wait too long for a subordinate to answer a call was part of the syndrome.

"Sorry, Colonel. Got absorbed in something here."

"No sweat. Look, how about lunch?"

In Washington, lunch was never just a meal. It could as easily be an assignation, assignment or assassination. Sandy Koppel had known that even before her transfer from Berlin. Especially if you were a woman, and most especially if you were a woman in Army intelligence, you prepared for a lunch in D.C. the way you would for a recon mission; carefully. Otherwise you could get blindsided. And in Washing-

ton, where careers took off and flamed out with equal
suddenness, that could mean trouble.

All this flashed through her mind in a jumble, and
she said, "Um, just a sec, Colonel, I'll check with my
social secretary to see what's on."

Chester chuckled again and she glanced at her
computer terminal, tapping the keys to call up her
schedule. She knew she had nothing going on for
lunch, but she needed the time to consider his invitation cum command. Chester's request might be purely
business. Or it might be camouflage for a sexual
overture. More than one middle-aged colonel like
Chester had used the same move on her. She didn't
think he was the type to hit on her. He seemed, in fact,
almost impossibly straight-arrow, perhaps cut from
the same cloth as her father, all crew-cut candor and
honest hard work. But she had been wrong about men
before, especially men who reminded her of her father. Her schedule, though, gave her no excuse to refuse.

"Looks okay, sir. What's the occasion?"

"Some people you need to meet."

"People." She made it half statement, half query.

"Yeah. I call 'em the over-the-hill gang. We meet
once or twice a month. This time, I thought you'd like
to attend."

"Sure. Uh, can you give me some background—"

"Way ahead of you. Come on into my office and
I'll brief you."

"Ten-four, Colonel. Now?"

"Right. Next ten minutes or so. I've got a meeting
at 1030."

"Be there in a flash."

"Fine," Chester said and chopped the connection. Sandy looked back at the screen. The numbers still wouldn't give up their secrets. She sighed again and tapped in her personal security code. They disappeared and the screen blanked.

She plucked her purse from its hiding place under the desk, fished out her compact and flipped it open. She grimaced as she saw what a few hours had done to her makeup, and set about repairing it. Working in civvies had its benefits, but it also had its drawbacks. If she were wearing her green Class A uniform, she'd have many fewer problems to contend with. But the focus group worked in secrecy, buried on an ELINT-secure floor of one of the many office buildings in Crystal City, across the Potomac from Washington. That meant she and the others had to look like the civilians who populated the building. And that meant she had to face the same problems of choosing clothes and a "look" as any other thirty-two-year-old single woman who earned good money in a semiexecutive position.

Washington was full of such women, and Sandy was heartened to see that most of them seemed to have as much trouble solving the problems as she did. You had to look feminine, but not too feminine. As a promising young manager, you had to exude charm, but also self-control and a certain executive stance. You had, in short, to do the almost impossible with your tribal costume. The men just bought Brooks Brothers and said to hell with it. After casting around for something a little more her own style—something European, slightly outré, maybe—she, too, said to hell with it and bought an entire wardrobe at Alcott and Andrews, a sort of all-female equivalent of Brooks Brothers.

She therefore looked like just another Washington up-and-comer, a five-foot-four blonde with lively, flashing blue eyes, and stylishly cut hair. She was clad today in a tastefully tailored gray two-piece suit and a high-collared white silk blouse that concealed more than it revealed of the figure she worked hard to keep fit and attractive. But she couldn't resist adding her mother's jade necklace and earrings; they, the expensive, almost too-sexy gray pumps and her bulging gray leather Gucci briefcase made clear to any onlooker that she was no secretary. Stepping out of her red Porsche 944 Turbo at her garage every morning, she knew the effect was right when the same lawyers and lobbyists who shared her parking area made it a point to flirt mildly with her. None of them, she knew, would guess that she was an Army officer.

She snapped the compact closed, slipped on her shoes and swept her little office with a swift look to ensure she left nothing classified in the open. Satisfied, she entered the buzz of the main office, locking her door behind her as she started for Chester's office on the other side of their floor.

The focus group's key officers each worked in small, closed offices like hers, not along the outside walls—which would have given them all nice views but also provided the bad guys easy visual access—but grouped together in the center of the suites. A casual visitor would imagine that it was perhaps just another law office; there was nothing visible to suggest otherwise. The classified data—the photos, the documents, the computer files—were all safely locked away.

Chester's office was bigger, but still in the inner core of the floor. He seemed to spend as little time in it as possible, moving around their cubicles like a professor monitoring the progress of his pupils. Sandy wasn't surprised to find him standing at the open door of Curt Fields's office, laughing and leaning against the doorjamb. She didn't know much about her boss, but she knew, after only her first few months, that Mat Chester liked to laugh.

He saw her and waved inside at Fields, simultaneously turning and inclining his head toward his own office. She went in and sat down.

They'd been given strict instructions about office decorations, warned not to give away their military backgrounds with the usual memorabilia each officer inevitably collected. Everybody but Mat Chester complied. He apparently found it impossible to resist hanging a North Vietnamese regular army map case casually over his coatrack. Only the most observant would see the small hole made by a round from Chester's M-16 almost in the center, or the faded words, "Hue, 1968" inked next to it.

Chester closed the door as Sandy sat down. He was one of those Army officers who could never be camouflaged, in Brooks Brothers or anything else. Today he wore a pink oxford-cloth button-down shirt with a yellow silk tie, but the way he wore it stamped him instantly and indelibly as military. He was handsome, Sandy thought, in a pleasant, even-featured sort of way, his eyes maybe a bit too close together for Hollywood good looks, his Adam's apple a tad too protuberant, his gaze too level. He didn't look like a movie star, he looked like what he was: a paratrooper who'd somehow crashed into intelligence and was determined to do well in it. The word among his staffers on this, his first focus group command, was that like all of them, he had *it*, the mysterious quality of insight that made all the difference between a man who looked at something and a man who saw it.

He sat down and pointed to the coffee maker on the nearby table.

"Need a caffeine spike?"

"No thanks, Colonel. Too much already."

He poured some into a battered mug and winced as a little of the hot liquid slopped onto his hand. He looked around for a napkin, found none, shrugged and sucked the overflow off his hand.

"Me too. What the hell." He sipped some and set the mug down. "Okay. The subject is lunch, and the object, as always, is better intel."

She relaxed invisibly inside. So much for him hitting on her.

"You ever hear of something called Hillbilly?"

Sandy blinked. "Uh, no sir."

He swallowed more coffee and grimaced. "*Damn*, that's hot. Good. That means some of our security people are on the job anyway. Hillbilly is the name people gave to the first interagency conference on restructuring our whole intelligence system. They called it that because the chiefs all got together in West-by-God-Virginia to discuss what ought to be done." He smiled at her. "Needless to say, not a damn thing got done. Except a lot of high-level staff time got wasted and a compartmentalized report got sent up to the

President, who was not amused, since he was the one who ordered the confab in the first place." He held up his hand as she opened her mouth.

"Wait. I know what you're going to ask. You're going to ask why he ordered it. Right?" She nodded.

"Fear, is why. Not fear of the bad guys on the other side, but the intel chiefs' fear of one another. Of course, that's not what the official line was. The official line from the White House staff was that the whole intelligence community had gotten too spread out to be controlled by the Director of Central Intelligence, let alone the President. The story was that none of the more embarrassing failures of the past two decades or so would have happened if we'd had a so-called rational intel setup." He paused, drank some more coffee and looked hard at Sandy.

"You recall the little screwup in Peru?"

"You mean the Delta Force's finest hour?"

"Exactly. That broke the camel's back. You know and I know that the DF guys did what they were supposed to. It wasn't their fault that the Shining Path weirdos decided to blow the train before the deadline. But as we also know, the DF troops got the blame for all those messy civilian deaths."

"Which explains a lot. Like why they were disbanded and Echo set up."

"You got it. And it also explains why the Hillbilly people went back to the hills with orders not to return until they had a new deal worked out. The idea was that all the roles and missions and turf wars would somehow be worked out and a whole new intel system emerge, one that the President could, ah, in his own words, 'rely on.'"

"So what happened?"

"The worst that could happen. The White House people ran the show this time around, and after five days, they came back with a proposal for a new National Security Act to replace the 1947 legislation that set up the whole American intel system in the first place. Nobody was happy with it but the geniuses who thought it all up. And none of them had to make it work." Chester leaned forward.

"Now, about here is where I expect you to be wondering what all this leads up to, since we both know the table of organization for the DIA hasn't changed a whit in the past few weeks. I'll save you the wondering. It leads to paralysis. What happened was, as soon as they left the conference, the biggies decided to freeze everything until they knew which way the wind would blow. Planned ops were canceled, ops underway were cut back, and everybody just pulled in horns and waited."

He took a swig of coffee again and regarded her closely. "Any of this connecting for you?"

Sandy smiled. "In a way. Thing is, it sounds like all this coincides with the op that I ran in Germany with the Recovery troops. Which means I'd have missed the buzz about it, having my hands full at the time."

"Correct. The von Grabow deal actually finished off any chance people like Blackie Lundberg might have had to uncork some new covert action. And that's where things stand today. Dead-ass stalled, until the brave legislators and the White House write us a new charter."

Sandy mulled it over for a moment, then said, "I guess it all explains why not much is going down on

the covert side. But how does this add up to the over-
the-hill gang and our lunch?''

Chester grinned. "It gets complicated about here.
What I'm going to tell you now is beyond compart-
mentalized, Sandy. It's flat-ass you-and-me secret.
Okay?''

"Sure. Shoot.''

"Well, thing is, a lot of folks weren't happy that the
covert side had to grind to a halt. Most of them were
folks you and I know. Career intel types, mostly military. A lot of my friends, probably some of yours,
even though you're just a youngster.''

She flushed. Thirty-two made her a youngster? She
didn't know whether to be flattered or feel patronized.

He carried on. "So these folks gradually figured out
what was happening—or rather, not happening—and
tried to correct things. But every op plan that called
for action seemed to get nowhere. Slowly, we got the
picture. The people upstairs were just not going to
play. Period. So we, uh, decided to play anyway.''

Sandy blinked. Chester caught her fleeting expression and sobered. "Understand here that we're talking serious stuff. We knew what we were doing, going
ahead on some of these things without orders. But
Christ, it had to be done. The other side sure wasn't
slowing down. In fact, our moles managed to alert us
to the fact that the bad guys seemed to know more
about the inside dope on what our chiefs were doing
than we did. That kind of frosted some balls, I can tell
you.'' He looked absently at the NVA map case.

"Nobody talked much about this in any organized
way. At first. But as time went on and our people kept

going facedown in the mud all over the map and nothing was being done, a few of us started meeting, very informally, for lunch. Just to talk things over in a general sort of way. To see how we might help one another out, maybe keep things moving until the ice broke up top.

"That's the over-the-hill gang. Folks like me. From DIA, CIA, FBI, service intel, National Reconnaissance Organization, State, the works. Most of us know one another from years of going to the same places, doing the same things. Nobody above a colonel or navy captain, no real heavyweights, just action types, close to retirement. Like me." He smiled wanly. "Sometimes we call ourselves the lunch mob."

"Beats being called the lynch mob," Sandy said, echoing his smile with her own.

"Yeah," he said and fell silent. He looked at her with hooded eyes. They both knew what he had just told her made her either his accomplice or accuser. There was no legal sanction for what Chester and his friends were doing. Just necessity, as they saw it. It could easily be seen as mutiny, should any military official care to bring charges against any of them. Yet as Sandy turned it all over in her mind, it was blindingly clear to her that key superiors had to know about how the covert activities were proceeding in spite of the official freeze. Chester was walking a very tight rope over a very large chasm. If he stepped off it—if one of his or his friends' ops got blown by the media or a jealous bureaucrat—nobody would save him. Now he wanted her to join him. And it might be too late to say no.

"So," she said, her voice a little less confident than she liked it to be, "what's the prognosis?"

"We figure the bozos ought to have it loosened up again inside ten months. The election's coming up and none of them want to have this hanging fire longer than that. But until then, we have to keep things running. Trouble is, as usual, it gets more complicated every day, harder to keep the whole thing completely informal and extracurricular. We need help. People like you."

"I see. You know, Colonel, this amounts to conspiracy."

"Hell, Captain, it doesn't amount to conspiracy. It *is* conspiracy. But what the hell choice have we got? Let the goddamn limp dicks at the wheels run us into the minefield? Shit. We even thought about getting the press on the case. But we just couldn't do it. You can't trust those bastards any farther than you can throw 'em. So all we can do is put our heads down and put one foot in front of the other. As an old infantry type, I'm sure you can appreciate that."

"Yes, sir. I can appreciate it." She wondered if he knew how close to the nerve he struck with that comment. Her greatest hurt lay under the heading of "infantry." She had been chosen to try out the concept of an integrated male-female infantry company, with her as the CO. It had been tough going, breaking into the last bastion of the Old Army, the Man's Army, but she and her people had finally done it, proving in exercise after exercise that men and women working together could fight as well and as fiercely as men alone. Too well, it turned out. The old boy network, alarmed at her success, and fearing too many females in combat

units, mobilized against her. The pressure was put on
her through all the dirty, subtle tactics about which her
father had warned her, but which she had never before encountered.

As she'd realized what was happening, she'd vowed
to fight them to the end. But in the end they'd won.
Their decisive blow had been the affair she'd fallen
into with her battalion exec. He had seemed not only
sympathetic to her and her cause, but also like a
younger version of her father: witty, strikingly handsome, brave. But he'd also been on their side. His job
had been to seduce her, then to scuttle her career by a
carefully arranged incident that would reach the ears
of the CO and compromise her, but not him. She'd
been blind even to the potential for such a thing until
a casually dropped hint from a fellow officer who
found the plot distasteful warned her to cool it with
the XO. His warning came just in time. When she'd
confronted the man she thought she was head over
heels in love with, he'd just smiled patronizingly at her
and walked out. Furious, humiliated, but still determined that they wouldn't win, she asked for a transfer to DIA. It made her even angrier when nobody—
not even the colonel—asked why. It was only at the
Military Mission in Potsdam that she began to get over
it.

"I can appreciate it, but I don't get it. Why do you
need me?"

"You're the best, Sandy. You see what others don't.
That's it, in a nutshell." He glanced at the clock on the
wall. "Look. I've gone on too long. Are you game?"

It was unfair to pressure her that way, and they both
knew it. She had every right—indeed, it was her

duty—to blow the whistle on him and his network.
But something held her back. Maybe it was the tan-
talizing lure of the forbidden. Maybe it was the fact
that since that incredible twenty-four hours with Max
in East Germany, she hadn't had much action, and
this was at least action of a sort. And it held a certain
revenge; if she could pull this off, she might be getting back at the old boys in some crazy, convoluted
way. And that clinched it for her.

"You bet, Colonel. But there's just one thing."

He held her eyes with his own. "What?"

"Why now?"

Chester looked at her without blinking for a moment, then turned away. "Something's going down in
Israel. A friend—guy you'll meet soon—filled me in
a little about it on Tuesday. Stuff we didn't know
anything about, officially. His price was our help." He
swung back.

"*Our* meaning the over-the-hill mob."

"Gang. Right. So I called this lunch a little earlier,
and wanted to include you."

"We can't handle it ourselves? Here?"

"No."

His flat refusal surprised her, and worried her a little. She waited, but he said nothing more. He had become inscrutable, his face unreadable. She decided
against asking more. She had done the thing her father had warned her against the day she went off to
Officer Candidate School. She had volunteered, and
as he warned her, when she did that, she began to lose
options. Especially in volunteering for something as
shadowy as this.

After a few moments, Chester cracked a thin smile, his eyes still deadly serious. "I'm not trying to be mysterious about this, Sandy. But there are reasons. You'll see."

Something clicked for her. When it flashed across her mind, it had that solid, *true* feel that all her best "connections" had. It was her knack, her specialty, the reason Chester had her here now. Her knack worked to deliver these flashes to her, sometimes on command, sometimes out of the blue. It combined her superb memory and extraordinary observational powers with what she knew professionally about the military and what she knew about people as a woman forced to excel in a man's world. She used to doubt the flashes, but no more. They had been proved too many times. Most recently in a Jeep Cherokee in the middle of a wild, pitch-black night in East Germany.

"I think I see part of it already. Your *friend* is Israeli, isn't he?"

Chester started, his eyes opening wider before he clamped his iron control on his features again. He cocked his head at her a second, then a slow smile spread across his face.

"Jesus, how'd you know—well, never mind. Trade secret, I imagine."

She reveled in scoring her bull's-eye. But she also knew she had to be careful. Chester wasn't just a member of this clandestine group, he was also her boss. He wrote her fitness report.

"It was easy, Colonel. I can tell you if you want."

He waved his hand, dissipating the tension as if it were fog. "Nah. Let's just say you got it right first time. That's what Uncle pays you for. And let's just say that this lunch is to help my—*our*—Israeli friend. So that he can help us again. That's how networks work.''

"So,'' she said wryly, ''I noticed.''

He wrinkled his tanned, leathery face into an enormous, genuine grin. ''You're right. When the pompous bull starts flowing so copiously, it's time for me to stop the lecture. Besides, my meeting is in three minutes. Let's get together at 1145 by the elevator and head over to El Brasero. We can talk on the way. Okay?''

"Okay,'' she said, and got to her feet.

Something about her look must have bothered him. He got up too, and said, before she opened the door, ''Hey. These are good people, Sandy. You won't be sorry.''

She tried to put on her cheeriest expression. ''I'm sure, sir,'' she said, and went into the main office again. But as she walked back to her own little cubicle, her smile faded, and a chill seemed to settle in her stomach. Most of the time, she loved the challenges of the Army. But there were times when she wondered whether life might not be easier and simpler if she were one of the Washington women whom she strove to impersonate with her Gucci shoes and briefcase and carefully tailored suit. As she unlocked the door to her small, sterile office, she realized this was one of those times.

She drew a deep breath, kicked off her shoes, keyed in her security code and called up the Soviet statistics. ''One foot in front of the other,'' she muttered, and stared intently at the numbers.

EL BRASERO WAS as Chester had briefed: a small beanery in the most run-down section of Arlington. Graffiti smeared the walls of the nearby storefronts, trash littered the unswept gutters, burned-out cars rusted in alleys. Two decades before, blacks had lived and worked here. They had been supplanted by Hispanics, and the Hispanics by Koreans and Vietnamese. As if cursed, the area resisted cleanup.

Yet Emilio Redaja's restaurant cleared a steady profit. Partly it was because he served good food. Mostly it was because he was a Cuban exile who'd worked for the CIA long enough to build a large network of friends in the Company and its allied agencies. Friends who patronized his restaurant when he bought it after he retired. And friends like Mat Chester who kept coming back because Emilio provided a "safe room" free of bugs when they needed it.

As Chester shoved open the massive door, Sandy shivered in the cold wind and relished the blast of hot air from the restaurant. She needed only a glance to see that this was no upscale Mexican-theme restaurant. Instead of the carefully backlit hacienda decorations typical of the genre, what little light there was came from a few sixty-watt bulbs behind garishly tinted glass screens along the walls. A ceiling fan sluggishly churned the stale, smoky air. A stereo somewhere blared Julio Iglesias through too many cheap speakers, covering what conversation might be going on among the two dozen or so patrons seated on a collection of ancient bentwood chairs at tiny, rickety tables. The customers studiously ignored the pair as they stood for a moment inside the cramped little foyer. Chester swept the group with a glance, then moved purposefully toward a side door almost hidden behind a small table piled high with dirty dishes. He nodded curtly to the head waitress as he weaved through the tables. An enormous woman with olive skin and an opaque gaze, she acknowledged his greeting with an imperceptible nod.

As Sandy followed Chester, she felt inquisitive eyes. Her cursory glance around the room told her volumes. It told her that these were not typical Arlington blue-collar workers spending a few of their bucks on frijoles. She didn't recognize any of the people, but she recognized their type. She had seen it enough in Europe, especially in Berlin. Dressed to be deliberately nondescript, trained to see without being seen, these men and few women were professionals. In her business. Like a jolt of unexpected adrenaline, it woke her to the reality of what she was doing.

Chester went through the door into a short, twisting hallway, opened another door and they stepped into a different world.

The room might easily have been lifted straight from a turn-of-the-century mansion. Ornate carved wood paneled the walls, as dark and richly polished as the long mahogany table and ten chairs arranged at it. Two chandeliers threw a pleasantly warm light on the room and the eight people around the table, who looked up almost in unison as they came into it.

"Mat," said a silver-haired man at one end, smiling as he did so.

"Ivan," Chester said, nodding as he peeled off his camel hair greatcoat. The others in the room fell silent as he and Sandy took off their layers of warm clothing and hung them on the nearby coatrack. When they were done, he seated her and stood for a moment.

"Folks, this is Sandy Koppel. About whom you already know. Sandy, these are some of our over-the-hill gang. From your left, Bob McCowan and June Ellis from State, Irene Hall from Navy Intel, Ivan Krug, Harvey Lane and Dick Amos from the Company, Larry Steele from the Recon people and Chuck Fender from NSA." He paused, clearly groping for the right thing to say next. "As you say, this lunch mob beats the hell out of a lynch mob."

Polite chuckles greeted this, and Chester sat down.

"A word of advice, Mat," said Ivan, lighting a pipe. "Stick to jumping out of airplanes if you're thinking about a career on the speech circuit."

Mat grinned, shook out his linen napkin and smoothed it on his lap. Instead of the cheap crockery and cutlery of the public dining room, the "special" table was laid with polished silver and crystal. A door almost invisibly set into the wood paneling opened and a small man with dark skin and a dark suit emerged. He darted quick black eyes around the room, met Chester's gaze and smiled, revealing crooked brown teeth.

"Colonel," he said, using Spanish accents on the word, "so at last you come. Welcome."

"Emilio. Thank you. This is Captain Koppel, my colleague. Sandy, our host, Emilio Redaja."

Sandy inclined her head and Emilio did likewise, still smiling. Sandy tried to match the small man with the violent life he had led as an anti-Castro agent. As with so many field people, he looked nothing at all like the kind of man who could kill with his bare hands and endure horrifying torture without breaking. Yet he had done both.

"Now that you are here, Colonel, your lunch can begin. Marguerite will bring your seviche. Enjoy."

"Thank you, Emilio," Chester said gravely. The exchange was obviously a ritual. Emilio nodded to the rest of the room and left.

What might have been an empty few seconds of embarrassment for Sandy disappeared as Dick Amos of the CIA said, "Well, Mat, what the hell is this about Mo Stein?"

Chester leaned back in his chair. Marguerite slipped in and began placing glass dishes of seviche before them.

"He's looking for a free-lancer. I told him we'd help."

"Why us?" asked June Ellis. She, like the others, did indeed seem to be about ten years older than Sandy. She wore her gray hair in a tight bun and looked more like a librarian than an action officer.

"He needs an American. Says that his op has led here, but he knows the Hillbilly problem and knows he'll get nowhere through channels."

"What kind of free-lancer?" Harvey Lane, who wore a perpetually cynical look, made his question sound menacing.

"Specialist in defense electronics, maybe somebody active in the commercial end, who can also handle the rough stuff if necessary and still bring home the bacon. Obviously he *wants* a superhero, Sherlock and Audie Murphy all in one, but like us he'll settle for a mere mortal. The idea is that the guy'd sniff around for Mo, looking for a tie-in with the incident they had at Har Mughara.''

"Umm," said Ivan, trailing pipe smoke. "We don't know much about what went on there. Will Mo help us if we help him?"

"That's the deal."

"How far will he go?" Chuck Fender, from the National Security Agency, was a former cop, and it showed. He tended not to believe anybody about anything. As Mat had explained to Sandy, Chuck and Harvey acted as balance weights in their group, damping out enthusiasm but providing in the process a vital service by keeping them from too-ambitious plans.

"I don't know. He hinted a lot. I've known Stein a long time, and he always delivers."

"Within limits," said Irene coolly.

"Sure. Within limits. But we're weak over there now, at least from what I know. Isn't that the case with everybody?"

Nobody disagreed. Fish forks clinked on glass and Ivan tapped out his pipe.

Chester wiped his mouth and leaned back, sipping the wine that Emilio had provided. "So. Anybody know any free-lancers who might fit the bill?"

The silence continued.

Chester looked around, then picked up his fork again.

"Problem is, Mat, as you well know, our assets are stretched too damn thin right now," said Ivan. "I can't speak for everybody, but I know the Company's right at the bottom of the barrel. I'm reluctant, frankly, to suggest somebody we might need more than he will.''

Nods followed from around the table.

"Understood. I warned Mo that it might be the situation. I certainly couldn't think of anybody we could suggest who would be able and yet uncommitted. My understanding from our guys is that everybody's who's any damn good is overbooked.''

Sandy had listened to the interplay without comment, as befitted her newcomer's status. Yet she had made a connection and wondered if she should bring it up. She broke off some French bread and munched it, watching the others and waiting for a clue. On one hand, she didn't want to stick her foot in her mouth. On the other hand, she was here for a reason, and it wasn't to eat and run.

"Mat, I just don't see it. Aside from getting a little dope on the Mughara thing, what's in it for us down the line?'' Amos leaned on the table and made his point with his fork. Next to him, Irene gently shoved his hand and fork back toward his plate, smiling faintly and rolling her eyes. He ignored her and stared at Chester.

"My idea was this. Last I heard, we're way down on recruitment. Even the funds have been frozen at DIA, and I guess from what Ivan said last time we met, that's the case at Langley, too. So I figured if we could come up with a likely guy, we could let him work for Mo—on loan, as it were—and check him out. If he proved out, we'd terminate the loan and set him up with us.''

"You mean by 'us,' the network,'' said Ivan, repacking his pipe.

"Correct. It'd be only part of a short-term deal, until they clear the gridlock, but we're losing enough people out there that we've got to do something. At least the way I see it."

Ivan nodded, puffing the pipe to life. "I see your point. But I'm afraid I still can't commit any of the few potential dossiers we've got. Hope you'll understand."

Chester glanced at Chuck Fender and lifted an eyebrow. Fender shook his head.

"If I might," Sandy said, "I have a suggestion."

They looked at her with the interest teachers give a promising student.

"Shoot," said Chester.

"I know a guy who might fit the profile. He even works for us in the Agency."

"Interesting," said Krug. "But if he's already in the system, isn't he on assignment? It would be hard to break him loose if he is."

"No. The last I knew, he was in training at Camp Peters."

"Hardly makes him a free-lancer," Amos said with a snort. "How could we use a guy already *in*?"

"No, wait a minute, Dick," said Chester. "Sandy's on to something. As you know, Lundberg got authorization for a bunch of people to go through training before the freeze hit. This might work. We know they'll go nowhere once they're through. Why waste a trained man? Go on, Sandy."

The interest of the group was now intense. They waited while she folded her napkin.

"Well, I knew him in Germany, in the von Grabow op. He's tough, smart, fast on his feet and good with his hands." She recalled the way he had held her in the shattered Jeep as the Soviet antiarmor rockets exploded all around. Recalled her uncontrollable shaking and how his hands calmed her. "Maybe best of all, his father's a retired Army two-star who runs an electronics company on the procurement people's 'A' list."

Nobody spoke. Then Krug pulled the pipe from his mouth and tapped it on the huge ashtray in front of him. The dull clonking echoed in the elegant dining room. "I'd say, Mat, that your colleague has solved your problem for you. *If* you can spring the guy, *if* Stein buys him and *if* he can handle this kind of assignment. Wouldn't you?"

Chester looked at Sandy. "Maybe," he said. "You think your man would play?"

She shrugged. "He's definitely not a team player. It should be right down his alley."

He stroked his chin and looked around the room. "Okay, let's give it a try. Nobody else has a better idea. What's his name?"

She picked up her napkin and smoothed it on her lap. His was one name she'd never forget, but she didn't want these people to know that about her. Or him.

"Moss," she said, her voice as neutral as possible. "Max Moss."

Across the table from her, the two other women exchanged swift glances. And smiled faint, knowing smiles.

CHAPTER SEVEN

BARTON PICKED UP his glass of beer, lifted it to his lips, and then paused. He stared into the amber liquid, made a noise somewhere between a grunt and a chuckle and drank. He set it down on the table with a clunk and looked blearily at Max.

Max looked blearily back. The party had gone on a long time. Probably too long for Mike's taste. The aviation people who'd come to help celebrate Max's successful license check ride took up a lot of room, and room was something Mike's Place didn't have. Since a lot of the flying types—some active–duty Navy, some civil, one former Air Force jock—had to fly the next day, they were judicious in their drinking. That meant fewer profits per occupied stool and chair. And while Mike, as an old pilot himself, enjoyed the familiar revelry, he was still a businessman whose business was making certain every person in his joint bought the maximum possible amount of product while he was there. So he was just as glad when, about ten o'clock, the pilots and their friends began to clap Max and Charlie on the back and leave; their going opened up the place to the regular, hard-core drinkers.

"So, Mr. Moss," Barton muttered thickly, "formerly by-God Captain Moss of the U.S. Square Force, finally gets his goddamn wings." He'd said something like that for the previous three hours, about as soon as he'd begun drinking seriously—as though he couldn't believe it.

Max ignored him. "Finally" was hardly the appropriate word. Max had blitzed through the written exam for his private pilot license weeks earlier with an almost perfect score. The check ride had been harder to arrange, but finally, today, the FAA's examiner had consented to go up in Ol' Blue with Max, and came back shaking his head, exclaiming at his airmanship with so few logged hours. But he'd issued Max his ticket, and the usual blowout party had ensued.

"Two goddamn months," Barton said to nobody in particular. "If I'd been—" He stopped himself, shrugged and drank again. Ever since Max's first flight with him, he'd been continually and vocally amazed at Moss's swift learning of the skills of flying. "*Two months!* Jesus! Moss, you realize how many guys can climb in a fuckin' SNJ and qualify in two months?" He didn't wait for Max to answer. He slugged more beer and looked at the TV set, where more silent colored images flickered. "Damn few, is the answer, nugget. Damn few."

Max did not take his half-jesting compliments too seriously. He'd been a little surprised at the speed with which he picked up the tricks of flying, but on reflection, he'd decided that it wasn't such a big deal, at least not at the level he was flying Ol' Blue. In aerobatics, he was about as sloppy as any neophyte, but the basics were a snap, compared to driving a race car

at Daytona. Especially since in Ol' Blue and other
trainers, there was somebody to coach you. In a racer,
you had to figure it out for yourself. Besides, most of
the legends about how hard the SNJ was to fly had
been made almost a half century before by young-
sters barely out of their teens; Max had a whole career's worth of handling high-speed, sophisticated
equipment, and had never even considered that there
might be some kind of vehicle that he couldn't master, had he the time and cause.

He poured more beer into his glass and wondered
again at the cause for flying Ol' Blue. In truth, it was
simply because it would pay off quickly in a way he
relished. Learning to fly was easy for him, just as
learning to drive racers had been easy. Much easier
than learning to live the way he was expected to live,
by his father and the others who thought of him as a
sort of social renegade when he recoiled from the road
map Eric Moss had imperiously issued him on his
graduation from Berkeley.

He smiled wanly as he sipped the beer and watched
Charlie ogle a cracker's pretty girl. Some guys never
grow up. By his own admission, Barton had narrowly
escaped a thousand scrapes with military and prime-
val male justice in his twenty years in the Navy, because he insisted on having as good a time as possible.
At all times. He was the quintessential, perpetually
juvenile fighter jock—superb in combat, useless on the
deck, except for roaming the earth in eternal search of
booze and women. And now, after everything, what
had he? A monthly check from Uncle Sam, a trailer,
a dilapidated airplane and a disreputable Corvette. His
family had more or less given up on him years ago, his

three former wives divided most of his retirement pay, and the rest he spent on avgas and beer. In pursuit of what?

The lesson wasn't lost on Max. As he'd flown with Charlie, he'd grown to love the man's wit, his worldly-wise charm, his story for every occasion, his youthful approach to everything. But in his soberer moments, Charlie had made no secret of his regrets. Where were his kids? he'd mused on one soft Keys evening, the kids he never had and never wanted. Or so he'd thought during his marriages to fast, flashy women, each of whom subsequently married somebody else and had *their* kids. Charlie had a license plate frame on his Airstream that read, Live to Fly, Fly to Live, and Max had thought about that message many times as they'd sat in the cool shade of Charlie's tattered awning outside the trailer, going over lessons and theory before and after Max's training flights.

With only a change of verb—"drive" instead of "fly"—it might have been Max's motto, too. And that shook him. Because as his blowup at Camp Peters had led, inescapably, here, so, too, did the realization that flying was just one more kind of escape for him, an escape to—where?

The jukebox, as it had all evening, broke his train of thought. But this time he was just as glad. From long experience, he knew that he had a lot more questions than he had answers, at least for the hard ones. The crackers that filled the place now began to grow rowdy, one of them swinging wide and knocking Charlie's chair as he maneuvered back to his own table, laden with a tray of beer mugs. Charlie lurched sideways and slammed his own glass down, trying to stand forcefully and confront the guy. But he was too soused, too old and too late; the cracker had never even noticed, and all Barton saw when he was erect was the man's broad, sweaty T-shirt disappearing between two other arguing T-shirts filled with Florida bellies and beer. He gazed at the man for a moment, then motioned Max to his feet.

"Time . . . time for an officer and a gentleman to be going, I believe," he said shakily.

Max nodded and got to his feet, almost as unsteadily as Barton. He rarely drank to drunkenness, but this was one of those rare times when he got very close. Too close for driving, he thought, and was about to warn Barton that neither of them was in shape to navigate the roads when he realized the older man had already begun to push through to the back door, not the front door. Max followed. Somehow they made it to Mike's house, fifty yards from the bar. Somehow they made it through the door. Somehow—he didn't know how, because he was fading too fast—they found beds.

And suddenly it was tomorrow, the bright sun lending force to a blinding headache. He awoke thirsty and nauseated and hungry and weak. He awoke with a cat on his face.

The cat looked at him as he opened his throbbing eyes, which seemed to be glued together with epoxy. It was a patently mean cat. It had to be because it continued to lie on him in spite of the fact that he was having trouble breathing.

"Mmmff," Max said bravely. The cat—narrow of eye, black of coat, long of claw—sniffed and stuck a paw out. The paw's claws dug into his nose. He blinked and repeated, "Mmmff!" and shoved the cat away with all his might. It barely moved. He gave up and closed his eyes again.

Later he awoke less traumatically. The cat was gone, and so was the sun. This time he realized the true meaning of "hangover." He realized he was going to be sick.

He rolled over and lost everything in his stomach in three enormous heaves. Tears gushed from his eyes with the effort. But as he lay back, tasting the vileness in his mouth, gasping, he began to feel better. He lay perfectly still and tried not to feel the pounding of the blood in his head. Time passed—it might have been a minute, or three hours—and he raised himself to see his immediate world.

Some smart soul had placed a very large plastic bucket square against his bed, obviously expecting him to do what he had done. He flopped back, relieved.

Only slowly did it come to him that the ceiling at which he occasionally looked was in his own bedroom, not Mike's. Somebody had dragged him out of Mike's and back to his place. He brought all his concentration to bear and tried to remember. He could not. It was not a problem he relished, so he drifted back to sleep.

When he awoke again, it was dark, and his nose was filled with the smell of something delicious being grilled. It smelled like steak. His stomach knotted, and he knew that at last he had to get up and bribe or kill whoever was grilling the steak to feed it to him. Fast.

But fast was not in the script when he tried to sit up. He groaned and levered himself up on one shaking elbow. The light was on in his kitchen. He could not see

who was there. Must be Charlie, he thought numbly.
Good old Charlie had recovered first, brought him
home and was fixing—what? Breakfast? Lunch?
Dinner? Who cared?

He did, more with every passing minute. But his
body was not obeying him well. He groaned again and
managed to swing his legs out of the bed. He noticed
with an odd sort of detachment, first the bucket was
gone, and second that he was naked. He rubbed his
jaw. It was coarse with stubble. He must have slept
through a whole day. The room stopped swaying and
he tried to get to his feet. He lurched to the doorway
of the dark bedroom, squinting against the glare of the
fluorescent kitchen lights, drawn by the irresistible
odor of the steak. He grabbed the doorframe and
peered into the kitchen through eyes open no more
than slits.

A figure stood at the stove; he could make that out,
and no more. He blinked and croaked, "Hey" so
weakly he wasn't even sure himself if any sound
emerged from his throat.

The figure turned to him and he realized the word
had indeed escaped his larynx. As his vision cleared,
he found himself staring at a woman. Not a man. Not
Charlie. A woman. A woman he had known about a
million years ago. He gulped.

Sandy grinned at him, and looked him up and down
appreciatively. "Hiya, Max," she said cheerfully,
"how are you feeling?"

He swayed and grabbed the doorframe harder.
"Uhh—" he said.

"Yeah," she said, nodding, "you tied one on. Well,
maybe you ought to have some coffee and chow, eh?"

She smiled wickedly. "But first maybe you ought to put on some clothes. You know how it is. The neighbors might get the wrong idea."

Max Moss had not been embarrassed many times in his life, and never to the point of blushing over his entire body. But as soon as he understood that he was standing stark naked in front of Sandy Koppel, he turned crimson from head to toe. And then he turned tail and scurried, lurching and staggering, back into his bedroom. Her gentle, tinkling laugh followed him, making him blush even more. At least she wouldn't see *that*, he seethed as he fumbled in his closet for his battered old English smoking jacket. He stepped into the bathroom, winced as he saw his reflection, splashed some water on his face in a hopeless attempt to appear civilized, squared his shoulders and went back to the kitchen.

Sandy was humming as she assembled the food. He stood for a moment in the doorway again, just looking at her. He had forgotten so much about her, and yet, she was in many ways unforgettable.

"Hello," he said, and tried to enter the room with some dignity. It didn't work. Naturally, just as she turned, he tripped over the stool by the phone. She grinned again and went back to her salad, keeping a weather eye on the beans boiling merrily away and the steak sizzling in the broiler.

"Here," she said as he leaned on the counter beside her, arms crossed, "eat this while I finish dinner. It'll keep you alive." She handed him some kind of flat cracker heaped with what looked like cottage cheese and paprika. He took it, sniffed and stuck it in his mouth. At first bite, his stomach heaved, then, mi-

raculously, told him to send it all down. He gobbled
it up in a few crunches. She glanced at him, handed
him another and pointed to a glass with milky liquid
in it. He ate the cracker and drank the liquid, which
was sweetly lemonish. When he'd done, he felt like a
new man. Or at least a new zombie. He confronted the
matter of speech with someone he hadn't seen in more
than a year.

"Uh, how . . . well, I mean—"

"Keep quiet. We can talk later. Sit down over
there—right, where the place mat is, with the napkin
and cutlery. I had a terrible damn time finding any of
that stuff—and don't try to talk or think until you
eat." He rolled an eye at her like a drunken porpoise
checking out the sky and managed to sit down as she
said. He marveled at the place mat. He hadn't known
there were any. But then, all he ever ate was micro-
waved food. By himself.

But not tonight. Sandy peeled off her apron,
plopped the platters down on the trivets—had he had
those, too, all this time?—scanned the table and sat
down. While he sat like a little kid in the doghouse,
hands limp in his lap, simply watching, she dished out
his food and handed him his plate. Then she smiled
and declared that even if he was too blotto to drink
fine wine, she had a bottle of Cabernet Sauvignon
from California and she by God was going to drink.
He was perfectly welcome to any if he so chose, the far
more prescriptive soda water in front of him notwithstanding.

He ate. He drank. Slowly he came back to life. She
spoke hardly at all, smiling at him occasionally. It was
at once the weirdest dinner and the best dinner of his

life. He felt as if he were a man who had been saved
from drowning, or death by asphyxiation. By the time
dinner was over, he felt marvelous.

Afterward, he helped her put the dishes away, she
directing again, he obeying, the domestic clink and
clatter providing the continuo to their dance. At last,
everything was stowed, and she flipped the dish towel
across her shoulder, plucked her wine from the spar-
kling counter and eyed him across the rim of the glass
as she sipped. He grinned.

"Now," he said.

She nodded. "Probably now is as good a time as
any."

"You first," he said.

"Okay," she said with a sigh, "but this is going to
be a long one. Why don't you take a shower first? *After* I pay a visit."

"Sounds good. *Nach ihnen,*" he said, waving in the
direction of the lone bathroom. She dipped a phony
curtsy and brushed past him to the bathroom. She left
a trail of scent that he did not recall from the time in
Berlin. Actually, he thought as he went back to his
bedroom to get some underwear, he recalled all too
little about Sandy from Berlin. He knew a lot about
Captain Koppel; he vividly remembered the way she
saved his ass with that Cherokee, braving rockets and
cannon to get him. What he didn't remember, and was
now astonished at not remembering, was Sandy as a
vibrant female.

And vibrate she did, as she gave him another smile
when they passed at the bathroom door. He paused,
pointing at the TV and sound system. "Television is
over there, and the radio—"

"I know. I'd plenty of time to figure it all out. Get in the shower before they arrest you for indecent odors."

In the shower, he let the surprise of her being here wash over him as fully as the hot water. A dizzying sense of unreality underlay the whole thing, but she was undeniably here, and he was undeniably about to ask her why, and how. And, he realized, for how long.

"Why?" she repeated. She sipped her wine again and regarded him from the rattan couch where she sat. "Well. That's a tough one. Sure you don't want to start with 'how'?"

"Okay," he said, settling back into his own chair. "How, then."

"Well. I started with Blackie Lundberg's office. You knew he was not at DIA anymore, didn't you?"

"Nope."

"Now he's chief of Special Operations Command, at MacDill."

"Ah. Hope he enjoys it."

"Max. The guy saved your bacon with that Coletto deal. You could have been shot for desertion or disobeying an order from the President—"

"Hey," he said, holding up a palm, "I know. General Lundberg has done me quite a few favors...a lot more than the CIC of the Agency had to for some guy from the Mission. I know."

"You hold him responsible for what happened to you at Camp Peters?"

"No. I guess I only hold him responsible for commissioning me, for knowing I'd be just interested enough to play the game. I figure that's how I wound up at Peters."

She frowned. "Weird logic. But never mind. Anyway, I traced you to Peters, where the XO at Lundberg's old office said you were being trained as an operative." She paused. He said nothing.

"I found out that your CO there accepted your resignation four months into training, when you only had another two weeks to go."

"That all you found out?"

"No. I talked to a Sergeant Wolfe—"

"Big Mouth we used to call him."

"—who told me the story of how you and three other guys broke into the motor pool, stole some ATVs and raised hell in the local burg until the MPs caught up with you. Wolfe said it took the entire camp MP company and two state troopers to net you."

Max lifted his shoulders a little and let them drop.

"Colonel Landreth said that as a result of the interview you had with him the next day, you jointly decided that it would be best if you terminated your commission."

"Shit," Max exploded, "we jointly decided squat! Landreth pulled my chain every day I was there, and I finally had it up to—and besides, what the hell harm was there in a little Honda ride through the goddamn Louisiana bush? We'd been through the wringer with those sadists. We'd learned fifty-three ways to kill with a telephone book and a toothpick, and could navigate with a wristwatch and a candle. Landreth was a pissant, as Ike used to say. A goddamn pissant."

"Maybe. Anyway, Lundberg's office concurred in his acceptance of your resignation—"

"What? Really? Blackie—Blackie agreed to it?" Max looked a little shaken.

"Apparently," she said soberly. "Landreth was only the camp CO, you know. Agency regs don't give him authority to cashier any trainee operative, or accept resignations from one. He had to get permission from upstairs. And he got it."

Max sat back, subdued. It was a blow to him to have General Lundberg—who really had intervened not once but twice to save him—finally agree that he was not special ops material. It gave his resignation an unwelcome poignancy; maybe he didn't quit so much as get fired. Sandy saw him chewing on it and hurried on.

"I got you as far as the bus to Mobile, and it took the state DMV to get me to your Chevy dealer. I lucked out and talked to Cindy, the gal who sold you the car—she remembered you, believe me, and you're lucky to have gotten away from her, boyo—and Cindy recalled that you talked a lot about breaking the One Lap of America record time to Key Largo. So I took a long shot, hooked up with the property management people—there aren't many, y'know, around here—and presto! Max Moss is found."

He looked at her with hooded eyes, a look she remembered from Berlin, and with no fondness. Max had the habit of changing moods entirely too quickly for comfort. "A lot of trouble just to turn up a drunk."

"No way. Besides, from what Mike said, you deserved it. Got your wings—and in a T-6!—in record time."

"You know Mike?"

"Now I do. And Charlie, too. He sends his best, by the way. Asks if you figured out how to hold your liquor yet."

Max snorted. "You've been a busy lady."

"You could say so. You didn't make it easy."

"So why do it? Why track me down?"

She considered him a moment, then folded her hands in her lap. She looked like a schoolmistress reviewing the misdeeds of a wayward pupil.

"You sure you want all this in one shot?"

"Damn sure," he said. "It's a safe bet you didn't go through all this because you missed me. Time you told me what's going down."

"Okay," she said quietly. And then she told him.

He sat silently through her thirty minutes and more of nonstop monologue. She was an excellent briefer, and knew how to tailor her briefing to the audience. Max, she knew, would be suspicious of everything— her motives, the Agency's interests, how "official" the whole crazy thing was, so she spent the greatest part of her time not in describing the free-lancer's role with the network, but in how and why it came to be. When she was done, she drained her glass and looked Max in the eye.

"Well?" she said.

Max had sat through her monologue, arms crossed on his chest, legs crossed, on a cushioned ottoman. He was feeling highly defensive. At her question, he uncrossed his arms, rubbed his face and smiled at her. "You probably want to know what I think," he said cheerfully.

"You're as fast as ever, Max. What do you think?"

"I think," he said, standing and stretching, "that it's time for all God's children to go to bed and think of many things. I think it's been a long couple of days. I'm pooped, kiddo. Flat wiped out. So where are you staying?"

Sandy looked up at him for a moment, unsure of his mood. Finally, she decided he was serious. Obviously, he needed time to think it all through. She stood, too, and stuck her hands in the pockets of her jeans. She grinned at him. "Is that a line?"

Max smiled back. She looked stunning, the pastel pink T-shirt hanging loosely from her breasts, the jeans tailored tightly enough to show how well arranged and cared for the rest of her body was. Ruefully, he shook his head.

"Unfortunately, Captain Koppel, *no*. And I ought to be shot for it. But you've given me too much to chew on. I really do need the time to think—alone. But if you've no place to stay, well, you evidently already know my place inside out, so—"

She looked a tiny bit crestfallen, but the look passed quickly. "No need. I'm checked in down the road at the Flamingo. Give me a call when you're ready to talk. No hurry. And no push, Max. If you need a lot of time, I'll go back to D.C., and you can call."

"Probably won't be necessary. Either I'll know tomorrow, or I'll never know. Need a ride?"

Sandy plucked her wineglass from the table and took it to the dishwasher. She placed it neatly on the top rack, locked the door and started the cycle. The whooshing of the water inside filled the little room. "No thanks. The taxpayers rented me a BDM."

Max looked blank and frowned. "A BDM? What the hell's that? New armored car?"

Sandy laughed lightly as she got her denim jacket from the closet and picked up her purse. She reached in, and just as Max had remembered from their first meeting on the Heldstrasse, pulled out her keys without conscious effort. She was still the only woman he'd ever known who could do that.

"No, silly. BDM stands for *boîte de merde*. G'night. Call me tomorrow. Maybe you can take me out to the Plantation Key Yacht Club." She gave him a funny, piercing look and was out the door before he had digested the French for "shitbox."

CHARLIE SWATTED AWAY a sandfly from his leg. His expression was unreadable behind his aviator's sunglasses and in the deep shade of his battered Navy baseball cap. About a hundred yards offshore, a big powerboat blared along, drawing his attention. Charlie watched the garish speedboat churn up white water and a massive wake until it turned the corner by the Nun buoy. As the noise of the big V-8 faded, Charlie looked back at Max.

"Well? What do you think?" Max asked.

"About what?" Charlie said.

Max leaned forward and put his elbows on his knees. The old lawn chair creaked. "About the whole deal."

Charlie returned his gaze to the luminous blue-green water of the bay. The sky was sheerest blue, almost the color of a pilot's sky at thirty thousand feet. A faint whisper of warm wind tickled them.

"Son, if you really want my advice, I'll give it to you. But you might not like it. Or me, after I'm done."

"Chance I'll take."

Barton peeled off his glasses and pulled up a corner of his Naval Academy sweatshirt to polish the lenses. He studied them carefully as he made little circles with the cloth.

"Let me tell you a story. Once upon a time there was this hot young stud. The kid was born golden. Everything he did was perfect. All-star at school, varsity at college, 4.0 student, cheerleaders stood in line to give him blow jobs, the works. Being so perfect, naturally the golden boy joins the Navy to fly fighters. And he does." Charlie held up the glasses and squinted at them. He continued polishing.

"Golden boy has *the* hot-shit career. At first. Sex, booze, the fast track, even becomes an ace. He's all golden: golden hands, golden dick, golden everything. Makes rank, up to commander, in record time. But then, things start to go wrong. He gets his golden dick caught in the wrong place, and the booze starts to get ahold of him, 'stead of the other way round. But he figures, hey, no biggie, I'll just fly like a sumbitch, and of course he does. And then one day, flying MiG Combat Air Patrol over a strike on a penny-ante bridge in the Nam, he kind of forgets something because he'd been a little too free with the bottle the night before. And four of his best buddies in the whole fucking world get blown away." Barton stopped and just stared at the lenses for a while.

"Now golden boy goes home and finds out that as lousy as things have been for him, they've been even worse in the World. Turns out the little number he'd married in a fit of stupidity some years before had gotten wind of the problem he'd had with his dick and his drinking, and it's *sayonara* dead-ass. Golden boy figures, sierra-hotel, I'm free now, and really gets serious about his fun times, and soon as hell, why he's hitched again. But something's wrong. Seems golden boy kind of missed the fact that everybody else was growing up while he was lookin' good in his F4. And what do you know? The Navy's not amused anymore. Fact is, nobody's amused anymore. But golden boy doesn't know any other way to act, see? So he just keeps on, throttle in zone five, and one day, well, one day it's all just ... over. And golden boy's all alone.''

He put his glasses on. ''Now this guy's no dummy, see, no matter how he ran his life. So after a sufficient amount of time has passed—say, ten years or so—in which the world has obviously not given a tinker's damn about whether golden boy is alive or dead, he figures a few things out.'' Barton held up a fist and ticked off the points with his fingers.

''One: flyin's fun, but in the end it doesn't mean shit. Two: potential doesn't mean squat. Words don't mean squat. What counts is the doing, not the talking. Three: women are not just for fucking; they're for loving. Four: making life is better than taking it. And five—well, five is simple, but it took golden boy a damn long time to understand what it means. Five is: there aren't any second chances.'' With that, Charlie settled back into his chair and looked stonily across the sand at Max.

''That answer your question?'' he asked in a flat voice.

Max shook his head after a while. "Nice story. I could match some parts of it myself. But it sure doesn't help me now."

Barton looked out to sea. A schooner lay heeled over, all sails set, making toward open water. He watched her for a few moments.

"Okay, Max. I live by pretty simple rules these days. One of them is, never give anybody any advice—especially anybody you like. But I'm going to break that rule today, because you're obviously in a world of hurt. So listen up, boy.

"As I understand it, these folks are okay types on our side, not theirs. What they want you to do is go to work for your old man as a cover and handle a few discreet affairs for them, affairs their own people for whatever reason can't handle. Way I see it, they want you to be a very unofficial subcontractor for the U.S. government—which, in my humble opinion, is a whole lot better than being a full-time employee of that same employer."

Max nodded. "All that's true. But—"

"Couple other points, if you don't mind my going on. Now, having screwed up my own life so well, I'm pretty good at spotting other folks engaged on the same project. And, if you'll pardon my bluntness, boy, you look set to take a hell of a wrong turn about now. I'm sixty-seven years old, kid; I've got an excuse. What the hell have you got? Young stud like you ought to be doing something worthwhile, but all I can see you got planned is a lot of nothing. And I'll tell you this," he said vehemently, "Charlie Barton never tells another man how to deal with a woman, but that lady Sandy is one *hell* of a woman. And she's got it bad for you, boy, real bad. That makes you about the luckiest man I've known for a good while. No female I ever knew went through what she did to get at me, for any reason. Now you may think otherwise, but fifty years of chasing pussy has taught me a thing or two, and one of them is that when you catch ahold of a twenty-four-carat woman, you don't *ever* let go. And that lady, mister, is *gold*."

He stared at Max. Max stared back. Neither man spoke until Barton got up and walked toward the ice chest. Midway there, he paused and looked back at Max.

"Key thing to remember, aside from always checking your six, is this," he said gruffly. "Nobody—and I mean *nobody*—escapes rule five. You got that?"

"I got it," Max said, gazing out at the disappearing schooner.

"NICE 'VETTE," SANDY SAID as she slipped into the passenger seat. "Separation pay special?"

Max grinned at her as she closed the door. "Yep. Mobile. I—"

"Ah, yes. Cindy of the dark eyes and lascivious look. I remember well."

"You yourself are looking mighty, uh—"

"Lascivious?" She laughed, smoothing her shimmering dress. "Nice of you to notice, Mr. Moss."

He flushed and put the car into gear. "What I meant—"

"Oh, shut up, Max. I'm hungry. Plantation Key?"

He flashed a grin at her as he backed out of the Flamingo's parking area. "Hey. You called it yesterday."

"So I did."

The weight that oppressed him began to lift under her brightness. She looked absolutely stunning, he thought, and she positively radiated something. Life, maybe. Or love of life. He didn't care. It was tonic for his malaise, whatever it was.

"This thing any good?" she asked as he accelerated out onto the highway. Max recalled Kelly and winced inwardly.

"Uh, yeah. Pretty good." He remembered Sandy's Porsche 944 Turbo and the way she kept and drove it. Sandy, he reminded himself, was not Kelly. Definitely not Kelly. She peered at the moonroof fittings.

"Saw in *Car and Driver* that they finally got the assembly up to q.c. specs. That so?"

Max allowed himself a tiny smile. Boy, was she not Kelly!

"Well, it hasn't leaked yet."

She cast a critical eye on the cockpit. "You really *like* those video game displays?"

"Yeah. I guess I do," he said somewhat lamely.

She shook her head as she pulled down the sun visor with its lighted vanity mirror. She switched on the light and eyed her makeup critically. Finally she pulled out her lipstick and touched up her lips. Satisfied, she switched off the light and said, "At least they give you a decent mirror. You'd think the guys from Zuffenhausen would figure it out too."

She adjusted her seat expertly and turned on the radio. Scanning the band, she settled on some dreamy New Age tinkling.

"So. Make any decisions?" Her voice was still bright, but an edge underlay it. Max was secretly glad. Sometimes her self-discipline intimidated him. He knew what kind of crap she'd had to endure in the Army, especially when she'd taken on that experimental all-female infantry company, and lost it to what was nothing more than the outraged male vanity of her brother officers.

"Maybe," he said.

"Ah," she countered. And the rest of the trip was made in silence. But Max drove at ninety, not fifty-five.

Dinner was an anticlimax. Max couldn't bring himself to talk about his jumbled response to her proposal, and she didn't push him. He slowly relaxed, drinking a tiny amount of wine with their huge shared slab of swordfish. She kept up a light patter of cheerful, inconsequential talk, about people they both knew from their days in Potsdam, about governmental squabbles and service rivalries, about her Porsche, about her sister's family in Ohio, about everything except what he was going to do.

The ambience made it easier. The club was an airy place, its dining room a glass-walled affair right on the water, surrounded by glittering, expensive yachts whose owners competed with one another to offer passersby a light show with lanterns and bulbs strewn along their decks and standing rigging. Soft breezes wafted through open doors, carrying the odor of the sea and sand. A small band had set up, and it began to play gentle dance music.

Sandy's eyes lit up as she watched them play. She reached across the table and touched Max's hand. He jerked as if a live wire had touched him, and she smiled, eyes luminous in the candlelight.

"Hey, Max. You know how to dance?"

He flushed again. "Not so you'd notice. Fred Astaire I'm not."

"Well, I'm not Ginger Rogers. Come on. Sweep me off my feet."

He would have protested, but she grabbed his hand and lifted him from his seat as if he were a child. He followed her to the dance floor, where some couples were already heart-to-heart, moving slowly on the polished wood.

Max hadn't danced since his father made him attend dancing lessons in high school. He suffered a panic-stricken moment as they stepped onto the floor, a feeling familiar no doubt to all men who don't dance often, but his reflexes took over almost immediately. Some automatic mental process scanned his performance files, selected the one coded "dancing" and instructed his body while he went along for the ride. The same genes that made it easy for him to operate just about anything mechanical also ran his body for him. Good thing, too, he thought, since if he'd had to do it consciously he'd never have made it. He relaxed a bit as Sandy came into his arms, smiled up at him and laid her head on his shoulder.

He relaxed even more as they danced through the next three tunes, still in the same embrace. Solid gold, Barton had said, and Max was beginning to see what he meant—and to wonder how on earth he'd missed all this back in Germany. Maybe it had been because she was his superior then, a captain to his first lieutenant. Or maybe—who knew? Who cared? He was here, now, and so was she. And it was delicious beyond all reason.

The band took a break after the third number and Max and Sandy broke apart, applauded and went back to their table. The dessert dishes and coffee cups had been cleared away and the bill lay discreetly tucked inside a leather wallet. Sandy pulled out a credit card and laid it on the bill, and a waiter picked it up immediately.

"Uh, hey! I was going to pay—"

"That's all right, Max. The taxpayers, remember? This is business."

"This is business? What's pleasure, then?"

She smiled at him in a way that melted his marrow. He blushed deep crimson. Luckily, the waiter saved him, bringing back the bill and the card slip. Sandy signed, jotted expense data on her copy of the slip and stood up. "Come on," she said, "let's see what your 'Vette's got."

She grabbed the keys from him as he began to unlock the car. He looked up, surprised.

"Mind if I try it?"

He blinked and nodded. By the time he got himself settled in the unfamiliar passenger seat, she had adjusted her own seat and the mirrors and had the engine running. He snapped his seat belt in and looked at her.

"Ready?" she asked, eyes bright. Max's heart beat a little faster. He wasn't used to being a passenger—had never been used to it.

The snick of the gear lever, the bellow of the engine and the spinning of the tires on the coral gravel an-

swered him. Sandy power-slid the big red Corvette out
of the parking area, and Max suddenly had some ap-
preciation for how Kelly had felt. He clutched the door
handle and grab strap and watched the big green
numbers on the dash display flick to ever higher
speeds. The twin-turbocharged engine pinned him to
the seat. Sandy slammed expert full-throttle shifts.

They whistled across the bridge Max had used to
stop the Cuban in his Benz, the speedo registering 135
and still climbing. Sandy smiled, hands loose on the
wheel, relaxed, a ridiculously small figure behind the
sweeping dash, fat leather wheel and huge leather seat.

At 155, she eased up. Max suddenly remembered
something unresolved from their time in Germany.

"Say. Where—where did you say you learned to
drive?" He had to speak loudly to be heard above the
wind and the tire noise.

"You remembered! Good for you. Well, then you
probably also recall that I never told you." She deflected the steering wheel deftly left and right to jink
the Corvette around a slow-going van. He tightened
his grip.

"Bondurant School. At Sears Point." She glanced
at him. "Know it?"

"Yeah. Good place. Which course did you take?"
He didn't move his eyes from the road, where the
brilliant halogen headlights were barely adequate, at
their speed, to paint the way with light.

"Formula Fords. Raced a whole season." She
flashed him a wide grin as he darted a wondering look
at her. "Took third in the series," she added with obvious satisfaction.

Max shook his head and deliberately moved his hands to his lap, where he elaborately folded them. "Solid gold," he muttered. Sandy did not hear him and concentrated on driving.

Florida's finest were elsewhere that evening, so they arrived at Max's condo very quickly. Sandy hauled the big 'Vette down and swung into his parking place. She switched off the engine after letting the turbos spool down and looked at him as the engine cooled, pinging in the sudden silence.

"I think it's time to talk," she said.

"I won't ask whether it ought to be at my place or yours," Max said. She lifted an eyebrow and climbed out. She tossed him his keys and followed him up the stairs. He unlocked the door and they went in.

He faced her in the little foyer and went suddenly mute. She stood a little apart from him, her expression mischievous.

"You know," he said finally, "I don't think you're taking all this very seriously this evening."

"Oh yes, I most certainly am. Very seriously."

They stood a heartbeat more, looking at each other, until Max's left hand, by itself, jerkily reached out and touched her shoulder. The smile faded from her face and she looked at him big-eyed. His vision seemed to blur momentarily. His hand, still acting without his direction, cupped her small shoulder and caressed her bare back.

She closed her eyes and swayed slightly. He stood like an idiot mute for a moment more before his mind completely shut down, and suddenly she was in his arms, lips parted, and he was kissing her.

They clung to each other for long seconds. He felt short of breath, dizzy, exhilarated and electrically charged all at once. He had never felt this way with any woman in his life. Her kiss was a symphony of exquisite nuances, now delicate, now forceful and demanding, now yielding. He broke away after he knew not how long and blinked at her. She smiled dreamily at him.

"I—" he began. She put a finger to his lips.

"Shut up, Max. Let's go to bed."

He smiled back—not the wry, cynical Moss smile, not the mocking, bitter smile, but the smile she'd known he had in him the day they met—and literally swept her off her feet. Cradling her in his arms, he carried her across the darkened living room toward the bedroom.

He tripped again on the stool. She laughed, kicked off her high-heeled shoes and kissed him softly on his neck as he regained his balance. "You Tarzan, me Jane," she whispered in his ear, and nibbled its lobe.

He paused by the bed and kissed her again. He laid her gently on the bed and said, "Not quite," but she pulled him down and nibbled his other ear.

"Close enough for government work," she whispered huskily, and only their bodies and souls spoke for a long time after that.

MOONLIGHT POURED through the bedroom window, painting them both pale blue-white. She was asleep, head cradled on his shoulder, but he was awake. She felt like pure silk to him, her skin alive and warm, radiating life. He wondered how he had managed to live without her. He wondered how he could not have fallen in love with her the minute he met her, carrying those groceries into the little apartment in Berlin.

He wondered many things, none of which had suitably convincing answers. But finally he slept.

He awoke to her kiss. The moon was almost down, the morning at the in-between stage of predawn quiet, when the entire world seems to be holding its breath, as if awaiting something momentous. She looked at him, traced the tiny scar on his chin and smiled once more. Her eyes seemed to be as big as the sea that washed gentle waves on the beach outside.

He gazed into her bottomless eyes for a long time. Finally he said, "If I do it, will we have time together?"

She lost a little of her glow, but her smile didn't slip. "As much as we can. As much as you'd like," she said.

He thought about it while the last rays of moonlight haloed her golden hair. He stroked her face and she laid her head on his chest. He thought he felt the warm wetness of tears, but he couldn't be sure.

"I could do it without joining up. I could just move up to wherever you are," he said. She lifted her head again and looked at him searchingly. He saw that they were tears.

"Oh, Max. They... *we* need you. Please don't give up."

For a dark, ugly moment, the nasty Neanderthal hunter who lived deep inside him wondered if all this were an act, a Mata Hari ploy to recruit him. But her eyes told him otherwise, and he felt ashamed of his thought. Still, to work again for his father, to operate as a free-lancer in the dangerous world of spies and counterspies, a world he had only had a brief glimpse of...all without sanction, without guarantees, without security. These were things that would tax him to the limit. Maybe beyond.

Barton rose suddenly in his mind, and unaccountably, the phrase he remembered most clearly was, "Flyin's fun, but in the end it don't mean shit." Who on earth had any security, in the end? Their only security lay in each other.

He kissed her fiercely, longingly, a kiss not just of passion but of emotions ineffable and unutterable. When he pulled away, her face was aglow.

"Put me in, coach," he said. "I'll play."

CHAPTER EIGHT

IT TURNED OUT that Max was wrong about many things. He had assumed that dealing with his father would prove difficult, that the old sparks would fly anew when Eric Moss learned that he had resigned from the Air Force, that Moss, Sr. would consider his son's request to return to Moss Electronics after an absence of more than a decade a request to be treated with derision. He had assumed that, basically, nothing had changed.

He was wrong. Major General Eric Moss, U.S.A.-Retired, seemed delighted to have his only son phone him from Key Largo and ask for a job. The whole thing had gone so smoothly Max wondered if it had all been orchestrated beforehand. Was Eric Moss, he wondered, as a former Army intelligence officer, still in the network? Was *he* a member of Sandy's over-the-hill gang?

He had a lot of time to brood over the connections and unanswered questions as he drove the Corvette from the east coast to the west. The trip was a five-day haze of motel rooms, endless highway and fast food. He noticed none of it, having engaged what he called his "road mode," that lifesaving detachment of intellect from body that made the vast distances of the

American continent bearable to one who had regularly to traverse them on wheels. And Max was that kind of man; as a racer, he had towed his race car all over the country, living the auto-nomadic life to the hilt—and beyond.

But when he arrived in San Jose, he was not prepared. The semisleepy southern bay town he recalled was gone. In its place was a megalopolis, a Northern Californian version of the Los Angeles basin, filled with smog, freeways, enormous tracts of prefab houses and equally huge developments of prefab factories. In the decade he had been gone, Silicon Valley had been born, come to age and begun to decay. It was a measure of the swiftness that underlay every aspect of the computer and microprocessor industries that the boom they provided could so quickly and so perilously turn to something like bust. Max rolled along the swooping interstates in his Corvette like a stranger. Which, now, he was.

He almost didn't find Moss Electronics. When Eric Moss had begun the company with a few key government contracts and a lot of venture capital, he had erected the company building in what was a deserted piece of undesirable real estate well southwest of San Jose. Then, the road had almost petered out a few hundred feet from the company door.

Now the road was four lanes wide, and Moss Electronics occupied what seemed like ten acres. Max drove completely around the site, stunned, noting the four different entrances—each guarded—the maze of buildings behind the triple rows of fences and wire, the elegant blinding-white main office building with immense windows of bronzed glass and the lush lawns

that offset the severe, camplike atmosphere almost
enough to make the casual visitor think he was near a
college campus. But the stony look he received from
the gate guard when he pulled into the parking lot
dispelled any sense of warmth, and restored the truth:
this was not just big business, it was also secret business. And one thing he knew had not changed—would
never change—about Eric Moss was his obsession with
security. Not even his own son would slide through his
gate unchecked; the guard saw to that.

Something not quite like déjà vu and yet not so different washed over him as he walked through the typical Santa Clara Valley autumn heat and entered the
cool splendor of the reception area. It was the
strangeness of it all, he decided; the prodigal son returns, and has to check in with the receptionist. He
smiled at the bright-eyed young woman, impeccably
made-up and dressed, and told her his name. She
smiled at him and said, of course, Mr. Moss, I'll tell
the general's secretary you're here. She toggled a
switch somewhere on her panelful of lights, spoke
softly into an almost invisible microphone and said
that Gerry, the general's secretary, would be coming
right out.

Max felt acutely uncomfortable, a stranger in a
strange land. He noted three other men waiting, each
exuding confidence, each relaxed on one of the artfully arranged blue velvet loungers, each a variation
on the successful corporate theme. The only differ-
ences seemed to be hair and suit color. By contrast, he
wore his ancient Harris tweed with the worn cuffs,
faded blue jeans, beat-up Vibram-soled walking shoes
and a red Stewart tartan sport shirt.

He was saved by the arrival of Gerry, who turned out to be a man, not a woman. Max was surprised again; Eric Moss had never been a man to avoid beautiful women. That was how he had come to marry Max's stepmother, after all. He bottled the thought and shook the strong, dry hand that this Gerry Anderson offered him.

Anderson was dressed as impeccably as the waiting corporados, and was also no kid. Max judged that he was only a little younger than his father, and something about him suggested the military: the GI-issue glasses, perhaps, or the ability to stand straight-backed but loose-kneed, the pain-saving knack of staff officer and line grunt alike. They went through the introductions and Anderson hesitated a bit before leading Max through the locked and camera-monitored doorway.

"Mr. Moss," he said in a low voice, "I just wanted a word before you saw your father. You know he's been ill?"

"No. Not since his stroke."

"Ah. That was a good while ago, now. So you haven't seen him in..."

"A couple of years. In Washington. Why?"

"I think you'd better understand, sir. Your father is in fragile health, but he does not admit it."

"He wouldn't." Max smiled.

"Perhaps not. But you should be aware of it."

"What's the problem?"

Anderson met his gaze evenly. "Basically, he's wearing out. The strain is significant. More so now."

"Now? Why now?"

Anderson shrugged. "All this—he runs it all. Business is very good, but without any help..."

Max frowned. "What about his XO? Or line staff?"

Anderson smiled. "Your military experience shows, Mr. Moss. Unfortunately, we have no executive officer right now. The board removed Mr. Uchida last year, and the general has not agreed with any of their choices, nor they with his. So you see how it is."

"I think so. We're talking about a seventy-three-year-old guy doing two men's jobs. That it?"

"That's it exactly. I just wanted you to know so you wouldn't be too surprised. The general had told me that you didn't know much about our operation these days."

"Thanks. I appreciate it. By the way, did he tell you anything else about me?"

Anderson stiffened. "No. The general keeps his family life strictly to himself, Mr. Moss. Now, if you'll follow me—"

Max followed. And when he was ushered into the big corner office with the view of the freeway, he saw at once why Anderson had warned him.

His father rose to greet him like a wraith rising from the grave. Anderson left them standing a few feet apart, discreetly closing the thick oak door behind him.

"Hello, Father," Max said. He swallowed and wondered what a son like him did to show belated affection for a father like Eric Moss.

The older man resolved the issue for him. He came around the desk and embraced Max with a firm grip, holding him for a few seconds. Then he stepped back and smiled. It lit up his face, but it also showed the deep scars that were the legacy of time and many trials. Where once his face had had the ageless, indestructible quality of tough leather, now it seemed to be made of parchment, almost translucent. Max smiled back, shaken.

"Damn! It's good to see you, Max. Sit down, please."

Max pulled up one of the Louis XIV chairs and waited until his father sat also. The older man sank back into his leather chair with obvious relief and some effort.

What was it, Max wondered, that so obviously had changed? Even when stricken by his stroke, which had left his left side partially paralyzed, Eric Moss had continued to be a dynamo. His hair was still thick, if now almost all white, his eyes still sparkled as greenly as Max's. And he was only a little thinner than when they'd last met at the club at Bolling AFB in Washington. Whatever it was, the change was dramatic and eloquent and it spoke of energy quickly draining away.

Yet his father had never been a man short of words, and was not now. "Good trip? Any problems?"

"None," said Max. "How are things here—"

Eric cut him off with an imperious wave. "Don't have much time for small talk now, Max, if you don't mind. Come over to dinner tonight—oh, damn, no, not tonight, we have the lieutenant governor tonight—anyway, when you can make it for dinner, we can share a brandy and chew the fat. Meanwhile, you've got a pile of work to get through, briefings to absorb, people to meet."

In spite of his father's frailty, Max was annoyed. It was precisely this imperious manner that had driven him from his father a decade before. He reined his anger.

"Fine. But tell me, what role did you see for me?"

Moss, Sr. stared at Max. "You haven't read your brief?"

"What brief?"

Eric closed his eyes as if counting to avoid swearing. "Somebody screwed up. You were supposed to get a full brief by FedEx. Last week. Before you left."

"Sorry. Never showed up."

A muscle twitched in Eric Moss's cheek. "Okay. I'll fill you in right now. Interrupt at will. One: your call was timed perfectly. So happens I'm skirmishing with the board over a number-two man here. They claimed the guy I wanted was too old. Guy they wanted was too dumb. Stalemate. So you call, and bingo! My problem's solved. I've got them half sold on the idea. Two—"

"Wait a minute. You want me to help *run* this place? Jesus, the last time I was here you wanted me to push a broom! How—"

"Hold it. I pulled your files; Blackie helped me out. You have a double-E degree so you speak our language; you know about computers; you know our market, we might even say, intimately; you've got some combat time and some leadership experience and . . . you're my son." He paused. "Long as I hold the majority in this company, that adds up to a persuasive argument. Because you own a substantial share, too."

"What? I never knew—"

"It's in a trust. Very complicated. Took it out when you went crazy and went off racing and whatnot. Figured someday you'd come to your senses, and when you did, you'd need a grubstake." He glanced at the desk clock and held up his hand again to forestall Max. "Back to the briefing. Two: I've bet the company on some products that combine artificial intelligence, high-res sensors and leading-edge hardware. We're at the go/no-go point right now, Max, under highest pressure. We need some sales of the flagship of this product line—and you're the guy who's going to take us over the finish line with it. The board agrees. As of right now, you're a provisional vice president."

Max shook his head. "A vice president? You know I have no corporate experience, no idea even what you're building back there—"

The older man leaned forward and pinned him with a burning look. "There's no other way, Max. Do you hear me, boy? No other way!" He sat upright and looked out the deeply bronzed window at the freeway, where the traffic sped silently by. "Do you have any idea how much it meant to me when you called? Christ, I knew the week you bailed out that you'd left the service; Blackie called me personally. I kept waiting, but you never even dropped me a postcard. I'd actually given up. I thought, this is it, the kid has finally blown his top, and was about ready to hire a PI to track you down. But then..." He stopped, and blinked. "Then you called. And the prodigal son returned."

By itself, the speech was not convincing to Max. He had crossed swords with his father too many times and emerged bloodied too often not to be wary of him now. Yet there was a tension in his body when he spoke that said to Max, This is true, this you can believe. The most obvious explanation was the simplest, and the hardest for any son to take: Eric Moss was dying. And he wanted the world right before he died; he wanted his son to reflect his best. Moss Electronics was Eric Moss's lifework, even more than his thirty years in the Army. What he was really saying was that he wanted his son to carry it on for him.

Good thing, Max thought wryly, that this son hasn't any other plans. Good thing Sandy pulled all this together. And a good thing he wasn't five years younger, or he'd have bolted by now.

He said none of what he thought, of course. Like much of what passed between him and his father, it had to be unspoken. The code demanded it. So instead of embracing the old man and speaking of love and mortality, he smiled and said, "Seems like a good plan, and I guess I'm your ball carrier. Shall we get on with it, General?"

THE MOMENT MAHOUD stepped into his mother's apartment, he knew he had been duped. He expected to find her on her deathbed, as the messenger had affirmed. But she was nowhere to be seen. Instead, he walked straight into the muzzles of four Uzis. Wisely, he stopped dead. Wisely, he did not resist when the men swiftly disarmed and bound him. Wisely, he did not ask who they were. He seethed inwardly and reconciled himself to death at their hands, whoever they might be. So near the Israel-Syria border, they might be anyone's thugs—Phalangists, Palestinian renegades, even Syrian soldiers in mufti. They might even be Israeli.

They were. He found that out when they finally removed his blindfold, hours after they'd taken him. He hadn't even bothered to try to pin down his location as they shoved him from the house, jammed him in some kind of vehicle and hauled him around through the night. He was fairly certain of their identity when the jolting of the back roads was replaced by the smooth ride of good asphalt. When he heard the car halt and men call to one another in Hebrew, he knew. And so he readied himself for death.

It was not to be. They were too good at their jobs. They handled him as if he were a patient in a hospital, not someone to be tortured. He was fingerprinted, eye-printed, denti-printed and stripped. He was locked in a clean, green-painted cell with a bunk. And left for some time. When they came for him again, he tried to lunge at them, as he had been taught, but they were too alert and too good. Coolly, they lashed him to a gurney and rolled him to an operating room. His last conscious thought before whatever they injected him with took effect was that this all scared him more than if they'd beaten him senseless.

"WELL, SIR, this is it. The Viper."

Max walked along the length of the tiny airplane. It resembled a model. A toy, almost. He ran a hand over its mat-gray surface.

"Uh, Mr. Moss, sir, would you please not touch the surface?"

Max withdrew his hand. "Sure, Duane. Why?"

The tech grabbed an unmarked spray bottle of some blue fluid, squirted some on the fuselage and wiped it down with a large tissue from a box standing next to the Viper on its launcher. "The oil from your hand, sir. See, it changes the radar reflectivity. We've got this baby almost invisible by now, and we like to keep it that way."

Max nodded. He continued his inspection of the unmanned airplane. Nothing about it gave away its importance to Moss Electronics. Yet in it lay his father's fortune—and maybe his own.

"Not very big, is it?" Max said. Duane tensed. Max glanced at him and smiled. "Did I say the wrong thing?"

Duane Horton grimaced. He was typical of that new breed of American worker, the technician-manager. Not quite blue collar, not quite white collar; somewhere in between. Max knew and respected his kind well, from racing and from the service; crew chiefs were made of the same stuff as were the best line maintenance officers. Education and social background did not define these men so much as their hands and brains. What distinguished them was that they could not only conceive of something, they could also make it. They tended always to be underrated by those who categorized by attire and speech; like his comrades, Horton neither wore a modish suit nor spoke eloquently. His eloquence was in what he did, not what he said.

"Well, Mr. Moss, I guess we're a little touchy about how the Viper looks. Seems like first thing every dodo says about her is that she's small."

"She *is* small, though."

"Damn right, and we worked like hell to get her that way, too. When you figure how much we've got crammed in her—well, I guess you already know all that."

Max peered at the tiny camera lenses faired into the body. "No, Duane, I don't. Why don't you take some time and tell me?"

Duane's eyes lit up. He ceremoniously withdrew a pointer pen, extended it and walked to the front of the Viper. Max caught his father's eye and winked. The old man smiled back and left, leaning heavily on his gold-headed ebony cane.

"Now, Mr. Moss," Duane began with what was obviously his briefing spiel voice, "what you see here is not an ordinary remotely piloted vehicle. What you see here is an entirely new kind of air-breathing, multimission, recoverable, truck-transportable, self-defending combination of hardware and software. It just *looks* like an airplane...."

"STEIN."

"Colonel, this is Captain Rabin, Section Two. I apologize for calling so late, but we have information relating to the incident at Har Mughara. We thought you might like it right away."

"And you were correct to think so. Go ahead."

"It seems that the raid was under the command of one Hassan el Jazzar. Of the Jihad. We have seen him before, under different names. Perhaps you recall—"

"Yes. I know him. Go ahead."

"Our information is that el Jazzar was acting in concert with the PLO."

"*With* the PLO?"

"Correct, Colonel. Some kind of deal was struck. Anyway, our information was that this el Jazzar met with Dr. Qidal. Personally."

"Anything else? The object of their operation, perhaps?"

"No, sir. Sorry. Our informant, ah, was unable to help further."

"I see. Who was your informant, Captain?"

"A subordinate of el Jazzar's."

"How did you select him?"

"Part of the dragnet operation. When we ran the cross-check program, he just came up on the computer. As did Hassan, of course. But we didn't think we could get to Hassan."

"Doubtless correct."

"Anyway, he was, let me see, number nine of sixteen. We have five to go before we close the file. We may get more, but we just thought you'd like this data early. It will probably be another two weeks before we close out the operation, and Colonel Levy felt that—"

"Yes. Thank you, Captain. And thank Colonel Levy. I'll return the favor one day. It seems as though Section Two is on top of things, as usual."

"Yes, sir. Thank you, sir. Good night, sir."

"Shalom, Captain."

As he switched off the bedside light and lay back in his bed, Moshe Stein was not thinking about Hassan el Jazzar or his lieutenant. He thought instead about the complications of the Mossad. About the way Levy in Two disapproved of the vague definition of Section Four's responsibilities, and how Levy never missed a chance to co-opt him. Rabin's call was useful; but who knew what Rabin had not told him?

El Jazzar was not Stein's quarry. The real quarry lay within the Israeli system, somewhere, either a mole or a turncoat. Yet he had nothing except el Jazzar to go on, now. So, in order to stalk the true prey, he had to run after the Iranian, just like Levy and Rabin.

He sighed and closed his eyes. Wherever el Jazzar was, there too was the Judah IV. And the link to the traitor, whoever and wherever he might be.

CHAPTER NINE

IN THIS PART of the Mediterranean, nobody took chances, so it did not surprise Hassan that the gunboat did not display a flag. After all, they were not flying a flag, either. The gray, ominously turreted boat remained abeam their dilapidated little coaster, pacing them at their steady seven knots through the cold water. He slipped down below the gunwale and turned to face the master, who peered through field glasses at the gunboat.

"Turkish? Greek?" Hassan asked.

A wave splashed over the side and the master ducked. Hassan grabbed a stay and held on. The wave swirled around the small deckhouse cum bridge, leaving the master dry but soaking Hassan.

"No. I think . . . I think Israeli."

"This far out?"

"Yes. The Bofors, I think. Only the Israelis mount the 40 mm in that way."

"Then try the signal."

"But if they are not Israeli—"

"It will make no difference. Only the IDF will recognize the signal. We must try it now, or not use it."

The master slowly put down the glasses. He nodded to the mate, a swarthy Turk who stood in the waist, one hand around a shroud, the other clutching a signal lamp. "Send Lima-Kilo-Lima," the master called. The mate braced himself against the roll of the coaster and put the lamp sight to his eye. He flashed the letters.

Hassan twisted back to watch through the gunwale. For a moment, the gunboat continued to pace them. Then its signal lamp flashed.

"Repeat the signal," called the skipper to the mate, before Hassan could ask what had been flashed. The mate clicked off L-K-L again, and this time the gunboat responded immediately. It flashed another lengthier message, then veered southward and roared away, slicing through the waves and trailing a broad wake.

"What did he say?"

The master lowered his binoculars. "Godspeed and good luck," he said. He looked at Hassan. "They were Israeli. Good thing you had the right message. They would as soon have blown us apart in these waters."

Hassan thought about the Judah IV, stored below in a crate marked Machine Tools and almost smiled. Had the Jews tried it, they would have gotten more than they gave, by about ten kilotons.

"Yes," he said, "it is a good thing." Wherever Qidal had gotten the code from, it was a reliable source. So far, the only hitch in the plan had come when Mahoud had been lured to his death in Syria, leaving against Hassan's own order. But the Israelis would pay for that, as they would pay for everything else—assuming everything went as well in America as it was going in Europe. He smiled, thinking of the black man. It would. One touched by Allah was charmed.

"HEY! JAMES!"

The black major's head jerked around and scanned the parking lot for the voice that would dare use his first name. Jefferson Paul Jones knew that behind the sunglasses, Major James Lenteen's eyes would be narrowing. He climbed out of his old Toyota and waved.

The Army officer saw him, stared for a few seconds, then broke into a grin. Jones slid up to him, dapped his fist and slapped him on the back. They danced the familiar dance of Army buddies long separated, now inexplicably reunited. Happened all the time.

"J.P.," exclaimed Lenteen, "where the hell have you been, boy? We haven't seen you in—"

"Now don't you say a coon's age, or one of us is gonna get mad!" grinned Jones.

"Say, you're out of the Army, no?"

"Yeah. Some time. But you still in, right?"

Lenteen shook his head ruefully. Under his gold-trimmed garrison cap, his tightly curled black hair was tinged with gray, as was his trim mustache. "Man gotta put in his time. Otherwise the chicken don't scream on paydays."

Jones zipped his nylon jacket against the cold November northeast wind blowing across the Francis Scott Key Mall parking lot.

Lenteen had grown up a mile or so away from the Jones family, but it might as well have been a continent away in status. The son of a prosperous grocer,

Lenteen shared nothing with Jones except street jive. He had actually gone to college, although Vietnam interrupted it and threw them together as warrant officers in the Air Cav. Afterward, Lenteen, responding to parental pressure, had gone to the University of Maryland extension college campuses on the bases to which he was assigned. Ultimately he was commissioned.

This was one difference between them. The other was that James Lenteen was basically not very bright. Jones hoped to use that deficiency now, because Lenteen had information he needed. As a battalion exec at Fort Detrick, he had access to a certain level of classified data. That data included a joint Special Ops Command/Federal Emergency Management Agency operation plan, recently issued to key units in the Washington area. Lenteen's was one of those units. That was why Jones had patiently used his nonflying time to shadow Lenteen. And why it had paid off today.

"Made chief, and that was that, James. You know how it was."

Lenteen swelled with obvious self-importance. He clearly felt superior to Jones, even though he had much less combat time—or maybe because of it.

"Hey. No big thing. You didn't get the breaks, is all."

Al-Shiran suffered his patronizing, and shrugged. "Yeah. No big thing. Say, why don't we grab some coffee. It's cold out here."

Lenteen turned to look back at the mall, putting his left shoulder board with its gold oak leaf insignia almost in Jones's face. "Surely, why not? Good place next to Sears—"

Al-Shiran smiled at his puffery. He had him. And soon he would have the frequency information he needed.

MAX SAT BACK in the simulator chair, dazed. "Jesus," he whispered.

"You okay, Mr. Moss?" Duane's voice seemed to be coming from right next to him, but Max knew he was fifty feet away. The fidelity of the binaural sound in the helmet was incredible. As was everything else about the system.

"Sure. No problem. It's just . . . this thing is . . ."

"Yes, sir. We all feel that way. Now you know why."

Max drew a breath, wiped his sweaty palms on his trousers and flipped up the visor. Instantly, he was dazzled by the fluorescent lights in the simulator room. He blinked and undid the helmet strap. Duane dropped off-line and soon was clattering down the metal steps. He helped Max untangle the umbilical cords that connected the helmet system to the computer.

"The field unit is much cleaner," Duane said as he swiftly disconnected the plugs. "We keep fiddling with this one, so it's kind of a mess. A lot of us have combat time, so we know what'll happen if we make it too complicated." He set the scratched and battered helmet down on a nearby Formica table littered with bits of electronica, the detritus of microchip creativity.

"You flew real good, Mr. Moss," he said.

Max slipped the knot of his tie up and worked it back into place. "Thanks," he said, "but it didn't seem like it to me. Those SAMs—"

"Hell, sir, you cleaned them like they weren't there. Smitty ran the toughest program we had, and he said—"

"Well, thanks, Duane. Anyway, all it takes, as the ads say, is one test drive and you're sold on the Viper system." He shoved back from the controls console and pulled his suit coat from the chairback. As he put it on, he looked over at the nine-foot Viper on its launcher. "Duane, what the hell is wrong with those guys in the Pentagon? Why won't they buy this thing? Somebody else got something better?"

Horton shook his head. "No, sir. Nobody's got anything like what we've got. Not the big guys like Lockheed, not the little guys. There's only one real explanation, Mr. Moss, and I hesitate to tell you, since they say you're a pilot."

Max motioned Duane to accompany him back to his office. Duane fell into step with him. "So I'm a pilot. So what?" Max said.

"Well, that's the problem, if you don't mind my being blunt. Pilots. As long as these remotely piloted vehicles were sort of dumb, long as they were obviously inferior to the so-called real thing, the pilots didn't mind 'em too much. And there was some money in the budgets for RPVs for battlefield surveillance, target tracking with laser designators, that kind of Mickey Mouse stuff."

They reached the computer-controlled access door. Max looked into the camera, the red light turned green, and he swung open the thick door to the office complex. A pretty secretary nodded, smiling to him as he passed.

"Okay," Max said as they walked on the soft, static-free carpeting. "So pilots feel threatened by it. So why can't we sell it to the people who don't especially care what the airplane drivers think?"

"We tried. Your father—the general—talked himself blue over the past year, trying to sell it to some of his old friends who were still in. But then we ran into another snag. The technology."

They rounded the corner to Max's office. He plucked the pink call slips from his box, waved at his secretary, Linda, and went in. He still was not used to having an office at all, let alone one so plush. Paneled in deep rosewood, with a computer terminal built into the rosewood desk and encompassing a miniature round conference table and four chairs, the room itself was bigger than anything he'd lived in during the past decade. He tossed the slips on his cluttered desk and sat in one of the conference chairs. Duane joined him.

Linda appeared at the door, holding a cup and looking questioningly. He nodded and she left to get coffee for them both. Some perks he enjoyed. Duane pulled a mechanical pencil from his pocket and began to sketch a set diagram. It showed overlapping circles.

"We're between a rock and a hard place. One set of buyers—the Air Force, the Navy aviation people, even NASA and the FAA—are biased against what the Viper system can do because they're pilots. Another big set is afraid of it because of the technology."

Linda put down two cups and left, closing the soundproof door behind her. Duane sipped the coffee and went back to his diagram.

"Even though the basic research for this system came from their own people—at Wright-Patterson, for the interactive display stuff, and Ames for the aerodynamics stuff—they think it's too advanced." He snorted. "Shoot. It's five years old now, at least, and we're still the only company who's got it all together in one package. Others could do it, but they haven't got the guts. The general knows better. He knows the country needs this system—and not just because Moss Electronics needs it, either. Hell, we could write off the money and go back to making avionics and spy cameras for satellites tomorrow. We wouldn't have any raises for a while, but we could do it." He sipped more coffee and looked out the window.

Max knew a little better than the technician how much of the company was riding on the Viper, and how much more was at stake than just raises. But he kept his counsel and urged Duane to continue.

"The decision makers are just too damn old, and too out of touch. They don't even speak our language. Fact is, they're just behind the curve on this stuff. That's where all this procurement-officer career path talk comes from; the guys with the power are afraid to make a decision, so they delegate it to a bunch of professional know-nothings who also don't buy the right stuff. But they make the right kind of noises while they do it." He picked up his cup, looked glumly into it and set it down again. He added a third circle to the other two on the notepad and said, "So when you add these pro bureaucrats, these so-called

procurement officers, you wind up with three inter-
locking sets of guys who either can't or won't buy
what they need. Their own troops in the field keep
telling them—but they won't listen. I guess it's just
going to take another damn war to break up this stupidity." He cranked the lead back into his pencil and
sat back.

Max swiveled the notepad toward him. "Looks bad,
Duane. But don't forget the key thing about set theory: it's not just where the sets overlap that counts, but
where they don't. That's where we'll hit them next.
Right where they don't expect us. I've got some ideas
on that one. So you guys hang tough, and keep improving the bird and the system, okay?"

Duane brightened. He had obviously not heard this
kind of booster talk in a long time, so beset had the
general and the company been. "I sure hope so, Mr.
Moss. We'll give it our best shot."

"That's all we need, Duane. That, and a good demo
in D.C. I'm working on that one now. Think you can
have it up and running for a show next month?"

"Next *month*? Hell, sir, we can have it ready next
week, if you want it."

Max got to his feet. Horton followed. "Good,"
Max said evenly, looking him in the eye. "Then have
it ready next week."

Horton blinked in surprise, then almost grinned. He
left with a spring in his step Max had not seen before.

AMSTEG WAS A TINY TOWN almost precisely in the
center of Switzerland. It perched precariously on the
verdant verge between the Reuss River and the craggy

scarps that turned Reuss Valley afternoons into perpetual shadow. About a hundred kilometers south of Zurich, the town seemed to prosper on providing food, lodging and fuel to travelers on the E9, the nearby superhighway. Stein had passed through Amsteg many times in his career, usually alone, and had settled into staying at the Hotel Stern, a fastidiously clean place run by the same family for centuries.

He stopped at the hotel now not only for food and lodging, but for information. His agents had tracked Hassan through here on his way to Zurich, where he was now holed up in the Muslim quarter. Alois Rumpelmann, the proprietor, would have noticed things about Hassan and his party of considerable value to Stein. Through the years, they had guessed that they were both in the business of information gathering: Rumpelmann for business, Stein for security. This bond aside, for some reason, they actually liked each other.

Stein pulled into the courtyard of the hotel and left the rented Fiat's engine running while he dashed through the falling snow and into the foyer. As always, Albert, the ever-present assistant, had the door open for him even as he dashed through.

"Herr Stein," the old man said, "it is a pleasure! Welcome, sir. I hope you are staying tonight?" He closed the door and brushed snow off Stein's jacket. Like Rumpelmann, he spoke perfect English—and as perfect French, German, Italian and Spanish.

Stein nodded. "Yes, Albert. The weather is not so good for making Zurich tonight, I think."

"Ah, but not so bad for Switzerland in November, Herr Stein. Please—the master will be with you in a moment. May I collect your baggage?"

"Of course. Just the blue bag tonight. And the car—"

"In the garage. We have plenty of room tonight."

Rumpelmann caught up with Stein at the small service desk. A short man of fifty-seven, he was dressed in the manner of a genteel if not especially upper class Englishman, in subtle tweeds and wool. He verged on the chubby, but his restless eye and swift movements belied it. As he had been up to Eton and Cambridge, his speech was as English as his dress. He was worth millions, Stein had discovered, yet he continued his family trade with humility and pride. Stein had never asked him why. It had occurred to him more than once that the hotel keeper might easily be connected with the Swiss secret service.

"Shalom, Mr. Stein." Rumpelmann bowed, beaming. "Welcome back to Amsteg. I hope you're staying with us tonight?"

Stein knew better than to extend his hand in greeting. They were as close to being friends as it was possible to be, yet the strict protocol that governed much about the Swiss prevented Rumpelmann from crossing the line of the professional into the personal. Instead Stein bowed in return, the faintly Prussian bow that Alois had perfected.

"Of course, Mr. Rumpelmann. I would no more visit your country without staying here than I would ask you to visit Israel without seeing the Temple on the Mount."

Rumpelmann swiftly wrote Stein's name in the book, checked a visitor card for Stein's passport number and handed him a room key. "Dinner?"

"Of course. I'm not too late—?"

"*Never* at the Hotel Stern. As you well know, having arrived yourself more than once at odd hours."

"Indeed. Perhaps we can speak after dinner?"

"My pleasure. But now, I must attend—"

"I understand. I'll hope to see you later, in the Rathskeller."

Dinner was superb, if simple by exotic tastes. The trout was grilled to flaking perfection, the vegetables *al dente*, the wine cool and dry. Stein had almost shoved Hassan el Jazzar and the Judah IV from his mind after his cheesecake and Irish coffee. He ambled from the small dining room to the narrow little stairs that led to the ancient cellar, from which the sounds of laughter and music emanated. He smiled and pushed open the gnarled old oaken door.

Smoke from the fireplace and the many pipes and cigars assaulted his eyes as the accordionist's chords clobbered his ears. The place was jammed; in Amsteg, this was where people gathered on cold winter nights. He shoved past an old couple swaying to the tune and found a stool unoccupied in the far corner, near the end of the bar. He sat down, enjoyed the music and the gaiety and waited.

Twenty minutes and another cognac later, Alois slipped through the crowd almost unnoticed and sat down across the scarred old table from Stein. He waved away the bartender and leaned on the table so that he could hear better.

"A good crowd tonight," Stein said.

Alois shrugged.

"Was it like this on Monday?"

"No. Fewer, I think. Were you looking for anyone in particular?"

"An Iranian. Possibly two or three."

"Ah. Mr. Ahmed, Mr. Hakim and Mr. Muhammed."

Stein nodded. "I wonder if you heard them talking?"

"Farsi is not a language of which I am a master, Mr. Stein. Besides—"

"I know. Propriety. These men are very dangerous, Alois. You could say they have the fate of nations in their hands."

"Or, perhaps, in their blue Volkswagen van, the one with the Essen plates and the large crate?"

Stein lifted his cognac. "I see you understand my meaning."

"To some extent. And although I do not speak their language, I must confess to more than mere curiosity when men of such obvious bad character make trans-Mediterranean telephone calls."

"Ah."

"Indeed, Mr. Stein, one might even say this curiosity of mine sometimes exceeds the limits of both taste and legality—at least as we construe them in Switzerland—and I find myself, to my shame, with a record of such telephone calls, even though I cannot—as I said—understand them myself." He looked around the room, smiling, and returned a wave. When he looked back to Stein, the smile had fallen as if off a precipice.

"By taking one of these records from me you would doubtless be doing my conscience a great deal of good. I would certainly sleep better were the evidence of my untoward curiosity removed. And, I daresay—" he looked shrewdly at Stein "—others would, also."

Stein finished his cognac and set down the snifter. "And the format of the record to which you refer—?"

"Microcassette, at one and seven-eighths inches per second. Monaural," Rumpelmann responded instantly and low-voiced. "With automatic line-gain matching to defeat bug sniffers."

Stein controlled his surprise. "I hardly know—"

Rumpelmann shook his head and leaned closer. "No need, Mr. Stein. I do this for peace. And for Isaac Rumpelmann, who started this enterprise three hundred years ago as a fleeing victim of a pogrom in Eisenstadt. We have not always been such staunch Lutherans, you see?" He stood and extended his hand.

Even more surprised, Stein awkwardly got to his feet. Rumpelmann shook his hand firmly and then held it as his eyes held Stein's.

"Shalom, Mr. Stein. And good luck with Mr. Ahmed. I think you will need it." With that, he dropped Stein's hand, and disappeared back into the jostling crowd.

The cassette lay on Stein's bed in an unmarked envelope when he returned to his room. He rummaged in his briefcase, pulled out his Japanese microcassette recorder and inserted the taped record of Hassan's call. He plugged in his earphone, sat down with a notepad and turned it on.

Ten minutes later, he switched it off, stared at the opposite wall for a moment and picked up the phone. If Rumpelmann was not an intelligence man, he should have been, Stein thought as he dialed. For the Swiss had even recorded the direct-dialing sequence Hassan had punched into his phone, enabling them to backtrack the call.

"Four-seven-six-six," a voice said on the phone.

"Prepare to ident and scramble," Stein said, enunciating the words clearly. Sometimes the computers refused to play when they had a bad connection or a fast talker.

"Ready," said the voice.

Stein picked up what appeared to be a standard Japanese-made autodialer and placed it against the mouthpiece of the phone. He punched in a nine-digit number and spoke into the other side when the tiny red LED turned green, indicating the Tel Aviv computer and the portable scrambler were in sync.

"Colonel Stein here. I have a tape to send, about ten minutes. And then I need to speak with Captain Chafaz."

"Yes, Colonel. We're ready to receive. And we're calling the captain now. Go ahead."

Stein replaced the tape machine's earphone cord with one that ended in another male plug. He slid that into the autodialer and started the tape. The green LED flickered, indicating a good send.

While the machines spoke to each other, he thought about what Hassan had said on the phone. About the airplane they were going to meet tomorrow at the small airfield near Zurich. And about their not needing to stop and refuel to get to Ireland.

Somehow, Moshe Stein doubted that Hassan el Jazzar was going to link up with the Irish Republican Army and use the Judah IV to devastate the British army in Northern Ireland. But what *was* he going to do? And why Ireland?

CHAPTER TEN

"NEXT WEEK? That isn't much time, Max."

"I know, and I'm sorry. But I had to catch those guys in Space Command off guard. As it is, I had a tough time getting a three-day window at Andrews."

Sandy paused. The line hissed. Max had had plenty of bad conversations with women over telephone lines that hissed like this one.

"Well, I was going on temporary duty to Yuma. But I guess Mat will let me slide that a week. Okay. You'll stay at my place, won't you?"

"Where else? Of course. Can't wait."

"Neither can I. Call me when you get your schedule firm, will you?"

"Natch. Uh...Sandy. I, um, I really miss you."

She laughed, a delight not even the telephone could make less appealing. "And I miss you. Bye."

Max hung up the phone less concerned by his continuing inability to articulate his feelings for Sandy than by the ticklish problem of getting three generals and their staffs to Andrews in the right frame of mind to understand what he was selling. Endlessly pondering how to get the defense establishment interested in the Viper, he'd finally struck on the new kids on the block: Space Command. More than any other group, they would immediately appreciate the value of the system, since they had the greatest difficulty in putting men into their equipment. Such was the intensity of the unabated internecine warfare at the Pentagon that it was a good bet once the Space Command guys got the Viper, there would be a me-too scramble by the Air Force and Navy to get aboard as well.

He sighed and flipped open the project folder with the detailed bio data on each general and his staffers. That was the plan, anyway. How it would actually play out was another matter entirely. He grimaced as the remorseless figures of the spreadsheet his father had so cheerfully shown him reminded him of how much was riding on whether his plan would work. If it didn't, Moss Electronics might be just another example of a company that bet its future on a single product and failed.

The thought of failure stirred him as much, he found, as the thought of losing a race, and with the same results. He dived back into the plan with renewed intensity.

THE SNOW CONTINUED to fall sporadically. The weak morning light of Zurich in November showed Stein that el Jazzar's blue VW van was still parked in front of the dispirited-looking apartments. He shifted in the Fiat's seat and sipped hot chocolate. Rising at 0400 had been the only way he could assure himself that he'd make it here from Amsteg before dawn. As with most stakeouts, nothing had happened, except that he continued to get colder.

His people had been in place at the airport since
0500. If Stein somehow missed el Jazzar, they would
pick him up at the small airport west of town.

He looked up and down the narrow little street for
the thousandth time. A few pedestrians with early-
morning jobs had doggedly plowed through the
thickening snow to their bus stops. Most of the Muslim workers who lived here would be leaving within the
next hour.

His portable car phone beeped. He snatched it off
the cradle and said, "Yes?"

"Nothing yet here, sir."

"Or here. Hopefully, they're still inside."

The phone went dead. He rubbed his hands and
wondered if he should have acceded to Chafaz's suggestion that they just go in and take el Jazzar. But the
risk of the ensuing firefight was too great; relations
with Switzerland were not so good that they wouldn't
be seriously damaged by Israeli agents killing inno-
cent Swiss in an attempt to retrieve something they
were not supposed to possess anyway. Besides, who
knew how well prepared or fortified the apartment
building might be?

He wished for the support of the Swiss, but Avrams
had vetoed it. This one they had to do on their own.

Just as he was about to decide to start his engine to
take the edge off the chill, people began trickling out
into the workday. A big truck ground past him,
throwing dirty snow onto his windshield. He quickly
reached out his window and swept it away. When he
settled back into the Fiat, the van's brake lights were
lit. Exhaust vapor stuttered out the tailpipe. The raspy
drone of a VW flat-four filled the little street.

He wiped a small section of the inside of his windshield to see better. Two hunched, heavily bundled figures clutching large cases ran awkwardly to the van from the apartment building. Stein plucked his phone from the cradle and punched the code.

"Yes," his man at the airport answered.

"They're leaving now. I'm following." He hung up and turned the key to start the Fiat.

Nothing happened. He tore his eyes from the van and looked down at the key. He turned it again. Only the dash lights came on. Nothing else happened.

"Shit!" he said, and thought furiously about the cause. The van's brake lights went off. Frantically, Stein sought the reason for the Fiat's failure to start. He had electrical power. He had gas. He had—

He had left the automatic gear selector in third gear. The interlock prevented it from starting in gear. Cursing, he slammed it into Park and savagely twisted the key.

The little Fiat whined merrily away. And did not start. The van lurched forward a foot as the driver fumbled for reverse. Stein mashed the gas pedal furiously, pumping it up and down. The starter whine slowed, then a brief cough announced that enough gas was present to make the engine hiccup. The van's reversing lights came on. It slowly worked backward against the foot-deep snow.

The Fiat coughed again. And again. The van paused. Its left-side turn signal flashed on, and it pulled into the street.

"Damn!" Stein raged. And suddenly the cold little Fiat stammered to life. He allowed it one second to warm up, then slammed the gear selector into first.

The engine promptly stalled. He turned the key again, eyes fixed on the van now threading its way gingerly between the snow-covered ranks of parked cars on the narrow street. Nothing happened. Again.

He remembered the gear-lockout and slid the selector back to Park, still twisting the key against the stop. The engine whined again, but this time roared as lustily to life as its anemic compression ratio and miserly carburetion allowed it to. Stein turned on the defroster, allowing the engine a few more seconds to run without a load, and strained to see which way the van was turning at the cross street. Left.

"Okay," he said, his breath condensing in the cold air. "Let's try it again." This time, he eased the gear lever into first and the car thunked into gear without drama.

He caressed the gas pedal to get it over the snow berm left by the predawn plowing. The Fiat's front wheels spun momentarily, then gained some traction, and suddenly he was on the rutted snow of the street. He pushed hard on the accelerator and the car stumbled, then gave him all it had. It wasn't much.

But it was enough to catch sight of the van at the corner. By the time he reached the cross street himself, it was turning right at another small intersection. He scowled and settled into the chase: close enough to see and follow, but not so close as to alarm. It was a ticklish business at the best of times.

Three minutes later, he realized two things simultaneously. First, this was actually the worst of times, since Zurich's infamous morning rush hour traffic had just exploded around him. And second, the van was not heading west, but east.

The Swiss are no more polite in cars than any other people, possibly less so. Certainly on a gray, cold, snowy Monday, no commuting worker will give way to anyone, anywhere. So Stein had to fight to keep the van in sight, even though it, too, was trapped by the inching, bumper-to-bumper traffic. He fumbled for the car phone and only succeeded in knocking it over on the floor of the passenger side. He leaned over to pick it up.

An insistent honking brought him back up. Behind him, a burgher in a Mercedes gesticulated angrily. He looked ahead and saw a couple of car lengths had opened up. He also saw that the van was gone.

He ignored the Mercedes and the phone, swung the Fiat out of line and put it up on the sidewalk. He leaned on the horn and accelerated, one set of wheels on the sidewalk, one set on the road. The Fiat snaked and slid, people shouted, cars hooted at him, but he got to the next intersection just in time to see the van turning down another street. He wrenched the car off the sidewalk and floored it.

The VW van driver knew Zurich. That much was obvious. But something else was obvious: he was not heading for Felshausen, the little airfield Stein had deduced they were using. As he sweated and worked the Fiat closer through the maze of snow mounds and traffic, he considered where they might be going—and came up blank. As far as he knew, there weren't any airfields east of the city.

If he could have spared a moment to use the phone, he might have gotten word to his agents. But the tail had to be kept, and even in the moments when they were both stopped at a light or in traffic, things began moving too quickly for him even to dial the number.

They were almost at the outskirts of town now, in a light-industrial neighborhood. The van was six cars ahead of him, and traffic was speeding up as the cars thinned out, feeding off into large parking lots.

The phone beeped at him just as the van pulled left and made a sudden left turn down a narrow, unplowed road. He ignored the phone and waited until the last minute to follow so that it would not be so obvious that he was tailing them. The phone continued to beep insistently as he swung the Fiat left. The front wheels spun for traction. He wrestled the wheel back and forth and just made the turn. The van was headed down the lane, gathering speed. He followed in the ruts, the snow so deep that it appreciably slowed the Fiat. He floored the accelerator and fumbled for the phone.

"Yes! I'm behind them now, heading east, not west," he barked.

"We wondered—"

"Don't wonder! Tell me—is there an airfield past the Kloss glassworks?"

"I—just a moment, sir. We'll check—"

But before they had an answer, the van slewed sideways ahead of him and took off down yet another unplowed road. How can they go so fast? Stein wondered. He came up on the turn and somehow made it. The Fiat fishtailed wildly but finally clung to the ruts the van had made. He picked up the phone again and cradled it between his jaw and shoulder, both hands on the wheel.

"—no, sir, we don't think so, but Ari says—"

He didn't even respond, because the van now turned right, a hundred meters ahead, behind a large industrial building of some kind. Stein saw that the road went over a little creek. The van wiggled a bit as it crested the bridge and disappeared behind the building.

The Fiat did more than wiggle as he steered it at its full snow-speed into the turn and onto the bridge. Too late he remembered that bridges freeze when roadways do not. Too late he remembered the methods of keeping a front-wheel-drive car in control when it begins to spin.

The Fiat swung first right, then viciously whipped left as he did precisely the wrong things with the steering wheel, throttle and brake. It slammed to a halt against the bridge railing, smashing him against the side window and door, and flinging the telephone against the other door. The engine died instantly.

Head buzzing, he blinked, released the steering wheel and collected himself. He looked in the rearview mirror to see where the van was, but the window was too frosted. He swore and unbuckled his seat belt, and popped the door open. He jumped onto the slick, snowy surface of the bridge and stared into the distance. The van was gone. But at least the snow had stopped, to be replaced with leaden gray clouds sluggishly moving from west to east.

He surveyed the car, saw that it seemed to be still all right, got in and started it. It fired immediately. He gingerly engaged reverse and slowly worked free of the bridge railing. Confidence restored, he hammered the car down the lane, following the tracks.

They led out of the industrial district into the countryside. Soon he was in a forested area, the road barely one car wide, trees looming on both sides. The visibility seemed to improve. The tracks veered suddenly left, and he slowed.

Cautiously, he allowed the Fiat to creep forward past the turning. He saw that there was a clearing not far from the roadway. Parked on one side of the clearing was the van.

He turned off the ignition and got out. He pulled the 9 mm from its shoulder holster and crunched in the new snow through the trees to the parking lot. He saw that a much larger area beyond it had been cleared not only of snow but of trees. He worked through the pines, breathing shallowly to slow the condensation of his breath, until the van was only a dozen meters away.

The lights were off, the engine off. The snow around the sliding door was heavily trodden. Tracks led to the recently plowed section of the lot. He hunched, pistol cocked and ran to the van.

Nobody was in it. The crate his men had seen was gone, too. He stepped around the van and looked toward the end of the cleared zone. A windsock, starkly orange, stood out against the snow-covered trees. The zone was no more than three hundred meters long. But it had evidently been enough for whatever airplane Hassan and his men had rendezvoused with.

He stood a moment longer, pistol in hand, looking around, when he suddenly realized that he was frozen to the marrow and his feet were soaking wet. He holstered his pistol and turned around to trudge back to his Fiat. As he passed the VW he saw a chrome badge on it that read Syncro 4WD. He snorted and shook his head, slipping in the damp snow, and made it back to his rented Fiat, which most definitely did not have four-wheel drive, as he found when he tried to turn it around in the narrow, snowy lane.

His feet were still cold, if not still wet when a Swissair 747 with him aboard punched through the low-hanging cloud over Zurich. But Stein was oppressed by the failures and chaos of the morning more than by his physical problems. When he'd reached the Israeli trade center in Zurich, he'd gotten a direct line to Avrams on the scrambler and had not attempted to minimize his own culpability in the loss of Hassan el Jazzar.

Avrams had not rebuked him. He had that to feel better about. And Avrams had agreed with Stein that there was little likelihood that the Jihaddin would use the Judah IV to threaten the British. That left only the United States as a plausible target for them.

It would be best, they agreed, for Stein to go in person to Washington and monitor events from there, while Avrams went himself to Britain to stand by in case they were wrong about el Jazzar's intentions. They could not afford, for Lorelei's sake, to inform the American or British governments of what might be happening.

Stein's thoughts were broken by the pretty young flight attendant's query about a blanket. At least in first class they noticed when you were cold. He let her tuck the blanket around his legs.

He reviewed again what might happen, what had happened, what the options were. The result was the same: they were still fumbling in the dark. He looked

at his watch and calculated the flying time to Washington. It would be a very long flight.

"IT WILL BE a very long flight. You know this."

Hassan drank the tea and swallowed his irritation.
Was this the best pilot they could find? he wondered.
A former Iranian air force pilot, they told him, a
specialist in low-level penetration flying. Perhaps. But
he was loud and irreverent, boastful of his prowess
and full of tales of how he had single-handedly de-
feated many Iraqi fighters. Ever since he had picked
them up in Switzerland in his highly modified Pilatus
Porter, he had been talking. All the way, it seemed, to
this windblown plateau on the west coast of Ireland,
where there was a deserted, rude field with kerosene
waiting for them, courtesy of yet another Jihaddin
connection.

"Yes, I know the flight is a long one. And difficult."

The pilot swept a hand over his slicked-back hair,
preening even in the middle of green nowhere. "No.
Not so difficult. I have made it in this airplane—oh,
seven times. But long. Very long."

"Commander," Ahmed called from the dark gray
airplane, "we have finished pumping. The tanks are
full."

The pilot spoke before Hassan, not realizing Ahmed and Feyda called Hassan "Commander" and not
he. El Jazzar gulped tea angrily.

"Good. We will board now." He turned to Hassan, grinning hugely, a white slash in his black-bearded
face. "You have pissed? No? I tell you, you must piss.
You will find it very difficult in the airplane. And I do

not like spilled urine in my airplane." He turned and stalked back to the Pilatus before Hassan could respond.

Instead of pissing, Hassan spit on the damp Irish ground. The big three-bladed propeller of the Porter's single turboprop engine was turning over when he jumped up into the doorway. In a few moments, the wheels stopped rumbling over the peat and the plane flew sluggishly out across the dark, rolling sea, climbing not more than fifty meters above the immense white-capped rollers into a murky layer of cloud.

Hassan shifted uncomfortably in the copilot's seat. In the huge internal fuel tank, the turbine fuel stank abominably, worse even than the urine the pilot fussed about. But with the tank full of fuel, the new satellite navigation system and the pilot's skill, they could make the westward crossing without stopping.

At least, that was the plan. As the Porter bucked and dipped sickeningly in the dark Atlantic cloud, Hassan had no doubts about the plan. The only unknown was the pilot's skill—and since the demands of the flight meant they had to sacrifice a real copilot to accommodate the three Jihaddin and the crate, everything rode on the skill of the single pilot. But he had gotten them to Ireland undetected, flying low over the land and sea, trusting his Allah-given luck and skill as much as the sophisticated—and stolen—American inertial and satellite navigation system.

Beyond him, Feyda suddenly succumbed to the sickening stink in the cold, cramped cabin and the uncomfortable motion of the airplane. He retched miserably, beseeching Allah between bouts for strength.

It would indeed be a long flight.

CHAPTER ELEVEN

"THIS IS NEVER GOING to work, you know."

Sandy snuggled closer. "Sure it will," she said sleepily.

Max stroked her soft, golden hair. "No. I can't see it. Long-distance love affairs never work. Believe me, I know."

She lifted her head and rested on her elbows. In the faint light coming through the open bedroom door, her naked skin seemed to glow eerily. Her breasts swung invitingly between her arms as she levered herself up to face Max.

"Oh really? You mean as in a certain English chemist?"

Max smiled ruefully. "You know about Christie?"

"I know all about you. And I also know why your thing with her fell apart. It wasn't distance, pal. It was lackawanna. Yours. Not hers."

He reached out and stroked one breast. She arched and presented them both to him, the nipples hardening. "Maybe, maybe not," he said. "But that certainly doesn't apply now, does it?"

"Mmm?" she said. And for a long while neither of them spoke, at least not in words.

Max awoke again before dawn, unaccountably nervous. Jet lag, he thought. He lay awake and listened to Sandy sleeping next to him. She slept soundly and deeply. He envied her. She had the ability to fall asleep quickly when she wanted to, a true soldier's knack for making the most of every moment's respite from the grind. She also seemed not to suffer from the destabilizing effect of sleeping with someone—not just making love, but actually sleeping—when not used to it.

He had neither knack. Somebody once had told him that he understood machines better than people. It had been said so long ago, he had forgotten who it was. Christie, maybe, back in Cambridge. Whoever said it, it was all too close to the truth.

With every mile the American Airlines L-1011 hauled him closer to Washington from San Francisco, he had grown more anxious about his ability to pull off what he had promised his father and the people in the company: selling the Viper to the generals. Not because he doubted the Viper, but because he doubted his own ability to sell people anything. Sandy had helped enormously, of course. She had been obviously as happy to see and hold him as he had been to embrace her.

Why she should have fallen for him was something he also could not fathom. Like most loners, he expected everything from people except love. When he got it in double handfuls—first from Sandy, then, even in his own form, from his father—he was disoriented. Happy, but disoriented. And not a little fearful, like a man waiting for the other shoe to fall.

Waiting for it, turning over the problems in his mind, staring at Sandy's bedroom ceiling, he finally fell asleep. He awoke again to delicious cooking odors, and for a dizzy moment couldn't place himself; was he back in Key Largo? Then he awakened more fully. He rolled over and squinted at the digital clock.

Even though it was still dark in the bedroom, the clock claimed it was almost eleven in the morning. Sandy was not in bed. He groaned. Today he had to begin the sales pitch with a preliminary briefing at 1500 at the Pentagon. Less than six hours away and he wasn't even awake. He breathed deeply and kicked off the inviting covers. "Jet lag," he muttered as he fumbled his way to the bathroom.

Sandy was dressed and humming as she prepared what was now brunch. Max walked up behind her quietly, cupped her breasts and kissed her neck. She closed her eyes and kissed him, then broke free to save her eggs Benedict.

"Finally up, I see," she said.

"Yeah. Should have been about three hours ago. How long have you been conscious?"

She handed him a steaming mug of black coffee. "About three hours."

He gulped the coffee and sat at her kitchen counter. "I have to brief the dummies today. How about you?"

"Yep. Have my own dummies to brief."

"Back for dinner?"

She laid a plateful of eggs Benedict in front of him, and kissed him on the nose. "Of course. About six. You're taking me out."

"I am?"

"Yeah. We're going to the Kennedy Center for the eight o'clock performance of *Swan Lake*."

"Ballet?" Max frowned. "I don't esp—"

"We're going to meet somebody there who is very interested in you. Then, after the show, we're going to a place in Georgetown where we can all eat and talk. After that . . . use your imagination."

"Yessir, Cap'n. Sold. Ballet, huh? Who—"

She looked at her watch and grabbed her purse. "Sorry to feed you and run. Gotta go. Make sure to reset the security system before you leave. And take out the garbage, will you? Thanks." She pulled on her Burberry, jerked open the front door and went out into the chilly gray day. Then she popped the door open again, rushed in and plopped herself down on Max's lap.

"I forgot," she whispered, "to say something else. I love you, Max Moss." She stifled his incipient grin with a kiss that made him lose all interest in his brunch, disengaged and stood up, all business again. She tore off a piece of his toast, smiled enigmatically and ran out the door.

Max looked at the door a moment. Then he picked up his fork and attacked his breakfast. His incipient grin became actual, which made eating slightly difficult. But it made the gray day sunny, and made him realize, almost with a jolt, that he didn't feel too bad.

THE CANADIANS WERE no less zealous at keeping unannounced aircraft out of their airspace than any other nation. But no radar system is perfect, especially in peacetime, and most especially in winter. Not even a drug smuggler, it was reckoned, would be brave or stupid enough to attempt low-level penetration in an Atlantic winter. So the sector controllers confined their attention to penetration by Soviet reconnaissance bombers, and Hassan's Pilatus Porter slipped through the Canadian air defense zone as easily as a minnow through a tuna net.

Most of a day after leaving Ireland, the Porter's pilot slipped the now-lightened turboprop down out of the low, scudding clouds to a short, rough landing on a farmer's field near the strip of French-speaking towns along the Fundy coast of Nova Scotia.

Waiting at one end of the soggy winter-wheat field was a twin-engined Piper. It stood under the tin roof of a dilapidated outbuilding, invisible from the air. Hassan saw it only as the Porter taxied across the rough field. Near the door of the big shed, the pilot spun the Porter around on its tailwheel and began to shut down the engine. He grinned hugely at Hassan as the gyros whined noisily in the sudden silence.

"You see? A long flight. But not a difficult one."

El Jazzar peeled the headset from his aching head. Under other circumstances, he would have liked to do many things besides agree with the irritating aviator. Yet he had done as he promised, they had arrived, thousands of kilometers from their takeoff point, almost exactly on schedule. Hassan did not waste time wondering whether it was technology or technique that had gotten them across the Atlantic in a single-engine aircraft with so little drama, albeit so much discomfort. Time was still of the essence; every minute they spent on the ground here they were exposed to the winds of fate.

Ahmed and Feyda had the fuselage door open and were outside before Hassan had finished gathering his gear. Although exhausted by the buffeting and vibration of the flight, they worked quickly to get the crate out of the Porter.

The Piper pilot left his place next to his airplane and ran to help the Jihaddin. Hassan did not hear what the pilot said to Feyda and Ahmed, but he recognized him immediately, and he felt that inner release of a tiny tension that all who plan complex plans feel when one more small part falls into place. He worked his way back along the fuselage of the now-silent Porter, past the almost empty fuel tank to the gaping cargo door, where the four men had wrestled the crate out to the ground. Hassan paused at the door and caught the Piper pilot's attention.

The pilot stiffened slightly and salaamed, saying in bad, halting Arabic, "Welcome, Hassan el Jazzar, Commander of the Faithful. Allah be with you."

"Allah be with *you*, Hadj al-Shiran," Hassan said, and jumped to the ground. "It is good to see you," he continued, in English.

Al-Shiran smiled soberly. "And to see you, Commander. Do you want to rest before we—"

Hassan shook his head. "There is all eternity to rest. Now we must move quickly. Let us load and be on our way." He turned to the Iranian pilot. "You will rest now?"

"Yes." He shrugged. "Until nightfall. When you leave, I will conceal the airplane in the shed. Then I will go back." He grinned again, a wolf's grin. "My way will be easier than yours, I think."

"Perhaps," said Hassan. "The way of Allah is never easy."

Whatever rejoinder the loquacious pilot was about to make died on his lips as the ferocity in Hassan's voice was matched by the sudden fire in his eyes. He had the look of a man about to enjoy some especially savage kind of sport.

FOR MOST PEOPLE an evening out to the ballet and dinner was enjoyment. For Max, it was a kind of mandatory performance, a time of camouflaged feelings and necessary politesse. He had learned early at important parties given by the ambitious Army officer his father had once been that his role in these affairs was not central; he was a spear carrier, usually to the women. There were aspects of Tchaikovsky's ballet he found interesting, but, though he tried to see congruences in the highly disciplined movements of the dancers and the brutal grace in the world of racing he knew so well, the attempt failed. Ballet was an alien world for him. Perhaps, he mused as the small talk swept around the table at the little Greek place in Georgetown, if one of those dancers were his daughter or sister or wife, it would be different. He smiled at the thought. He'd known a guy once, an Army intel type, who'd married a dancer. It had not turned out well. He pursed his lips absently, trying to remember the guy's name.

"Max!" Sandy said insistently. He put down his coffee cup and blinked back into the table talk. Obviously, he had missed something; Mat Chester, Sandy's boss, and his plain but pleasant wife, Katie, were both looking at him. Sandy was slightly flushed.

"Yo," he said weakly. "Sorry. Just thinking about the ballet."

Chester grinned. "I know the feeling. Happens to me, too. You leave, thinking, wow, that was fine, and then an hour later it's all a blur and you wonder where your forty bucks went."

Katie smacked Mat's shoulder in mock anger. "Hey! That's not true at all. Why, I remember well the—"

"Me, too," said Sandy. "Wasn't Odile just *fabulous*? I mean, I saw this back in Paris, oh, five years ago, and—"

Katie nodded eagerly, leaning forward, her eyes owllike behind her ornately rimmed glasses. She and Sandy slipped into the female frequency. Mat caught Max's eye and indicated that they get up. Chester mumbled something that suggested he and Max were going to the john and Katie waved her hand, still engrossed with Sandy.

The two men made their way through the crowd jammed into the restaurant. In the john, they went to adjoining urinals.

Chester carefully scanned the dirty little bathroom. They were the only ones in it. "Well, what do you think?" he said.

"About what?"

"About the network. Surely Sandy's told you."

"Some. Not all."

"Interested?"

"Sure. Otherwise I probably wouldn't be here." He zipped his pants and went to the washbasin.

Chester joined him at the basin, pulling out a comb and running it through his short hair. "Good. We'll follow up later. Glad you could join us."

Max shot him a sharp look. Had he in fact joined anything? Or was Chester referring to the evening? Chester met his gaze evenly, then turned and opened the door into the noisy roomful of people.

The two couples said good-night on M Street, Georgetown's main drag. As always, rain or shine, it was packed with roaming bands of kids, looking to score something, anything. While Max had said a polite good-evening to Katie Chester, Mat had pulled Sandy aside and spoken low into her ear, almost to the point of embarrassment of his wife and Max.

"Home?" Max said as they watched the Chesters navigate through the crowds to the subterranean parking lot.

"Sure," she said and took his hand.

They didn't speak on the short drive back to her place. Something about the evening was bothering both of them. Maybe, thought Max, it was his ill-concealed dislike of the ballet. He resolved to do better next time.

He tried to kiss her in the foyer, but she eluded his grasp. "Nope. Not now. We've got work to do first. Drink?"

He shook his head and peeled off his jacket, tossing it on a chair. He loosened his tie and sprawled on the sofa, legs outstretched, head back.

"Okay. What work?"

She kicked off her shoes, folded up her legs and wriggled into place in the big chair across from him.

She sipped on a gin and tonic and regarded him seriously.

"First things first. Have any luck today with the dummies?"

"The Air Force? Maybe. I got the tactical guys nervous that the Space Command people were going to watch the demo day after tomorrow. I figure that's a good start. If it works well, they'll be sure to demand their own hardware to make damn certain no space cadet steals a march on them in the budget."

She sipped again and cradled the drink. She stared into it, stirring the ice with her little finger. When she looked back at him, her demeanor had changed; now she was solemn.

"I'm glad." She paused again, as if uncertain exactly how to proceed. "What did you think of Mat Chester?"

"Your boss? Seemed like an okay guy. Why?"

"Well, you know the evening was arranged so he could check you out himself. Before...before we went any further."

Max frowned slightly. "I guess that makes sense. It's no crazier than any of the rest of this crazy stuff."

"Max! This isn't crazy stuff. We—that is, they, well, *we* have a lot of problems. As I told you in Florida."

"Actually, kid, all you told me in Florida was that the government wanted me to act on the QT as a kind of free-lance agent. You didn't say much else, if you'll recall."

"No...I guess you're right. I couldn't. But Mat wants me to fill you in some more tonight. He liked you."

"Well, goodie for me." Max got to his feet, somehow rankled by the direction this was taking. He went into the kitchen and popped a beer. Sandy was looking uncomfortable when he returned. He flopped back onto the couch and slugged some beer. "So? What's next? An IQ test?"

"Listen, Max, this isn't easy for us—for me, either, you know. We have to do it this way, because of how screwed up things are in the system. But it's just temporary. Mat says—"

"Get on with it, will you? What's next?"

"Mat would like you to try a job."

"A job. Fine. What kind of job? Want me to break into the Watergate? Steal some secret documents to send the Russians? What?"

"Calm down, Max. Nothing like that. Just simple stuff. For..." She paused and drank some gin and tonic. "For a friendly government."

He looked at her a long time, impassive, then set down his can of beer with exaggerated precision. "A what?"

"A friendly government."

"You must be kidding."

"No. We—they—"

He exploded to his feet and jammed his hands in his trouser pockets. He glared at her, then paced around the little living room. She bit her lip and watched him.

He drew a deep breath and sat down again on the sofa. He picked up the beer can, raised it to his mouth, then set it down, apparently fixing all his attention on getting the label perfectly aligned with the coaster.

When he looked back at Sandy, the color had drained from his face. It made the scar on his chin stand out.

"I want to get this perfectly straight. I need to understand every part of it. Now. You came down to Key Largo to sign me up as a knight-errant for the poor old beleaguered U.S. of A., right? Our intelligence capability is seriously impacted by the pols, right? Those were your words, I think."

"Something like that," she said stiffly.

"So there's this network of old pals, colonels most of 'em, professionals, who figure that they can run things until the pols get their rocks off and put everything back the way it's supposed to be. Until then, Uncle needs old Max to run a few errands, some of which might be fun for a crazy kind of guy like old Max, who after all is one weird kind of dude, what with being a Recovery jock and racer and like that." He grabbed his beer and slugged some down, face now flushed.

"Okay so far? So old Max buys all this—not least because the lady they send down to recruit him manages to knock the son of a bitch's socks off—signs up again with his old man's company as a cover and makes his first pilgrimage to Mecca here and finds out—hey, presto—that it isn't *Uncle* who wants him, it's a *friendly government*!" He sat back and stared hard at her.

"Well. A few points, Sandy old girl. First. You may recall, since you participated, what getting entangled with so-called friendly governments leads to. Think back to a certain Jeep Cherokee, a certain day in which every swinging dick with a rocket launcher was trying his best to kill us both. That's first. Second, consider this: old Max may be crazy, but he's not stupid. He has a pretty good memory, and recalls fairly well how those guys who got recruited by Reagan's people to run goodies to the grunts in points south got railroaded when the shit hit the fan. At least they had the consolation of working for Uncle, or at least what they thought was Uncle. Where would I be with your 'friendly government' if things went south for me like they did for them? Shit creek, that's where."

She swallowed and set down her own drink, a prelude to speaking. But he continued, leaning forward, eyes glittering.

"And last, there's this. Things have happened to me you don't know anything about—regardless of your clever investigations and your contacts. I make up my own mind about things. Especially things that involve—" he looked away, searching for the words "—the bottom line. Stuff like duty, and honor. Even stuff like what you owe your country and what your country owes you in return. I'm not sure I have any kind of philosophy that you could write a book about, but there are a couple of things I know for sure, and one is, if I'm going to put myself on the line for a country, it won't be for any but my own."

Silence arose like a wall between them. As he talked, she had at first been surprised, then gradually angered by his tirade. She let the silence stretch uncomfortably, hands tightly clasped in her lap, legs folded, regarding Max calmly. When she judged he was beginning to cool down, she spoke.

"You must think I'm either some kind of Mata Hari, or a patsy. You're wrong if you think either. Let's get this straight right now, or we're never going to make it, as you claimed this morning. When I went down to Key Largo, I went officially. Jesus, Max. You think you're the only guy they're looking to hire? You rate yourself too highly. Anyway, I went for you because I knew you... and, dammit, okay, because I thought from our time in Potsdam, that there were some things we didn't get done. Or said. And I was proved right. But that's *us*.

"As far as the job is concerned, it would have been all the same to me if you'd not taken it. We'd have gotten our thing worked out somehow, whether you went back to your dad or not. But I knew—*I know*—just enough of what Mat Chester is saying to be true that I thought you were one of the right men for the job. It's a tough, screwy, no-win kind of job. But I thought that's what Max Moss was all about. So when you agreed, I figured you understood that signing on meant that the work you'd be asked to do was... unconventional." He started to say something, but Sandy unfolded and stopped him.

"Don't bother. I know: 'unconventional' is certainly the word for helping out a government we've decided needs the help. Well, it's your call. You're a volunteer—you can drop out any time, now or later." She jerked her glass off the table, hand trembling. "But dammit, there's one more thing. I really don't appreciate your implication that I—and my friends, like Mat—have the morals of the Nixon White House, or Reagan National Security Council. *You* make up your own mind about duty and honor and patriotism? Damn, Max, what do you think I feel? What makes you the only person in the world with a conscience or an ethical code? What—" She waved her glass and sat back. "To hell with it." She slugged down the remains of her gin and tonic. "You don't want to play. I'll tell Mat. Right now."

She slammed down her glass and stood up, slightly unsteadily. She waited for Max to reply but he just looked at her. She finally shook her head, stalked to her bedroom and slammed the door. Max stared at the table.

In the bedroom, Sandy calmed herself before she dialed Mat's number. She knew Katie would understand the late call; it was a permanent feature of her life married to a Mat Chester.

He answered the phone on the second ring, as usual.

"Colonel."

"Sandy. What's happening? Anything wrong?"

"No, sir. But I have to report...I have to report that Moss won't do it."

"Won't do what?"

"He won't work for our friend."

"Why not?"

"He says...well, he just says he won't work for anyone but Uncle."

"No chance of changing his mind?"

"I don't think so."

"Hmm." The line was silent a moment. "Well, win some, lose some. We'll deal with it tomorrow. Too bad. He seemed like a good guy."

"He is, Colonel. But he's stubborn."

Chester chuckled. "He's also got a foot in your door, hasn't he? Never mind—none of my business. Look, Sandy. Don't worry about it. We'll get another guy."

Sandy chewed her cheek. "Uh, sir, I wonder if...look, he's been under awful pressure on the coast. And this is all kind of sudden for him. Before we scratch him off the list, even if he won't do the job for our friend, why not still consider him for other things?"

"Your loyalty is admirable. But I don't think so. We can't afford the time and energy; we need people who'll deliver. And we don't need guys who won't trust us to decide what's got to be done and what hasn't. But, tell you what. Let's just leave him on ice for a while. Who knows? He might change his mind. Okay?"

"Okay. Thanks, Colonel. And thanks again for the evening."

"No sweat, Sandy. See you at the office."

When she opened the door again, Max saw in her pale, strained countenance the mirror of his own conflicting emotions.

Unaccountably, he grinned at her, a wan, pale grin, but he had to begin somewhere. She looked a little startled.

"Hi," he said. "Want to try again?"

She almost smiled, folded her arms and looked at him quizzically. He got to his feet, grabbed her gin and tonic glass and took it back to the kitchen. He poured her another drink, took it to where she still stood eyeing him, handed it to her and leaned back against the kitchen counter. She took the drink and waited.

"So," he said brightly, his voice only cracking the tiniest bit, "how did you like the ballet?"

CHAPTER TWELVE

FREDERICK COUNTY AIRPORT was deserted when al-Shiran landed the Piper Navajo at just past two in the morning. He had known it would be. Flying charter so much, he had come to know the habits of the airport, just as a commercial fisherman comes to know the cycles of activity of his harbor. He had not needed the sophisticated navigation system to tell him when he was over the little airport; he knew it well, and the night was clear enough for him to line up on runway 19, click his microphone five times on the unicom frequency to activate the automatic runway lights, and drop the big Piper down with hardly a squeak from its tires.

Frederick was ideal for their purposes. It was an "uncontrolled" airfield, meaning that it had no FAA-operated control tower to regulate traffic, yet it was big enough that al-Shiran was able to secure the right airplane from his employer, County Aviation. Slade thought he was on an overnight charter—a common activity for the pilot he called Jones.

The flight from Nova Scotia had been long and dangerous, in its own way more difficult than the trans-Atlantic flight Hassan and his two men had endured. Al-Shiran had made it a point to secure as many Canadian charters as possible, to stay current on the weak spots in the border radars, just for this night flight. Luck had been with them, again, in that the weather had stayed calm and mostly clear. The forecast was for three days of high pressure and clear weather.

Al-Shiran brought the big twin to a halt inside the fenced area of County Aviation. Beside him in the copilot's seat, Hassan had managed to stay awake the entire trip. Al-Shiran admired his grit; not many men who had made a nonstop Atlantic crossing in an airplane like the Pilatus would have given up the chance to relax in the Navajo's velour cabin seats. Ahmed and Feyda had thrown themselves into the seats almost as soon as the crate was jammed through the aft door and lashed down.

"The airplane will be secure?" Hassan asked as soon as the engines had been shut down.

"Yes. It will be locked. No one will disturb it."

"You have the van?"

"There—in the lot. You see?"

Hassan followed al-Shiran's finger. A Ford van stood under the sole mercury lamp in the virtually empty airport parking lot. Al-Shiran had rented it earlier in the day.

They off-loaded the crate and their gear bags into the van when al-Shiran brought it around, and in minutes the Navajo was locked and they were driving out the airport road to Interstate 70.

Tractor-trailer trucks roared past them as al-Shiran brought the Ford van onto the interstate, heading west. Ahmed and Feyda sat on the floor of the van's box, legs wedged against the crate. Hassan again sat in the passenger's seat.

They drove in silence until al-Shiran came to his exit. A couple of forlorn gas stations stood across from each other like ancient fortresses at the exit, one flanked by a 7-Eleven store, the other by a Mc-Donald's. Hassan peered at them with thinly disguised interest.

"Your first time in America?" al-Shiran ventured. Making small talk was not in his nature, but the strain of the long flight, the excitement of the operation finally begun, the whole amazing *fact* of it really happening made him bolder than usual with a Commander of the Faithful.

Hassan did not reply. Al-Shiran understood and continued driving. So far, they had exchanged perhaps two dozen words, beginning with Hassan's query about the status of the preparations and ending with his concern about the airplane's security. If he sensed that al-Shiran needed—craved—reassurance he did not show it. Perhaps it was because he was himself exhausted. Perhaps it was because it was his leadership style to ignore weaknesses like those in al-Shiran that begged for approval. But perhaps it was simply because he was Hassan el Jazzar.

When they finally arrived at al-Shiran's rented farmhouse, they entered it as if it were a military objective, stealthily and silently, conscious always of the need not to be seen. After the American showed them their beds, the bathroom and the kitchen, he found himself alone in the hallway, under the single bare forty-watt bulb, with el Jazzar. The bulb swung slightly as it responded to the creaking of the floor above, throwing strange shadows across el Jazzar's haggard, fierce countenance.

"We are almost there, my brother," el Jazzar said. There was no smile.

Al-Shiran swelled to be called brother by el Jazzar. "Yes, Commander. I must work tomorrow, and I have the airplane booked for a charter tomorrow night that will last through the next day. You and the brothers can rest and make ready. No one will disturb you here."

More could have been said, but neither man said it. Hassan merely grabbed al-Shiran's muscular biceps and squeezed it hard, looking into the black man's face. Then he released him and went upstairs.

THE BAR WAS A JOINT, if not quite a dive. Mat Chester was a little surprised that Mo Stein would know of such a place, maybe even more so that he would come here often enough to command a booth in the gun-fighter's corner.

"Didn't know D.C. had places like this," he mused, sipping his J&B. The rocks rattled in his glass. "Flanagan's in Boston is sort of like it. Maybe Danny's in Murray Hill. How'd you find it?"

Stein simply shrugged while he made wet circles on the stained old wooden tabletop with his beer bottle.

Chester echoed his shrug internally. Okay, he thought, if we're going to be coy, two can play. He'd known Mo a long time—and really had saved his ass— but times change. And so, he realized as he looked at Stein's receding hairline, do people.

"Mat, we've got a problem," Stein said suddenly.

"Jesus, who doesn't? Don't feel like the Lone Ranger."

"No, I'm serious. You know last time I was here, when I asked you for help with a free-lancer?"

"Yeah."

"The situation has...changed."

"Don't need him?"

"No. I don't think so."

"That's no problem, Mo. We haven't busted our gut to get you a guy."

"Good. Thanks. But that's not what I mean about a problem. It's related, but not the issue."

"So what is the issue?"

"I can't tell you. Not now, anyway. But I have to go this far: be very alert. We think—that is, I think—a certain Jihad leader has entered the States." He glanced around swiftly as he raised his bottle of beer, a professional's appraising scan of the room.

"Ah. The Jihad." Chester set down his whiskey. He looked past Stein's shoulder, letting it sink in. The Israeli wouldn't tell him this unless the man involved was someone very special, much beyond the threat posed by the average terrorist, domestic or imported.

"Can you give me any details?"

"No. I should not even be telling you this. We traced him to Ireland, then lost him. He...must be carefully watched."

"Got a name, at least? Our people probably know all about him."

"I'm sure they do. But I don't think they realize what he can do. Otherwise, I'm sure you, in your position with the interagency working group, would have known about it by now."

"'It'? What 'it'? I thought we were talking about a man."

"We are. His name is Hassan el Jazzar. Krug will have the complete file on him, almost as good as ours."

Chester frowned. "Doesn't ring a bell, but then I don't spend much time with the Arabs."

"He's not an Arab. He's Persian. Was a leader of the Revolutionary Guards brigade that took over the embassy. He is very smart, very tough. Very dangerous."

"Got it," said Chester and pulled on his whiskey. "Anything else?" He looked at his watch. "I promised Katie I'd take the kids to a movie in—holy shit!— less than an hour."

Stein looked for all the world to Chester like a man who wanted to say something else, but couldn't. His professional self-control was obviously strained. He fiddled with his beer, looked Chester in the eye and then dropped his gaze again.

"No," he said, "nothing else. Thanks for seeing me. I hope you won't be seeing el Jazzar."

"Yeah," said Chester, pulling on his coat and getting up. He flipped a five out onto the table. "Me too. See you later, Mo."

"IT WASN'T AN especially good day for me, either." As she spoke, Sandy took Max's overcoat and hung it in the closet. He set his briefcase down and stood a moment, his face made paler by the cold outside and the lousy day he'd had. She wore her Class A uniform, the one she'd worn when he met her in Berlin, and looked used up herself.

Suddenly he smiled wryly. "Well, here we are, husband and wifelike, comparing notes on who had the worst day at the office."

She ran a hand through her hair and pulled out the pins she used to keep it compact under her garrison cap. "Except we're not mar—"

He cut her off by the simple expedient of putting his hands on her shoulders and kissing her. From there on, the evening got a lot better. They spent it making chicken stir-fry together, he in his favorite old smoking jacket, she in her oversize Ohio State jersey that almost covered her fanny, except when she reached for something. Max found a lot of excuses to have her reach for things.

They decompressed, he from a day passed wrestling with the USAF and FAA bureaucracy to ensure that his Viper demonstration would not be hindered at the last minute by either organization. She had spent the day patiently explaining to congressional staffers how intelligence gathering at DIA differed from the same activity at the CIA, NRO and other agencies. Hillbilly Two was in full swing.

They finally sank into a tubful of hot water and mountains of bubbles. Max lay back against the tub's rim, legs outstretched. Sandy nestled in, her back to his chest. Steam clouded the mirror in her bathroom, and they let the heat and bubbles soak away the day.

"Max?" Sandy asked finally in a soft voice.

"Mmm?" He didn't open his eyes.

"What about your stepmother?"

"What about her?"

"You never talk about her, y'know."

"Not much to say."

"Well, I mean, is she nice, or nasty, short, fat, tall, skinny—"

"She's a nice lady. Fifteen years younger than my father. Dresses like a million bucks, knows everybody who counts, gives parties they write newspaper stories about in the society pages, and loves my old man, I guess."

"Sounds like you don't like her much."

"I don't dislike her. Not anymore. She had me over to their place in Carmel a couple of times last month." He recalled Katharine's obvious need to gain his trust, if not his affection. She knew he had not given her either ever since Eric Moss married her, only weeks after his first wife's funeral. Max had never enjoyed Katharine's company, but this time the two of them had been like secret allies in a campaign to save his father. They had reached a sort of understanding at that last dinner at the Moss weekend house on the beach in Carmel, an understanding that both would work to take the heat off his father. Eric's life obviously depended on it.

"She have any kids?"

"No. Hey, what's all this about, anyway? More dossier stuff?" Max shifted in the tub uneasily, setting loose a small tidal wave.

"No, no. I was just wondering. You know. You must wonder about my parents, too, sometimes. Don't you?"

Max realized with a start that he never had. And that made him realize that Sandy had embarked on a chain of thought that led to—what? Marriage?

The idea didn't seem as absurd now as it always had before. After all, now he was a semirespectable businessman, not a stock car racer or agent in training.

Or was he? Some part of him might be, but he didn't feel any different from the guy who knew how to take the high line at Darlington or fake out the Vopos in Potsdam.

Sandy interrupted his musings. "Well? Do you?"

"What?"

"Do you *wonder*? About my family?"

Could he level with her? Would she understand? He knew she wouldn't. Not yet. He smiled wolfishly to cover up his own unease. "Kid, right now the only thing I'm wondering is how long I can stay awake. We've got a big day tomorrow, y'know. I got you your pass from the Andrews guys, the weather looks good, and *we* have to get up at the crack of dawn if we're going to have the Viper humming when the brass arrives."

She sighed. "I know. It's just—sometimes I wonder what it would be like to have a normal American life."

Max suddenly slid out of the tub, allowing her to slosh backward. He stood, glistening wet and naked in front of her, arms spread and said, "Hey! This is *it*, Captain Koppel! This is as normal as it gets!" And before she could respond, he'd plucked her from the tub, water splashing everywhere, and run with her, laughing, into the bedroom.

IT WAS ALMOST MIDNIGHT when Chester made it back from the mall with Sharon and Mike. He undressed quietly, brushed his teeth and slipped into bed, kissing Katie's neck without awakening her. He began the process of rerunning the day and planning the next.

As he recalled Stein's conversation, he remembered that he'd intended to call Sandy to tell her Moss was off the roster, since Stein didn't need him. He played with the idea of calling her now despite the hour, then decided against it.

There would, after all, be plenty of time tomorrow.

CHAPTER THIRTEEN

IF THEY HAD NOT made love, there would have been plenty of time. But the same chemistry that kept Max semiconscious all night, turning over in his mind all the possible scenarios for the demo flight also ignited his testosterone when the morning light caressed Sandy. He was helpless against his own hormones. So he awakened her not with coffee and microwave pastry, but with nibbles, kisses and body heat. She responded all too well, and by the time they almost sank back into a delicious slumber, the dawn had become day.

He noted the time almost absentmindedly, mumbling, "Hmmph...6:53," and rolling over. Next to him, Sandy was beginning to breathe deeply and rhythmically. The digits rolled around his mind looking for meaning. Suddenly they found it. He jerked awake.

"6:50-*what*? Holy shit. Sandy. Sandy! Wake up, kid. Time to move!"

She opened one eye and watched him scramble to the bathroom. The eye moved to the clock, stared at it and closed again. She rolled over and caught a few more precious minutes of satisfied sleep. She knew what he did not: they had missed the window.

"The what?" he asked fifteen minutes later while he gulped coffee and crunched on toast.

"The window," she said, calmly buttering her own toast. "No need to go crazy. You miss the window, you're screwed. Might as well relax."

Max made certain none of the apricot jam had gotten on his silk tie. "I don't get it. What window?"

Sandy smiled ruefully. "Boy, what a businessman you make. Don't even know about commuting, do you? Well, Mr. Vice President, the fact is that while you've been out raising hell in race cars, America has gotten gridlocked. No place worse than Washington."

"Yeah? So? San Jose's not exactly an open prairie. My commute from Los Altos—"

"Doesn't even make the minors, kiddo. Here, if you don't get on the Beltway by six-thirty, no matter which way you're going, you've missed the window of opportunity. That means you get to go bumper-to-bumper for at least an hour.

"Now," she continued, relishing the chance to lecture him, "from here I can get to the Pentagon parking lot in, say, thirty minutes—but that's because I stay off the Beltway. To go to Andrews, though . . . you get it."

He looked at the kitchen clock. "So we missed the dreaded Beltway window. Seriously?"

"Seriously."

He looked worried. "Wonder if I should call Duane and tell the boys we'll be late. Or maybe call the Air Force guys—"

She reached over to him and patted his arm. "It's okay, Max. Everybody around here understands the

Beltway. You were shooting for a ten o'clock takeoff, right?''

"Yeah. Briefing at 0930. I wanted to get there around eight."

''No sweat. We'll be there a little late, but you can launch on time and brief on time.''

He still looked worried. Prerace jitters, he well knew. But so much had never ridden on a race as rode on this flight. Not for the first time since he'd taken this job he began to have some sympathy for businessmen.

THE SUN SLOWLY WARMED the frigid metal surfaces of the Piper Navajo as Hadj al-Shiran carefully inspected the airplane. He had learned the hard way, two decades before, about preflight inspections. You had to look, really look at the airplane while it was on the ground if you wanted it to keep you alive in the air. Many pilots as experienced as he had kidded him over the intensity with which he checked out everything; but more had died, surprised, when some vital system had failed in flight. You flew, al-Shiran knew, only by the grace of Allah and the integrity of your airplane.

Hassan fidgeted in the cockpit while Ahmed stood guard, his Uzi concealed beneath his voluminous gray overcoat. Feyda, the technician, completed the wiring hookup. The ramp at County Aviation was quiet, and only a predawn courier flight broke the chilly silence. When they'd arrived, with the sun, they could hear the traffic on Interstate 70, a couple of miles away. Although only forty-five miles northwest of the Washington Monument, Frederick was still a rural town—perfectly suited to their needs.

Al-Shiran knew Hassan was impatient. But today, the airplane had to be perfect, so al-Shiran worked slowly and methodically. His walk-around was performed to the occasional clunk or grunt of effort as Feyda worked on the Judah IV. Ahmed, standing by the tail, shifted his stance and spit at the ground. Al-Shiran ignored him.

Suddenly a Chevy pickup came down the little road from town. Al-Shiran motioned Ahmed and Feyda into the cabin and watched the small yellow truck approach.

"It's the line boy, Commander," he said. "As planned. Please stay quiet inside." Al-Shiran waved at the lanky blond youth as he climbed out of his pickup, sipping on a huge cup of coffee from 7-Eleven.

"Yo, J.P.!" said the teenager. "Up early, huh?"

"Damn straight, Ben. Got to fly to live, man!"

The kid waved and went off to start the fuel truck. Al-Shiran stood by the port wing and glanced at the cabin. No one was visible inside.

The truck with the faded Chevron logo ground slowly over to the Navajo from the fuel pumps, where it was kept full and locked. The airport manager controlled the fuel, not Slade, so al-Shiran had been unable to schedule fueling any other way. But the risk was small.

Ben halted the big diesel truck with a squeal of brakes and jumped out, leaving the engine running to provide power for pumping the avgas. Although he was only nineteen, Ben had been the line boy at Frederick for three years; he knew all the airplanes and all the pilots by heart. He was a cheerful kid determined to be a pilot someday, and al-Shiran had found himself drawn into a kind of friendship with him.

Ben attached the static ground wire to the main gear of the Piper, slipped in the big nozzle and started pumping. The pungent aroma of aviation gasoline filled the air.

"What you got this mornin', J.P.? Another run of bearings for Detroit?"

"Nah. Got some people to pick up at DCA. Charter."

Ben grinned at him. "Say, you wouldn't have room for a deadhead, would you?"

"Not this time, kid. Next time, though. I promise."

It was a perennial dialogue. Ben always tried to scam rides with the pilots whose airplanes he serviced.

Al-Shiran signed the credit card receipt and waved as Ben pulled the truck away. Somehow, it had not occurred to him until this very moment that what he was about to do might have some effect on Ben's life; he saw Ben as somehow outside the white man's vicious world of lies. He didn't pursue the thought.

"Is he gone?" hissed Hassan from the cockpit.

"In a moment," said al-Shiran, hoping today wouldn't be the day that Ben had enough time to hang around for the takeoff. He was lucky. As soon as the boy had parked the truck, he ran back to his beat-up Chevy, jumped in and roared off, back toward Frederick. Al-Shiran relaxed slightly. There had been little danger that Ben would prove too inquisitive. But things could not be allowed to go wrong now. Not now.

"THIS IS CRAZY! Look at this mess."

"I'm looking. I look at it every day." Sandy sighed and flipped open her newspaper.

Max pulled Sandy's red Porsche 944 Turbo into the creeping line of cars waiting to edge into the clotted artery of the Beltway. There was none of the semi-calm that pervaded Los Angeles traffic jams on the major freeways; Washington was too frenetic a city for that. Instead of cars smoothly moving at a walking pace, Beltway traffic lurched and halted. Max had been in jams all over the world, but none had the sense of Sisyphean frustration that five minutes in this mé-lange of vehicles with District, Maryland and Virginia plates had. As he fretted and chewed his cheek, checking the clock too frequently, he began to wonder if some of the failures of America's leadership did not somehow derive from the Beltway.

A PROFOUND SENSE of unreality began to overtake al-Shiran as he started the Navajo's engines on the ramp. It was all so normal. Events had proceeded precisely as planned. In the familiar routine of starting the engines, he had often found comfort from what was to follow. In Vietnam, in Iran, in Latin America, he had mastered the art of allowing the banal to create the important. Yet never before had he felt this peculiar dislocation of action with results; he knew that starting the Piper's two 540-cubic-inch turbocharged Lycoming engines would change the world. He *knew* it. And yet the aviator in him was simply…starting the engines.

He looked at where Hassan stood in the phone booth with Ahmed slouching nearby. Hassan could have called on the flight telephone on board, but it used radio, not land lines. Hassan had not told him what the call was about. Only that it had to be made at the moment they were committed, and not earlier. As the engines warmed, Hassan hung up and jogged with Ahmed back through the County Aviation gate to the Navajo. The two men climbed into the airplane up the aft airstairs. Al-Shiran heard the clunk of the door being secured. A second later, Hassan edged through the little passageway between the cockpit and the cabin and squeezed into the copilot's seat.

Hassan shot al-Shiran a sharp look as he allowed his hand to linger on the prop control for the right engine and his eyes to rest on the tachometer.

"Brother al-Shiran. You are all right?"

Hassan spoke English with an accent, but al-Shiran caught the warning tone.

"Yes, Commander. Please fasten your seat harness. We will take off soon."

"How soon?"

"We have a flight plan calling for wheels-up at nine past the hour. In seven minutes."

Hassan checked the pad he withdrew from his gear bag. He nodded as he found the entry. The noise of the propellers and engine made discussion difficult without headphones, so Hassan plugged his in. Al-Shiran heard the click of his mike jack.

"How do you read me? Al-Shiran? Ahmed? Feyda?"

They each acknowledged, al-Shiran last. He glanced at Hassan.

"Brothers," said Hassan, "I have just spoken with our command. Everything is ready. We are ready.

They are ready. The world sleeps, not knowing what awaits. But we do. And Allah is with us. Let us not fail to do our duty to Him and our cause.''

He spoke in Arabic, but al-Shiran's knowledge was good enough to catch the meaning. He inclined his head at Hassan, who pointed ahead.

Al-Shiran released the brakes and advanced the throttles. The sense of unreality had gone.

STEIN WAS SHAVING when the call came. He cursed as he nicked himself in his hurry to grab the phone.

"Stein," he barked into the receiver, smearing shaving cream on the plastic mouthpiece.

"Chafaz, sir," came Chaim's voice over a long distance line. "Colonel, we do not have a scrambler on this line. But we must warn you."

Stein wiped shaving cream off the receiver. "It can't wait until we get secure communications?"

"No, sir. I don't think so. You remember the call we traced from Amsteg?"

"Yes."

"We placed a monitor on the number. We were unable to get anyone to the actual location, which as you recall is in—"

"Yes, never mind, Chafaz. I remember. Go ahead."

"Our signal intelligence people report a call was made to that number a few moments ago. They sent the tape to us. I just played it."

"And?"

"Colonel, I don't know how much to say on this line—"

"Say what you must."

"In that case, it is our friend from Amsteg, Colonel. He reports to the person at the called number that the plan is going ahead."

"What plan? Did he say?"

"The Love of Allah, he called it."

"And when is it under way?"

"Now, Colonel. He said he is boarding the airplane now."

"Could you trace the call?"

"Only to the U.S.A. Our equipment interface with the Americans, ever since—"

"I know, Chafaz. But you could not localize it?"

"No, Colonel. We know only that the call came from the States."

"How long ago?"

"About ten minutes. I have the time hacks on the printout . . . exactly eleven minutes now. Section One was very good about getting this to us—"

"Thank them later, Captain. You are in the control center?"

"Yes."

"Stay there. Contact General Avrams in London. Tell him we have found the quarry. Tell him where. Tell him to stand by for data from here. You do the same. Activate the crisis staff in the command net— but don't tell any of the Knesset people. Just the PM and Defense. Got it?"

"Yes, Colonel. Do you think—?"

"I think this is it, Chaim. I think all hell is about to break loose. Keep a line clear for me. I may be able to use a secure American line when I get to the Pentagon, but if not, we'll have to hook up through the embassy."

"Do you want me to tell the ambassador?"

"No. Not yet. He knows nothing. Leave it that way. If we have to tell him, I'll do it through Aronson, the attaché. Anything else?"

"No, Colonel. Good luck."

"Shalom, Chaim. We're going to need it."

The line went dead. Stein thought swiftly about how he could shortcut the system to get the key Americans up to speed on what might be about to happen— without compromising his own operation. There was only one slim possibility. Chester.

Still lathered with shaving cream, he punched in Chester's home number. It rang and rang. Finally, a sleepy female voice answered.

"Listen, Katie. This is Mo Stein. I'm—"

"Mo! Good to hear from you. Gee, Mat just left. He—"

"For where, Katie?"

"Um, let's see…the Pentagon, I think. Yes. He had some sort of meeting."

"Katie, it's vital that I get to him as soon as possible. Does he have a car phone?"

"Gosh, we couldn't afford one of *those*."

"Okay, sorry, Katie. Now: do you know where in the Pentagon he's going? And when his appointment is?"

"Nope. Sorry. You know Mat. Doesn't talk about that with me. Or anybody, I imagine."

Stein closed his eyes and thought furiously. "Okay, fine. Look, if he calls for some reason, please tell him I *must* speak to him as soon as possible. This is critical, Katie. I'm going to the Pentagon now, too. Tell him to meet me or call me at the press office, okay?"

"Sure, Mo. Hey, sorry I couldn't—"

"No time now, Katie. Thanks. Bye."

He slammed the phone down. He had checked the wall clock when Chafaz gave him the time el Jazzar had made the call. Four more minutes had slipped by. He had the sense that he was in a race, but did not know where the race began or ended—only *when* it began. And knowing that, knew also that he was already losing it.

CHAPTER FOURTEEN

AL-SHIRAN LEVELED the Navajo at three thousand feet, pulling back the throttles to cruise power. As the two big props changed pitch, the noise level in the cabin dropped considerably. It was a crystal-clear day, and he scanned for air traffic as he lined up on Sugarloaf Mountain, his initial point for the funnel into Washington National Airport.

Hassan reached into his gear bag and withdrew an unmarked medicine vial. He popped the white plastic lid and scooped out a small handful of tiny red capsules. He expertly channeled them into his mouth and swallowed them in a single gulp.

Al-Shiran looked away. He busied himself with setting up the radios so that Hassan could work the special UHF comm transceiver while he worked the VHF radio. He did not allow himself to think about what Hassan might have fed himself. For a few moments he found calm in the engrossing job of flying. Then when they were almost abreast of Sugarloaf's gentle peak, covered now in dense forest with no leaves, he toggled the intercom.

"Commander. We are about to begin. Shall we continue?"

"Yes."

Al-Shiran switched the small toggle on the nav/comm control panel to COMM-1. He checked the frequency displayed on its LED readout, cleared his throat and spoke.

"Washington Approach, Navajo Nine-Six-Niner-Foxtrot is with you at three thousand inbound squawking 0230."

"Roger, Navajo Six-Niner-Fox, radar contact southeast abeam Sugarloaf. Expect River Approach runway one-eight. Maintain present heading." The controller's voice crackled through, revealing the bored cadences of a man who spent his working hours staring at huge green radar screens, for whom al-Shiran's airplane was simply another coded target to be inserted into the maze of air traffic around Washington.

As al-Shiran repeated the controller's instructions, Hassan glanced back into the cabin. Ahmed and Feyda were sitting in the forward-facing seats, across the small center aisle from each other. The Judah IV's aluminum casing was strapped securely onto the floor between the seats, and four thick wires led from it to a small black box at Feyda's feet. A red light glowed on the top of the box. On the seat next to Feyda was a palm-size plastic pistol grip, a single slender wire leading to the box at his feet.

Hassan studied Feyda. He was pale, his untrimmed beard jet-black against his skin. He wore a thin green nylon jacket and blue jeans. Across the aisle, Ahmed played with his Uzi, looking outside. Like Feyda, he was unusually pale and nervous. Hassan toggled the intercom.

"Feyda. The electronics are working properly?"

"Yes, Commander. All functional." He patted the grip. "I am ready."

"Good. Ahmed?"

"Ready also, Commander." But Ahmed's deep voice sounded troubled, despite his expression. Hassan studied both men a moment more, then turned to face forward again, watching the suburbs of Washington emerge from the morning ground haze.

"Commander?"

"Yes, Feyda?" He did not look back.

"It is . . . cold. Can we not have some heat?"

"Yes. I will see to it." He flicked on the cockpit intercom. "The men are cold, Hadj al-Shiran."

"Ah," al-Shiran said. He flipped a switch on the panel. In response, the gasoline-powered heater in the nose of the aircraft instantly activated. Doors opened in small ducts in the nose; one fed the combustion system of the heater with ram air, the other poured cooling air to its shroud. In seconds, warm air poured through ducts in the floor. "Commander...we should not run this heater too long. It uses gasoline. It will upset our endurance calculations a little."

Hassan looked at al-Shiran, and the black man winced as he saw the Jihaddin's large pupils and detached expression.

"No doubt you will ensure this does not become a problem," Hassan said and slowly looked out the cockpit windshield again.

"I—" began al-Shiran and then closed his mouth. He would fly. The rest was up to Hassan el Jazzar. And the honkies on the ground.

EVEN SANDY FINALLY admitted that things were worse than usual on the Beltway. They had not moved more than a hundred yards in twenty minutes. Max tried to practice self-control, and failed.

"Okay. This is nuts. We *cannot* afford to sit here any longer. Maybe there's a monster accident up there, or maybe it's just the final gridlock. Whatever. We have to get to Andrews. Is there any way to do it on surface streets?"

Sandy pulled out a map from the glove compartment. "Well, sure, there is. But it could take—"

"How bad can it be? Jesus, we've been in this sucker for half an hour, going nowhere."

"Okay, relax, Max." She studied the map for a moment. "Got it. We'll get off at the next exit, then—"

"The next exit? Sorry. We're turning this thing around. Now."

Before she could stop him, Max had steered the Porsche out of the left lane onto the shoulder, and had engaged reverse gear. He swung his head and shoulders around, set his mouth and hit the throttle.

Sandy jerked as the car accelerated backward. "Hey, Max! You can't do this! *Hey!*"

"Sorry, Sandy. If I bend it, I'll fix it. But I remember a break in the concrete barrier about a mile back. We're going back there and cut through to the other side."

She, too, craned her neck and watched as dumbfounded drivers saw the Porsche zooming along backward, debris trailing it in a minivortex. Gritting her teeth, she set herself hard against the seat, awaiting the impact. She stole a glance at the speedo. It read zero. But the tachometer showed 4500 rpm.

"Max! This thing—"

"Is just fine. Quiet. Cars work just as well in reverse as they do going forward. You just have to steer a little more care—"

He swerved suddenly where a driver was opening his door to dump coffee on the shoulder. Max whipped the Porsche past an inch from the open door. The coffee was swirled up into the guy's face by the speed of their passage. Sandy watched the man's eyes open wide as the Porsche shot past the line of halted commuters.

Suddenly Max slowed, then hit the brakes. The antilock system pulsed and the car halted as if it had slammed into a wall of sand. He snapped the gearshift forward into first and accelerated into the small opening in the barrier that Sandy had not even noticed. The opening was barely wide enough for the Porsche to fit through, but Max aimed the nose right for the edge, hit the brake with his left foot and the throttle with his right, spun the steering wheel and all at once they were on the other side of the Beltway, accelerating along the outside shoulder and meshing with the speeding traffic. In a moment, they were headed north instead of south.

Sandy let out her breath. Max glanced in the mirror. "Okay. Do we have to go all the way around this ring road, or can we cut through somewhere?"

Sandy collected the map from the floor and spread it on her lap. "You want to stay on asphalt, or go off-road?" she asked acidly.

"Doesn't matter to me. Long as we keep moving."
He grinned.

"Sounds like the story of your life," she muttered.

STEIN WALKED SWIFTLY past the ambling denizens of
the vast complex of linoleum floors and overcrowded
office space that was the Pentagon. At this hour, the
evening watch was coming off, groggy and red-eyed,
and the morning troops—for they were almost all, at
this time, military and not civilian workers—meeting
them with their own red eyes and insufficient-coffee
pallor. None of them paced Stein as he moved past the
guards, waving his pass, up the E-ring connector and
along the ring to the press office.

Few people were in the office. The morning briefings did not begin for another two hours. All the news
from yesterday's service dumps was pinned on various boards, press releases from the seemingly unlimited number of military PR offices filing dozens of
pigeonholes in what was known as the correspon-
dents' wailing wall.

Stein swiftly searched the interconnected offices,
waved to one correspondent he knew and went back
to the corridor. He sighed. The only chance he had
was that Chester might have been going to see the
deputy director of the DIA, who maintained an office in the building. He pulled out a much abused copy
of the locator book and began wading through the tiny
type.

Inside, he felt the clock ticking off the precious seconds.

"OH, NO." Max said it with enough feeling to make Sandy look up from the map. "Not *again*," he groaned.

Ahead, a wave of brake lights announced another Beltway bottleneck. Max slowed the Porsche and finally ground to a halt behind a pickup. He looked at Sandy. "Now what?"

"Now we wait," she said.

"THE WAITING IS OVER," said Hassan. Al-Shiran glanced his way and saw the man's left hand tremble slightly on his notebook. Al-Shiran returned his attention to flying.

"We are almost over the Chain Bridge," the American said.

"I see it," Hassan shot back, tracing the route on the plan, sketched out all those months ago in Qom. "Feyda. You will ready yourself."

"I am ready, Commander," said Feyda.

"Stand by to activate on my command."

Feyda was silent. He picked up the pistol grip and gingerly held it in both hands. Next to him, Ahmed wiped his palms on his trousers.

The Navajo was flying south at two thousand feet over the Potomac River, part of a stream of air traffic that included more than a score of jets and turboprops, all headed for landing at Washington National a few miles downriver. The FAA, responding to the anger of residents along the approaches to National, had decreed that when possible, pilots would use this River Approach, which would keep them over water and not densely populated neighborhoods. The effect was to crowd the airplanes into a traffic jam as annoying and demanding for their pilots and the air traffic controllers as any segment of the Capital Beltway. The task took all of al-Shiran's concentration.

"United four-seven, cleared for the approach, contact tower one-nineteen-one—*break*—Delta six-eight-bravo, slow to 200, thank you, sir—*break*—Eastern eight-eight, sir, you're drifting west, please maintain River centerline—*break*—Navajo six-niner-fox, increase speed to 200 knots for separation—"

Like the other pilots, al-Shiran did not acknowledge the controller's directions; there was no time and no space on the frequency. He shoved the throttles forward and eased the nose down.

"Passing the reservoir," he said on the intercom.

Hassan nodded. He checked the frequency dialed into the UHF transceiver again. There was no way to know for sure whether the special modifications for which he had paid so heavily—and secretly—would work.

"—Eastern eight-eight, contact tower nineteen-one—*break*—Navajo six-niner-fox, increase speed to 210 if able—"

Al-Shiran increased power once again and banked the Piper sharply left, then right to follow the twists in the river. Ahead on the left, pointing like a white needle into the sky, the Washington Monument was clearly visible. And behind it, the dome of the Capitol building glistened whitely in the morning sun.

"MAT!"

Chester turned and saw Stein approaching. He smiled and said something to the two-star general he was addressing and stepped toward Stein.

"Mo. Surprised to see you. How—"

"Mat. Listen. Something has come up. May we talk?"

Chester glanced at the general, now studying a folder held out by his secretary. "Well, it is a little awkward. Tell you what. Just give me five minutes with the general. Sheila? Would you get Colonel Stein some coffee?"

Stein fought the impulse to grab Chester and tell him five minutes might be critical. After all, he told himself as the general and Chester went into the general's office and closed the door, five minutes might not be critical at all. He accepted the coffee and sat on a leather armchair.

MAX WILLED THE digital clock to slow down. It did not. He willed the pickup in front to disappear. It did not. He willed his nerves to calm. They did not.

Sandy scanned through the preset radio stations until she got to the AM-band all-news station, hoping for something about the massive traffic tie-ups. But there was nothing other than the usual weather reports and cheerful announcements that traffic was "heavy" on the Beltway. She sighed and sank back into the leather seat.

"I think we'd better call on your car phone," Max grated.

Sandy looked at the clock. "Not yet. We've still got plenty of time."

"I hope so," Max said.

"NOW," AL-SHIRAN SAID a little uneasily. "*Now*. We are passing the last checkpoint—the Memorial Bridge.

We're less than two miles from touchdown." He cycled the gear back up, advanced the throttles and began a gentle bank to the left.

"Feyda. Arm it. Now!" Hassan barked. He licked his lips and waited for Feyda's response. It came almost instantly.

"Armed and ready. Verified on the detonator box, Commander."

"—Navajo niner-six-foxtrot, say your intentions, sir, we show you deviating from approach path, do not, say again, *do not* overfly prohibited area 56—"

Hassan smiled and toggled to COMM-2 from the intercom. "Attention," he said, watching the little red Transmit indicator flash as he spoke, "National Military Command Center. This is the Islamic Jihad. Over."

The cabin radio speakers crackled, but not with the NMCC response.

"—six-niner-foxtrot, we say again, you are straying toward the White House prohibited zone! You are in danger! You will be shot down unless you immediately turn away—"

The UHF frequency that al-Shiran had worked so hard over drinks to winnow out of Lenteen continued to hiss as if there were no human activity on it. Hassan keyed the mike again.

"I say again: attention NMCC duty officer. This is the Islamic Jihad. You have ten seconds to respond to my call or we will detonate a ten-kiloton nuclear device over your White House. Over."

"—say *again*, Navajo, you are—"

The controller was abruptly cut off by Hassan's frequency cutting in. The noisy static of VHF went dead as the UHF blanked it.

"Ah, this is Colonel Kimball of the United States Army. You are in violation of federal law. You are advised to clear this frequency immediately."

"Colonel Kimball of the U.S. Army, this is a commander of the Islamic Jihad. You will listen to me very carefully. We are now approaching the White House in an airplane containing a nuclear bomb, which we will detonate if you do not immediately abort the White House defensive system and clear all aircraft from our area. Over."

Six miles away in the National Military Command Center, a network of offices and conference rooms deep in the Pentagon that served as the nation's funnel for military crisis management, Colonel Ron Kimball looked at his senior duty officer, General Thomas Luciano. Both men were near the end of their long shift. Around them, each of the support staff paused almost in mid-breath, keenly aware that something very strange was going on. The frequency on which the call was coming in was strictly set aside for federal emergency use, known to very few people. In addition, special signal encoding and decoding devices—supposedly strictly classified—were required to communicate on the frequency. Nothing in their threat books prepared any of the nine people in the control room for how to deal with what they were hearing.

An Air Force senior master sergeant snapped out of the daze first.

"General, I'll check with National and the air defense people if that's okay—?"

"Do it, Dwight. Ron, call them back. Tell them what they want to hear. Stall them while we figure out what the hell is going on. If we've got a real one..." He let the sentence trail off.

"Islamic Jihad. This is the NMCC. We understand your demand. We are checking to verify. Stand by." Kimball clicked off and looked at the senior master sergeant, who was nodding and jotting something down quickly as he spoke into his phone. He slammed it down and wheeled around to face the duty officers.

"Sir, we have verification from National. A Piper Navajo is almost at the prohibited area, and the Stingers are aimed and ready to fire."

"Holy shit," whispered Luciano, sitting down heavily. "Holy *shit*. Why did this happen on *my* watch?" He blinked. "Okay. Ron, talk to them. Tell them we've shut down the Stingers. Dwight, tell the launchers to stand down until further notice. Hanley, get me General Jacobson, and alert the NSC liaison. Tell them we've got a goddamn situation here, and we need the crisis staff in place pronto. Everyone stand by for a possible DefCon upgrade. *Move!*"

They moved. And so did Hadj al-Shiran, taking the Piper Navajo into the forbidden airspace above the nation's capital, imagining as he did so that he could see into the very heart of the gutted ghetto where he had been born.

CHAPTER FIFTEEN

MAX FINALLY EXPLODED. He pounded the steering wheel and swore in two languages that the guy who designed the Beltway was the product of an incestuous marriage. He glared at Sandy, who sat stone-faced through his tirade. When he cooled down, he pointed at her car phone.

"Mind if I call Andrews and tell them we're going to be late?"

"Suit yourself," she said.

He unclipped the Mobira phone and keyed in the long code. The pickup truck ahead lurched forward seven feet. Max didn't even bother to move the Porsche. Behind him, somebody in a Toyota beeped angrily. He ignored the beep and the beeper.

The base operator put him through to Operations. He got the noncom who answered to track down Duane. By the time Horton got to a phone, the pickup truck was five feet farther along. Max grudgingly slipped the 944 into gear and idled forward.

"Duane. This is Max."

"Oh, Mr. Moss. We were wondering—"

"Yeah, well, I'm trapped on the damn Beltway. Did Colonel Howard get there yet?"

"Yes, sir, but he—"

"Can you put him on?"

"No, sir. Colonel Howard and his boys showed up about twenty minutes ago, and we were all having coffee and doughnuts, waiting for you in the ready room, when this captain rushes in and says something to Howard that makes him jump like a scared rabbit. Then he told his guys to forget the demo and get back to the Pentagon ASAP."

"They went back to the Pentagon? Why?"

"He didn't say, but he told me to apologize to you and said that you'd understand when you found out—"

"Damn! Did he say when he'd be back?"

"No. And funny thing, he and his men came in a van but they left in a chopper. You know, a Jolly Green, we used to call them in Nam—"

"Curiouser and curiouser. Okay, Duane. You hold on there. Is the Viper set up?"

"Yeah, the ops and maintenance people have been real good to us. We got the van right out in the middle of the runways, antenna's all set up and everything. Now all we need is the damn Air Force."

"And your vice president. Swell." He glowered into the tailgate of the rusted pickup truck. "Oh, well. I'm going to call Howard's office at the Pentagon. You stick close to a phone, but tell the men to stay ready. We still might be able to go today."

"Yes, sir, Mr. Moss. I'll be right here."

Max hit the flash button and savagely punched in Howard's number at the Pentagon.

"What's wrong?" Sandy had only heard his side of the conversation.

"My space cadets disappeared. Took a helo back to— Hello? Is this the project office for the advanced space systems? What— Hello?" He pushed the button again. "Damn. Must have gotten a wrong number." He redialed more carefully and this time got a recorded message that all circuits were busy.

He looked at Sandy. "Something strange is going on. Why don't you call your office and see if any of your spooks know what it is?" He handed the phone to her. Eyebrows raised, she keyed in her work number and waited. Finally her call was answered.

Max chewed his cheek and fumed while Sandy spoke in low tones to her co-worker. She flashed off and caught his eye.

"You're right. Something *is* going on. But nobody knows what. Mat Chester is in the Pentagon now. I'll try there, at the DIA liaison office."

She had to dial three times to get through. By then the traffic had mysteriously loosened itself, and Max was actually driving again, albeit at ten miles per hour.

"Sheila? Hi, this is Captain Koppel. You haven't seen Colonel Chester this morning, have— Oh. Can I speak to him? Thanks." She covered the mouthpiece. "He's there, with General— Colonel? Morning. We're stuck out on the Beltway, trying to get to Andrews for the demonstration of the Viper—you know, Moss's RPV—and we just got the screwiest message about the project officers being called back via helo— What?" She glanced at Max. "Well, sure, I guess. We could. Yeah. If you think— Certainly. We'll be there soon. We're not far. Out." She hung up the phone and looked oddly at Max.

"Well?" He shifted into second with gusto and waited for her response. She sat still, hands folded in her lap, staring out the windshield.

"*Well?* What'd he say?"

"Max...he said they're about to raise the DefCon state. And that I should get back to the Pentagon without delay."

Max looked around the five lanes of commuters. They all wore the same irritated expressions. For them, it was business as usual. He looked at her. "He said that on an open and unsecure radio telephone line? Is he joking?"

"Mat jokes sometimes. But not like that. This is serious, Max. I have to get back. Please...that exit ahead, the Little River Turnpike—take it. I can get us to the Pentagon in about ten minutes that way."

The gravity in her voice stopped him from complaining. He mulled it over for about five seconds, then pursed his lips.

"Okay," he said, "hang on." And then he downshifted and cut across three lanes of traffic to the exit, hitting the potholed concrete off ramp at about eighty miles per hour.

"COLONEL KIMBALL, THIS IS the Islamic Jihad. You are ready to listen?"

"Ah, Commander, this is General Luciano, speaking on behalf of the Joint Chiefs of Staff. As you can see, we've advised the National tower to do as you ask, and rerouted all air traffic from your vicinity. In addition, the air defenses of the prohibited zone are on hold. We're ready to listen to what you have to say."

Hassan ignored al-Shiran, who continued to fly in a lazy orbit at one thousand feet along the Mall, turning at the Lincoln Memorial and behind the Capitol, then making a bulging left turn to the White House. He could see security people on the ground tracking him with various antennas and optical scanners. He felt the odd sense of detachment he knew so well from Nam, when the gooks would hose him with 23 mm and 37 mm AAA, all in vain. He hadn't taken a serious hit then, and he wouldn't now. He flicked his gaze from point to point ceaselessly, not really hearing Hassan, not really even aware of how he was flying the airplane.

Hassan shuffled his notes and keyed his mike.

"Excellent. Let me tell you, General, how it stands now, so you will not think we are lying to you. Ten months ago we liberated a nuclear bomb from the secret Zionist arsenal at Har Mughara. That bomb is on this airplane, wired so that if we choose to, we can detonate it any number of ways. Do you understand?"

"So far, I've got that you claim to have stolen an Israeli nuke—which they claim they don't have, by the way—and claim to have it in that light plane. That correct?"

Hassan's eyes narrowed. He licked his lips. "General. I detect a skeptical tone in your voice. This is not good. For you or for anyone else. We are prepared to prove to you how wrong you are if you think that we Jihaddin are not willing to blow up your capital city. Do you wish this?"

"No, no. Go ahead."

"Our situation is simple. We have a nuclear bomb—the Judah IV. By the way, General, in case your Zionist friends wish to dispute the point, ask them about that name. We will detonate this bomb if we are molested in any way while we fly over the capital—*in any way, General!*—and we will detonate it by flying our airplane into your White House when our fuel is exhausted if our demands have not been met by that time. Do you understand?"

"Roger. You want us to meet your demands by the time your fuel runs out. How long is that?"

"About six hours, General. A long time to do some simple things to correct the many evils you have committed."

"Six hours. Understood. What are your demands?"

"Very small for such a large nation as yours. First, you will cause to be air-shipped to Libya ten of your Pershing II intermediate-range nuclear missiles, complete with support vehicles, spares, launchers and warheads. Second, you will insist that the Zionists immediately release Abu Khaddim and all those imprisoned with him. Third, after our people have verified you have done this, you will provide a Lockheed C-130 for our use at Andrews Air Force Base, to which we will transfer ourselves and the Judah IV—which will, I assure you, still be armed. Do you understand these?"

Silence greeted his question. He waited for a few moments, then said, "General, I asked you a question. Do you understand?"

"Roger. We understand. Now, you must know I am not empowered to negotiate with you. Even if I wanted to." The distaste was obvious in his voice.

"General. We know your table of organization. We know whom you will have to contact, what committees of emergency action you will have to form, the alternate scenarios for defeating us without giving us what we want . . . we know all this. That is why we are being more generous to you than you have ever been to us: we are giving you six hours to proceed with your foolish maneuverings. We are prepared to wait. We are the Jihad."

Hassan released the mike switch with a flourish and looked over at al-Shiran, his eyes wild, his lips edged with spittle.

The radio was silent for a moment more. Then it hissed to life. "Understood," said General Luciano.

CHAPTER SIXTEEN

SOMEHOW, THE MEDIA got hold of the story. Maybe it was a panicked NMCC staffer calling his wife, telling her to get out of town with the baby. Maybe it was someone with equipment he wasn't supposed to have monitoring the frequency used between the Jihaddin and the Pentagon. Or maybe the leak came when the executive branch got involved or when the National Security Council emergency action staff was activated. At any of these junctures, leaks were possible. And one happened.

The first pathway of the leak was to the local television news. Somebody tipped off somebody else that something extraordinary was going on at the Pentagon. The newsman who called on the tip got a harried press relations officer working for the secretary of defense's office—and a flat "no comment." But Washington insiders know how to circumvent the bureaucracy; the next four calls the newsman made began to clarify the picture for him, so he took a chance and called the tower at National Airport. Nobody had thought to tell the FAA people that they should not verify that an "incident" was in progress involving an airplane overflying the Mall. The news-

man could see the Mall from his office, and with a pair
of borrowed binoculars, he saw the airplane itself.

That was enough to break into the morning talk
shows with a news flash—and the news flash, as de-
void of detail and almost innocuous as it was, activated the powerful competitive instincts of the
Washington media. All over the area, news directors
in television, radio and print went into high gear to dig
out the story. From then on, it had a momentum of its
own, as each station monitored the others, one-upping
the last tidbit. Within half an hour, the word had
spread on the airwaves of a dozen radio and TV stations that Washington was under a nuclear threat—
even though no official announcement had been
made.

The dissolution of order was widespread and immediate. The District and the two adjoining states had
long-standing and frequently updated disaster management plans, coordinated with equally long-
standing Federal Emergency Management Agency
plans, but they all suffered from the realpolitik of the
region. No one ever took the nuclear-disaster scenarios seriously enough to commit significant assets to the
programs. This failure included key people to run the
centers, which were in fact functional—if only they
were staffed.

They were not. The absence of coherent government response after the sensational leaks fueled confusion. To some extent this, too, was a result of
Hillbilly One's freezing of the governmental arteries
of security, but it mostly derived from the President
and his key staff's being in Europe, leaving only
backup players in command at the scene. The vice

president was informed of the crisis while brushing his
teeth in the official VP's mansion at the Naval Ob-
servatory, but his effectiveness was hampered by a
surprising squabble among the NSC and NMCC and
JCS staffs about precedence in establishing a crisis
management center. While these internal affairs were
being furiously fought out, the engine of rumor was
lit off and gathered so much momentum that it could
not easily be stopped.

It did not help matters that the situation began before any of the apparatchiks who normally would have
issued soothing nostrums to the press hounds had actually gotten to work. There were duty officers in all
the key government agencies, but they were uni-
formly at the end of their duty cycles, tired, dispirited
by their own lack of information and generally unable to dispel the growing panic. The "first team"
players were either in Europe with the President or
trying to get through the increasingly jammed streets
to their work.

But some were not. Alerted by their own staffs or
the station, these people simply bugged out, emulat-
ing the highly trained and supposedly dedicated troops
of a Strategic Air Command base who, during a genuine nuclear emergency in the mid-sixties, dropped all
pretense at handling the emergency as the plan dic-
tated, and jumped in the cars, jammed the roads and
phone lines and evacuated the base. Studies had been
commissioned to determine ways to halt the exodus of
key people in such situations in the future, and supposedly astute changes had been made in the way operations were arranged throughout the governmental
agencies involved in emergency management. To no

avail. When the threat seemed real enough, immediate enough and the threat involved not just the workers but their families, the bug-out impulse was too strong for many to resist.

Panic spread not by official action or inaction, but in spite of it. And it spread too quickly to be contained. Fed on a steady diet of fear of the bomb for half a century, the citizens of the Washington area needed no additional stimulus to lose their cohesion when the threat of annihilation seemed real. Black, white, Hispanic, Oriental—the social fabric of the area began to unravel as the word flashed from mouth to mouth. Traffic immediately went to impossible and impassable on every road leading outward from the city and suburbs. Accidents happened, desperate people came to blows, and soon all sense of order was lost.

It never required much stimulus to set the ghettos ablaze at any time, even on a chilly November morning. Used to confronting death on a daily basis, the black motorcycle gangs soon coalesced and began systematically indulging themselves. Rival gangs clashed, fighting first over looting the stores. Policemen were killed, and killed looters in retaliation. The cops on the beat were soon swamped by the tidal wave of terrified citizens, left unable to cope with the professional leeches trailing in their wake, looting and raping and burning.

Emergency action quickly became impossible, but local fire stations, hospitals, police and National Guard units began to rally anyway, seeking order in the chaos. It was too late.

The six hours given by the Jihaddin as their deadline came and went as the city below their airplane went into paralysis. The emergency action teams had decided on a strategy midway between placating the terrorists and making some sort of assault on their airplane. It seemed inconceivable that they could be held hostage by a few men in a small airplane with a bomb the Israelis had only just admitted they had built, stored and then lost. More than a few of the Washington movers and shakers simply did not believe the Jihaddin could do what they claimed, although a sophisticated nuclear "sniffer" used by a joint FEMA/DoE team verified that there was nuclear material on board the airplane.

The urge to inaction, to stalling, to "cutting a deal," finally used too much time. The chairman of the Joint Chiefs of Staff counseled caution, but the President, conferencing with the emergency action team in the NMCC, decided that the two battalions of Special Operations Command troops stationed permanently at the Marine base in Quantico, Virginia, be readied for some sort of action—although what the action might be, nobody knew. Air Force fighters from Langley, Virginia were scrambled to ready status, armed and "cocked," waiting only the go order to blow the little Piper twin out of the sky.

Yet the massed might of the military was patently useless against the threat; if the Jihaddin were to be believed, they would detonate the bomb on any provocation. No one doubted the willingness of the Islamic madmen to die for their cause, but few actually believed the terrorists would use the bomb. Most thought the operation was simply another high-stakes publicity stunt by the string-pullers in Iran. Thus, hours were wasted while supposedly secure lines of communication to the ayatollahs were used to attempt to halt the operation at what the power brokers in Washington believed was its source—the holy city of Qom. Men trained to believe that everything is negotiable, that nothing is what it seems, and that anyone—even a mullah—has his price, will not soon admit that a threat like the one droning endlessly in racetrack orbits over the Mall was real.

But it was real. And as the minutes ticked by, as the wise men argued and schemed and contacted reliable sources and wriggled in the trap, nothing actually happened. The mullahs ignored them, refusing even to engage in a dialogue. The cocked weaponry remained cocked, useless. As the six hours of fuel time slowly drained away, as the clever psychological tricks failed to produce any results in "talking down" the Jihaddin, the wise men asked for more time, claiming difficulties with gathering the necessary material for the shipment of the Pershings, claiming difficulties with Israel over the release of the prisoners, claiming difficulties with the C-130 the Jihaddin wanted at Andrews. The tactic of the grind-down had always worked before.

It did not work this time. As the last of the Piper's fuel was fed to its engines, Hassan el Jazzar did not do as he had threatened and dive the airplane into the White House. Enraged, he decided to use the bomb to make the dirtiest possible explosion: a low-altitude airburst.

The ten-kiloton bomb detonated at 1800 feet almost directly over the Capitol building. The first overpressure wave, which produced shock pressures as high as ten psi, flattened every structure within a one-mile radius, including the so-called "hardened" sites touted as bombproof. People within this zone were incinerated by the heat, which, as it flowed outward and upward from the explosion, "canalized" down the city streets of Washington and the encircling communities. This had the effect of raising the temperatures of the air being driven through the "canals" until fire storm conditions were reached.

The fire storm erupted almost as soon as the overpressure wave passed through the two-mile mark, a few seconds after detonation. At three miles from the airburst, the overpressure had dropped to four psi, which was enough to knock down frame structures and destroy the less well-reinforced concrete buildings. People in this zone died quickly from the pressure wave or from the debris driven through them by the wave or from the heat.

Thirty seconds after the airburst, secondary atmospheric effects began to loft radioactive debris into the swelling cloud. The temperature difference between the various shell layers of the fallout cloud "shaft" and the surrounding air contributed to the violence of air-mass movement, which fed the fire storm. As the pressure wave propagated and to some extent dissipated, the lethality of the airburst actually intensified with the continuing canalization of the superheated air and the accelerative effects such channeling produced. Fifty seconds after detonation, the pressure wave had dissipated, but was still killing, and the fire storm was rapidly accelerating behind the pressure wave.

One minute after the airburst, more than one hundred thousand people had died, the fire storm was still in its formative stage, and the millions of cubic yards of radioactive debris hurled skyward by the intense convective forces unleashed by the detonation were only beginning to spread. The most damaging radiation had been released by the blast itself—the Judah IV was a "dirty" bomb, deliberately designed to kill by direct irradiation as much as by blast effect—and had already doomed one million more people to death within twenty-four hours.

At SAC's Iron Mountain command center, a satellite view of the explosion showed in startling detail how the blast effects were magnified by the airburst's height and location. The same satellite view also had been available to the National Military Command Center in the Pentagon, but the NMCC had ceased to exist only seconds after the airburst. At Iron Mountain, stunned SAC officers watched in horror as the zone of death expanded, shown in ruthless detail by the real-time satellite link. The angry white-yellow-red of the fireball slowly dimmed, but it was replaced by the roiling crimson of the ground fire storm spreading out from what had been Washington.

The picture on the screen froze. The fire storm halted before it got to Baltimore.

Silence pervaded the darkened room. It seemed no one dared breathe.

Finally, an Air Force general spoke. "Very... effective, Mr. Johnson. I don't think I've ever seen quite such a, ah, *succinct* briefing."

Next to him, an admiral sat upright and pulled his tunic straight. "Roger that, Mr. Johnson. We'd heard about the capabilities of the briefing system that your people and the Cray folks had put together, but until this morning, I don't think we fully realized its power."

Johnson switched off the large-screen video monitor sitting at the end of the table. "We were scheduled to brief the JCS in a couple of weeks. We'd already demonstrated the system to the NSC and the President and his staff. But we were ready when the variables were programmed. And I must say the variables were, ah, challenging. None of our models combined a tactical weapon of this yield with an airburst detonation and, ah, this location." He paused. "Still, despite the uncertainties, we're confident the NM-2 profile is reasonably accurate. It's taken four years to program for baseline scenarios, and you know how much staff and time it takes to keep it current. But there are times, we feel—and the President agrees, which is why, I gather, he wanted this simulation run—that it is the only real tool for examining options."

General Jacobson, at the head of the table as befitted his status as chairman of the Joint Chiefs, remained silent. He looked at the clock on the wall behind the video monitor.

"Yes. It was impressive, sir. But as was so clearly shown by your simulation of the scenario we asked you to input, our time is running out. Without being offensive, Mr. Johnson, I wonder if you'd leave us now—with our thanks—and allow us somehow to avert the very situation your computer so, ah, well portrayed."

Johnson snapped closed his briefcase and stood up. "Of course, General. I'll leave the NM-2 material here, if you don't mind, in the interests of speed—"

"Certainly. Thank you. Captain Anderson will escort you out." Anderson, sitting along one wall with the other staff, jumped to his feet and walked with Johnson to the door. The thick, soundproofed, snoop-proof door shut again and Jacobson looked around at the other service chiefs and their key aides.

"Well. In case any of us need reminding, that's what the stakes are. There's really only one question the President wants us to address, gentlemen. And that is, what can we do about it?"

MOSS SLID THE PORSCHE to a halt outside the old River entrance to the Pentagon. A burly MP, armed to the teeth, jumped out and held up a hand. When he saw Sandy, he snapped to attention and threw her a salute. As she scrambled out of the car, he said, "Beg pardon, ma'am, but this area is sectioned off for now—"

"I know, Sergeant," Sandy replied, returning his salute. She fished out her all-points Pentagon pass. The guard acknowledged it, carefully checking her photo with her face. "You may pass, Captain. But the gentleman—"

Max got out and showed his contractor pass to the guard. He looked dubious. "I dunno, sir," he said. "I got no orders to allow any nongovernmental civilians through."

Max looked across the car to Sandy. She pursed her lips, then said to the guard, "Sarge. Stand by one, will you? We'll get Mr. Moss authorization to enter."

The guard looked uneasy, but there was no other incoming traffic, so he stood by while Max and Sandy got back in the Porsche.

Sandy already had the car phone in her hand. She dialed quickly.

"Sheila? Captain Koppel. I'm at the River entrance. Look. Mr. Moss from Moss Electronics is here. He needs to get in to see his project officer. I figure Colonel Chester can—what? Oh. Thanks, Sheila." She clicked off the phone.

"What?"

"Sheila's going to have Mat call security. They'll notify him to let you in."

Max looked back at the guard, who lifted the small microphone clipped to his overcoat to his mouth, spoke briefly, then stepped to the car on Sandy's side.

"Okay, Captain. They just called me. Mr. Moss can proceed, but he's to check in with the security DO when you get inside."

"Never changes," Max muttered as they swung the Porsche through the gate and started looking for a parking place. Finally they found one in Sandy's DIA liaison zone, almost a quarter mile from the pedestrian entrance.

They hurried across the windy parking lot, saying little. At the door, another MP—not the usual rent-a-cop—again scrutinized their credentials and passed them through, again directing Max to the main security officer. He turned out to be a harried young major seated at what was usually the main information booth on the mezzanine level of the Pentagon's old arcade floor. He verified Max's ID, then issued him yet another temporary pass and cautioned that under "current conditions" he would have to be escorted by a uniformed officer at all times. Sandy agreed to do the job, biting back a tiny smile.

The corridors were almost empty. Those few people who were in them hurried with a distracted look that slightly unnerved Max; he had seen the look before, in Germany when things were really going to hell fast.

"What," he said quietly to Sandy as they neared the DIA liaison office, "is going on?"

Sandy was about to reply when they saw Mat Chester emerge from the general's office with Mo Stein. Her answer died on her lips when she saw the look on both men's faces.

CHAPTER SEVENTEEN

THE TENSION, INEVITABLY, ebbed, but the work load for al-Shiran did not. Flying the Navajo at the most economical airspeed for the low height was physically and mentally demanding. The twin wanted to be taken high and given its head, to cruise at 250 knots or better; yet here he was with it at two thousand feet in a tight racetrack pattern, keeping it below 120 knots, in the flight regime twin-engine pilots dreaded; low and slow.

Hassan seemed not to notice the passage of time. He seemed lost in a reverie of some kind, occasionally trading sharp words with the NMCC staff, who continued their pathetic and ill-disguised attempts to talk them down, as though Hassan were a desperate bank robber holding a teller hostage.

Ahmed and Feyda said little, save to discuss the small things as the flight wore on. Food, primarily, occupied Ahmed's thoughts, and an hour and a half after taking off, he was rooting around in the supplies bag for fruit. Feyda passed the pistol grip from hand to hand continually, growing less easy with it and the bomb it would detonate. Whether it would actually detonate the bomb or not he did not really know. He had simply been handed the stolen Israeli documentation along with a scribbled Farsi translation and a hastily drawn wiring diagram—presumably from the technical people in Tehran—and told to fabricate the required device for detonation. He was almost finished before they told him he would actually be required to go with the bomb and detonate it himself if necessary.

His dedication to the Jihad was keen, but that final piece of direction had shaken him. Sensing his mood, perhaps, the Revolutionary Guards had taken his wife and new son into their care. He understood the message clearly, and his outward fervor increased dramatically.

For Feyda and Ahmed, the endless series of left turns began to produce a strange destabilizing effect, almost hypnotizing and nauseating at the same time. Their ceaseless scanning of the ground and sky—ordered sternly by Hassan—in search of hostile aircraft or unusual ground activity, began inevitably to flag.

THE MEETING COULD have been awkward, but the palpable tension that electrified the entire Pentagon carried away the moment of awkwardness. Chester and Stein halted as Max and Sandy approached. Chester handled the introductions swiftly, and Sandy immediately asked what was happening.

Chester looked pained; Sandy realized that Max—and maybe Stein—were technically outsiders. So did Max.

"Hey," he said. "If you need privacy to talk, Colonel, no sweat. I've got to find my SPO people anyway and see if we can reschedule—"

"I wouldn't hold my breath," Chester said. "Chances are your people are caught up in the same thing that we are." He hesitated. "Oh, shit. Look, let's go into the conference room and I'll give you a quick flash on what's going down. Mo? You already know, but if you want—"

Stein nodded and they hurried to a small adjacent conference room. The long wooden table was scarred by cigarette burns and cup rings, and four cups with cold coffee still stood around the table, along with pads and pencils in disarray. Last night's detritus had not yet been cleaned up.

Chester shut the door and quickly summarized the situation. "At least," he closed, "that's as much as I was told by the general, and he was at the first NMCC emergency staff meeting. He's acting as DIA lead, so he ought to know. Questions?"

Max and Sandy took it differently. Sandy sat upright, as if at attention, making notes furiously on the pad. Max slouched against the back of his chair, legs outstretched. Both were silent.

"Max," Chester said, "although nobody will probably give a damn, and although you've been in the system until just recently, keep in mind that this is still classified." Max nodded, a tiny smile on his face. Chester grimaced. "Yeah, I know, but I had to say it anyway."

"Anybody got any ideas?" Max asked laconically.

"Not that you'd talk about. Snake eaters immediately tried to think up ways to grapple with them, fighter jocks immediately wanted to splash them, AAA guys wanted to blow them out of the sky and the feather merchants wanted to talk to them. Usual stuff."

Max sat a little straighter. "Anybody find out anything about the terrorists?"

Mo interrupted Chester. "I was able to help there. The man with the trigger is Hassan el Jazzar. He probably has a couple of his people from Iran and Syria with him."

"And the bomb?"

"Judah IV. We still claim we don't have any nukes, but . . ." Stein shrugged eloquently.

"Yeah, but what I mean is, can they set it off that easily? They told us in nuke school that you don't just light a match on these sweeties. You need a lot of gadgets just to pop it."

Stein looked uncomfortable for a moment. "They were well informed when they broke into our arsenal. They took not only the bomb, but the vital accessories and documentation, too. And . . . this particular weapon is designed to be . . . flexible."

"Sort of like the backpack nukes we use, but with a bigger bang. Much bigger," added Chester.

"Sir? Is there any chance they'll get what they want?"

Chester spread his hands on the table. "Right now, the betting in the crisis center is that they'll have to. Jacobson is in contact with the President and the VP is on his way here to take over the crisis team. Last I heard, nobody had any better ideas. It's really up to the President and Israelis. They've run the military options up one side and down the other, and everybody's still buffaloed."

"Seems crazy," Max said, doodling on the note-pad. "I mean, here's this dinky little Piper twin and we can't do *anything*. We can blow the world up three times over, but we can't stop a couple of guys with a bomb threat?" He paused. "I suppose nobody's se-riously considered just letting them run out of gas and try to pop the nuke. It might not go off."

Chester ran a hand over his hair. "Get serious. Yeah, of course they thought of it. Hell, at first everybody thought it was just an empty threat. But then Mo here, with his ambassador's consent, filled us in. CIA already knew something had gone down at Har Mughara, but the Mossad's pretty tough to pry information out of, and we didn't know about the bomb." Stein looked away from Chester. Max caught the sense of something prickly unsaid between them, a flow of angry electrons that under other circum-stances might have erupted in something ugly. It passed.

"How about the pilot? Who's flying the thing? And how did they get the Jihaddin and the bomb here in the first place?" Sandy asked.

Chester pulled out a paper from the folder he car-ried. "We got a make on the plane and the pilot fast from the FAA, using its registration number. Pilot's an ex-Army flier named Jones, Jefferson Paul. Re-tired as a chief warrant officer. Combat time in Nam, Iran, Nicaragua, the works. Lots of decorations, lots of covert work, good fitness reports. Retired a few years back. Had a job as a flight instructor in Fred-erick—that's up the road a piece, Mo, in Maryland—and the word we got was that he'd checked out the

airplane yesterday for a charter." He scrutinized his
notes, then added, "Oh, yeah. He's black."

"They got him at gunpoint?" Max leaned back
again.

"No, not that we can tell. CIA guys erected an optical scanner in the Washington Monument and we've
got good photos, computer enhanced, that make it
look pretty clear he's not being threatened. At least
not directly. FBI ran a make and found out they're not
holding his family or anything, because he hasn't got
any family. Psywar types wanted to work on him, but
nobody could figure out how to get around el Jazzar,
who's the one doing the talking."

"And *he*'s not vulnerable to persuasion." Max
made it more a statement than a question.

"No. He is definitely not one to be persuaded,"
Stein said.

Silence settled on the table. The event taking place
in the skies over Washington was too big to digest
quickly, too big to fully understand. Even in the rar-
efied atmosphere of the Pentagon, Max was having
trouble connecting with it. A few moments ago, it
seemed, he was struggling with traffic on the Beltway.
The dislocation of realities was too severe.

"Any thought of trying an evacuation? If they've
given us six hours," Sandy said, "maybe we could get
everybody out of town."

Chester looked down. It was as if he were embarrassed. "That was the first thing the crisis staff asked
the President when they got through to him. And he
wanted to do it. But the FEMA people claimed it
couldn't be done. They'd done a quick check and
found that the systems they thought were in place to

make it happen were just camouflage. A lot of corruption had screwed the pooch. They said that if he tried to evacuate, there'd be a bigger disaster than the bomb would create.''

"That's crazy, Colonel," Max said. "On one hand you've got thousands, maybe millions of people blown away, radioactive shit spread over the whole damn country, the government paralyzed by the loss of everything in D.C.—and on the other side, all you've got is some traffic jams. Which you people here have all the time anyway. What's the problem?''

"Panic's the problem, Moss. If we let just one word of this out—just the *hint* that that airplane people can see over their heads is doing what it's doing—the guys who know at FEMA say that we'd have chaos that would make those Hollywood disaster movies look like kid stuff. So they convinced the President we had to try to keep this one in-house and quiet.''

Max carefully placed his pencil on the notepad, channeling his irritation into the precision with which he aligned the pencil and the edge of the pad. "I don't agree. I'm not a guy in the know—whoever that might be in a situation like this—but I think letting this go down without telling people is pure chicken shit. I think you owe it to everybody out there to blow the whistle and let them take their chances running.''

Max knew as soon as he'd said it that he'd gone too far, that his mouth had engaged itself yet again without consulting his brain. Chester paled visibly, then reddened as Max spoke. Max was aware, as he glared at Chester, that Sandy was in distress, too. Stein looked away.

"You know," Chester said slowly and carefully, as if barely restraining himself, "a lot of guys would take what you just said all wrong, Moss. A lot of guys would just take your goddamn teeth and shove 'em down your ass for you. But I'm not one of those guys. I'm one of the few guys in this building who knows what you've been through, knows how you've done your bit for Uncle . . . so I'm not going to take it personally. But I *am* glad—real glad—that we in the network decided we don't need your services. Because you're still not a team player, that much is obvious." He paused and carefully rearranged his folder.

"Some of us might agree with you about what you said, no matter how tactlessly you said it. But you don't have the right to know that anymore, mister, because you checked out. You hung it up back at Peters. You're on the outside now. So you better get this straight: for the duration of this emergency, you're in quarantine here in the Pentagon. You now know too much, and with your attitude—well, I was wrong to tell you anything, I know that now, but I'm sure not gonna fuck the monkey by letting you out."

Max started to stand up and speak. Chester beat him to it, shooting his chair backward and meeting him, eyeball to eyeball across the table. "Captain Koppel," he grated, "you are ordered—*ordered*, Captain—to ensure this civilian does not contact anyone outside the Pentagon and does not leave until I say he can. Have you got that?"

Sandy stood up, too, obviously distressed. "Yes, sir," she said.

"Hold it, Chester," Max began. "This isn't legal—"

Chester collected his folders and turned to Max, now standing only inches away. His eyes were narrow and red, nostrils flaming.

"Mr. Moss, you better shut up, or I'll show you how legal this is. When I want your advice again, you can rest easy on this: I'll damn well *ask* for it."

Then he jerked open the door and stalked down the hall, his heel taps slapping on the old linoleum like the angry rapping of a snare drum urging troops to battle.

THEY ATE IN SILENCE and near-solitude. The Pentagon cafeteria was usually full of doughnut grabbers and break takers, but the nonessential civilians had been sent home with the terse explanation that an alert was in progress, and the remaining military and essential civilian people were working under what boiled down to wartime conditions. Rumors flew in every office, but the building was effectively sealed, both physically and electronically.

One effect was to depopulate the usual centers of hanging out. The tightened regime kept the doughnut grabbers in their workplaces, wondering what was going on and not gossiping in the cafeteria.

Max bit down on another piece of jelly-filled pastry. Sandy watched him over the rim of her coffee cup. The faint tinkling and clatter of the cafeteria kitchen echoed strangely through the large, almost deserted room.

"Hey," she said at last. Max hadn't spoken in more than monosyllables since they'd agreed to cool off with some breakfast.

He chewed slowly and looked at her. His color had returned, she saw, his green eyes no longer blazing.

"He's under a lot of pressure. He didn't mean it the way it came out."

Max continued chewing.

"Besides, you deserved it. You acted as if you were his boss or something."

Max wiped the sticky crumbs from his face with the paper napkin, and dusted some off his tie and suit. He drank some orange juice from the plastic container.

"I know. But it seems so... unnecessary."

She frowned. "What do you mean?"

"It's typical of these guys—" he waved his hand to encompass the Pentagon, or Washington, or them both "—that they can't just tell the truth and let the people act on it. They think they know it all."

"In this case, they do, don't you think?"

"Nope."

His attitude began to annoy Sandy. She felt as though he were indicting her along with "those guys." "Oh? What don't they know that you do, Mr. Terrorist Expert?"

"I'm not a terrorist expert. But I think I know a way to complicate the problem for the guys in the Piper."

"Sure."

Max picked up another bear claw pastry and studied it. He bit into it and looked away from Sandy.

"Okay. So what's your plan?"

He finished off the sticky chunk and lifted an eyebrow at her. "Is this official?"

"Come on, Max. Quit being an asshole. What's your plan?"

He swallowed the last of his orange juice and carefully cleared away his paper plate and plastic utensils. He smoothed out his napkin and began drawing. She watched, trying to understand the upside-down drawings. He worked for a long time, first using all his napkin space, then plucking hers away from her. When he finished, he handed the sketches and attendant notes across the table to her, sat back in his chair and drank his coffee.

Sandy laid out the napkins in their numbered order and studied them. At one point she frowned, then said, "What's this word?" He glanced at it and said, "Telescoping." She nodded and continued to pore over the napkins. She halted often to purse her lips or take a swig of coffee. Max ignored her, rocking back in the flimsy chair and staring off into the cafeteria's fluorescent space, hands folded on his belly.

Sandy at last sat up. She took out a nail file from her black leather purse and began trimming one of her nails, giving it intense attention.

"Do you really think it would work?" she asked, not looking at Max.

"Depends on the heating system in the Piper. If it sucks outside air, I *think* this would work. I'm not sure. But it seems right to me. Seemed right when I thought of it, back in the conference room."

She blew the nail dust off her finger. "Why didn't you tell Mat Chester?"

He rocked forward and looked at her. "You heard him, kid. 'Speak when spoken to' or words to that effect. Screw them. This place is probably better off as a crater anyway."

"You don't believe that, Max."

"No, I don't. But one thing I've learned in lo these many years of government service is that there's no percentage in being a crusader."

She put her nail file away and snapped her bag shut. "Maybe not. But there's certainly no percentage in being dead. So here's what we're going to do. You are going to swallow your goddamn male pride and go back to Chester with me and explain all this to him. You're going to do this not only because it's your duty, but because I want you to. If that still means anything to you."

It was probably not necessary, she thought, to add the last bit of blackmail. Max's sense of duty was far too strong to let him spend too much time sulking. But she had her needs, too. And she was scared, badly scared, by the sense she had picked up from Chester that things were way out of control.

CHESTER LOOKED UP from the number-three napkin with a strange look in his eye as Max finished speaking. "You sure?"

"No. Like I told Sandy. It depends on a lot of things."

"I'd have to check with—"

"Aerodynamics types, chemical warfare people, RPV specialists—if you can find any around here— and probably Air Force jocks, too. And the Piper people, if you can be circumspect enough about what you ask them and still get what you want to know."

Chester glanced at Sandy. "Does this sound crazy to you?"

"Very crazy, Colonel. But then, this whole thing is pretty crazy."

"Assuming we could verify that this has a chance. Assuming all other efforts fail and we try it. How much time would your people need to get ready?"

"Depends on how fast the special hardware can be fabricated, and that's something only Duane Horton would know. Also, we'd have to have access to the canister pretty damn fast so we'd be able to run the center of gravity problems through the computer."

"And you could do it? Yourself?"

"Nobody else is qualified."

"You'd be willing to do this, even though you'd be at the strip yourself? And everyone else evacuated?"

Max shrugged. "Sure. What the hell. I'm not a team player, Colonel. Remember?"

Chester reddened. "Okay, so I let my mouth write a check my butt has to cash. I'm sorry about that, Moss."

Max said nothing while Chester looked back down at the napkins spread out on the conference room table.

"If this were normal times, I'd say my career would be riding on this nutball idea. But nobody's career means shit right now. Max, I'm taking this to Jacobson. You stay put with Sandy." He gathered the napkins and stuffed them in his red folder.

Halfway to the door, he turned and stuck out his hand. "Thanks. Even if they laugh me out of the place, thanks. I was wrong."

Max shook his hand. "So was I. Forget it."

Chester spun and hurried out into the corridor.

Max sat down again and unbuttoned his tie. He sighed. "Same old shit, in uniform or out. Hurry up and wait."

Sandy smiled thinly. But she found it less and less easy to joke about what hung over them all.

CHAPTER EIGHTEEN

DAVID BAR-LEV SUCCEEDED admirably, he thought, at controlling his expression when Colonel Weizmann finally got through his tedious background data and explained to them what was happening in Washington. He allowed surprise to register, partly because he really was surprised; he had thought they would try something long before this. The pattern of PLO raids and Israeli counterraids had not changed at all since his secret meetings with Daud Qidal. Nor had the Jihad shown any slackening of its not-so-secret war against the PLO leadership, which occasionally spilled over into armed clashes in Lebanon and Syria.

As time had passed, Bar-Lev had come to think something had gone awry with Qidal; perhaps, he had thought, the dignified old professor had somehow failed to neutralize the Jihaddin, somehow failed to blackmail them to his cause, at least for this operation. The months had sped by and nothing more than an occasional rumor had surfaced about the Judah IV, neither Stein nor Avrams having the slightest idea—or so they said—where the weapon was. Like the other five members of the select committee on security, Bar-Lev had begun to think of the affair as closed, pushed aside by the daily press of Middle Eastern thrusts and counterthrusts.

Weizmann was a pompous Section One officer, wounded in the October War and vainglorious of his slashed forehead, which Bar-Lev was certain he used to good advantage with the women. Certainly he pushed the wounded-lion shtick a bit too far with them, not realizing that every graybeard around the oval blond table had been literally blooded as a member of the Hagganah while Weizmann was crying in his diapers. And Bar-Lev knew only too well how far he and the others in the Hagganah had gone to turn their beliefs into rivers of British blood. As Weizmann droned on about what the Americans thought and didn't think, and about what Colonel Stein thought, Bar-Lev, as old men will, connected this event with others far in the past and mused again that treason was indeed a matter of dates.

The thought led nowhere, though, except to other similarly relativistic—and therefore operationally useless—musings. Yet he seemed today not to have interest in anything other than musing. He forced himself to focus on the tall, dark officer and his tiresome self-importance. He obviously considered this a major moment in the drama of his life, a moment in which he held the starring role. Don't we all, though? Bar-Lev reflected. He almost physically shook himself when he realized he was doing it again. He *must* force himself to sit up and pay attention, to stare at Weizmann as intently as did his five colleagues.

Weizmann didn't make it easy.

"...so, gentlemen, I believe that is the situation as of about twenty minutes ago. Which is when, as I mentioned earlier, Colonel Stein's report came to us."

More like forty minutes, thought Bar-Lev, considering how long you've been going on about all this.

"The prime minister has been told?"

"Of course." Weizmann sniffed. "He is with the cabinet now, discussing the issue of the prisoners. He will undoubtedly ask your counsel next."

Ashkenazi, seated next to Bar-Lev, snorted. "He need hardly bother. He knows what we will say. We will say as we have always said: go to the devil."

"Ah, Yitzak, you're such a dove," the obese Lubich said, chuckling. "Always trying for the peaceful way out." The others chortled. Weizmann looked embarrassed, as if such senior members of the government—privy as only a few were to such information—should not act in this way. He looked, thought Bar-Lev, like a constipated schoolmaster.

Abramowicsz, as that month's leader, gathered the reins of control. "Gentlemen. Let us get on with things. No doubt, Colonel, you have matters of gravity to attend to?"

Weizmann looked confused for a moment. It took him that long to comprehend that he was being hooked offstage. He composed himself quickly and drew himself to his full, impressive height. "Yes, Minister. If you need me—"

"We know where to find you, Colonel. Don't worry."

The colonel collected his papers and stalked out.

Sunlight filled the room, making it almost too hot. Six stories below, the traffic of Tel Aviv snarled and honked like traffic anywhere. A fly buzzed, a mineral water bottle top popped, someone drummed fingers.

"So," Abramowicsz said finally, "now what? David? Any ideas?"

Bar-Lev heard his name, but there was something odd about it. He could see Abramowicsz, his lifelong friend and comrade, silhouetted against the sunlight streaming through the window. But it was as if he were drifting backward, back into the sun. Bar-Lev squinted and tried to make him out better. He saw Abramowicsz speak again, his lips moving, but no sound seemed to come out. Bar-Lev found that fascinating, in a remote sort of way. He mused on it awhile, as Abramowicsz and Lubich, acting in slow motion, got to their feet and, mouths still working, came toward him. He felt a curious sense that he should pay more attention, as he had felt he should with Weizmann. But now it was simply too hard. Everything was too hard. Even getting the horizon straight was too hard. He noted it in an amused sort of way as a strange buzzing seemed to drown out everything, including his own heartbeat. The sun at last seemed to blot out everything, even the hands that he now saw were reaching toward him through the golden haze and the pounding noise of something, something trying to happen inside him. He felt a splendid calm, such as he had felt never before in his life, and as the hands drew closer and the horizon fell on its side and he found it perfectly all right, he sought for something to say to the others to make them understand that it was all right and he was all right and the golden haze and the buzzing was all right, too....

"WHAT? WHAT DID HE SAY? Did you get that, Yitz-ak?"

Shaken, Ashkenazi stood up from Bar-Lev's body just as the medics rushed through the door with a clatter of boots and medical boxes. They shoved the old men who were standing around out of the way and went to work on the old man on the floor.

Ashkenazi shook his head as they connected electrodes to Bar-Lev's chest and injected powerful chemicals into his bloodstream.

"I don't know...it sounded like, well, it sounded like he said, 'It's all right. Treason's just a matter of dates.' But I must be mistaken." He watched them work on the body of the man who had saved his life in a gully in 1948 by killing two Arabs with his bare hands, and shook his head again. "Yes. I *must* have been mistaken."

CHESTER RETURNED to the conference room almost an hour after he'd left Max and Sandy there. After the first fifteen minutes, Max had grown increasingly tense, pacing the little room, sitting down, standing up, picking up magazines and books from the bookshelves, not reading them and putting them down again, only to continue pacing. Sandy had stood it for half an hour, then gone to the ladies' room, stopping by to ask the general's secretary about Chester. When she returned to the conference room, Max had settled down a bit. He half sat and half lay in the end chair, his feet up on the neighboring chair, suit coat bundled under his neck, tie loose, eyes closed. He was in that pose when Chester exploded through the door.

"Moss!" he barked.

Max jerked, his feet crashing to the floor. "What—"

"No time for that now. He wants to see you."

"Who?"

"Jacobson."

"Chairman of the Joint Chiefs?"

"Right first time. Sandy, you take this list and get started on the calls for me. I've marked the ones that are top priority. And—"

"Why does he want to see me?"

"—be sure to make good notes, we've got about ten four-stars who want everything in triplicate before they agree to anything. Why? I'll tell you why. It seems the chairman is highly interested in your plan, but he frankly doesn't believe you can pull it off."

"So why waste my time and his—"

"Because things are going crazy upstairs. The Israelis are giving us grief over the prisoners, and every minute it gets harder to keep a lid on this whole thing. MPs caught a couple of people trying to sneak out— they'd heard some rumors that were too close to being true. We've got to move, and fast. Come on, Moss."

Max went. He hurried along next to Chester as he burst back through the conference room door and gulped the corridor in three-foot strides. Max adjusted his tie and pulled on his jacket as they raced down the almost empty corridor.

"Anything I should know before I go in?"

Chester walked like a boxer leading with his chin, eyes fixed somewhere past the curving wall. "No. Yes. Try not to call Jacobson a damn fool."

"Seriously."

"Seriously, remember that he's got his hands full of shit. No matter what happens, it won't be good for him. If they pull the pin on the bomb, we die and that's bad. If some other harebrained scheme gets tried—and Lordy, you wouldn't believe some of the crap the snake eaters are trying to sell him—and it fails, we die and it's still bad. Even if something—like your scheme, God help us—works, and we all somehow get out of this alive, his career is kaput because the pols will want somebody's scalp, and they'll figure that it might as well be his. They'll say the goddamn military dropped the ball and let this all happen in the first place. So keep that in mind. All that can happen to you is death. Jacobson's got a lot worse fates to face. Win, lose or draw."

Max had no time to respond, because they came to the first of the security checkpoints leading to the emergency action center of the National Military Command Center. With each of the unforeseen crises of the past decade, the center had grown as its role had grown, and now it was a complex of its own, a mini-labyrinth inside the monster labyrinth of the Pentagon.

Max allowed himself to be scrutinized by tough-looking MPs at each checkpoint. Finally they cleared the last one, Chester moving virtually at the double, and came to another green-painted steel door with another covered keypad, another staring fish-eye camera focused on the person who might use the keypad and a couple of small lights at eye level on the doorjamb. Chester keyed in a lengthy code, the green light flashed twice, a dull clunk sounded in the door and it swung open.

Inside, bedlam was in progress. A large room, maybe forty feet by twenty, held a long table butted against a shorter one in a T. Uniformed men sat in chairs along every side of the T, the ranks displayed on their collars and sleeves rising as the ends met at the junction. Telephones rang incessantly. Six doors led to other parts of the complex, and most seemed to be full of people scurrying in or out, clutching papers and looking harried or nervous or just plain scared. Along the high walls, rear-projection status screens displayed force data: troop deployments, ship positions, satellite locations.

At the head of the T sat an Air Force general in a long-sleeved light blue shirt. His dark blue shoulder boards bore four big silver stars each; he wore a pair of command pilot's wings on the left breast, and below on his buttoned pocket was a command missileman's badge. He wore no name tag. He was an athletic-looking man of about fifty, with the standard-issue gray crew cut and a pair of what looked like dime store reading glasses perched on his nose. He pored over a computer printout being held on one side by a Navy two-star and the other by a Marine colonel. Chester wove between the hurrying troops and stood just behind the Marine colonel.

"—this is *it*, Jake?" The four-star looked up at the admiral over his half glasses, his tone clearly accusatory.

"Sir, we just didn't have the time. If we had known—"

Jacobson dropped the printout and peeled off his glasses. "Yeah. Well, if wishes were horses, Jake. But they're not. Maybe you and Bill can come up with something else. The President's going to call back in five minutes."

The Marine colonel scooped up the printout. "We'll have it for you, sir."

The admiral, who looked dubious, straightened up. "Right. We'll be ready."

"Good. Get cracking. And Bill—" He looked up at the Marine and saw Chester.

"Ah. Colonel Chester. Is this the man?"

"This is the man, General."

Jacobson peered intently at Max for a moment. Max felt as if he'd been x-rayed.

"Good. Let's go to C-1, okay? I can spare a minute now."

He pushed back from the table and got to his feet. Max saw that he had to snap his left leg into place by hand as he rose; the leg was a prosthetic device. It didn't slow him down. He moved quickly to the conference room at the end of the main room. This one had no locking door, but it did have a wall of glass that faced onto the main room. And it was empty, although the evidence of many meetings remained in the form of plastic cups half-filled with coffee and the usual debris of discussion.

General Jacobson slipped himself into a chair at the end of the white Formica table. Chester sat at his left and Max one chair down.

Jacobson waited until the door closed. Then he leaned back and eyed Max again. "Mr. Moss, Colonel Chester told us of your idea. I must say, it's audacious."

"Thanks, General."

"But as a pilot, I can't see it working."

Max stared evenly at Jacobson. "Why's that, sir?"

"Lot of things. But first, you'd get zapped by the formation problem." He smiled the kind of smile a man uses who knows the weight of ignorance of another man is so great he must be gentle in exposing it. "You got much time in flying formation?"

"None, General."

Chester stirred uncomfortably.

"Ah. Thought so. Had a quick look at your file. Must say, it's very... interesting. Too bad you decided to leave us, Mr. Moss."

"Some are called, General."

"And few are chosen. How true. But back to my point. Quite apart from the technical problems, you intend to pull off an incredible feat of airmanship here, and you admit you've got no experience in the required maneuvering?"

"None whatever, sir. At least not in the real world."

Jacobson laughed. "Son of a bitch, they were right about you, Moss. What do you mean, the real world? What other kind is there?"

Max smiled back in what he hoped was the duplicate of the patronizing smirk Jacobson had used on him. "Know much about computers, General?"

"Some. Get to the point." Max saw he'd scored a bull's-eye. Jacobson was pre-personal computer. His kids lived in a world completely unfathomable to him.

"Point's this, General. I've got maybe a couple hundred hours flying the virtual world, including formation work."

Jacobson mulled this over a moment, having stopped himself from making some caustic comment.

Something about what Max had said had triggered a memory. Max waited, then helped him out.

"The virtual world, General. Your people at Wright-Patterson quantified it a decade ago when they began work on the bio-cybernetic project. You recall the A-10F. Well, before the jock lobby killed it off and the Army got the ground-attack mission, the project proved the concept with a man-machine interface they called the Jesus Box. Your F-16 pilots are training with it now, in the advanced Super Cockpit version. The human engineering types at Wright-Pat figured out how to integrate the optics, terrain data bases, performance profiles, everything necessary to recreate flight on the ground...or to fly any airplane properly equipped from the ground. As of last week, there were, I think, seven Department of Defense programs working with the virtual world the systems create."

Jacobson swiveled his chair around and stared out at the bustle in the control center. He tapped the arm of his chair. Finally he swiveled back to face Max.

"There's a couple of things I've found out in twenty-five years of flying, Mr. Moss. Most important is, if you keep it simple, it might work. This leg is courtesy of trying to fly an F-4 too deep into a target zone, chasing a missile that needed more guidance than they said it would. When the goddamn SAM popped, it wiped out Stan in the back seat and rearranged my lower limbs, I flew that sucker back to Da Nang just so I could prove that what we were telling the brains about their so-called standoff missile was true. I felt then that there was no substitute for a good pilot in a good airplane, and I still feel that way." He paused and looked out the window again before continuing.

"Thing is, that was then and this is now, as my kids are always reminding me. In my book, Mr. Moss, you are a novice pilot, a civilian pilot, with no real experience trying to pull off something I wouldn't have tried when I thought God had never put a better stick on earth. In my book, what you propose is impossible. I can't prove it, because my in-house geniuses can't come up with the numbers to prove it can't work. But the fifteen thousand hours I've got in every goddamn airplane in the Air Force tells me so." He leaned forward against the table and fixed Mat with an ice-cold stare.

"But my book isn't the only book there is. I've had my ass handed to me too many times not to have finally figured that out. It's just faintly possible that what you are is the future and what I am is the past. It's just possible that this scheme of yours can work—in the same way it was possible, but incredibly unlikely to the point we never even programmed our wargame computers with it, that these Arab bastards would pull off what they're pulling off now. In normal times, I'd show you the door, Mr. Moss. But, as my daddy used to say, these ain't normal times. So what I'm going to do is hold you and your plan in reserve. I'm going to let you put it all together, and when the time is right—which means, when everything else is wrong, when the politicians have dropped the ball and none of the high-paid whiz kids in this city have picked it up—I'll let you give it your best shot." He held up a hand, palm outward.

"But understand this. If you get the go sign from me, things will be as bad as they can get. All my personal views notwithstanding, Mr. Moss, if you hear us call for help, *we will need it*. You will be *it*, man. The only thing between those crazy bastards with the bomb and a whole lot of dead Americans. Okay?"

"Okay," Max said, and in another second, Jacobson had levered himself up, looked hard into Max's eyes again, shaken his hand and gone out the door.

As it hissed closed, Max watched the general move to his chair at the center console again and begin calling aides to his side, jamming on his reading glasses and plucking a red telephone from its cradle.

"Now," Max said, "I understand what they mean when they say 'leadership.'"

"Yeah," Chester said, "that's the real McCoy, all right. For a goddamn *pilot*, that is."

Max shot him a glance that made Chester laugh. "Come on. Just kidding. You ready?"

"No. How about you?"

"Never was, never will be. Why should today be any different?"

"No reason," Max said, and followed Chester to the door. Outside, chaos reigned. But now, Max didn't need the reminder from the turmoil of the troops in the emergency action center. He had his own signals, the old, familiar chemistry of adrenaline flooding through his body. Christie, the English biochemist he'd loved a century or so ago, had once measured his system and marveled at it. His body, she'd said, was continually set on a chemical hair trigger, always ready, as she and her colleagues put it, for fight or flight.

Today he wouldn't be able to fight. But the flight had to be perfect.

CHAPTER NINETEEN

"THE LINES ARE OPEN to the Zionists and Americans?"

"Yes. The American President can contact us at any moment. Our communications specialists confirm that."

"And from Israel—"

"The same."

Daud Qidal nodded his approval. He hated waiting more than anything. Especially waiting for something like the Love of Allah to finish. He checked his Japanese digital watch and mentally subtracted the time zone difference. In two hours, it would be over, one way or another. The Jihad would have achieved a crushing victory or succeeded in blowing up the most important city in the Western world.

The secrecy surrounding the individual segments of the plan had taxed them all to the utmost. Only he and three others in the PLO knew the entire plan, and only six in Iran. He corrected himself. With Hassan el Jazzar in Washington, only five.

If the plan failed, the world at large would never know the full story. But that would be little comfort to the Palestinians condemned to another lifetime of misery in the camps. Nor, he thought, to him; as the inheritor of Arafat's messy legacy of chaos and failed worldwide sabotage, he had tried to buy time by building the strength of the PLO rather than squandering it in hopeless hijackings and vengeance bombings. It was a policy he knew would work, given time and support from the barely reconciled factions among the Palestinians. But should the Love of Allah result in failure, he knew, too, that retaining his power would require monumental efforts; the few who knew his part in the plan would waste no time in pointing out that he had missed the chance to use the bomb directly on the Israelis. Or that he had enlisted the aid of the despised Jihad.

He got up from the desk and went to the window overlooking his small corner of the wreckage of Muslim Beirut. Somewhere beyond the immediate area, about five kilometers west, a fire burned, throwing up a dark smear of smoke. He no longer even wondered what such things meant.

He did wonder as he stared out at the jagged moonscape of gutted buildings, what Bar-Lev was doing at this moment. Was he even now meeting with his committee to decide the prisoners issue? Was he wishing he had not begun this chain of events? Or was he, as old men are wont to do, simply trying to get through the wearisome day, striving to live just a while longer before death took his cares from his aged and stooped shoulders?

Qidal turned from the window. His aides' eyes followed him with the youthful fire that didn't know the meaning of failure. The aides followed him because they thought he was wise and tough and lucky. Not because they understood what he believed in. Their glistening eyes were momentarily too much for him and he wrenched his gaze away, to flick restlessly from object to object in his meanly appointed office. Seeking what?

A resolution, he decided. An absolute in a world too relative. He flinched inwardly as he found himself again so far, mentally, from the issues at hand. What kind of leader was he, to be arguing relativism when brave men staked their lives on *his* plan?

There was, as always, no answer, from Allah or anyone else. He sighed and sat down again.

The shimmering digits on his cheap watch had changed. But not much. And the phones were stubbornly silent.

"COLONEL KIMBALL."

"Yes, Commander. We read you. Over."

"There is an aircraft approaching us. Do I need to remind you what this can mean?"

"It's not one of ours. Let me contact National. Stand by."

"Hadj al-Shiran. What do you make of that aircraft?"

Al-Shiran followed Hassan's finger. At about two o'clock, a single-engine Cessna was closing fast. As they continued on the longest leg of their three-legged racetrack pattern around the Mall, the Cessna banked right, then flew parallel with them to their turning point. Al-Shiran eased the yoke left and their lower wing obscured the Cessna.

Hassan clicked to the cabin intercom. "Ahmed! Do you see an airplane to our right?"

"Yes—yes, I see it. He is turning with us, Commander."

Hassan was about to give an order to al-Shiran when the radio came to life.

"This is the NMCC, do you read?"

"We read you," Hassan replied.

"That Cessna is a civilian airplane, not under control of the National tower or other air traffic centers. National has been trying to contact him, but the pilot does not respond."

"Colonel, this is a childish ruse. Tell your pilot to fly away from us immediately or we will carry out our threat."

"Negative, Commander, we're unable to comply. That guy is on his own. What do you want us to do—shoot him down?"

"If necessary, yes." Hassan clicked off the mike button with satisfaction. He switched back to cockpit intercom. "Hadj al-Shiran. Is this possible? Could an airplane do this—fly so close and not be under their control?"

Al-Shiran nodded, continuing the wearying task of flying the racetracks. "Yes. A student pilot, maybe, or just somebody who doesn't believe in following procedures."

Hassan watched the Cessna pace them from about a mile away, turning with them. "What kind of airplane is it?"

Al-Shiran glanced at it. "Cessna 210. Single-engine, four-place."

"Come in, Jihad." It was the radio again.

"Yes, this is the Jihad."

"Commander, the only thing we can do is send one of our fighters over to escort the Cessna away. If we shoot him down, there will be immediate public concern as to why—and we cannot afford that now."

"Yes. Very good, Colonel. Let us see your fighter move him away from us. But I warn you; if you try to trick us and attack with your fighter, we will detonate the bomb. It will gain you nothing."

Kimball's voice was tired and irritable when he spoke. "Listen, el Jazzar, we know what your threat is. We're trying to resolve the situation. This is just some joyriding private pilot. Just take it easy. Our fighters will come from the south; there will be two of them in a section. One will go up high, the other will slow down to attempt to signal the Cessna to leave. If this fails, we will send up a helicopter to try. All right?"

"Yes. But no tricks."

"No tricks. Out."

"He knew my name," Hassan said. Al-Shiran glanced at Hassan. Something about the way he spoke alerted the pilot. Hassan's brow furrowed. Al-Shiran saw that he was sweating, despite his sparing use of the heater. The drugs. Whatever el Jazzar had gobbled more than four hours ago was wearing off. He was crashing, becoming emotionally destabilized. Al-Shiran silently cursed. Of all the times for the leader to come unglued.

"Commander! There! To our left—combat fighters!" Feyda's voice betrayed intense nervousness. Hassan and al-Shiran snapped their heads around and looked for the aircraft.

Al-Shiran spotted them first—two pinheads low on the horizon, flying up the Potomac, their exhaust barely visible as a faint smudge.

"F-16s," al-Shiran said. "Probably from Langley, in Virginia."

"Are they attacking?" Hassan's voice now quivered slightly.

"No. See—the leader continues and the wingman pulls up. Now, the leader will make a slow pass inside the Cessna and rock his wings—there, you see?"

The gray-blue F-16 flew past the Cessna with its gear and flaps extended to enable it to slow-fly better. Both airplanes were too far away for the terrorists to see the pilots. But the Cessna weaved in its flight path, as if the pilot were startled.

The F-16 pitched up in a steep bank and split-essed back and down, parallel to the Cessna. High above, the F-16 wingman flew in a tight circle. Al-Shiran grudgingly admired their flying. He came up to his turning point and banked the Piper over again, blanking the view of the F-16 leader closing with the Cessna.

When al-Shiran rolled out on his new heading, they craned their necks and saw that the Cessna and F-16 were flying off together at an oblique to the Cessna's previous flight path.

"Hello, Jihad," Kimball called.

"Yes," said el Jazzar, still watching the two airplanes heading north.

"We have contact with the civilian airplane. He's heading away. Do you see?"

"Yes," said el Jazzar. "It is good you did not try anything, Colonel."

A long wait preceded Kimball's reply. "Roger," was all he said, but the tone of his voice spoke volumes.

STEIN BRUSHED PAST the security man and sat at the plain little desk. On it stood a white telephone, nothing more. The tough-looking embassy security guard closed the door to the small, soundproof cubicle, and Stein was alone. He picked up the phone.

A click sounded, followed by a beep. Then the prime minister came on the line.

"Colonel Stein."

"Prime Minister."

"You are aware of the demands the Jihad is making on the Americans and on us?"

"Yes, sir."

"I have just been speaking with their President. He is very concerned. I might even say desperate. His military people have told him there is no way other than capitulation, to be followed with one of several operations to be mounted later to recapture their weapons and our prisoners."

"So I understood."

"But he does not like this solution. Their success rate with such operations has been poor."

"Indeed."

"In addition, I am under pressure from some here to accede to the prisoner demands."

"I can easily imagine, sir."

There was a pause. The secure satellite link was working perfectly between the embassy and Tel Aviv. The pause came not from technical problems but from the speakers' coolness to each other. Stein did not like the PM, and the feeling was mutual. Yet they respected each other, and the PM had always supported Stein when Section Four got into trouble inside the Mossad or out.

"We could easily short-circuit this whole affair, Colonel Stein."

"Yes, sir. We might be able to. But at what cost?"

"That is why I am calling. I want your assurance that the cost is not too high."

"It is not. I assure you. General Avrams—"

"Avrams is on his way back from London now, but out of secure communications, unfortunately. My decision must be made before he returns. There will be much confusion and the Americans will be very angry when I refuse the Jihad's demands. I must be certain the strain on our relations will be justified."

"No one can be certain, sir. But we have no real choice. We must proceed as planned. Or Har Mughara was all for nothing."

The silence returned to the line. Stein could picture the white-haired old man, wizened as an ancient desert tree, blue eyes bright and piercing, sucking on his omnipresent pipe and pondering the options. They had clashed many times on many issues, but they had agreed absolutely on Lorelei. He did not expect the PM to renege now.

He did not. "I do not require you to instruct me in values, Colonel. But we are agreed that our investment is too great to discard—at this moment. Thank you for your assessment. You will be available at the embassy?"

"I asked permission to remain at the Pentagon, but my contacts were not able to clear it. So, yes, I will be here. We have good communications with the NMCC, though, so neither the ambassador nor I will be too out of touch with events.''

''Good. Shalom, Colonel.''

''Shalom, Prime Minister.''

Stein replaced the receiver in the cradle.

Should he tell them? If the PM had not backed him up, it would be a different game entirely. But the Americans were out of options, and with Israel's continued refusal to discuss release of the prisoners, there was little likelihood the Jihaddin would compromise.

He got wearily to his feet and glanced at his watch, knowing what its message would be. Time, it said, was running out.

CHAPTER TWENTY

THE ALL-BLACK HUEY swooped down, pitched up into a hover and touched down on the concrete outside the hangar at Andrews AFB, where Max and his team worked feverishly. Engrossed in helping Duane Horton, Max did not notice the Army lieutenant hop out of the chopper and run toward the hangar. He carried a red cylinder about the size of a large thermos bottle, along with a sheaf of papers.

A burly Air Force security policeman in fatigues barred the officer's entrance at the open door of the hangar. The noise of the helo's engine and rotor blades, added to the four huge heater blowers warming the immense hangar, covered their conversation, but Sandy noticed them. She ran across the hangar and asked the SP what the problem was.

"Sir, the lieutenant doesn't have the right pass. He—"

"Captain, uh, Koppel," the young lieutenant said, reading her name tag and saluting, "I'm Lockwood, from Fort Detrick. I've got the canister—"

"Sergeant, let the man through. He's got the only pass he needs."

The SP looked dubious, then stepped aside and saluted the lieutenant, who waved a sloppy response and followed Sandy.

"You guys sure took your time," she said.

"It was harder to get the C-6 in this size than we thought when they called from the NMCC. Computer showed we had it, but it was stored in the wrong place."

"Well, you made it anyway. There—that's Mr. Moss, in charge. And Horton, chief engineer."

Lockwood halted and surveyed the scene. Max, Duane Horton and six other men were dispersed around the Viper, each up to his elbows in machinery. A lathe in the hangar workshop whined as the bit ate metal. A drill press added its shrill voice. Air Force enlisted men, led by a stocky master sergeant, worked alongside Horton's men.

"Uh, who's senior here, Captain?"

Sandy had gotten ahead of Lockwood. She turned and said, "What? Why?"

He looked embarrassed. "Well, ma'am, I've got these releases and transfers, and they have to be signed—"

She jerked them out of his hand, pulled a black GI ballpoint from her jacket and scribbled her name on all the manifold copies. She thrust them back.

"There. Now, give that thing to Mr. Moss so they can get it fitted up. And hang around; we may need you."

"C-6 is potent stuff, ma'am. You have to know how to handle it. If you break the cap seal, you might KO everybody in the county."

"Sure, Lieutenant. Thanks for the warning. Max?"

Moss looked up from the gaping cargo compartment of the Viper. He saw the lieutenant in his camos
and waved him over.

"Sir? This is the—"

"About time. Duane, look at this will you? Looks
like the damn thread pitch on the neck isn't what those
bozos told us it was." Horton ignored the lieutenant,
plucked the canister from his arms and examined it.

"You're right, Mr. Moss. This isn't a 12. Hey, Willie! Get me a thread gauge!" He gingerly set the canister down in the Viper and scratched his cheek,
eyeballing the fit.

Max straightened up and wiped his hands on a rag
stuffed in a pocket of his Brooks Brothers trousers.
He'd peeled off his tie as soon as the CH-53 had de-
posited him and Sandy on the ramp outside the
hangar, having flown them from the Pentagon almost
two hours ago.

"Thanks, Lieutenant. Any special precautions before we connect it up?"

"Well, sir, I don't know what you plan to do with
it, but it's dangerous stuff."

Max frowned. "It's not flammable, is it? They told
us it acted inert even under combustion."

"Oh, no, sir. It won't explode or anything like that.
It thinks it's xenon or argon. Why, you could pump it
into one of those heaters over there and it wouldn't
change a bit." He smiled, proud of his chemical warfare knowledge.

Max nodded. "Good. That's just what we're going
to do."

The lieutenant's grin slipped. But Max ignored him,
leaned on the Viper launcher wearily and picked up a

plastic cup that had once had hot coffee in it. He sniffed it, wrinkled his nose and tossed it into the big trash drum nearby.

"Any news?" he asked Sandy.

"None."

Reflexively, they both looked at the huge twenty-four hour clock on the maintenance officer's balcony over the workshops at the end of the hangar.

"Less than an hour now. You'd think they'd call."

"No reason, yet, Max. They're probably still trying to talk them down."

"Yeah." Max snorted. "Say, Lieutenant, you came down by helo from Frederick?"

"Yes, sir."

"Notice anything odd?"

"How do you mean, sir?"

"Well, like around National Airport."

The lieutenant thought, then shook his head. "No, sir. Nothing. Usual traffic, I guess."

Max looked at Sandy. "So they're still pulling it off. They're still allowing traffic in and out. Nobody knows yet. Jesus, that's amazing."

"Can't hold much longer. Somebody's going to get too curious."

"Yeah, well, soon it won't matter. It'll be all over one way or the other."

The young lieutenant knew better than to ask what was going on. He'd learned already that when somebody wanted him to know something, he'd be told. He stood and watched as the technicians fitted the red canister to a complex mechanism in the cargo bay of the Viper.

Horton nodded to the master sergeant, left him in charge and went to Max.

"Mr. Moss, we got a problem. Small one, but a problem."

"You mean, 'another' problem, Duane."

"Hell, we didn't expect to have to rig all this up when we came out here. Anyway, problem is, the claw action isn't what we'd like to see. The actuators weren't hard to jury-rig—Willie there stole them from a landing gear set—but they work a tad slow. That means you'd have to hold her steady while they bit. And that might be too tough."

"You let me worry about that, Duane. I'll fly it. You build it."

Horton shrugged. "Okay." He looked at the clock. "I'd say we can have a dry run of the system in about half an hour. Turned out Willie had some telescoping Kevlar tube, so we cut some time off."

"Sounds good, Duane. You guys are doing a hell of a job."

"What the hell, Mr. Moss. Beats working for a living."

Max smiled and watched Horton dive back into the Viper's guts.

"Good thing he's on our side," Max said.

"Who?" asked Sandy.

"Never mind. What's the weather like?"

"Still good. Winds about ten miles per hour, right around thirty-eight degrees, no clouds."

Max nodded absently and walked slowly over to the big Moss Electronics van parked near the Viper launcher. Sandy paced him. The lieutenant, abandoned, hesitated a moment, then went over to the Viper.

Max climbed the fold-down stairs into the big box van. Inside were three compartments, and three chairs. Two were normal electronic-tech consoles, with swivel chairs facing counters and boards full of communication control equipment, mainly for the antenna array mounted atop the van.

The third and farthest forward console was different. It was almost fully enclosed in sound-deadening material, including the lowered ceiling over the chair. The chair itself was a recliner, almost a couch, with swing-away armrests that incorporated handgrip controls. Only a few instruments faced the chair from the console. But emerging from it was a large, thick cable attached to the back of a black pilot's helmet with a mirrored visor. The helmet was hung over the headrest of the couch.

Max nodded to Arnie Axelsson, the chief mobile van technician, who sat at his master console, frowning at the readouts, a headset with a mike slipped over one ear.

"Okay, Arnie?"

"Just fine, Mr. Moss. Are we going to go today?"

"Hope so. Keep it up and running. We'll only have a few minutes' notice when we have to go."

"No sweat, sir. All systems are five-by."

Max absently smoothed a piece of silver duct tape holding a wire loom in place, gazed around the van again and ducked back through the door to where Sandy stood.

"All okay?"

"Yeah." He shoved his hands in his pockets. Then he took them out and cracked his knuckles.

"This waiting sucks, you know that?" he said.

Sandy wanted to put her hand on his arm, but this was not the place. "I know," she said.

THE NEEDLE DIDN'T BUDGE when al-Shiran tapped the fuel gauge. It showed empty, but he knew it wasn't right. There had to be more fuel yet. He had been forced to sacrifice some fuel to compensate for the large load, but his calculations couldn't be that far off.

Hassan watched al-Shiran calmly. The fuel quantity gauge was on his side of the cockpit, so the pilot had to reach over to tap the glass.

Al-Shiran sat upright and continued to fly.

"There is a problem?" Hassan asked.

"No, Commander. I don't think so. The left fuel tank shows empty. But I don't think it is."

"We expected six full hours, no?"

"Yes." Al-Shiran mentally ticked off all the things that could be wrong. There were many.

"Yet it has only been slightly more than five hours."

"Yes."

Hassan frowned. Al-Shiran found Hassan's scowl unnerving. It must be the length of the flight, and the tiring hand-flying, he thought. He had almost missed some of the turns; the repetitive racetrack was more enervating than he'd ever imagined. This had turned out to be the toughest flight of his life.

His life. His *life*. Some part of his mind, the part that was not involved with the problems of aviation, rebelled at the thought that after all this life, he would end as fiery dust when the bomb went off. He realized he had never really believed that it would. He had always believed they would cave in, as they always had when things got too tough for the white men. What sustained him was Allah; he knew that, but he knew also that Hassan's serene certainty also sustained. Now that el Jazzar began to look concerned—what could that mean about everything else?

Hadj al-Shiran didn't know. But the hypnotic laps of Washington had taken their toll on his physical and mental alertness; that he did know. And he also knew that he would not allow el Jazzar to see his fear of death. He gritted his teeth and mentally took up the prayer again, the prayer that had saved him so many times before and would save him now.

In the name of Allah, the compassionate, the merciful...

"ANOTHER HELO COMING, Max," Sandy said. He looked up from the Viper just as Duane twisted the last fastener on the cowling. Another all-black Huey settled on its skids on the ramp just outside the door. There couldn't have been more than three feet between the rotor tips and the massive steel doors of the hangar.

Two men in dress uniforms jumped out. Max recognized them as the Marine colonel and the two-star Navy man from the NMCC. The sentry snapped to attention and this time did not bar their entry. Max jumped down from the launcher and jogged over to meet them, accompanied by Sandy.

The admiral and the colonel halted and regarded the Viper behind Max with impenetrable expressions.

"Mr. Moss?" the admiral said.

"Yes."

"General Jacobson sends his compliments. And this." He handed Max an envelope. Inside was a typed order, in the classic five paragraphs taught at West Point. Max read it, reread it slowly and put it back in the envelope.

"Thanks," he said simply. "We'd better get started."

"Yes. You'd better," said the admiral.

Max's reply was cut off by the maintenance officer yelling from his office, "Mr. Moss! You have a call on scrambler!"

Max nodded to the two JCS officers and ran back to the office. The portly colonel handed him the phone and ducked out. The scrambler switch on the receiver was on, and the light was glowing.

"Moss," Max said.

"Jacobson. Have my people gotten there yet?"

"Yes, General. Just arrived."

"You got the order?"

"I got it."

"Okay. We're out of options. I convinced the President personally to authorize your plan."

"Thanks, General."

"Don't thank me, Moss. Just do it."

"Sierra Hotel, General."

Jacobson laughed. "Maybe you are a pilot after all. Good luck, son."

Before Max could reply, the line went dead. Max hung up and opened the office door.

Everyone stood grouped around the door in a silent semicircle. Max swept his gaze around their solemn faces and said, "Looks like we're on. Arnie, get the van outside and into position. Duane, get the launcher powered up and ready. We've got a mission to fly."

For a moment, no one moved, then Arnie, the cool, unemotional Swede, whooped and ran to the van. In seconds, the hangar was filled with noise and frantic movement.

CHAPTER TWENTY-ONE

MAX SLIPPED ONTO THE COUCH with a feeling of profound relief. He had never been any good at waiting. For anything. It was always a joy to act rather than think about acting.

Arnie helped him with the helmet and the armrests. The helmet had been molded for him, so it fit perfectly, the dense, closed-cell foam warming to his skin immediately. The underchin locks stabilized the helmet as he snapped them closed, the mike also snapping into place.

He saw nothing in the blacked-out inside surface of the mirrored visor, since the density control was set to full opaque.

Arnie powered up the helmet. The sound system hummed briefly, then the sense of vast spaces began to engulf him as the binaural computer opened up each quadrant of his surroundings.

"Hello, Max," said the associate.

"Hi, Missy," he said absently, reacquainting himself with the feel of the handgrips. "Missy" was an artificial intelligence, an "expert system" designed to handle the routine chores, to warn him of problems in the system, to be his guide when he forgot the capabilities of the Viper's technology. She was activated whenever the bio monitors in his helmet detected his presence and identity. Each Viper pilot had an associate whose name, voice and involvement level he selected. Max had chosen Missy out of whimsy and stuck with her. He thought of her not as a person, but as a kind of ultrasophisticated autopilot. There were pilots who thought of their associates as people. They had trouble adjusting. Max did not.

"Missy, visor up half," he said while still wriggling in the couch to get a kink out of his back.

The visor cleared so that he could see the console. He craned his neck and saw Arnie at his chair.

"Hey, Arnie, how do you read?"

"Five-by, Mr. Moss. System okay?"

"Seems to be. Give me a second to allow the collimators to warm up." The helmet incorporated small cathode ray tubes above each eye to project images into the inner surface of the visor. A tiny laser tracked and measured Max's eyes to assure precise adjustment of the CRTs, so that the images were stable and correctly aligned. The result was, depending on the sensor input fed into the computer generating the images for the CRTs, a "window" about 120 degrees wide and 80 degrees high, something like a TV screen or video game display. This window showed Max whatever world the sensors could display, the "virtual" world.

"Collimation complete," Missy's artificial voice reported.

Max checked the console; everything was green. "Missy, visor down full." The visor went black again. The effect was eerie. The computer-enhanced sound system made Max feel as if he were standing in the

middle of a huge hangar in total blackness. The sense
of enormous space was overwhelming, yet he could
not see anything. This was because the binaural sound
was not yet connected to any sensors other than the
simple comm net, which he and Arnie, his controller,
shared.

Arnie spoke, and the voice seemed to come from his
relative position. That was the point of the system: to
allow the pilot to use his hearing as a spatial locator.

"Mr. Moss, Duane says they're ready. Sensors are
hot."

"Okay. Missy, power up and sensor connect."

Gradually, the blackness was replaced by the view
from the nose of the Viper. The high-resolution TV
camera had a unique range of capabilities, from zoom
to tracking. Max controlled it either by hand or voice.

"Missy, sound up," he said. As the video had come
slowly to life, the audio came up. He heard the technicians at the Viper launcher talking, the clink of their
tools, the rasping snarl somewhere over his shoulder
of the van's auxiliary generator. The Viper's sensor
suite included audio for recon missions, but it was always useful. A small speaker allowed Max to talk to
people near the RPV.

"Missy, sound to external. Hey, Duane. How do I
sound?"

"Perfect, Mr. Moss. We're almost ready."

"Good. Let me know and we'll start the engine."

"Stand by one, sir. I want to check the probe and
claws one more time."

Max waited while Duane tugged on the Kevlar tub-
ing and the four steel claws projecting through the top
of the cargo compartment doors. He almost felt

Duane's hands, as if the sense of touch were present in the virtual world, too. He had noticed the effect almost as soon as he'd begun flying the Viper; like much else in the system, it was eerie.

The Viper was a relatively simple airplane, nine feet long, with a wingspan of seven feet. It was powered by two tiny ultrahigh bypass-ratio turbofans contained in small pods, like those on a McDonnell-Douglas DC-9, along the aft fuselage. This allowed almost the entire dorsal section of the main fuselage to be used as a cargo bay. In this bay, Moss Electronics proposed that any of the Department of Defense's agencies—or the intelligence agencies—could put their secret payloads, from simple electromagnetic detectors to gas sniffers. The clear nose cone of the Viper housed the full-motion TV camera used by the pilot to "fly" the Viper. The rest of the compact fuselage was packed with electronics, almost all of it designed and built, like the airplane itself, in San Jose by Moss Electronics.

Eric Moss had run into Bruno Kostiakowski after Bruno had been laid off at a huge defense contractor. As an old hand in intelligence, Moss had been immediately entranced by the bitter engineer's ambitious theories. Kostiakowski sought to combine the emergent technologies of the virtual world, the pilot's associate and the remotely piloted vehicle. His theory was that with the use of a ground-based pilot, the abilities of the airplane could be dramatically expanded, since it would have no "organic" limitations in maneuvering. A pilot might black out from excessive G force, but Kostiakowski figured he could build an airplane that a pilot could fly far beyond the cur-

rent range of human tolerance. The engineer also figured the defense and intelligence communities would
love it. But he was wrong.

Pilots feared the Viper. Insofar as Eric Moss or
Kostiakowski could figure it out before the latter died
of cancer, the pilots somehow felt that it reduced their
role to being video game jockeys rather than, as Kostiakowski acidly put it from his deathbed, "sky gods."

Now, with his right hand, Max moved the tiny
joystick that controlled the TV camera to full right,
then full left and full vertical. The scene shifted accordingly. He moved his hand back and gripped the
larger joystick that replicated the control stick in a
conventional airplane. "Missy, control surfaces up,"
he said, and a plan view of the wings, elevons and
rudder appeared on his window. He waggled the ailerons, pitched the elevators up and down and kicked
the rudders. The images all moved appropriately.
"Missy, surfaces down," he said, and the images disappeared. He swung the camera toward the right,
where he heard Horton talking.

"Okay, Duane? We better light the fire."

"Looks good, Mr. Moss. Tie downs are clear.
Ready to go."

"Rog. Tell everyone to stand clear." He hand-
selected the command frequency. "Arnie? Is Andrews tower ready? Are we clear for takeoff?"

"Clear, Mr. Moss. Wind's steady out of the south,
eight knots. We've got the launcher pointed right into
it."

"Great. Okay, let's go, then."

Sandy came in and sat down at the console next to Arnie. She shook her head when he pointed to the microphone, and just slipped on a headset.

"Missy, full systems check."

"All ready, Max."

"Okay. Missy, give me flight data display."

A ghostly green overlay of lines, circles and vertical bars appeared on his visor. These were the vital airspeed, position and direction cues, taken by the computer from the laser gyros inside the Viper, his virtual cockpit displays.

He swiveled the camera so that the direction cue was centered on his takeoff line. He licked his lips. His pulse speeded up and his palms went clammy.

"Missy, left engine start."

"Left engine, Max." A luminous green dial appeared on his screen. It showed the percentage of power being developed by the left engine as a solid pie slice. Max heard the engine start behind his left ear. It sounded good, and the slice rapidly expanded.

"Missy, right engine start."

"Right engine, Max." The same thing happened.

"Missy, rocket ignition on my downcount from three."

"From three, Max."

"Three." The engines accelerated; Missy knew that he would need full turbine power to fly once the rocket assist pod fell away.

"Two." A rocket status display lit up, showing seconds of burn as a bar graph.

"One." The rocket ignited, and suddenly Max was flung into the air, the roar of the rocket motor seeming to come from right under his chair.

The flight data panel came alive. Max steered the Viper up into the cold blue sky while the short-lived rocket booster burned its five seconds and fell away, down onto the large grassy verge of Andrews's runway 19 Right.

Max back-zoomed the camera to wide view and pitched down again. He had climbed to 3500 feet, but he needed to be no higher than the treetops. He banked the little airplane steeply right and flew northwest across the field.

"Missy, terrain data overlay, treetop hazards."

A computer-generated grid materialized over the sunlit Washington suburbs as he flew over them at 200 knots. Above the glowing grid, bright concentric circles highlighted towers, buildings and other obstacles that rose up to be potential threats as he continued lower and lower.

"Arnie. How do you read?"

"Five-by, Mr. Moss."

"Can you bring up the target location on the God's eye view?"

"Stand by."

Max gently nudged the stick and shot over the town of College Park.

"Where do you want it?"

"Give me a scale rep lower quad, translucent."

"Here you go."

A chunk of screen dissolved to become a map of the Capitol area. The ground track of the Piper Navajo flown by the Jihaddin was highlighted in yellow, the Piper itself was a small red triangle.

"Back-zoom to show my location."

"You got it."

Max concentrated on avoiding the towers of the Mormon Temple in Kensington and cranked the Viper into a hard left turn back to the south. He pulled back the throttles and the Viper slowed to 170 knots.

He studied the map for a moment. "Missy, give me an intercept with the target from a constant six."

It took the computer only a moment, then it displayed an arcing path from his location to the projected position of the Piper as it made its racetrack turns.

"Okay. Missy, take it to the intercept. Maximum evasion."

"I have the controls, Max."

Max relaxed his hand on the grips.

"Arnie, what's the time to intercept?"

"Seven minutes, fifty seconds."

Max sat and watched as the computer flew the Viper over the Beltway, then in toward Washington along the Potomac River, barely above the water and under the bridges. He used the time to turn over in his mind the techniques he had to use.

"Max, intercept imminent. Target visual."

Max put his hands back on the controls. He saw the Piper now, above and to the left, completing a left turn, its wing effectively shielding him.

"Missy, I have the airplane."

"You have it, Max," the computer said.

If he were flying a fighter, he could rip the Piper's belly with cannon. But he could not do that. He had to close, and not be seen.

He brought the Viper up under the Navajo, accelerating and climbing in trail behind the twin so that his period of visibility to the occupants would be minimized. He slotted in formation about twenty feet below the Navajo.

"Missy, maintain position here."

"Hold position, Max."

He studied the belly of the Piper. He was not concerned that they would hear the Viper; those huge props churned out enough decibels to cover even a conventional small jet engine, but the Viper used heavily shielded turbofans in which the hot, noisy effluent was cooled and mixed by the enormous volume of bypass air the engines swallowed. You could barely hear the Viper on the ground when it passed right over you only ten feet overhead. As a recon probe, it had to be quiet.

"Turn coming up, Mr. Moss."

"I know, Arnie. I want the long leg coming up."

"Got it."

The Piper bent slowly into another left turn and Missy followed. Max chewed his cheek and wondered what he had forgotten. He rested his hands gently on the controls, waiting until the planes stabilized on the longest leg of the pattern.

AL-SHIRAN SCOWLED and rapped hard on the glass of the gauge again. The needle actually fell a bit.

"Commander."

"Yes?"

"I believe we do have the fuel in this tank to make six hours. I would like to try something to verify it."

"What?"

"A maneuver. Instead of turning left, I will turn right suddenly in a steep bank, and we will reverse our pattern, crossing over the Mall."

Hassan shrugged. "It is all one to me."

Al-Shiran set his feet on the rudders.

THE PIPER'S TURN caught Max by surprise, and Missy, too. The big twin cranked over to the right and the computer did not react for almost a whole second. Max grabbed the controls.

"I've got the airplane—"

"You've got the airplane, Max," the female voice said, infuriatingly unaware of what was going on.

Max snapped the Viper into a hard right turn, pulled back the throttles desperately in an attempt not to overshoot. The edge of the Piper's wing loomed above, and he seemed to be slipping ahead of it.

"Missy, deploy spoilers!"

"Spoilers out, Max."

The Viper slowed as if it had run into a wall in the air. The angle-of-attack indicator flashed at him, warning that at this airspeed, this bank angle and this pitch attitude, he faced an imminent stall. He held the stick back and up still, trying to detect what Charlie called the "nibble" of the air rushing over the wings trying to separate and steal his lift.

AL-SHIRAN SHOT A LOOK out the left window in the middle of the bank. Something was there. He knew it. But what?

"Hold on," he said to Hassan and the others on the full intercom.

He took the Piper over in an even harder bank, jamming the throttles forward. The twin surged and yawed as the thrust pulled unevenly across the wings. Al-Shiran kept it banking farther and farther until even Hassan looked alarmed. Just past halfway through the 360-degree turn, the Navajo seemed to judder as it approached a stall. Al-Shiran eased off on the yoke and the shudder faded. He craned his neck as he had learned to do in Nam and Iran, looking for whatever was trying to kill him. Because his combat sense told him that his vision had picked up *something* that was trying to kill him.

He completed the 360, then pitched the nose down suddenly, picking up airspeed. Hassan glanced at him.

"What are you doing, Hadj al-Shiran—"

"Shut up," he grated, concentrating. Then he yanked the yoke up and cranked it hard left.

The Piper nosed up hard, squashing them all into their seats, creaking and groaning as it reached and exceeded the G-limits to which it had been built, then slowly it performed the falling turn he asked as he fed in differential power to help it over the top.

Now we'll see you, you bastard, he thought as the nose fell through the horizon.

MAX PUT ALL OF HIS concentration on the belly of the Piper. He imagined that he was tethered to it by a six-foot length of cord. He tried to imagine that he was the pilot; what would he do next?

The Viper bucked as he drew closer to the underside. Prop wash from the counter-rotating props churned the air into an invisible sea of raging turbulence. He felt as if he were being physically thrown as the view port was kicked from side to side by the buffeting.

"Missy, help me stabilize in this location," he said, almost gasping.

Sandy darted a look at Max from her chair next to Arnie. She could see what he could on a conventional CRT in the console. Max's body was drenched in sweat and he twitched and jerked with each slam of the Viper in the swirling vortices.

"Engaging active control, Max," the computer said.

Active control meant that the computer acted as a motion damper, canceling out the errors of his control inputs while also solving the positional problems he was trying to overcome. The view stabilized, but the cost was some microseconds of response to Max's inputs.

When the Navajo jerked up suddenly, Max pulled up, too, falling slightly behind, below and into clean air. He saw the ailerons of the Navajo above clearly, and saw the deflection that meant the pilot was going over the top.

"Missy, spoilers!" he shouted.

"Spoilers, Max," the computer replied calmly.

The Viper slowed, seemed to hang in space while the Piper completed its overhead turn, and then Max slammed the throttles forward, shooting under the Piper.

He crossed as its nose fell through the horizon, then savagely slammed the stick hard right. A human pilot in any airplane capable of making the turn would have been blacked out by the thirteen Gs it induced. But the Viper stood on a wing and slid around, using its gimballed engines to comply with the turn Max wanted to make. As the Navajo went into a shallow dive, Max was slotted back under its belly like a lamprey on a shark.

CHAPTER TWENTY-TWO

"WHAT'S GOING ON?"

"I can't tell, General. Looks like they're playin' tag or something."

Jacobson stared at the slightly out-of-focus TV picture relayed from the Washington Monument. He watched a moment, then smiled grimly.

"Son of a bitch *is* a pilot, after all."

"Sorry, sir?"

"Nothing, son." He looked at Kimball, up at the command console. "Any commo?"

"No, sir."

He looked back at the screen. Around the emergency action center, everyone else did likewise. There was nothing else to do, now, but wait. And pray.

AL-SHIRAN SWIVELED his head frantically, looking for the shadow, the telltale, the giveaway. But there was nothing. He flattened out the Piper's shallow dive and resumed his airspeed and level flight.

"I'm sorry, Commander. I thought...I thought—"

"We are all tired, Hadj al-Shiran. But we shall rest soon, in the Love of Allah."

Hassan looked at the fuel gauge. "Nothing has changed, al-Shiran."

It had not. The pilot shrugged. "Then we do not have much time, Commander."

Hassan did not answer. Instead, he pulled out the vial and peeled back the plastic lid, spilling out a handful of red capsules into his palm. He gobbled them greedily, actually chewing some. Red liquid stained his lips.

They flew silently for a time, backward along the pattern they had pursued so long that morning. Al-Shiran gently made the turn over the Lincoln Memorial.

Hassan's nostrils flared. "Yes. *Yes.* Now is the time, my friends. They must agree or die." He toggled the mike switch and said, "Attention. This is the Jihad."

Kimball's voice came back immediately. "Yes. Go ahead."

"Our time and yours are running out. The pilot tells me we have very little fuel left."

"What? You said we had six hours. That's…thirty minutes from now."

"We have made a mistake, or our airplane has been too hungry. As you have been, all over the world. But there is still time. If I receive the call from my superiors on our flight telephone, as we established, I will deactivate the bomb and we will land at National Airport. We have fuel enough for that."

"We know, Commander. But the Israelis—"

Hassan laughed suddenly, a semihysterical laugh, the sound of a hyena, not of a man. Al-Shiran flinched.

"The Israelis! Always it is the *Israelis*—"

MAX SLOWED DOWN his heart rate and brought the Viper back up into position again as the Piper stabilized in level flight.

The prop wash was just as bad, but now he knew how to handle it. He engaged the computer and slid into position. He studied the view under the white nose of the Navajo. Just where it was supposed to be, a triangular depression forward of the cockpit bulkhead showed the location of the air intake for the combustion heater. He drew a deep breath.

"Arnie. I'm in position. Do you see?"

"Yes, Mr. Moss. Looking good."

"Okay. Let's get going." He spoke to himself as much as anyone. Nobody else could do much. It was all up to him, now.

"Missy. Maintain position."

"Position, Max."

"Right. Missy, open compartment doors."

"Doors open, Max."

The Viper wobbled as the sectional doors rolled back along their tracks into the fuselage. The airflow over the cargo bay disturbed, the airplane tried to fly up into the Piper. The computer stabilized it. Max waited until it was correctly in formation again.

"Missy, deploy probe."

"Probe deploy, Max."

The Kevlar tube Duane had liberated was raised by a hydraulic servo into the airstream. Again the computer adjusted the airplane to allow it to stay in position.

"Missy, extend probe to my mark."

"Probe extension to your mark, Max."

Slowly, into Max's wide-angle view under the
Piper's belly, a black pipe extended. It was attached to
a strong alloy rod, also telescopic, that guided it
through the center of the maelstrom being kicked
backward by the big prop blades. The tube was about
an inch in diameter at the base, tapering to less than
half an inch at its full extension. It ended in a U-
shaped nozzle, aimed backward.

"Keep going, that's it, yeah, go on, go on, a little
more—*hold it!*" The rod stopped. It wavered back
and forth, buffeted by the turbulence. Max wet his
lips.

"Missy, give me the airplane."

"You've got the controls, Max."

The Viper lurched a little as he took the stick. Even
augmented by the computer, he was not as steady as
it was. But only he could bring it into position.

With his left hand, he took the camera control. He
slowly zoomed the view until he was looking straight
at the back of the heater intake. The view wobbled
fiercely as the Viper bucked in the wind wake. He
pulled back the zoom until the end of the pipe was also
visible.

"Okay," he breathed, "now do it right, Max."

He pulled up with his fingers on the stick so slightly
he might have imagined the action. But the U-shaped
nozzle on the pipe moved closer to the heater vent, still
blowing back and forth, held in check only by the
strong alloy rod. He willed the Viper up another inch.
It complied to his faint finger pressure. The nozzle
bumped up into the shallow duct area, then pulled
down again as the airplanes moved apart. He held his

breath and put all his concentration into the nozzle and the duct.

"Missy," he whispered, "stand by to blow canister."

"Canister blow, standing by, Max."

He zoomed a little tighter. He needed almost four full seconds for the canister's two gallons of compressed C-6 to blow through the pipe. He counted to himself, watching the nozzle dance into and out of the duct. If he allowed it to blow and miss the duct, the whole thing was over.

"Thousand-one, thousand—" The nozzle moved out. He swallowed and eased up a tiny bit. The nozzle scraped the bottom of the nose cowling. He hoped they couldn't hear it, but it was too late now.

For a moment, the air seemed to smoothe. He held his breath, concentrated as he had never done before and said, "Missy, blow canister—*now!*"

"Canister blow, Max," the computer said calmly, but he knew it had by the tiny fuzzing at the edge of the pipe as the charge of compressed air expanded through it.

"—thousand-four! Okay. Missy, retract pipe." He back-zoomed the camera and saw the pipe slowly pull back past his visual field.

Now, you sucker, he thought, let's see what happens now.

A FAINT SMELL OF IODINE caught al-Shiran's attention. He sniffed and looked around while Hassan raged into the microphone at the Pentagon.

Iodine. Something about iodine. His memory thrashed, looking for the connection.

No. It wasn't just iodine that counted. When you smelled iodine and the tang of oranges—

"...so when you smell iodine and the tang of oranges, gentlemen, you are smelling the carrier for C-6, the most potent nonlethal gas in our entire arsenal..."

Fort Detrick, 1982. The chemical warfare course...

C-6! Somebody was—

He never completed the thought. He slumped backward, mouth slackening, eyes closing just as Hassan, too, fell against the cockpit window, his straps holding him almost upright.

MAX HELD THE STICK almost as tightly as he held his breath. The gas couldn't affect him; he knew that. He was on the ground, miles away from the Viper and Piper. But it felt as if he was there. It always did.

"Missy, time since injection of gas?"

"Twenty seconds, Max."

Twenty seconds. At Camp Peters, they'd said C-6 worked almost instantly. That was Army talk for within about fifteen seconds, if it was going to work at all. Give it another few seconds for blowing through the heater pipe, the floor and ceiling vents and throughout the whole cabin. Say thirty seconds.

He watched the nose ahead. Did it seem to veer slightly to port? Was it his imagination, or was he flying under an uncontrolled airplane now?

"Arnie. Contact the NMCC. See if they have a visual on the Piper. We need to know if it worked. See if they can spot anyone in the cockpit."

"Roger, Mr. Moss. Stand by."

Max flew alone for a few more seconds. Here came their turning point, the White House. Would they turn? Or would—

"Mr. Moss. They can't see. Sun angle's wrong."

"Shit. That means we have to take a look. Okay. Missy, deploy spoilers."

"Spoilers deploy, Max."

The Viper slowed suddenly. The undernose view he had became a view of the entire underside again.

"Missy, retract spoilers."

"Spoilers in, Max."

Max cautiously edged the Viper up into the clean air off the left wingtip of the Navajo.

"Missy, retain position."

"Position hold, Max."

He twisted the camera to the far right. Nobody moved in the cabin. He zoomed it up close and thought he saw a man slumped against the port rear seat, but he wasn't sure. He moved the view along the fuselage and stopped when he came to the pilot's window.

The pilot's head lay against the window.

"Missy, move to the other side, same relative position."

"Execute symmetrical maneuver, Max." The Viper rolled over the Piper and slipped into position on the right wing. Max zoomed in again and saw another man slumped in his harness.

"Arnie—you get that?"

"You bet, Mr. Moss!"

"Tell those guys in the Pentagon the gas worked. Tell them we're going ahead."

"Yes, sir!"

"Missy, I've got the airplane."

"You've got the airplane, Max." Cool as ever.

He back-zoomed to normal view, realigned the camera and brought the Viper back under the belly of the Navajo.

"Arnie? They ready?"

"Roger, Mr. Moss. They say Dover's been evacuated and everything's as planned."

"Okay. Here goes nothing." He edged back along the fuselage of the Navajo until he spotted the telltale rivets of the bulkhead that gave him his reference point.

"Missy, deploy claws."

"Claws up, Max."

Inside the cargo bay, four steel claws manufactured in the hangar workshop by Horton's men and the Air Force machinists slowly moved into the airstream. Each claw was about a foot from base to point, and each had two fingers. They were powered by gear actuators, whose hydraulic pressure would allow them to punch through the soft aluminum of the Piper's belly with ease.

Unless I slip away at the wrong point and it just knocks the airplane off center and into a spiral, thought Max. The twin was in stable level flight. But like all airplanes in such a condition, it could be made to depart stability with the wrong input. Their computer had crunched the numbers supplied by Piper in Vero Beach, but who knew?

Not anyone. Yet, he thought.

"Full deployment, Max." That meant they were well clear of the vertical fin on the Viper.

Max eased up toward the belly again. "Missy, give me centering marks."

The computer calculated parallax lines and displayed them on the screen for Max. When they were even, he was centered under the Piper. He moved the stick left, then right a bit.

"Okay. Missy, open claws."

The claws opened, and the Viper bobbled again as the changed airflow affected its stability. He corrected and eased up to the belly.

"Missy, announce contact." He couldn't see the claws, since they were behind his screen view. But Horton had wired a simple switch into diagonally opposed claw tips.

"Contact, Max."

Max held the stick up and yelled, "Missy, close claws! Fast, dammit! Now! *Come on!*"

The powerful actuators moved the linkages and the claw tips penetrated. But not evenly. The right rear set slipped, then caught and dug in at a riveting line. The Viper yawed into the airstream as it did so.

"Missy, correct yaw! Hold position!" Max jockeyed the stick while the slow claws bit through the aluminum and finally halted.

He let out his breath. They were coupled now. For better or worse.

"JESUS, I DON'T BELIEVE IT. Look at this, General."

Jacobson put on his glasses and moved closer to the TV monitor in the console, where the CIA surveillance team's signal from the monument was relayed.

"Looks like a hang glider fucking a 747," somebody said. The room exploded in laughter, more the result of bottled tension than the humor of the image.

Jacobson joined them with a faint grin. But now he really began to worry. Because now, for the first time, he began to think—to hope—that Moss might be able to pull it off.

"HEY, ARNIE! I think I got 'em!"

"I think you do, Mr. Moss."

Max experimented gingerly with the controls. The theory behind his plan had been that it would take very little to move the combined aeronautical vehicle that the Viper-Piper now was, at least horizontally. The Piper pilot had trimmed the twin for level flight before he had lost consciousness, so the airplane was balanced and could be easily maneuvered.

The control deflected, but it took a long moment for the Piper to respond. The claws shifted in its fuselage. Max centered the stick again. He would have to be very careful, or the Viper would simply rip itself free of the Piper rather than moving them both. He would have to make tiny movements. And slow ones.

"Missy, flight time to Dover."

"Twenty-three minutes, Max."

"Missy, give me visual cues to the shortest flight path."

"Cues up, Max." A sort of shadowy highway leading to his left showed the fastest path.

Max swallowed and wiped his fingers. Part of him wanted to allow the computer to fly the path, but he worried about its ability to sense incipient separation. It was only the visual clue of the Piper fuselage slewing that told him anything about its attitude.

He rested his hands on the grips again and turned left, very slowly, very slightly. At first, nothing happened. Then, the combined mass and aerodynamic

drag was overcome by the Viper's little ailerons, and
the coupled airplanes began to turn.

He carefully centered the stick. They rolled out, and
the joint held.

"Arnie. Get hold of ATC and have them clear this
route. I don't want to make any more turns than I have
to."

"Roger."

Max thought furiously. The plan called for him to
fly the coupled contraption across the Chesapeake Bay
to Delaware. There, he would try to land at Dover
AFB, which, except for a handful of security people,
had been evacuated. That way, in case something went
wrong and the bomb blew during approach or landing, a minimum of people would be affected. But if it
worked, they could contain the incident easily, since
they'd have the airplane on the ground at an empty Air
Force base. All he had to do was—

"Holy shit!" Max jerked the stick right. The nose
of the Piper yawed left. "What's going on? Arnie!
Arnie! What's happening?"

"I don't know, Mr. Moss. It looks like—"

"The left engine is dead! Christ, Arnie, the goddamn Piper is running out of gas!" Max struggled to
hold the Viper and Piper together. But the Piper's
right engine was turning them into a left turn, yawing
the coupled aircraft so that the force of the wind
would almost certainly decouple them, and send the
Piper into a spin.

"Missy! Full left engine power! Now!"

"Full left power, Max," the computer replied sto-
ically. Max tried to remember his multiengine training. Step on the ball. Fly into the live engine. But none

of the homilies worked when you were trying to move a big airplane with a little airplane's controls.

Slowly, inexorably, the Piper rolled left, against the powerful thrust of the Viper's turbofans. Max fought it as much as he could, trying to sense the point at which the claws would rip from the Navajo's belly.

Just as he was about to give up, the right engine of the Piper lost thrust. He detected it as a slowing of the turning force, then he saw the prop blades slowing down until they, like the left engine's, were turning over simply by the force of the wind. The planes' turn stopped, but their airspeed began to die.

"Arnie! We've got to get this thing down somewhere, and fast. Missy, full emergency power both engines!"

"Full power, Max. Caution: turbine hot section overheat potential after fifty seconds full power."

"I know, dammit. Arnie?"

"I—just a minute, Max—"

"Okay, call the Pentagon, tell 'em what's happened. Missy! Alternate airports within gliding distance?"

"None, Max."

"Okay...uh, Missy, alternate airports within turbine-overheat distance?"

"Andrews Air Force Base, Max," the computer said.

"Oh, shit. Well, we've got no choice. Missy, visual cues for a route to Andrews with approach to landing."

The Piper seemed to sink the little Viper like a whale sitting on a seal. Max kept pulling back on the stick, but even at full power, their speed kept falling. The route cues popped onto his screen. He gingerly turned right to follow them.

"Missy, calculate approximate stalling speed of the coupled aircraft," he said, sweating.

"Unable, Max," the computer said sweetly.

"Oh, wonderful. Arnie! What's happening?"

"Pentagon says try for Andrews, Mr. Moss. We've got no choice."

"Can they evacuate?"

"They're trying now. Listen to the horns!"

Long-unused, the air-raid sirens wailed out over the suburban Maryland air base. Security police rushed out and began shepherding startled civilian and military workers and families off base. Traffic jams instantly formed, but brutal measures slowly cleared them.

Max glanced at the altitude readout on his screen, but he didn't need it to tell him he was losing the battle to stay aloft. The altered dynamics of the coupled airframes meant that the Piper twin now was unbalanced without its thrust. Max was grappled into the fuselage too far aft for good control without power. The nose kept falling, and he had to keep pulling back on the stick to correct it. And all the while, the speed dwindled as quickly as their altitude.

The cue bars guided him at last to within sight of Andrews. He saw at the far left corner of the screen the approach end of runway 19.

"I have the airfield! Arnie—do you see it on the monitor?"

"Yes, Mr. Moss. We see it."

Sandy, transfixed, watched as the van she was sitting in became visible at the midpoint of the grass between the two 10,000-foot parallel runways.

"Okay, Arnie, everybody. This is my last chance to talk before we come down the chute. I'm going to try for a landing on 19-Right. Maybe you guys should bug out now."

"No way, Mr. Moss. We're with you all the way."

Sandy reached over from her chair and squeezed his arm. He jumped, startled from the virtual world of his helmet to the physical world. She picked up the mike.

"Don't sweat it, Max. You can do it."

"Thanks, Sandy. Yeah. Sure. Okay, here we go, gang. I'm showing just over 100 knots—and this Navajo stalls at about 80. Hang on!"

He rolled out the airplanes on final, just as he had a thousand times before. But this time the ground was rushing up to meet him much faster than he had ever experienced. He shoved the throttles all the way forward into the military power zone.

The turbine overheat warning lit up on his view screen. He ignored it. He crossed the airport boundary, barely fifty feet in the air, just clearing the instrument landing system lights planted in the grass.

The right turbine failed catastrophically, eating itself as the overheated hot section threw one blade, then all the others, slicing through the engine nacelle, cutting off some of the electrical power to the Viper. Half of Max's view screen abruptly disappeared. He pulled up on the stick as hard as he could, willing the airplanes to fly, trying to keep them airborne for another few feet.

"Come on, you bastard, come on, I know you can do it—"

The left engine followed the right just as he skimmed over the grass onto the concrete arresting gear area. For a long second, nothing seemed to happen. Then the Viper slammed onto the runway, exploding in a huge, roiling ball of flame.

Max yelled and jumped in his couch as if electrocuted. Then his head pitched forward on his chest.

The Viper, sheared away from the Navajo, smeared itself along the runway while the Piper sailed forward another hundred feet before impacting the ground, one wing low. It pivoted on the wingtip, spun around on its belly, instantly bent a prop and circled crazily down the smooth concrete, spinning like a huge top.

The Navajo stopped five hundred yards from the parked control van.

Sandy leaped to her feet, ripped off her headset and frantically began trying to pull Max's black helmet off. Arnie joined her, and yanked it off his head after he unclipped the chin clamps.

Max's face was white, covered in sweat. His eyes were wide open, unseeing, pupils dilated. A look of sheer terror stamped his features.

Another explosion from the Viper shook the van. Arnie looked at Sandy.

"Is he—"

"I don't think so." She put her ear to his chest. "No. He's alive. Get a doctor."

Arnie ran to the comm console. Sandy studied Max a moment, then slapped him, as hard as she could.

His head jerked, and his flesh reddened where she struck him. He gagged, then retched and jerked forward. He shook his head and looked around.

"We're . . . what—"

"You got it down, Max."

For a moment, he looked blank. Then relieved. Then he remembered. "—fire! Jesus, where's the Navajo?"

"Max, relax. It's just down the field. You have to rest. They'll take care—"

He lurched to his feet.

"No! I saw a fire start. If it goes—"

She paled. "Okay, but let's call the—"

She was too late. Max shoved past her and staggered out the door of the van. He blinked in the afternoon sunlight, spotted the smoking Navajo and began running toward it.

CHAPTER TWENTY-THREE

"WHAT HAPPENED? Dammit, *what happened?*"

Kimball switched channels and spoke into the mike. Others along their consoles did the same. Jacobson jerked up his own phone and started punching numbers into it.

Kimball got through first. He nodded, dropped the mike and called, "Sir! General, we have Andrews tower. They say the RPV separated at touchdown and exploded. But the Navajo is okay. They're sending their crash units."

"What about Moss?"

"They're at the far end of the field, down by the Piper, sir. Tower says they can't quite see what's happening down there, and they're out of contact with the commo guy on his team."

"Okay. Make sure they wait until our people show up before they enter the airplane. Anybody screws around with that bomb before we get the right guys to it...*damn!* Why couldn't he have made it to Dover?" He pounded his fist on the console. Everyone nearly jumped.

"We ain't out of the woods yet, people."

Nobody replied. They didn't need to be reminded.

MAX POUNDED ALONG the runway, running in a
groggy haze. But each step cleared from his fogged
brain a bit more of the disorienting experience of
crashing the RPV. Still awash in adrenaline, his body
gave him running speed he hadn't known he pos-
sessed. He was aware, vaguely, that Sandy ran behind
him somewhere, but all his concentration was on the
Navajo—and the flash of fire he'd seen as the RPV's
right engine exploded. Somewhere in the aft fuselage
of the Piper, a fire was smoldering. He had to put it
out.

Far down the two-mile runway, yellow-painted crash
and rescue vehicles rolled out of their shelters. But in
the confusion of the evacuation, key people had been
allowed or ordered to leave the base, so deployment of
the rescue units took much longer than it should have.

Max focused on the Piper. It sat on its belly and
bent prop at the end of a long series of deep, curving
gouges in the runway. Its cabin and cockpit seemed to
be filling with yellowish smoke. Far behind it, the
flames of the wrecked Viper sent a big plume of black
smoke into the cold November sky.

Suddenly Max was standing next to the airplane.
The smell of scorched metal and burned paint filled
the air. The airplane's electric gyros still whined at
thousands of rpm. Max ran all around the Navajo,
looking for evidence of internal fire. There was none.
Sandy puffed up to him as he paused on the left side,
next to the airstairs door.

"Max—what—"

"I saw a fire start in there. It's got to be put out.
And the bomb—"

"Max! Just wait, dammit! The rescue guys and the bomb specialists—"

He stepped to the door. "There won't be anything left if we wait too long. You ever see an airplane fire?" He didn't wait for her answer. "Stand back. The C-6 might still be active." He twisted the outer locks and pulled.

The door gave an inch, exhausting foul-smelling vapor into the air. Max ducked away from it and pulled again. It was stuck, jammed by the twisting of the fuselage on impact.

"Give me a hand," he barked. Sandy grabbed the edge of the door with him. "On three. One, two, three—"

They hauled and the door squealed, then popped free, making them reel back. A gush of yellow smoke and heat poured out. Something inside went *crump* softly.

Max squinted into the fuselage after the worst of the vapor was out. He couldn't see well enough, so he held his breath and jumped inside.

Sandy hesitated a moment, glanced down the runway to check the slow progress of the vehicles and hauled herself in after him.

Max was kneeling at the aft bulkhead, working at the cargo door. Behind him, Sandy looked around. She saw Ahmed and Feyda, limbs akimbo, strapped into their seats like dummies. Their eyes were closed, heads hanging limply. She spotted Ahmed's Uzi on the cabin floor and picked it up automatically. She peered forward. But the smoke was thickest there, and she could tell nothing.

While Max pulled on the cargo compartment door, she gingerly examined the bomb. It was in a large aluminum case. The trigger mechanism had fallen from Feyda's hand onto the floor. She eyed it for a moment, saw its umbilical to the intermediate control box, noted the red and green lights and decided it was beyond her competence to attempt to deactivate it.

She turned back to Max just as he pulled over the access door. A huge gush of smoke and some flame erupted. They reeled back into the cabin, coughing, then Sandy found the door and half-crawled, half-jumped out. She fell on the ground a few feet below the door, still clutching the Uzi, and continued to cough. Her eyes seemed to be glued shut. She forced them open and wiped them fiercely. She looked around for Max.

He was not outside.

"Max!" she called hoarsely. "Max! Are you—"

He rolled out of the door and almost knocked her down as he fell the two feet to the runway. He held a small Halon fire extinguisher bottle to his chest, which he held out to her as he tried to get up.

"Quick—pull the trigger pin and give it back to me—come *on*—"

She took it and did as he said while he staggered to his feet. Tears ran down his face from eyes that were no more than slits. His face was covered in yellow soot. He grabbed the Halon bottle from her and put his foot back on the dangling airstairs.

Sandy grabbed him. "Dammit, Max, just wait—"

"No time," he croaked and plunged up the stairs and into the cabin again. She began to follow, but the acrid smoke was too much. She lurched backward, overcome by a spasm of coughing that seemed to tear her guts apart.

"RESCUE ONE FROM TOWER."

"This is one, go ahead tower. We're almost there."

"Understand, rescue one. New orders. They want you to hold short of the aircraft until the special weapons team arrives by helo."

The rescue officer looked down the runway a quarter mile to where the figure of the female Army captain was retching on the ground near the airplane. "Say again, tower? We're almost there, I tell you!"

"They want you to hold short of the aircraft, rescue one."

"But we can see smoke from the plane, tower—"

"Those are the orders, rescue one. Hold short until further notice."

The driver glanced at the rescue officer as he put down the mike. He slowed in anticipation of the order to halt.

The rescue officer looked at him. "What the hell you doing, Stewart?"

"But Cap'n, they said—"

"This is my fucking operation, Stewart. Get this thing moving!"

Stewart dropped the hammer and the big diesel groaned back up to speed.

SANDY FINALLY GOT some clean air to her lungs and rocked back on her haunches. The swirling smoke seemed to be thinning in the doorway. She craned her neck and, seeing the rescue truck still coming, she waved her arms.

"Come on, you bastards! What the hell are you waiting for?" Then she got to her feet and went back to the airplane. She put her wobbly foot on the bottom of the airstairs, grabbed the hand line and looked up.

Max appeared above her. He looked like a vision from hell, covered in soot, face smeared. But he grinned at her. He held up the Halon bottle.

"Found the source! Sprayed it good. Think it's out."

Sandy smiled and they just looked at each other for a heartbeat. Then Max put a hand on the ladder line and started to descend. As he did so, the plane rocked. He paused and turned to look into the cabin.

Almost as if it happened in slow motion, Sandy saw Max pitch forward toward her. He hit her with enough force to knock her backward off the ladder and onto the ground.

She saw stars for a second, then levered herself up and saw a real vision from hell.

In the doorway knelt a huge black man. His face was contorted in fury, the whites of his eyes blood-red, his hands knotted into massive hammers. He glanced at her and then leaped down onto Max, who was shaking his head as he got to his hands and knees.

Max grunted as the big man kneed him in the back. He collapsed to the ground and Jefferson Paul Jones pinned him to the runway. Jones raised his huge fist to smash Max.

Sandy knew she should be doing something, but she seemed to be moving in molasses. She remembered the Uzi, now lying on the ground nearby. As if in a dream, she reached toward it.

The fist fell on Max's back. He gave a choked cry. Sandy felt the Uzi's cool metal clip. Her fingers took forever to crawl up the clip to the plastic grip.

The black man raised his fist again. He made an unearthly howling noise.

Max suddenly and explosively thrust himself off the ground with his arms, unbalancing his attacker. The black man fell backward a bit, then grabbed at Max to get him down again. But Max wasn't there to be grabbed. He had rolled out from under Jones.

Max knelt on one knee a few feet from Jones, breathing hard. His eyes were narrowed. They stared at each other a few seconds, then simultaneously leaped.

Sandy finally got the Uzi into her hand and managed to lever herself up.

The two men were a tangle of sooty clothes as they struggled. The black man was taller and more powerful. But he had been under the influence of C-6. Max had not.

Sandy watched, bringing the Uzi to firing position and cocking it as they fought. Some part of her—the Army officer part—icily noted that they used many of the same moves on each other. Both had obviously been trained under the same doctrine. But they were not quite equals.

Max was not only younger, he was freshly instructed in the art of killing with the hands. He had not practiced the art until now. But as the best training does, it surfaced when needed.

The black man got him into a choke hold and began exerting enormous pressure with his forearms on Max's throat. There were several solutions to this hold, Max's instructor at Camp Peters had pounded into them. Max used them all. One worked.

Jones reeled back, gasping. Max spun around and wasted no time; he kicked the man's groin hard. Jones doubled over in pain, as expected. But as Max prepared the second blow of the one-two, his adversary swung from the doubled position into a swift, wide-arcing kick that gave his boot tremendous speed and momentum.

Max ducked aside in time to avoid taking it in the head. But the boot caught his shoulder and spun him into the trailing edge of the Piper's wing. Max recoiled, trying to regain his balance and confront his enemy.

He was too late. Jones swung his other leg in a classic karate move and got Max in the back. Max jerked and stumbled to his knees. Almost instantly he got his hands up in the guard position, but Jones was readying himself to administer the coup de grace.

He never got the chance. Sandy's finger tightened on the Uzi's trigger and seventeen slugs ripped through the pilot's chest before he knew he had been hit. He staggered backward, arms dropping, wobbling like a stringless marionette. He bumped into the fuselage, stood a moment staring wide-eyed at them, then slid to his knees and pitched forward on his face with a sound like a side of beef dropping to the butcher shop floor. He left a smeared trail of blood on the Piper's white fuselage.

Max blinked and breathed hard for a few seconds, not moving. Then he got to his feet and limped around to face Sandy.

They looked at each other.

"Good shooting," Max said finally.

"Thanks," Sandy replied.

The rescue vehicle ground to a halt twenty yards away and men clad in full-coverage yellow suits clambered out. Their leader hurried toward them, his suit hindering his swift movement.

"I'm Captain Green. You people okay? Captain?"

Sandy got up, helped by Max. She slung the Uzi on its strap over her shoulder.

"Yeah, I think so. He's not," she said, pointing to the body by the fuselage.

Green looked and then peered up at the doorway. "Are there any others?" he asked, his voice made unreal by his protective helmet's speaker system.

"Yeah," Max said. "But they all took a dose of C-6. This guy—" he inclined his head at the dead man "—must have been one tough dude. Usually C-6 knocks you out for hours."

Green surveyed the wisps of smoke that emerged from the doorway. Max followed his gaze. "There was a fire. Out now. But there's a shape inside.... You guys nuke handlers?"

Green shook his head, making his helmet bob. "No. We're supposed to wait for the special weapons people. They—"

A shout from the rescue truck interrupted him. "Hey, Captain! Tower just said the helo's on approach over the north end here— There he is!"

They all looked north and saw a pair of big CH-53 helicopters driving in toward them at high speed and low altitude. They would arrive in less than a minute.

Green turned back to them. "Looks like we're going to get this thing wrapped up. Why don't you folks climb in the vehicle and let Saunders check you out? We'll coordinate with the special weapons crew and take care of these people." He waved at the Piper.

Max put his arm around Sandy and nodded. "Yeah. Sounds good to me."

She smiled at him and they walked slowly away from the Navajo, saying nothing. The din of the diesel and its auxiliary power generator filled the air, counterpointed by the rotor slapping and engine noise of the choppers as they began to land one hundred yards north.

Max kept his arm around Sandy, heedless of what people might think. She walked a few feet concerned about it, then rested her head on his shoulder.

At the door of the big rescue van they stopped. Saunders, the young paramedic, reached a hand out to them. Max waved it away. Saunders saw how Max was holding Sandy and grinned, ducking back into the van.

Max turned her to face him. She looked up, eyes wide and serious, face as grimy as his, hair filthy.

"You," he said, "are one beautiful lady. And I love you."

She closed her eyes, and he kissed her. The shouts of the special weapons team disembarking, the noise of the multiple engines, the stench of the smoke and the horror of the killing all faded from their senses. They clung to each other for a long, breathless kiss.

A shout, much louder than the others, brought them out of it.

"Hey! Look out. There's a guy—"

The sharp crack of a pistol shot, followed by three more, split through the cacophony. Everyone froze. Max and Sandy jerked back to look at the Piper.

A yellow-clad rescue worker and a couple of uniformed special weapons men lay on the ground outside the door of the Navajo. A man lurched drunkenly into the doorway, brandishing a pistol in one hand and something else in the other.

"He's got the trigger!" Sandy said.

Hassan el Jazzar looked around at the stunned Americans. Nobody moved for a couple of heartbeats. Then Max pushed Sandy aside and started back to the Piper.

Hassan caught sight of Max. He looked at him with the eyes of a madman. Max had only gone two paces when Hassan raised high the trigger, holding it as if to offer it to Allah.

The ripping snarl of an M-16 on full automatic froze Max in his tracks and kicked Hassan back inside.

The soldier who'd fired lowered his weapon. Nobody breathed. Nobody moved.

Except Hassan el Jazzar. He staggered to the doorway once more, a bloodied handful of rags. And still holding the trigger. He fell to his knees in the doorway and raised the trigger again.

The soldier brought the M-16 back to his shoulder and sighted on Hassan, his weapon toggled to fire single shots. He put his finger on the trigger of the M-16.

He did not have time to squeeze it. Hassan rolled his eyes, cried, *"Allah il allah! Allah il allah! Allah—"* and squeezed the Judah IV's trigger.

"Oh, shit," Max said.

And then the world blew up.

CHAPTER TWENTY-FOUR

DAUD QIDAL JUMPED when the phone rang. So. There was still time, yet. Perhaps they would agree after all. Perhaps there was hope.

Khan spoke on the phone, nodding. He was the most phlegmatic aide Qidal had ever seen. Impassive in joy, sorrow, health, sickness. Sometimes he drove Qidal mad. As he did now, when Qidal could not tell from his murmurings into the mouthpiece what was happening.

He composed himself, and turned deliberately to stare out the window at Beirut. He was the leader. He must appear in control at all times, as though he had ice water in his veins.

Khan tapped him on the shoulder. Qidal started. He had not even heard the man get up from the desk.

He looked at the young aide. Khan gave nothing away by his gaze.

"And?" Qidal said. "Who calls?"

"New York. They have word from Washington."

"And it is?"

"Hassan. He set off the bomb."

"Ah." Qidal felt his blood freeze, felt his stomach knot, turn over and devour itself. He felt a sickening of his entire being. It was not what he had steeled himself to feel should it come to this. But now it had.

"There is more," Khan added after a moment. "I will let them tell you. They are on line one."

Qidal stared at the blinking light on his phone. Slowly, he reached out and picked up the receiver.

THE WORLD SEEMED TO consist of a pulsing blur. He watched it for a while, maybe a year or so, maybe a few seconds, idly wondering what it might be. It grew larger and smaller, like a flower opening and closing. It amused him to watch it.

Slowly the blur began to change, and that did not amuse him. He did not like it changed. It was a pleasant thing as a rhythmically expanding and contracting circle of light, but as the light grew brighter it was less pleasant.

He had the sense that there was something important about the light's growing brighter. It drew him toward it, relentlessly, as it swelled in size and brilliance. He knew he was supposed to want it, but still resisted, remembering the pleasant, soft glow it had exuded at first, recalling warmly the almost loving quality it had seemed to have.

Finally the light took him through itself. Finally he could not resist its pull anymore. He approached it reluctantly but it drew him with too much force. He gave up and allowed it to swallow him.

MAX'S HALF-STRANGLED cry brought Sandy awake. She jerked in the uncomfortable chair and blinked for a moment, trying to orient herself. She looked around with the wall eyes of the person who has been through too much too soon and cannot locate herself quickly.

A hospital room. His hospital room. In George-town University Hospital. She rubbed her eyes and tried to figure out what had awakened her.

Max cried out again, an anguished, inarticulate cry. She got painfully to her feet and hobbled to his bed. She only barely beat the floor nurse.

"Is he—?"

"He's all right, I think. Pulse is fast. He isn't really conscious yet. But he must be coming back."

Sandy leaned on the railing of the bed and looked at Max's heavily bandaged face. Both eyes and his entire cranium were swathed in white bandages. A drain was taped to one side of his head. Tubes led to his nose, both arms and his urethra. One leg was splinted, the other wrapped tightly in elastic bandages to retard embolisms.

They watched him for a while longer. Then his pulse settled down and the nurse made a note on the chart. She scrutinized Sandy.

"How are *you* doing, Captain?"

"Okay."

"Hmm," the nurse said, eyeing Sandy critically. "I don't know. I'd like to see you back in your own bed. Doctor's orders," she said, as if that clinched it.

Sandy hobbled back to the chair, favoring her broken ankle. "No thanks. As long as I have the cast, I'm okay here. Besides, I outrank the doctor."

The nurse sighed and left.

Sandy shifted into a more comfortable position and picked up the magazine she'd been reading when she'd fallen asleep. She leafed through it awhile, then tossed it down.

She looked at Max. And hoped.

HE BEGAN TO DREAM, or maybe to live. He wasn't sure. People appeared as phantoms who moved through scenes half-familiar to him. They seemed to be speaking, but he could not hear them. One scene drifted into another, one dream session into another.

He had no sense of himself. He could not direct the scenes, only witness them. Sometimes they were happy scenes, and if he had had lips to use, he would have smiled at them. And had he had eyebrows, he would have frowned at the sad scenes.

Someone who might have been his mother kept appearing. She had the aspect of a gossamer butterfly, and seemed to be in constant distress. There was no reason he could discern, until the Other appeared. The Other seemed to be a man, who might have been his father, if he had had a father, and if that father had been huge and threatening.

The gossamer woman and the threatening man danced or flew or whirled around him until he could no longer watch them. They coalesced into something that pulsed. Something that rhythmically swelled and contracted, a bright spot in a dark maelstrom.

He recognized it suddenly as the light that had drawn him somewhere he did not want to go. Somewhere he had been. Somewhere cold and hot and painful. But it drew him on. And he was powerless to resist. Until finally he was engulfed in the pulsing spot of light.

MAX AWOKE SUDDENLY, as if from a long deep sleep. Sensation flooded him. From fingers to toes, from back to front, from mouth to eyes.

Eyes. He opened his eyes and felt the eyelashes brush something covering his face. He suffered a panicked moment of near-suffocation, then realized his nose and mouth were free, although something hard and cold ran up his left nostril and something else almost filled his throat.

Awareness of the tube in his throat made him gag. He retched and a surge of pain almost sent him unconscious again.

When the reflexes subsided, he lay, gasping, and began a serious inventory. It was painful. Almost everything he tried to move hurt abominably. His arms were not even free. They seemed to be strapped to boards. He wiggled them slightly and felt the deep-buried node of not-quite-pain that signaled an intravenous needle.

After a few moments of exploration, he was soaked in sweat and still blind. But he noticed that the blindness varied in degree; in some directions it was lighter. He experimented, slowly closing his eyes and then opening them, trying to determine if it was the covering that made him blind or some wound.

The verdict was split. But he thought—he hoped—he could detect light when his eyes were open.

It wasn't much. But it was a start. He thought about trying to talk and then gave up the idea. Just being awake drained him utterly. He closed his eyes and slipped quickly back to sleep.

"HEY," MAX SAID. Sandy dropped her book. She looked at him, wondering if she had imagined what she heard.

"Hey," he said again, weakly but as clearly as he could around the tubes in his nose and mouth. "Anybody there?"

She choked back the sudden cry she felt and got to her feet. She went to his bedside.

Carefully she placed her hand in his right hand, which lay strapped to a board, palm up, so that the IV connection would not be broken if he moved. His hand closed around hers.

"Hey... who's there? Sandy? Is that you?"

She swallowed hard. "Yes. Max. It's me. Don't try to talk. Just stay quiet. Okay?" She wiped a tear from her face with her left hand.

What might have been a smile distorted his mouth. The tubes made it hard to tell.

"Sandy. You're... *we're* alive."

"Yes, Max. Alive."

He was silent awhile, just breathing. It hurt her to listen to him breathe. He gurgled slightly. She glanced at the biomonitor screen. His pulse and blood pressure were up, but not enough to trigger the alarm. When he had come out of the operating room, and for the first week in the intensive care unit, the alarms had gone off every time she was allowed to visit him. She had begun to think of the alarms as the cause of his being here, in a strange kind of logical reversal. If they would leave him alone, the reverse logic went, he'd get better.

"I think I have to sleep now," he said in a hoarse whisper.

"Yes," she said. And she stood there a long time, holding his hand with both of hers, until she was sure he had really gone to sleep and not died.

THE SNOW WAS DEEPER than the last time Chester had met Stein at the bar. But the neighborhood wasn't improved by the accumulation, nor was Chester's state of mind. He slogged through the gray slush on the uncleared sidewalk and shoved open the door to the joint.

The same people might have been sitting at the same places. In the gloom, it was hard to tell. Mo Stein was certainly at the same spot, the gunfighter's table in the far corner. He acknowledged Chester's curt nod with a tilt of his glass.

Chester slid into a rickety chair across from Stein. They just looked at each other until a waiter appeared. Chester called for a Scotch and soda. The waiter left and Chester pulled off his greatcoat.

Stein saw that he wore his winter green uniform. The medals and the silver eagles on his shoulders glittered in the dim light. The waiter slouched over and set down the glass of Scotch. Chester handed him a five and waved him away.

He lifted his glass. "Absent friends," he said. Stein saluted with his bottle and they drank, eye to eye.

Chester carefully set down the glass. He arranged it very precisely in the center of an ancient stain, then looked up at Stein. His face was unreadable. In the background, the jukebox played "Kansas City."

"You didn't tell us," Chester said.

"No." Stein drank some beer.

Chester took a hit on the Scotch and looked around. Nobody sat near them. The closest customer was ten feet away, head down on a table.

"Care to share with me why not?"

"No."

"Ah." Chester took a long swig of the liquor. "The forensics boys did a good job," he continued.

"I'm sure," Stein replied.

"I saw the report yesterday. Turns out the Judah was a phony. Gelignite wrapped up in radioactive junk metal. Not even plutonium. Just a cesium casing to fool the sensors, the lab people say. It certainly fooled ours."

"Did it?"

Chester began to lose his composure. He jerked the glass off the table a little too quickly and some slopped. He drank again. So did Stein.

"Officially, nothing's going to be said. Officially, nothing happened except that a civilian aircraft crashed at Andrews during an exercise. NSC memo says that nothing is even going to be said to your ambassador."

"I see."

The liquor he'd drunk too fast began to work on Chester. But it didn't have too much to do; he had already built up a serious head of steam.

"You do, huh? Yeah, you probably do." He slugged down the last of the Scotch and waved the glass at the barkeep. When he came over to the table, Chester said, "Another S and S, and my—my *friend* here will have whatever the hell he wants."

The barkeep's opaque expression did not change. He looked at Stein, who raised the beer bottle. The barkeep went away.

They looked at each other again in stony silence while the jukebox changed to another country tune. The barman returned and laid down their drinks. Stein gave him a ten. He kept it.

Chester raised his glass, looking across it at Stein's impassive features. Then he crashed it to the table and leaned forward.

"Jesus, Mo, why the hell didn't you *tell* us?"

Stein slowly set his bottle down. He placed his hands around it as if it were a neck he wanted to strangle.

"I can't tell you," he said, low-voiced.

Chester remained hunched forward for a second, then turned his head and spit into the corner. He shoved his chair back and grabbed his coat.

"Great," he snarled. "See you around campus, pal."

Stein stood up. "Wait a minute, Mat. Please sit down. I can try to explain. A little."

Coat half-on, Chester eyed him. "A *little*? Twenty years of friendship, Mo, and all it gets me is a little?"

"Yes, Mat. I'm afraid so. Please sit down."

Chester slowly unwound, like a spring uncoiling itself. He tossed his coat off and warily sat down again.

Stein did not look at him as he began to speak. He stared at the top of the bottle, which he turned around and around.

"We had an operation. Highest classification. The Judah IV was the . . . bait. Har Mughara itself was a trap."

"But you lost people there!"

"Yes," Stein said slowly. "It was a calculated risk."

"Did *they* know that?"

"Who?"

"The poor bastards in the trap."

"No. Of course not."

Chester sat back. After a moment, he slugged down some Scotch. "You got some code of conduct, mister."

Stein flashed an angry look. "We learned it the hard way."

"Yeah? So did we."

"And you are still learning."

"What the hell's that supposed to mean? What are we, a bunch of little kids?"

Stein didn't answer for a moment. He looked back at the bottle and kept turning it. "You don't understand, Mat. You will never understand. For you, there is respite. Not for us. We can't take chances. Not with the Arabs, not with anyone." He looked up and fixed Chester with a strange, piercing gaze. "Not even with you. Perhaps *especially* with you."

Chester grimaced and drank. "Report I read—and we're talking maximum compartmentalized classification here—said not even the damn President knew it was a fake. Christ, man, couldn't your people even tell the fucking *President*?"

A cynical smile crept across Stein's handsome face. "Think about what you just said. From our perspective, your president is a leak waiting to happen. Not just this president. All of them. Your system promotes it. No. We cannot afford it." The trace of a smile slipped off his face. "We could not even afford to tell anyone in your network. For the same reason."

"You wouldn't trust us in the network? Not even me?"

Stein was silent. When he looked up there was the first hint of emotion written in his face.

"No, Mat. I'm sorry. We do not believe in networks, you see. We believe only in results. Your network is a fantasy. A luxury we cannot afford. In truth, you cannot afford it. If you only knew—well, if you knew how many in your network were working against you, you might understand."

"So you never believed in us at all."

"No. You—they—were a tool." Stein plucked up the beer and drank deeply. He set the glass on the table with exaggerated care. "Mat, you are fooling yourself with the network. Others will use it against you."

Chester looked away to cool himself off. "You think we're so goddamn naive we can't sniff out our turncoats? You think—"

Stein interrupted him. "I think my best American friend, who saved my life, is in grave danger because he believes too much in what he cannot see." He leaned forward and a fierce energy shone from his eyes as he sought to ensure he had Chester's entire attention. "To *survive*, Mat, you must always believe only what you can see."

Chester might have struck another man at that point. But he discerned in Stein's manner a truth of sorts, a distasteful one, perhaps even an alien one. It stayed his anger. So he allowed the words to fall unrebutted. He drank a little more. So, eventually, did Stein.

After a few moments, Chester caught the Israeli's eye again. "Your operation. At least tell me if we went through all this shit to some end. Was it successful?"

Stein wearily wiped his face. "Yes. It was successful."

Chester took a stab in the dark. "You had a leak. In your own government. Somebody who was helping the Arabs."

Stein jerked involuntarily. He suppressed the reaction instantly, but Chester smiled a thin, bitter smile. "So we're not the only ones. Surprise, surprise. Who was it, Mo? The goddamn prime minister?"

"No. But not far from him. An old man. Ill, sick of war. A man with a delusion. A man who believed in things he could not see."

Chester raised his glass. "Sounds like my kind of guy. Here's to him, whoever and wherever he is." He gulped Scotch and looked at Stein. "Is he dead?"

Stein inclined his head.

Chester snorted. "Killed by his own country. What a joke."

"No. We didn't kill him. We let him die. He was being kept alive by machines. He wanted only to explain and die. So we gave him to death and the grace of God."

"God? What's this 'God' crap, Mo? You don't believe in God, do you? Shit, that would mean you believe in something you can't see!"

Stein knew Chester was drunk. He chose to reply anyway. He drank the last of his beer, set it down carefully, pulled close his overcoat and got up. He stood looking down at Chester, who squinted up at him, red-faced.

"I see God everywhere, Mat. It is man I don't believe in."

Chester watched him leave, weaving skillfully between the tables and the drunks sitting at them. In a moment, Stein was gone.

Chester slowly turned back to his drink. He picked it up and held it out to the empty chair across the table.

"To the network," he said and downed it in a single long gulp. Then he got unsteadily to his feet, shoved himself into his greatcoat and followed Stein into the cold gray snow.

CHAPTER TWENTY-FIVE

SLOWLY, IN TINY STEPS, he came back to life. One day, they removed the tubes from his nose and mouth. A few days later, they began unplugging the IV drips, giving him back his arms. They left the urethra catheter in because of his legs; with one in a splint and the other still wrapped in an Ace bandage he couldn't have gotten himself to the bathroom if he wanted to.

But it was his eyes that obsessed him. Daily he asked the nurses when they would unwrap his head. Daily they evaded the question.

Not even Sandy could get a straight answer. He understood that it was the blow from the chunk of Piper smashing into his forehead that they were concerned about. The famed neurosurgeons at Georgetown had spent ten hours working on him.

He took it as he had always taken bad news about damage to his body. Somehow, it seemed to be happening to someone else. It was a story he heard, not one he lived. He had always had this reaction, starting when he was a kid in the base hospital, being treated for a possible case of polio. It wasn't—couldn't be—happening to him.

But as the days went by and Sandy talked of everything in the world but what had happened and what might happen to him, he began to sense a creeping fear he had never known. It was not the rush of heat washing over him in a race or combat. It was an icy chill that started near his heart and slowly ate into every part of his body. There were nights it woke him up, and he had to struggle not to cry out. To be alive; yes, this was astounding. But to be blind forever, and who knew what else—this gnawed at him, day in and day out, as his body worked overtime to repair itself.

Then, suddenly one day, the chief neurosurgeon examined him and announced it was time. They propped him up and while two interns supported his head, the chief surgeon began unwrapping the bandages.

He told himself it was no big deal; they changed bandages often. But they always stopped at the two massive pads he called the blinders, pads that covered his entire eye sockets.

Nobody said much as the surgeon unwound the gauze. The chief grimly told him to keep his eyes closed as they worked, and not to open them until he gave the word.

Max felt his pulse quicken, as the weight came off his head. He sensed when they were down to the single strap that held the gauze blinders in place. Then that one came off. He felt deft fingers prying up medical adhesive tape, and next to his right eye, the skin pulled in protest as the tape was peeled back. He felt a cool rush of air on his closed eye as the pad came away.

And—was that light he saw? Light through his eyelid? He fought the impulse to open it and see. He trusted these men, who had pieced him back together and saved his life. But it was the hardest thing he had

ever done to keep his eyes shut while the doctor gently
lifted the pads away.

The air caressed his head and face. He relished it. It
felt as though he were taking a cold shower.

Hands examined his head, face and eye sockets.
Much of the feeling in his scalp was gone, but he
sensed their touch, sensed when a practiced finger ran
along a still-raw scar. It was like the feeling he had
under a local anesthetic when the dentist filled a tooth;
he knew the pain was there, but it was being stopped.
It would come, he knew.

"Okay," the gruff surgeon said, "this is it, Max.
Here's the deal. We took a lot of metal out of your
head. Mostly your skull—your lovely face was pretty
much untouched." An intern chuckled.

"Your head's doing fine. Your thick skull saved
your brain, not to mention your ass." More chuckles.

His tone grew more serious. "But your eyes are
going to be a different story. The optic nerve doesn't
like being screwed with. We don't really know what's
going to happen when you open your eyes; you may
be blind in one or both. You may be able to sense light.
You might even get some signal through. We just don't
know. But we've got to begin somewhere. You game
to start?"

He thought his role called for a smartass remark. He
couldn't think of one. This wasn't just a story anymore; this was *him*. "Sure, doc. Let's go."

"Okay. Now, I want you to open your right eye
first. We've pulled the shades and turned off all but
one overhead light, so it may seem dark. But don't
give up if it does. Keep looking, and the signals might
get through. Ready?"

"Ready."

"Fine. Go ahead. Open your right eye."

Max thought he had done some tough things in his life. He had gone hard and fast in cars and airplanes, he had seen men die, even killed with his own hands. But nothing was as tough as making his eye open. It was as if his brain refused to face the bad news. It took an almost physical effort. But suddenly, the lid was up.

At first, nothing happened and he wanted to sob. But slowly, the faint pulsing light he had seen in a thousand dreams appeared. It throbbed with his heartbeat, opening and closing. Then it began to break up. And the light coalesced. It became . . .

It became the hospital room. It became a single overhead fluorescent light illuminating three men in lab coats. As the image congealed, his eye darted from object to object, as if relishing the shapes, the colors, the textures.

He grinned.

The chief—a balding, thickset man, not at all like his voice—held up his right hand a foot from Max's face.

"Do you see this? How many fingers am I holding up?"

"Nine," Max said. And the ice melted in his belly as they all laughed.

"SO IT WAS A PHONY." Max fought the impulse to scratch his head. He had little hair, but a lot of scar tissue.

Sandy nodded. He found himself dwelling on her with his gaze; his weeks without sight reminded him of what a gift it was to see. And what a gift she was to be seen. She flushed slightly.

She made a final pass on her fingernail and put the emery board in her purse. She sat in the single chair in his room, her ankle cast gone, replaced now with a bandage.

"Yes. A phony," she said. "Mat told me yesterday."

Max looked at his broken leg. Even the cast was fascinating to look at. He knew he would eventually tire of *seeing* things, but it would take a while.

"I don't get it."

"Neither do I."

"What about Chester? What's he think?"

Sandy frowned slightly. "I don't know. He has some idea, I can see that. But he won't share it."

"Anyone else in your lunch group got any ideas?"

Sandy colored again. But not with pleasure. "We...they haven't met since the incident."

"Why not?"

"I don't know. But I think it's related."

Max snorted. "I bet. Chester have anything to say about it?"

"I don't know. I haven't asked, and he hasn't said. Besides..." Her voice trailed off.

"Besides what?"

"Besides, I've gotten orders."

Max felt his blood freeze. Sometimes, it was possible to forget Sandy was an officer in Uncle Sam's Army. Sometimes. But Uncle Sam had a way of reminding him, brutally.

"Where to?" He tried to make it sound light, as if it didn't matter.

She put her hands in her lap and looked out the window. "Does it matter a lot to you, Max?"

He swallowed. "Sandy. They told me about how you slept in that chair. They told me about how you spent whole nights in the chapel downstairs. They told me how you'd stay here until they made you go away. What kind of man do you think I am?"

She turned to look at him, and he thought he'd never seen her so solemn, so beautiful. Her golden hair was haloed by the winter sunlight coming through the eighth floor window, light that was only intensified by the Georgetown University playing field below his window.

"I don't know, Max."

"Well, I do. I'm the kind of man who will say, 'If you want me to, I'll follow you anywhere, Sandy.' But only if you want me to."

She stared at him, then opened her mouth to speak.

She didn't get the chance. A solid knock on the door interrupted her. Max scowled.

"Yes?" he said.

The door opened and General Jacobson stuck his head in. He glanced from Sandy to Max. Being in uniform, Sandy jumped to her feet.

"Not interrupting, I hope?" said Jacobson.

"Not at all, General," Sandy said quickly. "I was just—just leaving."

Jacobson shot her a shrewd glance. "Rog. Well, tell you what, Captain. Why don't you just wait outside a sec? I won't bother Mr. Moss long."

"Certainly, General," she said, gathering her hat and purse and hurrying to the door. He held it open for her and then stepped inside.

He limped to Max's bedside and showed him a small Norfolk pine in a pot. There was a blue ribbon and a card with it. He set it on the floor and said, "This is from all of us at the NMCC, Mr. Moss. Not much, but we figure there's no real way to pay you back. Besides, it's a nice little plant." He shoved out his hand.

Max slowly shook it. "Thanks, General. Have a seat."

Jacobson shook his head. "No. I remember all too well what I was thinking when the PacAF CINC showed up at my bunk in the hospital at Okinawa. Guy made a damn speech at me, smiled for the photo opportunity and left me a damn medal. Last thing you need is the same deal." He paused and grinned. Max found the grin impossibly infectious.

"Notice I don't ask how you're feeling. I know how you're feeling. Lousy, right?"

Max nodded.

"Yeah. Staff told me. But tell me this, you up to a little business?"

"Sure. What do you have in mind?"

"That Viper. I think you proved your point. Air Staff thinks so, too. Or at least most of them do, now that I've persuaded them a little." He grinned. Max could only imagine the kind of persuasion this man could bring to bear.

"What I'd like to do is issue a request for a proposal that only your system could meet. People in Systems Command tell me yours is the only one that could meet it anyway. I'd like to get some of these out into the experimental wings and see what some *Air Force* pilots can do with them." His smile took the sting out of the allusion to Max's civilian training.

"I got a little taste of that when I went out to Wright-Pat and tried their system. You know the one. You delivered a good-size lecture to me on it."

Max flushed.

"It was the right thing to do, Moss, and just in time, too. I couldn't believe it. I could pull, fifteen, seventeen Gs—" He stopped. "Anyway, point is, I think we need this virtual world integrated into our doctrine, and damn quickly. My term runs out in two years, and the next chairman might just be a Navy man. You know what *that* means."

Max nodded.

"So by the time you're on your feet again, your company will have a shitload of work to do for us, and pronto. I'm going to make it part of the covert programs so we don't have a bunch of congressional pukes standing behind every engineer. That okay with you? I mean, you don't mind us going around the system a little, do you?"

Max shook his head.

"Didn't think so. Blackie told me you were a crazy SOB. In my book, that makes you one of us, Mr. Moss." He glanced at the door. "I think I'm overstaying my welcome. Besides, they expect me at the Senate."

He stuck his hand out again. "I just want to repeat it, Max. Thanks. For everything."

Max shook his hand again, and felt the surge of Jacobson's personal magnetism flood through him. The general dropped Max's hand and went to the door. Holding the knob, he turned.

"One more thing. That was one *hell* of a fine piece of flying." He paused as if to say more, then grinned, waved and went out the door.

In a few moments, Sandy returned. She was blushing a little. "Wow!" she said.

"Yeah. Quite a guy, isn't he?"

"I mean, Max, how many guys get a personal visit from the chairman of the Joint Chiefs?"

"I don't know. Do you?"

"No. But I do know how to answer your last question to me before he arrived."

"Ah. About me following you?"

"Yes." She picked up his hand, but lowered her eyes. "It means a lot to me, Max. It really does. *You* mean a lot to me. But I think I understand more about you than you do."

He frowned. It made his scalp pull oddly.

"What do you mean?"

She met his gaze. "I know the sentiment is there, now. But you're too restless. I don't need a doctorate in psychology to figure that out, Max. So I don't want you to promise something you'll regret. Something that *we'll* regret. Remember how you said, 'This'll never work'?"

"Yeah."

"Well, it won't, not if we go at it wrong. Your pledging to follow me like a puppy is wrong. But our meeting when we can—that's right."

"Listen, Sandy, I'm no dummy. I know about my character. But taking over the company from my dad has changed me, somehow. I think so, anyway. It's the first thing I've done that I ever thought I might stick with. It, and you."

She caressed his hand. "I feel the same. But both of us are too old to play moonstruck lovers. We can *be* lovers. But I don't want to play anymore."

"Neither do I," he said gravely.

They looked at each other for a long time. Sandy drew a deep, shuddering breath. "It may be a moot point anyway," she said with a tiny smile twitching her lips.

"What do you mean?"

"My new orders. They're for Fort Ord, in Monterey. I'll be less than an hour from you, Max!"

He was going to say something brilliantly witty like *Hot damn!* or *No kidding?* but she cut him off by embracing him as best she could. It wasn't easy, across the bed rail, but they managed.

Just as, he thought as he inhaled the wonderful clean smell of her hair, it would not be easy in California. But they would manage there, too. He knew that, as he had never known anything else before.

MAX WAS ABOUT TO switch off the bedside lamp when a light tap sounded on his door. He stayed his hand and checked the time. Visiting hours were almost over.

"Come in," he said.

A tall man dressed immaculately in a gray double-breasted suit entered. He looked swiftly around the room and addressed Max with a faint smile. "Mr. Moss?"

"That's right. Have we met?"

"No. I'm William MacLeod. Here's my card, sir." He handed Max a crisp white business card. MacLeod's name and an 800 phone number were all that were printed on it.

"What can I do for you, Mr. MacLeod?"

MacLeod eased the door closed with a motion that seemed almost too practiced. Max cataloged the man's totems of status; he wore gold double cuff links in a French-cuffed shirt, a titanium and gold Heuer chronograph and a deep red silk tie, knotted perfectly in a half Windsor. His black hair was fashionably cut for a man his age, which Max guessed to be about forty-five. He was tanned and fit looking, his movements smooth, oiled, athletic. He seemed not to have the telltale swelling under the arm of his jacket of a man with a shoulder holster.

"Perhaps, Mr. Moss, quite a bit." He pursed his lips and considered Max a moment, as if he were weighing him in the balance.

"Do you know a man named Charles Barton?"

Max thought quickly. Charlie ran near to the edge of the law in some of his doings. Probably his income tax was none too worthy of close scrutiny.

"Of what concern is it to you, Mr. MacLeod?"

"Captain Barton has, ah, worked for us on occasion, Mr. Moss. He stands very high in our esteem."

"I see. And who are 'we'?"

"A group of, shall we say, concerned citizens. Americans."

Max rubbed his eyes. "Mr. MacLeod, if you'll forgive me, your oblique manner is too much for me tonight. As you may have figured out, I have taken a few lumps lately. My stamina for gamesmanship isn't what it might be. So if you'd just get to the point, I and my raggedy-ass body would greatly appreciate it."

MacLeod smiled widely. It didn't surprise Max that he had a perfect smile and perfect teeth.

"In fact, Mr. Moss, I know all about your lumps, and how you got them. They are part of why I am here. Charlie Barton is part, too."

"Great. Keep going."

"Gladly. I am an information broker of sorts, Mr. Moss. Washington being the center of the information universe, I base myself here. I bring together people who need something with people who have it.

I do this only for select clients. Some of those clients occasionally need men and women of very special talents. Skills, attitudes, abilities that do not appear on résumés."

"Ah. You're a headhunter."

"If you like. Of a very specialized sort. Consider Captain Barton and you will see my point."

"Charlie's retired."

"Is he, Mr. Moss? That will be news to us—and to him."

That stopped Max. What did he know about Charlie, really? An old guy with a trailer, a Stingray and an airplane. And lots of stories. Who knew how many more he had that Max had never heard?

"Touché. So what's the deal, here, Mr. MacLeod? You fronting for the leftists, the rightists, the save-the-world guys or the blow-up-the-world guys?"

A certain bleakness came into MacLeod's face. "Mr. Moss. You are too tired and too ill to ask me to discuss theology and morality, which seems to be the thrust of your question. Let me put it to you this way tonight, and when you are better, and if you wish, we will continue in more depth.

"I do not work for any government, ours or anyone else's. My clients are Americans who know right from wrong and act accordingly. You have, of course, no way of knowing this now. I will not ask you to trust my truthfulness, trust being a rare commodity." He paused.

"My goal with you tonight, Mr. Moss, is simply to acquaint you with me and what I and my clients do."

Max smiled thinly. "So far, I know precious little about what that is."

"Think of it this way, Mr. Moss. We simply work to ensure that our children do not say of us, as was said of the vast majority of Germans under Hitler, that all that was required to defeat the evil was to refuse passivity."

"Oh, yeah; 'all that's required for evil to triumph is for good men to do nothing.' Heard it before, Mr. MacLeod. What particular contemporary evil do you—and your clients—have in mind that Max Moss might be able to help quash?"

MacLeod considered Max soberly for a moment. "Barton told me you were a hard case. Most men would find my offer at least intriguing, Mr. Moss. You seem to find it humorous."

"Maybe not humorous. Maybe melodramatic. Or self-conscious. Like that."

"I see."

"Not sure you do, MacLeod. What bothers me about your deal is the 'concerned citizen' thing. In my experience, that's a code phrase for somebody who thinks he knows what the rest of us poor slobs ought to be doing. And I think that guy usually has a personal stake in it somewhere—some way to profit by his 'concern.'"

"You're a very cynical man, Mr. Moss. I won't try to convince you otherwise. But I'll leave you my card, the invitation to call when you feel like discussing the matter further and this observation of my own, the result of my few more years of living: not all men are alike. Some, incredibly enough, can be trusted."

Max might have had a retort, but MacLeod gave him no chance to use it. He inclined his head and was out the door with another precisely measured group of smoothly oiled motions.

Max picked up MacLeod's card again. It was all too preposterous. And yet...and yet was it, really? He thought of himself, tonight, sitting in a hospital bed as a result of what? Where had all this begun? With his racing? With Recovery work in the Mission? With the DIA? With—

The reduction could not be done. His life—perhaps everyone's life—was a string of coincidences, woven into a fabric of wild threads impossible to predict.

But that did not make him anybody's knight-errant. He was a modern American, not some medieval free lance. He was—

What?

The final question stopped him. He stared at the pristine white business card. He closed his eyes and rested his head against the pillow. The short hair on the back of his skull prickled where they had shaved him, reminding him of how close he had come to not being here to be amused by MacLeod.

He put the card on his bedside table and switched off the light. Outside, the whistle of a jetliner flying the River Approach to National Airport echoed off the hospital buildings.

Maybe he was a knight-errant. Maybe he was an adventurer. Maybe everyone was, in the adventure of his own life.

He closed his eyes again. He'd think about it to-morrow.

If he stayed lucky.

EPILOGUE

THE DRIVE FROM the hotel was interminable. No matter how many peacekeeping groups struggled to rebuild Beirut, it remained a city at war with itself.

Daud Qidal said nothing during the trip. Neither did Khan. There was nothing to say anymore.

Maybe there never had been. Maybe his ouster had not been engineered because of the Love of Allah, but because of who he was, what they thought he stood for.

They wanted blood. It was so much easier. So much simpler. Solutions required mental effort, compromise, adult behavior.

The meetings had sounded fair, but he'd known the minute he entered the conference room that he was out. The PLO's executive council was not a large body, but it was usually noisy. Today it had been too quiet.

For good reason. Mohammed Mussein had finally managed to pull together enough backing to accuse him of softness and get away with it. And somebody had given Mussein enough damning information about the Love of Allah to make Qidal seem a fool.

Qidal rested his head on the Mercedes's headrest as the driver threaded the bombed-out ruins. The motorcycle escort picked its way among the rubble, and the armored cars ahead and behind slowed them even further.

He dreamily recalled when Beirut had been a bright city, a city of wide boulevards, carefree nightlife, thriving, alive, intense. Now, it was a battleground, a refugee camp.

Beirut. All over the world, the name conjured the same images; fear, death, disease, endless combat.

At least, he thought, I did my best. Not often in life have I been able to say that of myself. Not as a lawyer, not as a judge, not even as a professor.

He lost himself in musing about the past. When the Mercedes rolled to a halt outside his apartment complex, he blinked in surprise. Khan got out and went to the door. He and the two guards went inside to unlock the lift.

Wearily, Qidal gathered his battered old briefcase and slid across the seat. The driver opened the door for him. He stepped out and began to walk the six paces to his door.

The first shots spun him around like a rag doll. He saw, out of the corner of his eye as he twisted and fell, that the motorcycles and armored cars were gone from their usual stations. He hit the sidewalk facedown and saw his driver pitch forward into the car, almost decapitated by a storm of bullets. He closed his eyes and the pain came like a sledgehammer.

Khan and the guards ran into the street from the apartment building. The guards ran in both directions in search of the assassins. Khan knelt by Qidal.

Tenderly, he turned the old man over. He wiped blood from his eyes and mouth and cradled his head in his lap.

Qidal opened his eyes.

"Who did this, grandfather? *Who*?"

Qidal summoned all his strength. He smiled gently at the young man. "We all did," he said, and died.

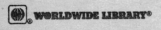

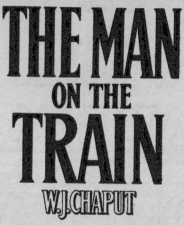